# LYING IN WAIT

## OTHER TITLES BY MICHEL BUSSI

*Nothing Can Erase You*

# LYING IN WAIT

A THRILLER

MICHEL BUSSI

TRANSLATED BY SAM TAYLOR

AMAZON CROSSING

Previously published as *Trois vies par semaine* by Les Presses de la Cité in France in 2023. Translated from French by Sam Taylor. First published in English by Amazon Crossing in 2025.

Published by Amazon Crossing, Seattle

www.apub.com



EU product safety contact:
Amazon Media EU S. à r.l.
38, avenue John F. Kennedy, L-1855 Luxembourg
amazonpublishing-gpsr@amazon.com

ISBN-13: 9781662520662 (paperback)
ISBN-13: 9781662520679 (digital)

Cover design and illustration by Jarrod Taylor

Printed in the United States of America

# CONTENTS

*On this, perhaps my last night, I am recording these words.*
*What will you, dear listener, remember of my story?*
*What does anyone remember of us, once our lives have been crumpled up?*
*We are made of nothing but rags and paper.*

*Milana*

*But you, listening to me now, you who are still alive . . . I have a secret to tell you.*
*You are the only ones who can write the end to this story. Beware everything you read.*
*Beware everything you learn.*
*Beware the invisible threads.*
*And beware those pulling the strings.*

# PART ONE

## Nanesse, Vicky, and Éléa

# I IS AN OTHER

Letter to Paul Demeny by Arthur Rimbaud

***Thursday, September 14, 2023***

# 1

## Katel

***Statue of the Four Sons of Aymon, Bogny-sur-Meuse, Ardennes***

High above the Meuse River, the four large rocks looked like four knights on horseback.

Or so people said.

Personally, Captain Katel Marelle saw nothing but four gray blocks of schist rising bombastically above a tired, miserable river that meandered, listless, between France and Belgium in the cold September rain.

*Going to work here at this time of year,* thought the captain, *is like being sent back to prison after you've already served your time.* Summer wasn't even over yet and it was fifty degrees Fahrenheit and pissing with rain. Meanwhile that hypocrite Sandra Mihiel had been transferred to the Côte d'Azur, and now—to top it all—Katel found herself with a corpse on her hands.

Or to be precise, the corpse was in the hands of two other cops. She had left it to her younger colleagues, Will and Mehdi, to jump over the railing that protected a monumental white stone statue of the Four Sons of Aymon and climb sixty feet down the steep hillside to take a closer look at the victim. As they leaned over the body, they shouted up their observations while she stood stock-still on the lookout point, behind the railing.

"Can you hear us, Captain?"

Her head covered by the hood of her parka, Katel nodded.

"He must have fallen from your side of the railing. Or someone pushed him. Either way, he must have been standing where you are now before he dropped down here. The trees stopped his fall. Otherwise we'd have found him all the way down there, on the cycle path that runs beside the river. Can you imagine, with all those kids riding past on their way to school?"

Yes, Katel could imagine . . . Why couldn't this guy have jumped a few miles away, in Belgium? From the Bayard de Dinant rocks, for example, or from the Château de Crèvecœur, straight into the Meuse? Nobody would have found his body for another month or two, and by then, with any luck, she'd have quit the police. Or jumped to her own death . . . although *she* would have been considerate enough to do it in a place where her body would never be discovered. The last thing she wanted to do was give her overworked colleagues even more to deal with.

"I found his papers, Captain," Will called, holding up a national ID card. "His name is Renaud Duval. He was forty-six and he was born locally, in Charleville-Mézières. You want more details?"

Katel nodded again. *The more details, the better, Will. In fact, if you could find a suicide note, that'd be perfect! Just so we can be sure that Renaud Duval jumped of his own free will, without anybody's help.*

The rain continued to lash down against her forehead, eyes, and mouth. Drops of water streamed over every bump and hollow in her angular face. Katel pushed the black curtain of hair away from her eyes and tucked it under her hood. She thought again about Sandra the traitor, the clerk from the commercial court in Charleville who'd waited until the end of August to inform Katel that she'd been transferred to the town of Cassis, on the Mediterranean shore; that everything was over between them; that she was no longer sure she didn't love men. *And what about me?* Katel had wanted to reply. *You really think you were my first, Sandra? You think I didn't date men before I met you? Well, I did! We simply weren't compatible, at least when it came to living together and not just sleeping together. But if I can't live with women either, what option do I have left? Adopting a cat?*

Katel sighed and forced herself to focus on her surroundings. The area consisted of a steep hill overlooking the small town of Bogny-sur-Meuse, built around a bend in the river. There was a promenade and a small parking lot in the woods, a vast meadow used for picnics and summer concerts, the four big rocks that people liked to climb, and a path leading up to the lookout where she now stood—the site of the huge statue celebrating the most famous of local legends: the Four Sons of Aymon.

Katel leaned over the safety barrier.

"Come back up, boys. Let the forensics guys play at being Spider-Man—they'll love that!"

The two police officers, perilously balanced on slippery rocks, did not need to be asked twice. While they climbed back up to the lookout, Katel thought through what they knew about the case. Clearly the guy had killed himself the night before. It happened all the time in this location. A group of joggers had called the police around six in the morning—some of those crazy people who woke before dawn to run up the steep path from Bogny-sur-Meuse to the four towering rocks. "Masochists!" Katel observed.

"Or you could call them maso-*schists*!" joked her assistant, Jérémy Bonello, approaching just then with a grin.

Lieutenant Bonello was jogging up at quite a pace himself. Katel admired his irrepressible energy. Jérémy was a joker and a morning person with a ridiculously optimistic view of life; he was a local who genuinely believed that the Meuse was as beautiful as the Danube, that the forested Ardennes region was the envy of Provence, and that Place Ducale, the historic central square in Charleville-Mézières, outshone the Piazza San Marco in Venice. He invited the entire brigade to a barbecue celebrating his wedding anniversary every year, and he was also capable of brushing off little Zoé's first day at school with a simple *you and Mom can tell me all about it tonight, sweetie, have a great day*. He was a perfect assistant who seemed always to be amused rather than upset by his boss's mood swings, and who played up the contrast between their personalities as enthusiastically as if a television company might one day use their partnership as inspiration for a detective series.

"Good news, Katel! I know how our man got up here." Lieutenant Bonello was the only person in the brigade who addressed her by her first name instead of "Captain," though he did still address her respectfully with the formal *vous*, and not *tu*. "This way, Katel . . ."

She cautiously followed her assistant down the greasy steps that led from the lookout and then along the plank path that ran beside the meadow.

"They organize medieval festivals here several times a year, you see, in memory of the legend of the Four Sons of Aymon. A dark tale of knights banished by Charlemagne—it's like our very own *Game of Thrones*! Watch where you put your feet here, Katel. Stay on the right-hand edge."

Katel caught sight of a huge hole about fifty yards ahead.

"The wool hole!" Jérémy explained. "That pit is deeper than a three-story building. It's the other place where locals like to kill themselves."

They walked for another hundred yards, across the parking lot, in the direction of an oak tree by the roadside. As they drew closer, Katel spotted a white Peugeot 307 parked under the oak's low-hanging branches.

"Apparently Renaud didn't drive a Renault," Bonello said.

Katel ignored the pun. She looked at the parking lot, which was empty except for their two blue, bureau-issued Renault Méganes.

"Why didn't he just park here instead of hiding his car under that tree?"

"I have a theory about that," said Jérémy with a conspiratorial wink that gave the captain a sinking feeling.

Katel did not believe in hunches or a sixth sense or any of those ideas invented to make people believe that cops become cops due to some sort of mystical calling. Even so, her assistant's knowing smile did give her a feeling that this investigation was about to go off the rails. She'd hoped that in Renaud she was dealing with some poor depressive, a guy who'd just been made redundant at one of the local sawmills or smelting works, or a divorcé stuck here while his ex took the kids and moved to the coast. Some considerate fellow who hadn't wanted to bother anyone with his problems, anyone that is besides the four cops whose job it was to clear up this kind of mess. A nobody, with the most commonplace name imaginable. *How many Renaud Duvals are there in France?* Katel wondered. And then, another thought struck her.

*But would a nobody who wanted to kill himself hide his hearse under the bushy leaves of an English oak?*

Jérémy opened the passenger-side door of the 307, put on his gloves, and began to poke around.

"There's nothing in the car," he said to Katel after he emerged. "No fast food containers, no parking tickets, not even a stick of gum. Either this guy was a neat freak or he cleaned out his car just before he jumped."

"Did you look in the glove box?"

"Yeah, just some papers."

"What kind of papers?"

Katel really hoped Jérémy wasn't about to hand her a stack of photocopied account books. Perhaps Renaud Duval was a crooked accountant who'd gotten bumped off. She had no desire to get embroiled in some shady financial dealings involving prominent local citizens.

The lieutenant gently closed the car door. The rain was still drumming on the roof of the car and on his police cap. He held out a transparent plastic pouch.

"Driver's license," he said.

Katel exhaled with relief.

"His name's on the first one," the lieutenant added.

*The first one?*

"I found two other licenses in the same pouch."

*Two others? His wife's? His daughter's? His lover's? His . . .* She began to read the licenses through the clear plastic. And then Katel Marelle stopped thinking. She stopped breathing. Because what she found, behind the raindrops streaming over the surface, was worse than anything she could have imagined.

The three licenses were for men with three completely different names.

*Renaud Duval*

*Pierre Rousseau*

*Hans Bernard*

Three men with different names but absolutely identical photographs! Not three brothers who bore a close resemblance . . . No, these men were exact copies of one another.

The captain wiped the water off the plastic to take a closer look at the documents.

*Renaud Duval, born January 29, 1977, in Charleville-Mézières.*

*Pierre Rousseau, born January 29, 1977, in the 18th arrondissement of Paris.*

*Hans Bernard, born January 29, 1977, in Mende, in the Lozère department.*

Katel examined the three ID photos again. She was able to spot some very small differences between the images: a slightly askew shirt collar for Renaud Duval, a round-neck sweater for Pierre Rousseau, a slightly shorter haircut for Hans Bernard. Renaud's gaze was aimed a little higher than the other two, Pierre's chin was lowered, and Hans hadn't shaved for a few days . . . They all had the same long face, the same square jaw, the same ironic smile, and—most tellingly—the same two pale gray eyes staring into the camera with the same disturbing intensity. They weren't the same photographs, but they were without a doubt photographs of the same man. Unless . . .

*Triplets?*

No, she had to accept the facts. Triplets tend not to be born in three different cities . . . And they usually share a surname and each have their own car. Besides, identical triplets don't exist in reality, only in bad detective novels. There was only one possible conclusion: This guy—Renaud, Pierre, Hans, or whoever he was—had been driving around with fake IDs.

"Looks like we've found the James Bond of the Ardennes," she said sarcastically.

"Not necessarily, Katel."

"What do you mean?"

"According to the papers Will and Mehdi found on Renaud Duval's body, he lived in Bourg-Fidèle, a village about twenty miles from here, on the Belgian border. There's even a photo of a woman in his wallet. His wife, presumably. Or rather his widow."

Katel Marelle took a moment to think this through. Jérémy was right: This Renaud Duval didn't look like a spy, and it wouldn't be hard to verify his identity. So then why was he driving around with two fake licenses? Why Paris? Why Mende?

"I suppose the first thing we should do is go to Bourg-Fidèle and meet Madame Duval," her assistant said.

"I'll go, Jérémy. Alone."

For the first time that morning, Lieutenant Bonello stopped smiling.

"Don't worry, I think you're a very good investigator," Katel reassured him. "But when it comes to delivering bad news, I'm better than you."

# 2

## Katel and Nanesse

***Bourg-Fidèle, Ardennes***

Katel drove cautiously on the narrow road that ran through the Ardennes Forest. Pine trees massed along both sides, leaning in like reckless spectators at the Tour de France, forcing her to keep to the center of the road to avoid the car's bodywork being scratched by the sagging, rain-soaked branches. The rain was pouring as hard as ever. The windshield wipers scraped across the glass, their screech reminding Katel of the cry of a sick seagull. From here, the closest beach was almost two hundred miles away, somewhere between Dunkirk and Ostend. Sandra had transferred to a beach—but a warmer one. The bitch had taken the sunlight with her, along with Katel's last surviving illusions about men and women. Where failed romantic relationships were concerned, she really was an equal-opportunity employer.

Katel put her foot on the brake as she saw a 30 mph speed limit sign.

She was entering Bourg-Fidèle . . .

*Faithful Town.* If Renaud Duval had been living here with a woman while living a triple life, he must have had quite some sense of irony.

The captain had done some online research before she set off. With 851 inhabitants, Bourg-Fidèle was the last village in the

Ardennes before the Belgian border and was known for its polluted soil, its below-average life expectancy, and its continental climate: freezing winters and baking summers.

The GPS spared her the hassle of making several U-turns in the middle of the village. As she drove past a school, the sound of children shrieking drowned out even her windshield wipers and the seagulls of Ostend. She went by a church as gray as the concrete parking lot that surrounded it, stopped to let an elderly couple cross the road to the Café des Sports, and noticed to her surprise a few houses brightly painted in red and pink amid the general dreariness, before realizing that she had already left the village. The GPS reassured her: *"Your destination is straight ahead in 0.2 miles."*

The house stood alone beside the road, without a neighbor in sight, as easy to spot as a gas station next to a highway. Katel took note of the brick walls, the privet hedge, the muddy sidewalk where she parked her blue Mégane. Renaud Duval lived in an ordinary house on a road that few people drive on and where nobody ever stops.

*Who are you, Renaud?* Katel wondered. *What are you hiding? If you hadn't jumped, who would ever have found you here?*

The captain spotted a light on in an upstairs room: a small yellow square sandwiched between gray slates and red bricks. She pulled the hood of her parka over her head and walked up to the door to ring the bell.

And then she saw something surprising.

The yard.

Instead of the small, neat lawn she was expecting, she discovered an amusement park. Or at least something that resembled one, given that it was no bigger than a fourth of an acre. It was a mini-Disney, a giant playground . . . Katel counted four slides, almost twice as many swings, three sandpits protected by sheets of corrugated iron, a merry-go-round, a climbing wall, and some climbing ropes: There was enough here to keep a whole class of schoolchildren entertained. Maybe triplets really did live here, and each one had a dozen kids?

"Can I help you?"

The upstairs window had opened and a face appeared: round cheeked, brick red, smiling. Madame Duval, presumably.

"I'm Captain Katel Marelle, from the police station in Charleville-Mézières. May I come in?" The captain stepped forward and began to thoroughly wipe her black combat boots on the doormat.

"Come in, come in!" Madame Duval urged her. "You'll be soaked to the skin."

The look she gave Katel was a mixture of anxiety and hospitality. The kind of look you might give Death if he knocked at your door, before politely offering him a cup of coffee. And, in a sense, it *was* Death knocking at her door: Under her police uniform, Katel was a messenger of the worst kind.

She entered, and as Madame Duval came downstairs and closed the door behind her, the captain looked around at all the photographs hanging on the walls of the entrance hall.

*Kids.*

Kids of all ages, from babies to young adults. Kids of all colors. In groups and in close-ups. Dozens of them, and no two the same. Lining up to take their turn on a slide, hair flying in the breeze on the merry-go-round, and—most often—sitting, in groups of three or four, in Madame Duval's lap.

"How many children do you have?" Katel couldn't help asking.

"Seventy-nine! My eightieth will arrive next week."

Katel's eyes grew even wider.

"I'm a caregiver," Madame Duval explained. "A foster parent, if you prefer. I look after children in need. Some of them stay just a few days, others a few years. For most of them, it's a few months . . . Were . . . were you sent by the child protection agency?"

"No, no," Katel stammered.

"Ah . . ."

Now the captain understood why the woman had not seemed surprised by her visit. She must be used to the police turning up at her doorstep. The parents of foster children often had lengthy criminal records, so it would be normal for the police to come here and question her—her or the kids in her care. Around the photographs on the walls, dozens of children's drawings were pinned: hearts, colored letters, golden glitter, a few of them saying *Thank you, Agnès*, and many more saying *I love you, Nanesse.*

Katel couldn't tear her eyes away from these happy photographs, these joyous scribblings. Agnès Duval was the kind of person whose humanity shines from her eyes, whose patience and tolerance are instantly visible in her smile; someone with an unshakable optimism. Now Katel wished she had sent Jérémy Bonello to deliver the bad news.

"Madame Duval . . ."

"Oh, everyone around here calls me Nanesse. Even the child protection magistrates! But don't feel you have to."

That sparkle in her eyes still shone. Katel knew that look; she had seen it, several times, in the mirror. It was the look of a woman in love.

"Ma'am, I'm afraid I have some very bad news . . ."

Nanesse wept. She had been crying for ten minutes now, without stopping. Sitting on the living room couch, the only words she had managed to speak between sobs were the same two questions:

*Are you sure it's him? Are you really* certain?

"Yes, Madame Duval," the captain said every time. "Yes, we're sure."

Nanesse had already confirmed this fact herself when she examined the ID card the police found at the crime scene and then the photographs of the body taken by Mehdi. Nanesse had recognized her husband's face, his clothes, his wallet, his keys, his car, his driver's license . . . Katel decided to wait a little longer before mentioning the other two licenses.

*What happened?*

This was the next question that Nanesse kept repeating. What had Renaud been doing at that lookout point above the Meuse? *Was it an accident? It must have been an accident!*

"We don't know yet, Madame Duval. We're exploring every possible lead."

Between Nanesse's sobs, Katel managed to ask a few questions and to note down a few answers. Nanesse had lived with Renaud Duval for twenty-eight years—in Charleville-Mézières for most of that time, then here in Bourg-Fidèle for the last five years. Renaud was calm, easygoing, attentive. A homebody, and maybe a little too house-proud, but those were his only flaws. With the children that they fostered, his obsession with everything being neat and tidy could make things a little difficult sometimes. But he was such a kind and patient man . . .

Katel felt certain that Nanesse was telling the truth. She couldn't believe that this was all some act and that she knew about the plastic folder containing the three licenses. The captain's gaze wandered around the living room. Nanesse was right: Everything here was in its correct place—the TV and the TV guide, the vases of dried flowers, the cushions on the couch, the knickknacks on doilies. Nothing strange at all—with one exception.

Those grotesque puppets that were staring at them!

The room was decorated with about twenty of them: string puppets, rod puppets, hand puppets. There was a Pinocchio balanced on one of the shelves of the bookcase; a wooden Guignol sitting on a stool; two marottes—sticks with heads on top—of Pierrot and Columbine shared the same glass vase; a ballerina, a male dancer, and a soldier wielding a saber hung from the ceiling.

The captain tried to ignore these curious onlookers.

"Madame Duval, did your husband sometimes travel?"

Nanesse sniffed. For the first time, a darkness occluded her eyes. So perhaps there had been trouble in paradise after all? Well, that was true for all couples, even those who were desperately in love.

"Yes, of course. For his work . . ."

"What work did he do?"

After another fit of sobs, Nanesse explained that her husband had worked as an engineer for Walor-Florennes, the largest manufacturer of machine parts in the Belgian Ardennes.

"What kind of machine parts?"

"All sorts—parts for watchmaking, complex gears, robotics. Renaud was head of quality control for customers. His sector covered all of Belgium, France, and Switzerland. He generally went away for one week every month, rarely more than that."

*One week every month,* thought Katel. Enough to build another life somewhere else. Maybe even two other lives. The captain slid her hand inside the plastic folder and touched the three licenses. After a brief hesitation, she decided to postpone the moment of truth.

"So tell me," she said, looking up at the puppets, "did those belong to your husband?"

The woman clung to this question like a life buoy. Talking about her family, about her husband, was clearly a way of keeping him alive a little longer.

"No, they belonged to my mother-in-law, Milana. She passed away six years ago. After a long illness, as they say. She lived in Charleville too. She was a great puppeteer, apparently, although I only saw her perform once. She had stopped performing for the public by the time I met Renaud, but she continued to take care of her puppets, and to create new ones, in the railcar she used as her workshop. Renaud was her only child, and she raised him on her own, so you can imagine how close they were. He was very attached to his mother, let's put it that way. He refused to leave Charleville while she was there. And after she died, he wanted to keep her best pieces close by. It's true that they're really beautiful, don't you think?" She gazed with melancholic eyes at the puppets, then added: "And my little protégés—as I like to call the children who come and stay with me—they love the puppets, even if they also find them a little bit scary. Especially that one, with his saber and the angry look on his face."

Katel nodded. It was true: The puppet soldier suspended above her head was a fearsome sight. She looked around for one last diversion, her gaze lingering uselessly on the TV guide and the dried flowers, then took a deep breath.

*Come on, Katel—you're good at giving bad news.*

"Madame Duval, do you have any reason to think that your husband might have been leading a double life?"

*Or a triple life, but we'll get to that later.*

Two teary eyes, as red as her cheeks, appeared from behind the embroidered handkerchief.

"No, not at all. Why?"

"But . . ."—another deep breath—"Do you think it's possible?"

"What do you mean by 'a double life'? That my husband had a mistress?"

"No, not necessarily. He might simply have possessed . . . another identity."

"Another identity?"

More teardrops filled the corners of Nanesse's eyes. But Katel couldn't drop the subject now.

"Your husband was often away from home. One week every month, you said."

Nanesse raised her voice. "I told you, he was head of quality control. He was home three weeks out of four. He was a loving, attentive husband and father, believe me—much more loving and attentive than most of the men who go home to their families every night."

"Are you saying you have children of your own?"

"Yes. They're grown-ups now. They work abroad. They left home when their grandmother died. That was a difficult time for everyone. They send us texts. And we video chat with them quite often. I can't complain—that's life nowadays. In the old days, there were only letters and phone calls when children left the nest."

The captain spotted two birthday cards on the dresser, their messages telling the recipient in glowing terms that she was a mom without equal.

"I understand. They come home just for celebrations . . . Or funerals."

Katel instantly regretted this ruefully ironic remark. Why was she making things worse? Poor Nanesse already had enough on her plate. The news of her husband's death; the revelation that he might have been living more than one life. For Agnès Duval, she knew, the worst was still to come: informing other family members, the visit to the morgue to identify the body, the autopsy, interrogations at the police station, a search of her home, the long wait before she was allowed to bury her husband . . .

Nanesse was looking out the window. The rain was cascading down the slides, hammering against the merry-go-round. An invisible ghost was riding the swings.

"Anyway, so your husband's frequent trips didn't bother you?"

Nanesse looked surprised.

"No. I was used to them. I loved living with him that way—three weeks every month. It meant we had a little more love to share each day we were together. It also gave me time to organize things with all the kids I foster. And it allowed Renaud to relax a little."

Suddenly she stared into the captain's eyes.

"I don't know many men who would have put up with my job. All those kids running around the house all the time. Renaud accepted it. He even helped me. And he never complained."

"Except about the mess . . ."

Nanesse gave a sad little smile.

"That was part of the job. Helping to educate these little ones. Teaching them values they had never learned before. Respect for others; the importance of making an effort; the importance of tolerance in family life."

*Damn it,* thought Katel, *this widow is giving me a lesson in love!* A siren wailed inside her head: an attack of sentimentality, from which she had to protect herself as quickly as possible by donning her armor of cynicism. She let a lock of black hair drop in front of her left eye.

"Yeah, that's great," she said. "Looking after other people's kids even after your own have gone . . ."

This counterattack seemed to bounce off Nanesse without inflicting any pain. She must have donned her own armor, of humanity. She turned to look at the dresser, where the heads of Pierrot and Columbine gazed at each other lovingly inside the glass vase.

"Have you discovered something, Captain? Was Renaud seeing someone else? Another woman?"

*This is the moment. But first, a brief respite before opening the trapdoor under her feet.*

"No, don't worry, we haven't found any evidence of another woman in his life. But . . . do you know the name Hans Bernard? Or Pierre Rousseau?"

Nanesse sighed with relief.

"No, I've never heard of them."

Katel had been examining the woman's face closely when she spoke those two names, but there hadn't been even a flicker of recognition. The captain could have sworn that this was the first time Agnès Duval had ever heard them. She slowly took the plastic folder out of her pocket and placed the three driver's licenses on the coffee table.

"We found these in the glove box of your husband's car."

Nanesse leaned forward, uncomprehendingly at first, and then the truth exploded like a grenade: photographs of her husband's face, linked to three identities, three addresses, one single date of birth . . . From the look on her face, she seemed to be trying to work out whether this was some kind of joke.

"Madame Duval, could you describe your husband to me? Physically, I mean."

Rain spattered against the windows. In the yard outside, Disneyland was drowning.

"Renaud wasn't really handsome," Nanesse told Katel, "but he had a charm all his own. His eyes were a particular shade of gray—you can't really see it in photographs. Pencil-lead gray. Very pale. He had pale chestnut hair, or dark blond if you prefer. And he had this way of walking, either hunched or too stiff, as if his spine could only exist in two or three positions. It was the same with his arms and legs—they were as straight as sticks."

"Like a puppet . . ."

Ignoring this, Nanesse explained: "Renaud suffered from calcification of the joints. Early-onset chondrocalcinosis, to use the medical term. It's incurable, but you can live with it. But yes, you're right, Captain—Renaud did move a little bit like a puppet. Clumsy and fragile. In my eyes, though, that unique walking style just made him even more irresistible."

*Except that you never noticed the invisible strings,* thought Katel. She forced herself to continue, encouraged by the realization that the worst part was now over.

She explained the next stages of the investigation's procedure in a detached, professional tone, drawing on her years of experience: Other colleagues would come this afternoon to interview her, there would be DNA testing to verify the identity of the body found near the lookout point, and Nanesse would be summoned to the police station; Katel would ask the fraud investigation team to examine the three driver's licenses, and she would search the government database of wanted people for information on Hans Bernard and Pierre Rousseau. This would take time, since the line at the government office was always longer even than at the emergency room at the hospital in Charleville-Mézières.

"More than a hundred people disappear in France every day, Madame Duval. There are almost seven hundred thousand names on the database, and . . ."

But Nanesse had stopped listening. She stood up, looking rather awkward and stiff-jointed herself, as if she was suffering from sudden-onset chondrocalcinosis.

"I'm afraid I have to get going, Captain. I need to pick up my children."

*11:50 a.m.*

Katel realized she was talking about her foster children. It would soon be lunchtime at the local school. Katel nodded, suppressing a fleeting impression: *This woman is lying to me!* There was no substantial reason for believing this, after all, and Katel had learned not to trust her intuitions. Mehdi and Will would be here in an hour at the latest. And Agnès Duval would need that hour to digest the news she'd just been given, to think it through.

The widow shook Katel's hand for a long time as they stood on the doorstep, ignoring the rain that poured down on them, apparently no longer in a rush to meet her children at the school gates.

"It was an accident, Captain," Agnès kept saying. "It must have been an accident."

# 3

## Nanesse

***Bourg-Fidèle, Ardennes***

Nanesse stood there in the rain, watching the police car disappear along the straight road that led to the center of the village.

She had lied.

Not about anything important, just one little detail. She did not have to pick up any children from the school. Eleven-year-old Ethan and thirteen-year-old Amine, who were staying with her this week, would not come home from middle school until late afternoon. She had five hours ahead of her. But no, actually she had only one hour. The police would return then, to question her, to search the house . . .

*One hour to kill.*

She had prepared salmon lasagna for two—Renaud was supposed to have come home that afternoon, to celebrate her birthday: forty-seven today. He'd been on a work trip all last week, in western France—somewhere between Brittany, the Val de Loire, and the Vendée—and he'd gone to Luxembourg yesterday morning. She always loved their reunions, when Renaud would open the door and drop his suitcase in the entrance hall, and she would urge him to the table before he even had time to take off his jacket. He always called her thirty minutes before he came home, so she had time to make sure that the meal was hot, ready, perfect.

But Renaud would never come home again.

Had he really been in western France all last week? And in Luxembourg yesterday?

Who were those two doppelgängers, Hans Bernard and Pierre Rousseau, whose names she had never heard before?

She had lived with Renaud for twenty-eight years. How could he have had another identity and kept it secret from her?

Nanesse went outside, barefoot in the rain. She sat on the merry-go-round and pushed it with her feet for a few seconds before letting the centrifugal force spin her around. The house flashed past in circles: the bricks, the yard, the sky, all of it spinning ever faster as the rain fell more heavily, lashing her face with ever greater force. She wished it would speed up even more, revolve as fast as a spinning top, to make the collision even more violent. She wished every raindrop would feel like a bullet, fired at point-blank range.

*Renaud will never come home.*

Was Renaud someone other than the man she had known?

She was dizzied by the circular motion, and her thoughts spun as fast as the blades of a fan. Renaud had always been there, in her daily life, but what did she really know about him? About his life before?

Everything? Nothing?

Their life together had started in 1995, at a chance meeting outside a Punch and Judy show at Place Ducale in Charleville-Mézières during the World Festival of Puppet Theaters. Renaud had been there with his mother, laughing like a little kid. That was what had first attracted Nanesse—his childlike laughter and his puppetlike body. She had been nineteen, and he'd been eighteen. She already knew what she wanted to do with her life: look after children. So what was one extra kid? Especially when this one was five foot nine—practically the length of her small bed—and had such lovely gray eyes. She had invited him home to her apartment on Rue Bourbon that very evening, and he had never left.

*And after that?*

A marriage, two children of their own, then dozens—seventy-nine to be exact—of *her* children. Twenty-eight years of happiness, three weeks out of every four . . .

*And before that?*

Before their encounter at Place Ducale? Nothing to raise any suspicions. Renaud had still been living with his mother on Rue de Wailly and studying mechanical engineering at the technology college in Charleville. Prior to that, he had graduated from Monge High School while she'd been a student at Chanzy High School; he had gone to Bayard Middle School while she'd gone to Rimbaud Middle School; he'd been at Citadelle Elementary School while she'd been at Kennedy Elementary School. They must have crossed paths frequently in that town of fifty thousand inhabitants without ever realizing.

They had loved each other deeply, in every room of their small apartment on Rue Bourbon. Neither of them had felt any need to keep seeing their old friends, but new relationships had become part of their life: colleagues from Ateliers de la Vence, where Renaud had been hired; educators and social workers at the child protection agency, parents of students; and some of her cousins—Renaud had no family other than his mother.

Yes, when she thought about it now, there was nobody—since her mother-in-law had died of uterine cancer—who could provide any information on Renaud's life or actions prior to 1995. But wasn't that true for everybody? Once you become a couple, you create a new family, in the process erasing all your old connections.

The merry-go-round slowed down. Nanesse's hair, sweater, and skin were drenched. She wasn't wearing a jacket. The icy water trickled down her breasts and onto her belly. She should go inside. She should look through Renaud's few belongings. She had to remember: There must be something—some kind of clue or witness—that could enlighten her about her husband's past. Renaud had grown up less than twenty miles away, in Charleville-Mézières. Someone was bound to remember him!

The rest of the day flew past. The police visit felt like a raid, and they took away all Renaud's computers, professional files, and personal objects. The awful identification procedure at the morgue crushed Nanesse's last slender hopes. It was definitely Renaud's body lying in that freezer drawer. The hours of interrogation at the police station were almost more painful. *We must explore every possibility, Madame Duval—accident, suicide, or even a crime.* Only Captain Katel Marelle's regular phone calls offered any reassurance. *We're searching, Agnès. We're trying to find out if these two other men—Pierre Rousseau and Hans Bernard—actually existed. So far, we don't have anything. We're also trying to reconstruct your husband's schedule, but one thing is certain—he wasn't in Luxembourg yesterday. Renaud lied to you; his boss never sent him there.*

*Renaud lied to you . . .*

Well, that was one thing she knew for certain now.

But what exactly did he lie about? Everything?

In the evening, alone with a bowl of mashed butternut squash, Nanesse turned on the TV to a music channel, just to break the silence. Ethan and Amine had gone away; she had asked the social worker from the child protection agency to pick them up. Trying to look after them, with everything that was happening, was too much. She preferred to be alone; she was used to it, one week out of every four, even if this silence was utterly unlike the silence she had known before—the silence of all those evenings when she waited for Renaud to call her.

She ate without appetite while gazing at the puppets around her. The man with the saber and the ballerina. Pierrot and Columbine. And, visible through the open bedroom door, one more: a woman with red hair and her woolen dog. All these companions, whose presence had comforted her for years, now seemed like scowling spies.

They were all liars! Who could she trust? The television? On the screen, Patrick Bruel was singing about meeting his old friends in ten years' time.

Nanesse turned up the volume, trying to fill the void and empty her head of all thoughts . . . And yet, something intrigued her. Something to do with the television. Not this program, or this music video, but a memory that she couldn't quite recall.

She racked her brains, seeking a way into Renaud's past. But the effort was surely in vain; even if she could discover one, if she could find someone who had known Renaud before her—one of his old teachers or coaches—what could they possibly tell her about . . .

*This TV!*

An image suddenly flashed in Nanesse's head. It was still blurry, but her mind's eye was bringing it into focus. They had bought this television set more than ten years ago—Christmas 2011, to be precise, in the Darty store at the La Croisette mall. Why, she wondered, did this fact seem so significant? She and Renaud hated the crowds that always gathered whenever there was a sale at one of the big malls. And besides, whenever she had foster children staying at the house, the television was never turned on. Why should this stupid 50-inch flat-screen TV with its HD resolution and its Dolby sound make her senses hum like this?

She had to rummage through her memory a few more seconds to finally locate what she was searching for. Once she did, she started to laugh, all alone in the living room. She felt almost certain that the puppets hanging from their strings turned toward her in surprise.

The guy who sold them this technological marvel—at least that was what he'd called it when recommending this model—had known Renaud!

The scene had lasted only five minutes, and millions of other memories had piled up on top of that one in the years since, but Nanesse had set it aside in a corner of her mind, probably because that TV salesman was the only person—out of all the people they had encountered during their twenty-eight-year relationship—who had known Renaud before she met him.

It was like clicking on a file inside her head. Everything reappeared, as vivid as if it had happened yesterday. The salesman had done his military service with Renaud, at the Colmar barracks, in the 152nd Infantry Regiment, just after Renaud passed his baccalaureate and qualified for college. Two young soldiers who had gone to the same high school . . . it was natural that they'd become friends. The man at Darty had been enthusiastic—*What are you up to? What a funny coincidence. We should meet up again*—but Renaud had been polite and noncommittal, and he'd tossed the phone number in the trash as soon as they got home. Nanesse had not found that suspicious. In truth, she might well have done the same thing if some old friend of hers that she didn't particularly want to see again had buttonholed her on the street.

From behind the flat TV screen, Patrick Bruel seemed to agree with her, singing about no longer having anything to say to each other.

She had to admit that the soldier in Darty hadn't sold them a piece of junk: In Dolby sound and HD resolution, Patrick Bruel's voice and eyes were as real as if he were in the room with her.

But how could she find that salesman, twelve years later?

She didn't even know his name and couldn't remember what he looked like . . .

She waited for Patrick Bruel to finish his song before turning off the TV. Then she ate the rest of her meal and went upstairs to bed, curling up under the sheets so she wouldn't have to see, staring at her from the nightstand, Manicka—the red-haired puppet—and her dog Zeryk. She lay there for more than two hours, eyes closed but wide awake, before getting out of bed.

As her mind had wandered through the fog of forgetting, an idea had come to her.

She went downstairs to the living room, knelt in front of the closet, and pulled out two old boxes. These boxes contained all their receipts for the past twenty years, organized in a series of cardboard folders. She opened the Electrical Goods folder, turned a few pages, and quickly found what she was looking for.

The warranty for a TV set.

*Philips 7PFL9603*

*990 euros*

*Darty at La Croisette*

*Salesperson: Bruno*

Nanesse couldn't bear the thought of going back upstairs, so she grabbed a blanket and lay on the couch. She would call Darty tomorrow, as soon as they opened. Even if this Bruno didn't work there anymore, surely one of his colleagues would remember him. She had a thread now, and she wasn't about to let go of it.

The only thread that connected her to Renaud's past.

*Renaud.* Was that even his real first name?

*Duval*, the surname that she had taken as her own—was that actually her husband's last name?

Or had she married someone else? One of those two doppelgängers with their handsome gray eyes.

Hans Bernard or Pierre Rousseau . . .

# LOVE MUST BE REINVENTED

*A Season in Hell* by Arthur Rimbaud

***Friday, September 15, 2023***

# 4

## Vicky

***Ruynes-en-Margeride, Cantal***

"Shit, what are you talking about? You've met him before! You even played pétanque with him at the Blueberry Festival! Hans Bernard, my boyfriend! Don't tell me you don't remember him!"

Sergeant Julien Murat frowned and looked up at the freshly repainted ceiling of the police station in Ruynes-en-Margeride.

"Of course I know your Hans, Vicky." It was a fact that Julien had played the French form of bocce with him. "But calling him your *boyfriend* . . . that's maybe a bit of an exaggeration, don't you think?"

"What the hell do you know about it? Have you been in my bed?"

Vicky Malzieu was annoyed. She often got annoyed when she ventured beyond the guesthouse she owned. It happened the moment she set foot in an office building, a hospital, a town hall . . . or a police station. And yet she had known Sergeant Murat for more than thirty years—since the day she was born, in fact. The two of them were the same age, had gone to the same schools, hung out with the same group of friends, gone to the same village dances. He'd even had a crush on her at one point. She sensed that Julien was about to say something stupid, along the lines of *Well, you never invited me into your bed* or *No, but I'd like to.* If he did, she would go straight to the police station in Saint-Flour and file a complaint.

"Calm down, Vicky," Julien said soothingly. "I'm just doing my job. That's what they teach us at the police academy—that we have to assess the seriousness of the situation. Like a doctor, you know: Should I call for an ambulance or just write out a prescription? To make sure we have enough time to solve real crimes, we need to filter out the less important ones . . ."

Vicky took deep breaths. She looked through the window at the peaceful curves of the Margeride mountain range. Green hills vanishing into the distance, illuminated by the late-summer sunlight.

"Okay, so here's the situation. I haven't heard from Hans in three days. This is the first time that's happened since we met."

Julien took notes with a red ballpoint pen, underlining certain words and crossing out others.

"And he's a truck driver, right?"

"Yeah. Self-employed. He delivers stuff all over Europe."

"So how often do you see him, roughly? Once a month?"

"He gets five days off in a row after working for twenty-one days. But what business is that of yours?"

"None at all, Vicky. It's your life. But going three days without hearing from someone who spends three weeks traveling anywhere from Gibraltar to Belarus doesn't seem like an emergency to me."

"I've called his cell phone dozens of times. He doesn't answer."

"Think about it, Vicky! Maybe his phone battery died. Or maybe he left his phone at a gas station somewhere. Or maybe he's stuck at a border crossing without a signal. Or maybe he just doesn't want to talk to you . . ."

Vicky looked through the window again. In the distance, the Garabit viaduct spanned the wooded hills like a straight red line drawn by an irritated teacher. She decided it was time to raise her voice. Lola, sitting in the next room, would hear her through the walls. But who cared? Her daughter was used to her temper.

"So that's your assessment of the situation, is it? I tell you that the man I live with has disappeared, and your considered analysis is that he must have dumped me?"

Sergeant Murat frowned and tensed his hand around the wireless computer mouse like a man squeezing a stress ball.

"That's not what I said, Vicky. I'm just pointing out that your boyfriend is . . . how can I put this . . . kind of nomadic? I mean, he turns up, he leaves again, you wait for him . . ."

"The perfect sailor's wife," Vicky muttered to herself.

"Sorry?"

"Nothing."

"Have you tried calling his boss?"

"He's self-employed—I told you that."

"Are you two married? In a civil partnership? Has he adopted Lola?"

Vicky shook her head. She was getting nowhere with this jerk. As far as she was concerned, he could go home right now to his wife, his kids, his pals, his mistresses, or whomever he usually went home to, if going home to someone was what he called love.

As she headed for the door, Sergeant Murat made one last attempt at pacifying her.

"Just wait a few days. Give him some time. If anything bad had happened to your Hans, we'd have heard about it."

Before leaving, Vicky flashed him a cursory smile—the smile she reserved for morons whose help she might need again one day.

Lola was waiting in the reception area, with Kasper sitting in her lap.

"What did the policeman say, Mommy? Does he know where Daddy is?"

"No, sweetie, he doesn't know. And we've talked about this: Hans isn't your daddy."

Lola thought about this for a few seconds. She appeared to put away each new piece of information in her five-year-old brain, like an archivist arranging files on a shelf. Then she picked up Kasper and clasped him to her chest. Vicky felt tears well behind her eyes and held out her hand to her daughter.

Lola took it and smiled reassuringly.

"Don't be sad, Mommy. Daddy—I mean Hans—will come back. He promised me he was going to fix Kasper, remember?"

Vicky sniffed, deeply moved by her daughter's optimism. She had to put on a brave face, to be strong, as always, for Lola. She had to look after her child the way that Lola looked after Kasper.

Her gaze descended to the strange doll, taking in his long red hat, his Scottish costume, his pointed nose and two big gray eyes. Hans had given Lola this toy for her fourth birthday. Kasper was not really a doll, in fact, but rather a sort of weird stringless puppet, with a mechanism inside his celluloid skin that theoretically enabled him to walk, to move his arms and lips, and to speak. Except that the mechanism had become jammed, so Kasper was paralyzed and silent. But Hans had promised to fix him . . .

She closed the door of the police station behind her and felt the September sunlight warm her skin. It was supposed to be eighty degrees today in the mountains—the kind of weather that usually spurred them to go swimming in the Truyère River or the Grandval Lake, or for a long walk up to Mount Mouchet. But not today. Vicky didn't want to stray too far from home, in case Hans called.

It took her less than ten minutes to get back to her farmland guesthouse, and she didn't pass a single car on the way. The summer tourists were already gone, leaving only a few retirees who were no doubt out losing themselves on hiking paths. The guest accommodations would be empty for a few weeks, until the All Saints' holiday. Every day in this rolling landscape between Lozère and Auvergne, she savored the joy of inhabiting a corner of paradise whose scents, colors, and charms were in perfect accord with her heart. When her friends who had moved to big cities, to Clermont-Ferrand or Toulouse, asked her if she wasn't bored, living alone in the countryside, she told them that she always had company here when she wanted it—either her neighbors or travelers passing through—but she could always find space and solitude too, which would not have been true in an overcrowded city.

The moment Vicky parked her Citroën Berlingo between the guesthouse and the meadow, two ponies came trotting up to the barbed wire fence. Lola rushed over to check that Rampion and Catsfoot still had straw in their feed rack. Vicky watched her for a moment before her gaze lingered proudly on the pale granite of the fully restored guesthouse. She had done that work herself last spring. The next step would be the roof. The slate shingles were stored in the outbuilding; all she needed to do now was put up scaffolding. Hans had promised to help her with that before winter.

She clapped her hands, encouraging herself to stay cheerful. Moping around anxiously was not going to make things better. Besides, that idiot Julien was probably right—not about Hans having abandoned her, obviously, but about the suggestion that his silence could be explained by something as simple as a lost cell phone.

The rest of the day went by quickly. She cleaned three of the rooms; she groomed the ponies; she played a game of UNO with Lola; she went through the account books while her daughter watched *My Neighbor Totoro* for the tenth time; they ate dinner; and then she fed the semiwild rabbits and hens before tucking Lola into bed and kissing her good night.

This was her daughter's favorite moment of the day for talking, in grown-up words, before Vicky turned out the light.

"Mommy, I've been thinking about what you keep telling me."

"About the importance of brushing your teeth?"

"No, about how Hans isn't my daddy."

Vicky sat on the edge of the little bed. Her daughter was just like her: Lola had spent the whole day pretending to be fine, but all the while she'd been thinking about him.

"It's true, my love. But that doesn't mean he won't come back . . ."

"Mommy!" Lola interrupted. "I'm five years old! I'm a big girl now. I know you made me with another man, that Hans isn't the daddy that you chose for me. But I don't care about that, because he's the daddy that *I* chose."

Vicky blinked back the flood of tears she could feel ready to pour from her eyes. *Don't cry! Not in front of your daughter.* Oh, Hans had to come back . . . She couldn't stand the thought of Lola growing up with this anxiety gnawing at her.

"And what about your doll?" Vicky asked, to change the subject. "What daddy did she choose?"

Kasper was sleeping beside Lola, as he did every night, with only his plastic head and his red hat poking out above the bedcovers.

"Mommy!" Lola sighed. "How many times do I have to tell you? Kasper might have pretty gray eyes and long hair, but he's a boy!"

Lola was sleeping, but Vicky wasn't. From the window of her attic room, she could see the stars and, below them, farther to the west, the illuminated girders of the viaduct—their own local, horizontal Eiffel Tower. To the north, the night was streaked with the red and white lights of traffic on the A75 highway. She had chosen the location of her guesthouse carefully: isolated amid the beauties of nature, in the heart of the Margeride mountain range, in an area with a population density of fewer than fifty people per square mile, but still less than ten minutes' driving from the nearest highway exit. Millions of tourists drove past on that highway every year, traveling from the north of France toward the south, and every year some of them would stop, lured by the landscape as they passed by . . .

Or because they were lost.

That was how Hans had ended up here.

It had snowed a lot that winter. All over the Margeride range, the snow had been more than three feet deep. The highway had been cleared, but every vehicle that ventured off it had ended up stuck, none more so than one particular eighteen-wheeler whose GPS hadn't given its driver any indication of how wide the roads were. Hans had found himself trapped, along with his truck and its cargo of tires that he was delivering to Clermont-Ferrand.

Vicky had spotted him from afar while she was shoveling snow from the driveway. She hadn't hesitated to help. In the mountains, during winter, solidarity is nonnegotiable. You can't just leave people to freeze by the roadside. Vicky had taken out all her equipment—chains, ropes, shovels. Hans's truck had finally skidded to a halt in a half-cleared parking lot, and naturally Vicky had offered him a cup of coffee afterward. Without any ulterior motives.

Vicky was always open and direct with men; she considered herself their equal, and she could come across as a little blunt and rough. That was enough to scare off most guys, despite the blond hair that she always wore loose, her big blue eyes, her natural complexion, and her tall, athletic body. A few of the bolder types would try their luck with her, but for her part Vicky was rarely attracted to overly confident men. And when she was, it never lasted long.

With Hans, it had been different from the start. He had the annoying maturity of a cautious adventurer.

They had made love almost immediately. While the kettle was still whistling, they had begun taking off their gloves, sweaters, and socks so they could dry them in front of the wood-burning stove. Then, in a somewhat pathetic striptease, the rest of their clothes had come off too, ending with the final item: the lacy underwear that Vicky wore under all her shapeless, farm-girl outer layers.

They had made love for a long time before falling asleep in front of the stove. Vicky had gotten up first because she needed to vomit. She left the bathroom door open, completely unashamed, then reemerged, naked, without even bothering to lower the toilet seat, the test strip in one hand.

"I'm pregnant."

"Wow, that was fast!" Hans smiled. "You must be one fertile chick!"

Vicky had instantly fallen in love with his offbeat sense of humor.

"Don't worry, you're not the father. I slept with the dad three or four times, about a month ago. And to be perfectly honest, he's the last person I'd want to raise a baby with."

"So you're not going to tell him?"

"No."

"But you'll keep the baby?"

"Yes. At my age, I don't feel like waiting around anymore. It's okay, I'm fully prepared to bring this child up on my own. It doesn't scare me. It can't be any harder than restoring a ruined farm, and I've done a pretty good job of that, right?"

Vicky had been hoping that Hans would tear his eyes away and admire the exposed beams, the lime mortar between the granite rocks, the hexagonal terra-cotta floor tiles from Raujolles, but his gaze had not wavered except to descend in a straight line from her breasts to her groin, staring fixedly at her naked curves.

"I could help you, if you want."

"With the farm?"

"Sure . . . and with the baby too."

Vicky was immediately smitten. You never know when such a thing will happen to you. It can happen even in a holiday house in the mountains in the middle of winter, even with a truck parked a hundred yards away that will have to be driven to Rotterdam, Lisbon, or Barcelona; even with someone else's baby in your belly. Sometimes, all it takes to make you fall in love is a pair of pale gray eyes and a body like that of an unstrung puppet.

They had talked for a long time that day. Vicky had sworn never to wait for him, never to wait for anything, not to become attached, never to ask him to stay, and she had sworn that when the day came that she'd had enough of him, she would tell him not to come back anymore. He had agreed to all of it.

Hans had moved in with her. One week out of every four. He was from the same general area, just a little farther to the southeast. He had been born in Mende, and had grown up somewhere in the Cévennes. He knew this region like the back of his hand: the Grands Causses of Méjean and Sauveterre, the valleys of the Tarn and the Lot . . . As a teenager, he had explored this landscape on his mountain bike; he took Vicky to all these places, on foot or on horseback. They loved the same kind of lifestyle: a somewhat melancholy solitude, Vicky in her guesthouse and Hans behind the wheel of his truck. But they loved meeting up too—on market days, at the blueberry festival or the Lozère Fair—and of course they loved spending time as a couple, renovating the farm, hiking, having sex. With every passing month, Hans gradually became her man, her lover. Her boyfriend.

Not that that prevented Vicky from keeping her promise. She never asked Hans to change, to stop, to stay longer. That rhythm—one week in every four—suited her perfectly. One week of happiness, love, and whispered secrets, and the rest of her time devoted to looking after Lola, the farm, her guests, the tourism office (of which she was the president), and the local association for rural development (of which she was the secretary).

Yes, she loved this alternating of intimacy and separation. She couldn't have stood the idea of living with a man permanently, because, no matter how handsome and sweet that man was, he would eventually have begun to make himself at home.

In the hit single "Dis, quand reviendras-tu?" the singer Barbara crooned that she wouldn't make a good sailor's wife, not being the sort of woman who would die of grief. Vicky had never been one to feel sentimental about a man's absence, but she was wavering now.

*Hans, when will you come back?*

# 5

## Éléa

***Boulevard Barbès, Château Rouge, Paris***

The first time Éléa heard about Pierre, she had been fifteen years old. She wasn't living in Paris yet; she was just a bored teenager in a village in Normandy, who knew nothing about the Château Rouge neighborhood. All her knowledge about the eighteenth arrondissement had come from postcard images of Montmartre—a far cry from her current tiny apartment in an ugly 1960s concrete cube that swallowed up 60 percent of the wages she earned as a secretary at a real estate agency, seventeen Metro stations and three changes of train away.

In fact, the first time, Éléa didn't hear about Pierre at all. She didn't see him either. She *read* him.

She had gone into that weirdly named bookstore in Alençon—Librairie Baou—by chance, almost in secret.

At fifteen, Éléa already had tattoos of thorny branches winding around her arm, and she never left home without a cigarette between her lips. She had been instantly drawn to one magazine displayed next to the checkout stand. A magazine that wasn't really a magazine at all; she would learn later that it was called a fanzine, a publication that circulates among the members of a community who share the same tastes, whether that be for manga, Korean movies, Mexican recipes, or poetry . . .

This fanzine was aimed at the French community of poets. Éléa had no idea how many poets there might be in France—dozens? thousands?—but there was something attractive about the fanzine's title.

*I Wrote Silences.*

Éléa didn't know that those three words had been written by a kid from Charleville-Mézières when he was nineteen: Arthur Rimbaud. She knew nothing of Rimbaud, of "The Alchemy of Words" or *A Season in Hell.* Éléa had simply found the bookseller a little weird: His head was shaved, except for a single tuft of gray hair, sticking up like a bird's crest; he wore a bowtie around his neck and a checkered Prince of Wales suit.

She had also found the man's bookstore weird, with those puppets hanging all over the place, between dusty old books: witches, African heads, Japanese dolls, Indian puppets made of wood, and Chinese dragons made of tissue.

Weird and attractive.

When Éléa had begun flicking through the fanzine, the bookseller had come over.

"Take it—it's free. I'm the editor. I collect poems by amateur writers who send them to me from all over France, and I publish them."

She had grabbed that fanzine and run out of the store like a thief.

*I Wrote Silences.*

In the solitude of her night, she had read the poems in the collection.

The poems were terrible! Thank God the fanzine was free . . .

The verses by those amateur poets were all pitiful. All of them except for the ones written by a certain Pierre Rousseau, who lived in the eighteenth arrondissement of Paris.

As soon as she set eyes upon them, the poems by that unknown writer had transfixed her. He expressed the inexpressible, he made the whirling world stand still. She had gone back to see the crested bookseller the next day to ask him if his fanzine had a letters page or something like that . . . you know, basically, if it was possible to contact one of the authors.

"Of course, my dear. Which one?"

"Pierre Rousseau, the author of *We, Poor Puppets*."

The face of that man who sold books of spells had cracked into a strange smile, as if he had already guessed which poet Éléa was going to name, and then he'd said: "Of course, my dear. Give me the letter and I'll send it to him. I feel certain he'll reply."

And that's exactly what had happened. This sorcerer had foreseen everything.

At first Éléa and Pierre each wrote the other a long, handwritten letter every month. Then it was every week. They exchanged a pile of more than a hundred such letters before Éléa gradually abandoned their paper correspondence in favor of electronic words on her cell phone. Éléa loved these new technologies. Pierre hated them, but in the end she managed to convince him to convert to the immediacy of the modern world, to letters that reached their addressee at the speed of thought.

This changed their lives.

Their exchanges went from weekly to daily, then began to take over their existence in real time. Not even three hours would pass without one of them telling the other what they were doing, eating, watching, or—most importantly—reading.

Even one day's silence would overturn their world.

Éléa and Pierre had never seen each other, never met, never exchanged a single photograph, but they knew that what they felt for each other was a deep romantic friendship worthy of the great epistolary lovers.

Or, at least, that was what Éléa believed.

At eighteen, when Éléa left her native province to live in Paris, although she didn't tell Pierre this from the beginning, she went to the capital for him—only for him. She took the first job she found—as a secretary in that real estate agency—and rented the first apartment she saw, in that supposedly working-class neighborhood at the foot of Montmartre. She never gave up either of them.

It was in that moment, when she left everything behind, that she realized she would never follow the classic model of starting a family and staying in touch with friends. In reality, she felt comfortable only with her own company, and with Pierre's words. She knew she was different.

After a series of tests, a doctor confirmed this hunch: She was on the autism spectrum—a condition rendered almost invisible in the eyes of other people due to her high intelligence. Éléa instantly felt as if she'd been cured of a disease that had been consuming her. Her diagnosis answered all the questions that she had been asking herself since she was born. Questions about her divergent thought processes, her anti-conformism, her narrow interests and intense passions, her inability to manage her emotions or to understand what other people were feeling, her painful awareness of injustice, and the need she felt for solitude and routine, which she had always imagined was just a form of selfishness.

Eager to know everything about the condition, she had read every textbook she could find, clicked on every website. Suddenly she recognized herself. She felt reborn. She even loved the name that those who shared this syndrome had chosen for themselves: autist. She was an autist.

It was also at this point in her life—just after her arrival in Paris—that Éléa started talking to her brain. At first she called it Brian, after Brian Molko, the beautiful singer of the band Placebo, but in the end she settled on the banal option of Brain. After all, what was more banal than talking to your brain? Éléa imagined that everyone, in the privacy of their skulls, discussed things with themselves, engaging in endless internal dialogues, debating shameful opinions. The world's greatest secrets were all hidden there, weren't they? In our heads. The last, the only truly uncrackable safe, in a world where everything else was filmed, monitored, recorded.

"What do you think, Brain?"

*Nothing much. I'm just listening to you monologuing. I find it relaxing.*

One morning, someone rang the doorbell to her apartment. Éléa never had any visitors, not even a pizza delivery. Nobody knew her address, except Pierre.

As soon as she heard the bell ring, Éléa knew who it was.

As soon as she opened the front door and looked out at the landing, its walls graffitied by the stairwell poets, she recognized the person standing there.

During all those years, Éléa had refused to imagine what Pierre might look like. She had never asked him about his age, his height, his weight, or the color of his eyes. Because she was worried that she would be disappointed, probably. Now life offered her an unexpected gift on her doorstep, a miracle standing there in front of her. Pierre was older than her, but not as old as she'd feared. And he was handsome. Oh, so handsome! Honey-colored hair. Eyes as gray as a moonlit night. A slender, muscular body—a dancer's body, she thought, the moment she saw him. Pierre moved in a unique, almost syncopated way, like a brilliantly articulated robot.

The moment she cried out in ecstasy, as they made love for the very first time, she knew he would be the first and only man in her life.

Afterward, as she caressed every inch of his skin, he told her that her guess was right: He was a professional dancer. He toured the world, interpreting his favorite—pretty much his only—role, that of Petrushka, the lead character in Igor Stravinsky's ballet of the same name; the most famous puppet in the Russian theater, madly in love with his ballerina.

Pierre—or Petrushka, as Éléa immediately started calling him: *my Petrushka*—could not stay. He was expected elsewhere. He caught airport connections the way other people change trains at Metro stations. But he would come back as often as he could, he promised. He loved her, he . . .

Éléa gently placed her palm over his lips.

"Shh, my Petrushka. Shh, no promises. Come back when you can. It doesn't matter, as long as you're mine. Mine and no one else's. I ask only one thing of you if you want me to be yours. Yours and no one else's. Write to me! Always write to me. As often as you can. Every day. Ten times, a hundred times a day."

He made no promises that night, but this was what they did, over the days, months, and years that followed. Their lives were punctuated by their messages to each other—sometimes brief, sometimes seeming to go on forever.

They always woke up to a note from whichever one of them had gone to bed last; a message to rock them softly to sleep, to comfort them in their dreams.

Every moment of joy or sadness, however small or intimate, was a moment shared between the two of them.

And whenever Pierre rang the doorbell of her apartment on Boulevard Barbès, which he did four or five times a year, Paris became a village where they would run, hand in hand, from theater to theater, from museum to museum. Pierre told her about every street, every monument; he had grown up here, and he knew every inch of the city; he knew the map of Paris better than the taxi drivers who drove them around.

Pierre showered her with gifts more expensive than anything she could possibly afford on her secretary's wages. Electronic appliances, mostly. Tablets, smartphones, computers that she used to listen to books and records from the local multimedia library. Éléa was fascinated by these technological marvels, each more advanced than the last; by the creative genius behind these miniaturized processors. This technology offered her a permanent connection with her Petrushka. Almost like an extension of herself. Pierre could see what she saw, feel what she felt. He could practically breathe the same air she breathed.

That night, though, she hardly breathed at all.

Pierre—her Petrushka—had not written to her for three days. Three whole days! This had never happened before.

Éléa pressed her forehead to the cold glass of her apartment's window and looked down at the hurrying world thirty feet below her on Boulevard Barbès. She listened to the hum of a world to which she did not belong. Behind her, in her tiny apartment, six blank screens illuminated the night.

"What do you think, Brain?"

*Do you want me to answer honestly?*

"No, not honestly and not dishonestly either. I want you to answer me objectively."

*Okay. Objectively, I think that Pierre is dead.*

". . ."

*I'm sorry, but based on the objective evidence at my disposal, that is the most logical conclusion. Pierre has written to you—well, to us—on average about ten times a day, every day, for years. The last time we didn't hear from him was on April 5, 2009, when there was nothing for nine hours after a major network failure. Right now, it has been precisely seventy-three hours, eleven minutes, and twenty-three seconds since we last heard from him. If Pierre had been having computer problems, or even if he'd had an accident, he would have found some way to let you know. The only other explanation is that he simply doesn't want to write to you anymore, but there is absolutely no evidence to suggest such a scenario. Agreed? So, to conclude, in the absence of any credible alternatives, my objective analysis is that Pierre must be dead.*

"You're a pain in the ass, Brain."

*I'm just analyzing the facts.*

"Well, I think he's alive!"

*You could be right. I would assess the likelihood of that at 11 percent.*

"Bastard!"

*Please stop pressing your forehead against this window. I'm cold.*

Éléa didn't move.

*You'll break the glass if you keep pressing it this hard. You're not planning to commit suicide, are you?*

"No. Not while I can still cling to that 11 percent chance."

At midnight, Éléa went downstairs to the street. She couldn't sleep. This was something that hardly ever happened to her. Her neighborhood wasn't sleeping either, but it appeared to be more used to its insomnia. Some smokers stood in front of a bar with dazzling neon lights; a line of people waited outside food stalls for their burgers and kebabs and halal fries; a few guys in sweatsuits guarded the entrance to the Château Rouge Metro station; and a crowd of noisy night owls were buying and selling at the foot of the white-walled Montmartre hill.

Éléa wandered aimlessly. Drunk men ogled her legs, her breasts, her ass, then forgot her as soon as the next woman entered their field of vision. Éléa liked walking through Paris like this, feeling desirable and untouchable. There were so many other pretty girls around that being sexy made her feel anonymous. She knew the power that her hourglass figure gave her over the brains of weak men. She fed on their lust, using it to stoke her libido, and every day she touched herself while daydreaming of her Petrushka.

For hours she lost herself in the local streets, praying and hoping, her only compass the illuminated Sacré-Cœur. The smart ring on her finger seemed to weigh a ton. This was the last present Pierre had given her. A technological miracle, even smaller and more discreet than a smart watch; every time she received a new message, the stone in the ring would buzz, chime, or light up, and she was able to choose between several thousand different colors for those lights, from sapphire to topaz. Of course her ring was connected by Bluetooth to all the other smart objects in the vicinity. Just by rubbing her finger, Éléa could listen to the voice messages on her smartphone or dictate a text. Her ring could also take her temperature, her blood pressure, her heart rate; it could measure the quality of her sleep, count the number of steps she took in a day . . . Pierre had presented it to her inside a red velvet jewelry box, as if it was a diamond engagement ring, and it was as dear to her as the One Ring was to Gollum.

Her own magic ring. *Her* Precious.

But tonight it was silent.

She went home via Rue Myrha and reached her apartment as the sun was rising. Exhausted.

During her long nighttime walk, the ring had not vibrated once. Éléa had thought about calling the police, but she knew they wouldn't take her seriously. They were hardly going to search for a man whom she often didn't see for four months at a time, just because she hadn't heard from him for three days. A man about whom she knew nothing beyond his name and his job . . .

And who, nevertheless, she knew perfectly.

"Shall we go to sleep, Brain?"

*It's about time!*

"Brain? Brain! Are you there? You're not asleep, are you?"

*I wish . . .*

"Brain, what time is it?"

*How should I know? Just ask your Precious! I need to get some rest. My performance levels decrease by 12 percent for every hour of lost sleep.*

"I'm sorry, Brain, I just can't fall asleep. Even with the curtains drawn and the shutters closed. It must be late morning by now, right? At least eleven o'clock?"

*It's 9:36 a.m.*

"Shit! Listen, Brain . . . About what you said yesterday. You know, your theory, and the chance that I was right. That . . ."

*That Pierre isn't dead? According to my calculations, the likelihood of that has decreased to 7 percent. Now go back to sleep!*

"If I sleep two hours, and Petrushka still hasn't called, what will my chances be then?"

*Less than 3 percent.*

"And by midnight tonight?"

*Zero. It'll be over. But it's over now. You know it is. You may as well throw your Precious and all those other smart objects in the trash. Forget it! What difference does it make whether Pierre is dead or he's dumped you? Either way, it's over. Stop loving a ghost.*

"Pierre loves me. And he's alive, I can sense it!"

*You're right. There's still a 6 percent chance. Now, sleep.*

When Éléa woke suddenly in silence and darkness, she realized that she had slept much longer than two hours, and that the last percentage points of her hope had vanished.

She sat up against her pillow. When she thought about it, it was quite simple. She just had to get up, open the curtains, open the shutters, open the window, and jump . . .

She had always known it would end like this. She did not possess a talent for living. And she had never been the most motivated person. Without Pierre, what was the point in continuing to exist?

She stared at the window, breathing calmly.

Just as she was about to stand up, she spotted a pink light under her sheets. And in that instant she understood what had woken her so suddenly from her dark dreams.

Her Precious was buzzing and flashing on her finger!

A new text. A message from Pierre.

With a brush of her fingertip, she connected her ring to her cell phone and her computer.

In Brian Molko's deep voice, the one that she had chosen to read out her lover's texts, twelve words emerged from the computer's speakers to chase away the shadows of death that had hung gloomily over her apartment.

*"It's me—your Petrushka! I'm sitting on my grave, waiting for you."*

# THE DAWNS ARE HEARTBREAKING

"The Drunken Boat" by Arthur Rimbaud

***Saturday, September 16, 2023***

# 6

## Nanesse

***Pont-à-Bar, Ardennes***

"Agnès Duval? Can you hear me? This is Captain Katel Marelle. Are you driving?"

Nanesse slowed down. The rain was drumming relentlessly on the roof of her old Clio. Amid the machine-gun noise of water on steel, she could barely hear the policewoman's voice through her phone's speaker. She spotted an open space by the side of the road, between earth and gravel, under a tired-looking plane tree, and came to a halt.

"I've parked, Captain. I can just about hear you."

"I received confirmation from the lab. The medical examiner sent me a three-page report. There's no doubt at all: The dead man was your husband, Renaud Duval."

Nanesse's eyes filled with tears. She stared at the moving wipers, as if it were her eyes and not the windshield that they were trying to keep dry.

"I'll spare you the details, Agnès, but it all matches up. The blood tests, the fingerprints, the DNA results, even his dental X-rays. Don't take any of this the wrong way—of course we believed you when you formally identified your husband at the morgue yesterday. But we're also investigating the two strangers, Hans Bernard and Pierre Rousseau, who appear to look exactly like Renaud."

Nanesse appreciated Captain Katel's frankness, even her lack of tact. She couldn't stand hypocrites and sycophants.

"We're making progress on everything else too. The judge wants to see you again, but I'm going to give you some advance warning: There are, let's say, a few gray areas in the file. First, the medical examiner couldn't find any evidence of violence on your husband's body. That is, the fall killed him, but it seems unlikely that he was pushed from the lookout point. He would have defended himself—we'd have found some traces of struggle. But of course nothing is certain . . . There could have been two people who threw him over the barrier, for example. We're still investigating that.

"Another complicating detail: We found the tire tracks of two other cars in the parking lot in the woods near where Renaud's car was left. The time of your husband's death has been estimated at around 8:00 p.m., so the people in those cars may have seen what happened. We also found some fresh footprints, different from your husband's. But only one pair of shoes, size twelve. You see the problem? Two cars, but only one driver. Don't worry, Agnès, we have some brilliant analysts who will get to the bottom of all this. With the rain and the mud, it's perfect for them. Although we can't rule out the possibility that someone could have erased their own footprints."

"So . . . Are you saying my husband was murdered?"

"Impossible to know. But one thing is sure: He wasn't alone up there. His car was hidden under a tree, but the other two weren't. We're trying to figure it out, Agnès. Your husband was a man who . . . well, let's just say he liked his secrets."

The longer this conversation went on, the less sure Nanesse felt that she really did appreciate Katel Marelle's lack of diplomacy. Whenever Nanesse had some distressing information to pass on to her little protégés—which was a common occurrence—she too tried to be honest, and she never lied to them, but she would often spend hours thinking of the most tactful way to convey the news.

"As far as your husband's identity is concerned," the captain continued, "it all checks out. He really was educated—from elementary school to high school—in Charleville-Mézières. And he did work three weeks a month at the Walor-Florennes plant on the Belgian side of the border, while he spent his nights with you. The fourth week he spent driving around France, visiting clients, but according to his boss, your husband was free to go wherever he liked during that time. Nobody policed him. We'll need to cross-check his work schedule with your personal memories to find out whether he was lying to you."

Nanesse turned off the windshield wipers. Better just to let her eyes drown in tears . . .

Suddenly she felt sure. Renaud had been stringing her along, all these years. He had a double life, even a triple life, that he spent visiting various mistresses . . .

"Agnès? Are you still there? As I'm sure you can imagine, we've also been investigating those two doppelgängers, Hans Bernard and Pierre Rousseau. We have their addresses on the driver's licenses, but we couldn't find any matches. There's no Hans Bernard living at 4 Rue de l'Espérance in Mende, nor is there a Pierre Rousseau at 17 Rue de Sofia in the eighteenth arrondissement of Paris. They could have moved anywhere; here in France, there's no legal obligation to declare your address to the authorities. We're searching for them, but there are more than sixty-eight Pierre Rousseaus listed in France. Only twenty-three Hans Bernards, but if you add in Belgium and Germany, you get another forty-eight of them. Do you want to hear the best part, Agnès?"

"No."

"According to my colleagues at the fraud squad, those three licenses are genuine!"

Nanesse remained silent.

"Yep, it appears those three men—your Renaud, plus Pierre and Hans—all actually existed. All three of them with the same face! So you can see why the judge wants to see you again, Agnès, as soon as possible, so that you can take him whatever documentation about your husband's life that you have."

"Well, that won't take long. He left me hardly anything . . ."

"Apart from about twenty puppets!"

"Yeah, and a receipt for a television."

"Sorry?"

"I found one of his old friends. It would take too long to explain, but I'm on my way to his house now, in Pont-à-Bar."

"Okay. Send me all the details. Name, address, and all that. And don't forget to call Judge Carignan to arrange a meeting. Agnès?"

"Yes?"

Nanesse wondered what terrible revelation the captain was going to announce this time.

"Take care of yourself."

Pont-à-Bar was submerged in fog. The village, consisting primarily of moored barges rather than rows of houses, was built along the Ardennes Canal, between Charleville-Mézières and Sedan. Between people strolling beside the locks and passengers on boats, it was usually quite busy here, but today the rain had dissuaded even the bravest bargemen.

*11 Chemin des Noyers.*

Nanesse parked her car beside the canal. The rain was falling more softly now, but the sky still hung so low that she was almost afraid she would knock her head against it when she got out of the car. It was the kind of weather to make you hang yourself, as the entertainer Patrick Sébastien once sang.

Bruno Pluvier's house stood facing her, a little isolated from the other buildings on the docks.

A charming little fisherman's house, she had imagined.

She'd been wrong.

Bruno Pluvier was a hunter.

# 7

## Vicky

***Hawkweed Guesthouse, Ruynes-en-Margeride***

The moment Vicky opened the curtains, dazzling sunlight lit up Lola's bedroom. A low, blinding sun, poking out from between the wooded peaks of the Margeride.

Her daughter practically leapt out of bed.

"Is Daddy home?"

Every time Lola woke up, her first question was always about Hans. *Is Daddy here? Has Daddy gone again? Is Daddy coming home today?*

Hans was the only man she knew.

Before Lola was born, Hans would place his hand on Vicky's round belly every month. And since her birth, he had not missed any of her birthdays. That was the advantage of being self-employed, he'd said: He could drive all the way across Europe in his truck without sleeping, from Copenhagen or Warsaw, to see his little princess blow out her candles. Hans adored Lola. And she, in return, had chosen him as her daddy . . .

"Is Hans here?" Lola insisted, pushing away her bedsheets.

"No, sweetie."

"Did he call?"

"No."

Trying not to cry, Lola turned to Kasper. In the small voice of a five-year-old mother, she reassured her puppet. "Don't worry, Daddy will come back—he promised. He'll make you better. You won't be broken all your life."

After breakfast, Vicky suggested to her daughter that they do some tidying up. Lola took on the task of going through her boxes of treasure: all the rocks, branches, dead insects, and wilted flowers she had collected while walking the paths of the Margeride that year. Vicky, meanwhile, went through her own belongings.

Or, to be more precise, through Hans's.

They were all kept in her closet: three shelves of clothes, half the hanging rail, and a cardboard box sealed with brown packing tape.

"Mommy, can I keep the ladybugs? Even if they don't have wings anymore?"

Vicky didn't answer. Her throat felt tight. She hesitated.

"Mommy?"

In one movement, she tore off the packing tape. Her gaze, and then her hands, plunged deep inside the cardboard box. She rummaged around, picking up each of the objects before putting them back, but there was no gold in Hans's treasure chest.

All she found were a few toiletries, a few frayed pieces of clothing, a ballpoint pen, a scratched pair of sunglasses . . . The kind of junk that you keep in a bag, then toss in the trash one day without even bothering to go through it.

Vicky kept searching. She unearthed an old toothbrush, a chewed pencil . . . not even a piece of paper, a photograph, or a key.

Hans had left nothing behind. Not a single trace of his past. No clues at all.

This time, Vicky couldn't push back the horrible sense of foreboding that had been haunting her for four days.

What if Hans had left her for good?

For five years he had lived with her in the guesthouse. But he had never sowed a single seed on the farm; he had been content to pass through.

His real home was his truck.

Vicky continued to half-heartedly go through the few relics that Hans had left behind. A couple of coins, a pack of tissues, a disposable razor. Hans had never tried to hide his life from her; he had told her everything. He was an only child, raised by a single mother who had died shortly before Vicky met him, in a village whose name she couldn't remember.

He had been with a few women before her, without ever becoming attached. Did he have a woman at every truck stop? Like a sailor with his ports, only less romantic?

Could he have abandoned her for one of them?

No, impossible! Every instinct told her that. Her entire body knew the truth: Hans loved her.

Oh, but what if she was wrong? Had she become so naive as to be swept away by a passing breeze?

She tried to reason with herself. She tried to convince herself that she would be fine without a man, even without her clumsy truck driver. She would forget him, she would survive, but . . .

But Lola would not be fine without her daddy.

Vicky taped the box shut again and put it back in the closet. She was irritated—with herself, above all. Hans was no materialist. She wasn't going to find him by searching through his belongings. She needed to search her own memory! Remembering the name of the village where he grew up would be a good start . . .

She tried to relive all those hikes they had taken together, projecting the film inside her mind and turning the volume up as high as it would go, so she could listen again to what her gray-eyed guide had been telling her. After sorting through this information, Vicky managed to run down a few clues. Hans had grown up in a large village with a steep-sided stream running through it, where he used to go fishing. By riding his mountain bike, he could reach the shallow slopes of the Causses, but also the steep hills of Cévennes. He knew those places better than she did. Vicky had been hiking with Hans often enough to be sure that was true.

"Mommy? Mommy, I'm done!"

Lola had not thrown away anything, not even a single dried-up fly.

"What time is it, Mommy? I'm hungry!"

Almost noon. And still no signs of life from Hans. Vicky thought about picking up her phone and calling Julien Murat at the police station again, but she felt sure the sergeant wouldn't take her any more seriously than he had yesterday. She had to present him with some new evidence: the name of a person he could contact, for example, or at least a place where he might begin the search. But where to start? If only she could recall the name of that damned village . . .

Lola was playing beside her. She had put Kasper inside a little cart pulled by a toy pony.

More out of idle hope than genuine expectation, Vicky asked her daughter: "Sweetie, do you happen to remember the name of the village where Hans—I mean, Daddy—grew up?"

How could Lola possibly remember? Her five-year-old brain didn't even know where Auvergne, America, or China was.

"Of course!" Lola replied, while continuing to play with her cart. "His village was Florine, like my friend."

"Florine?"

Vicky grabbed her cell phone. *Florine?* Like Florine Sérénac, her neighbor's daughter? She checked the internet connection and furiously typed in those seven letters. Then she waited, biting her lip.

Nothing. Lola had just made it up! There was no village in France named Florine.

Unless . . .

Vicky tried searching for villages beginning with F-L-O-R . . .

*Florac, Occitania region, Lozère department,* her phone told her.

Florac! Of course!

Vicky cursed her porous memory. It all came back to her now. It was in that village on the edge of the Tarn—the gateway to the limestone plateaus known as the Causses and the mountain range of the Cévennes, in southern France—that Hans had spent his childhood.

"Are you hungry, sweetie?"

Lola jumped to her feet like a puppet jerked by its strings.

"Yes!"

"I'm going to make us some boiled eggs and sandwiches. We're going on a trip."

"Where?"

"To find Hans!"

# 8

## Éléa

***Boulevard Barbès, Château Rouge, Paris***

*It's me—your Petrushka! I'm sitting on my grave, waiting for you.*

She jumped out of bed and pulled open the curtains and the shutters to let in the noon sunlight. The white domes of Montmartre were barely visible against the chalk-white sky, making the Sacré-Cœur look like the Taj Mahal without its minarets.

"Brain, wake up! I have news!"

Éléa shook her half-asleep head. In the mornings, her thoughts were always slow to form. It would take a few minutes for her Cartesian mind to reorganize itself and start interfacing with her emotions.

"Brain? Come on, you heard it as well as I did . . . Pierre wrote to me! So—"

*So, based on the data in my possession, I would say there is a 97 percent chance that he is alive.*

"Only 97 percent? He wrote to me!"

*You know that it's possible to program a cell phone to send a text days or even months later.*

"Oh, don't be such a sore loser! Just admit that I was right. Pierre is alive!"

*I'm simply being rational. A corpse can continue to send messages if those messages were written prior to his death. Lots of people do that on social media, to give themselves a kind of eternal life.*

"Oh, stop it!"

Éléa quickly stripped off the rumpled clothes she had worn to bed the previous night and placed her Precious on the nightstand. Standing naked in front of the mirror, she spent a moment admiring the brambles tattooed around her arm, the rose blooming on her chest, and the fallen petals near her navel, as black as her spiked hair.

Her Petrushka was alive! She was going to see him again! She had to make herself pretty for him . . .

She went into the shower cubicle: a cramped little recess, black with mold, where—if she was lucky—a thin trickle of water might eventually warm up. She waited for a few icy drops to fall on her head before calling out to her brain again.

"Okay, are you awake now?"

*No! I have to remind you of this every morning: When you're in the shower, I'm allowed to rest. You stop thinking and you focus on your body, like a normal girl. You check that your stomach is nice and flat, you feel how long the hair on your legs is, you examine your fingernails and toenails . . .*

"But I'm not a normal girl! And I need you, Brain. Pierre wrote 'I'm sitting on my grave.' What is that supposed to mean?"

*That he's dead.*

"Don't be silly. A dead man doesn't sit on his grave."

Éléa weighed her breasts in her hands while Brain thought this over. She had always thought they were too small, but Pierre adored them. She would put some perfume on them after she had dried herself.

*It's me . . . I'm sitting on my grave, waiting for you,* he had written. Was this some new game her lover had invented?

He didn't need to come up with such a cruel trick to make her want him, though.

Éléa leaned down to sniff the moisturizers on the edge of the shower. Tahitian gardenia or honeysuckle?

Brain, having considered her question, did not give her time to make a choice.

*Hang on, I've noticed something. The message says: "It's me—your Petrushka! I'm sitting on my grave, waiting for you." It doesn't say: "It's me, Pierre."*

"What difference does that make? Pierre or Petrushka, it's the same!"

*Maybe not. Where is Petrushka buried?*

"Petrushka isn't dead. You said so yourself. There's a 97 percent chance that he's alive."

Éléa slid her hands over her belly and spread her legs a little bit. She imagined her Petrushka kneeling between them, his mouth moving closer to the depths of her desire, his cheeks rubbing against her skin, his lips kissing hers. She remembered the scratchy feel of his stubble when he would meet her after a ten-hour flight, after catching a taxi to come and see her without having time to shave.

*Um, hello?* Brain said sharply. *Are you listening? I'm talking about the real Petrushka.*

"The real Petrushka is a puppet. A character in a ballet. He's not buried anywhere, and he's certainly not sitting on a grave."

*I'm not so sure about that.*

"Well, go away and think about it in silence. And leave me in peace for a minute. Weren't you the one who said we're not supposed to talk when we're in the shower? Just do some thinking. And hold on tight, Brain, because you're about to hit some turbulence . . ."

Éléa gently moved her middle finger to the edge of her clitoris, where it pressed, rubbed, twirled. The pleasure came almost instantly, overwhelming her. Too fast. That was Pierre's fault for playing with fire—their sacred fire.

She rinsed herself off, dousing the fire's final embers with cold water.

"Brain? Brain? Are you there?"

She stepped out of the cubicle and walked carefully on the wet tiles.

*Yes. And while you were having fun, I found it.*

"Found what?"

*An old and deeply buried memory. It goes back to the first few times we researched Petrushka.*

"On the internet?"

*Do people search for information anywhere else?*

"Well, I'm pretty sure my grandparents didn't use the internet. Anyway, what did you find?"

*Remember how you thought Pierre looked like a dancer? A Russian dancer. Vaslav Nijinsky. The greatest dancer of his generation, and his most famous role is Petrushka.*

"Okay, but everyone knows that. Even people who aren't lucky enough to have you, Brain. What's your point?"

*Do you remember where Vaslav Nijinsky is buried?*

"I don't know . . . Moscow? London? Saint Petersburg?"

*Nope.*

"Ah, then Paris! Where? Père-Lachaise? Montparnasse?"

*Wrong again.*

"Oh, is it here? Up the hill, in the Montmartre Cemetery?"

*Yes!*

"Thank you, Brain! I love you!"

Éléa jumped up and down, and the lid came off the tube of Tahitian gardenia moisturizer, spilling half of it over her breasts.

Of course . . . that must be it! Her Petrushka was waiting for her on the Russian dancer's grave, only a few hundred yards from where she stood right now.

She had spent the last few months thinking of nothing but seeing him again, pondering the different outfits she might wear, imagining a thousand different types of weather . . . and now that it was time to choose, she felt paralyzed by indecision. High-heeled boots or ballet shoes? Strappy camisole or low-cut blouse? Lace bustier or lace-up corset?

When it came to solving these dilemmas, however, Brain was no use at all.

# 9

## Nanesse

***Pont-à-Bar, Ardennes***

"Shit!" muttered Bruno Pluvier, sinking even deeper into his chair. "I haven't seen Renaud for more than ten years, but it's still really strange to think he's gone."

Bruno seemed upset. A little too upset. His 220-pound frame was hidden under an oversized sweater and a pair of khaki sweatpants. Nanesse felt uneasy in this house. And yet the former TV salesman had ushered her inside unhesitatingly, even a little impatiently. She'd had no difficulty persuading his former colleagues to give her his phone number, and Bruno had immediately invited her to come and see him.

"Of course I remember Renaud. Who could forget him?"

Pluvier had explained to her that he'd quit his job at Darty and set up his own business as an electrician, earning three times as much money for half the work. Which left him plenty of time to do the things he loved. This, Nanesse guessed from a few seconds' observation, probably meant hunting deer, partridge, and wild boar. There were hunting rifles hanging on every wall and cartridge belts slung over the back of the couch. A pair of damp-looking boots stood in the entrance hall.

Nanesse blew on the cup of coffee that Bruno Pluvier had warmed up for her. There was something about the décor in this house, something about this old friendship, that struck a false note. Renaud was the exact opposite of a guy like Pluvier. He hated all forms of violence and was physically repulsed by guns. In Bourg-Fidèle, half the village's men would meet up sometimes to go hunting, but Renaud was never one of them.

Bruno Pluvier caught Nanesse staring at his collection of rifles.

"I bet you're wondering how Renaud could ever have been friends with someone like me, aren't you?"

Nanesse blushed. At least Bruno Pluvier didn't beat around the bush.

"Well, there were almost three hundred of us called up to the 152nd Regiment, from all over France. Renaud and I became friends because we were from the same town, Charleville-Mézières, and we'd been to the same schools. That was often how it worked, in the army: First you made friends with people from your area, and then you found people you had more in common with."

"So you were already friends with Renaud before you were called up?"

"No, not really. We weren't in the same class. But we knew each other's names and faces, you know. And we recognized each other when we started in the regiment. Renaud was kind of famous because of his mother. She was an artist who made puppets in a railcar. Or at least that's what I remember . . ."

Nanesse nodded. She continued distractedly noting the names of the rifles on the walls. Chassepot Model 1866. Lebel Model 1916. Berthier Model 1939. You'd have thought Pluvier was expecting France to be invaded at any moment.

"But when you were in the regiment together, you did become real friends?"

"Oh yes, you could definitely say that. The other soldiers called us the Charleville buddies, Nono the Sniper and Renaud the Chameleon."

"Renaud the . . . Chameleon?"

Smiling at the look of surprise on Nanesse's face, Bruno leaned forward. His breath stank of alcohol, and she recoiled. He was the kind of guy whose children she looked after, she thought unkindly.

"Yeah . . . the Chameleon! I get the feeling your husband didn't tell you much about himself. Everyone called him that, because he had this amazing ability to act differently depending on who he was with."

"What do you mean?"

"Well, it's simple. When he was with me, and our little circle of beer-drinking gun nuts, he would hang out with us for hours, laughing as we shot bullets at tin cans or told the kind of jokes that would land you in prison these days! And the same evening, he might buddy up to a group of NCOs who all talked about literature and philosophy, before spending the later part of the night sympathizing with some conscientious objectors who were trying every trick they could think of to be sent home. He was at ease with everyone, Renaud—that's what I admired about him. He had a sort of gift, you know, for adapting to his surroundings. He would just blend in. Tell you exactly what you wanted to hear. He could have been a spy, I swear. Maybe he was, at that . . ."

He exploded with laughter, and a bit of his alcoholic spit landed in her cup of coffee.

"Here's another example to show you how hard it was to pin down Renaud. I remember he was taking a degree in mechanical engineering, but he also took advantage of his military service to get his truck driver's license, and several times I caught him reading poetry magazines. He used to hide them inside porn magazines so nobody would make fun of him."

Pluvier raised his cup to his guest's face.

"To your health, Renaud the Chameleon!"

Nanesse did not clink cups with him. She couldn't help feeling troubled by this conversation. She'd known nothing about Renaud being a truck driver or liking poetry. And what this Bruno called his chameleonic nature, she had always thought of as empathy. It was what had made her love her husband during all those years: the way he would always try to understand what another person was thinking, to put himself in their place. Such a rare quality . . .

She waited for Bruno to finish drinking.

"Did Renaud ever talk to you about his life before you met him? His childhood, I mean. Anything that might . . ."

Bruno flashed her a disturbing smile.

"It's really true then! You didn't know your husband at all. Then again, nobody knew the Chameleon. I was never the sharpest tool in the drawer, but even I understood that. Let me give you an example . . . There were lots of rich kids from Paris in the regiment, mostly NCOs; well, Renaud could reel off the names of all the Metro stations in the neighborhoods where they lived, the number of bakeries in each arrondissement, the opening hours for each museum, as if he'd lived there for years. There was a guy from Lozère there too—or maybe from Tarn? I can't remember—with a really thick accent, and Renaud would spend hours chatting with him about the hiking paths in the area and all these godforsaken villages so tiny that they make Pont-à-Bar look like Paris."

"Do you think maybe he had gone there on vacation?" Nanesse asked.

"Maybe. It must have been a really long vacation, though!"

"And that's all? About his childhood, I mean. You didn't ever see him again, once your military service was over?"

"No. Renaud cut off all contact as soon as we were sent home. Not that I was surprised. That's the Chameleon's technique, you see. He was probably sick of khaki, so he chose some other colors. Yours, apparently."

His gaze lingered on Nanesse's rainbow-colored patchwork coat, then on her pretty, round face, with its discreet pastel makeup.

"And you really never saw him again?"

"Just once. About twelve years ago, when I was working at Darty. But you know about that. I realized that Renaud had no intention of inviting me over for aperitifs, that he would toss my phone number in the first trash can he passed. And yet . . ."

"What?"

"Well, he did call my number once before."

"When?"

Bruno flashed her a conspiratorial smile.

"Two or three years after we got out of the army. Back then, the internet was just starting to become a thing. Renaud was clueless about it, but I was already part of the computer business. I know it doesn't look like it, but I'm a bit of a whiz when it comes to technology. He called me because he wanted some information."

*Information?* A shiver ran down Nanesse's back. This was it, she thought: the key that would open the door to her husband's past. Pluvier, though, did not seem in any hurry to tell her more.

"Do you remember what it was about?"

"Vaguely. It was a long time ago. And the information he wanted was about something that had happened long before that. Before we were born, in fact. He wanted me to find a copy of an old newspaper. A local edition."

"Did you find it?"

"Yeah, this collector had it. He must have sent it to Renaud."

"Did you really need the internet for that?"

"Oh, definitely! Renaud was looking for a foreign newspaper, you see."

"Foreign?"

"Czech, I think. It wasn't a Prague newspaper—some other town, with a weird name that I've forgotten."

Nanesse's patience snapped.

"That's too vague, Bruno! No year, no place name. This could be important!"

"I'm sure it was. Why else would the Chameleon have come down from his branch?"

"You don't remember any other details?"

"Just one thing. I feel like the name of that Czech town reminded me of something. The name of a beer. No idea which one, though." Bruno took his time drinking the last of his coffee, then added: "Although . . . I could look back through my archives. I have a record of everything, on hard disks that I keep in the cellar. It's the three rules of computing, you know: Back up, back up, back up. There was no cloud in those days, so you needed cardboard boxes and plenty of shelf space. Come back tomorrow, if you like, and I'll find what you're looking for."

Nanesse thought about the phone call from Captain Marelle: She needed to arrange to see the judge. She decided now was the right time to come down from her high horse. Leaning forward, she spoke to Bruno in a friendly voice.

"Couldn't you find it for me now?"

There was a gleam in the hunter's eye.

"If you insist . . ."

"I insist."

"Okay, I'll go and look now. Help yourself to more coffee. But don't touch any of the rifles. They might just be loaded . . ."

Bruno heaved himself out of the chair and disappeared through the open door that led down to the cellar. Nanesse waited. If he was as organized as he claimed, this shouldn't take long. She tried to go over the information she'd gleaned from their conversation. Surely Bruno Pluvier had been exaggerating? Renaud, a spy? Oh, what nonsense! He had simply been intelligent enough to adapt to his surroundings, and with a little general knowledge it wouldn't have been that hard to sprinkle the names of a few Metro stations or villages into a conversation.

But how to explain those three driver's licenses? And who did those other two cars belong to—the ones that had been parked below the lookout point at Bogny-sur-Meuse, while Renaud's had been hidden under a tree?

He'd had a meeting with Death that night. But what face had Death worn in those final moments?

Nanesse's thoughts continued to wander as she waited.

Bruno still hadn't come back.

She waited another five minutes, watching the hand of the clock on the wall, where it hung between an ultramodern sniper rifle and a double-barreled shotgun. Finally, she became impatient and stood up.

She went to the top of the stairs and called down: "Bruno, have you found it?"

No answer.

The staircase light had gone out, and the cellar appeared completely dark. A wild thought ran through Nanesse's head.

What if Bruno had run away? What if he'd disappeared through the back door, leaving her here alone?

*Ridiculous,* she told herself.

"Bruno?"

No answer. She pressed the light switch and the staircase was instantly illuminated. Still she heard nothing from below. She glanced back at the double-barreled shotgun and wondered if she should grab it. Suddenly she felt frightened.

*Stop being so silly!* she told herself. Bruno was probably just concentrating on his task, annoyed with himself that he hadn't yet found the file he was searching for.

She descended the first few steps.

"Bruno, is everything okay?"

Silence.

Beyond the bottom step of the staircase, the cellar was in total darkness. There were two narrow basement windows facing the street on the canal side, but the rain and fog outside meant that almost no light filtered into the room. Was Bruno hunting old memories the way he hunted game? Unseen and unheard?

Nanesse kept walking down the stairs, her hand touching the wall, until she came to another light switch. She turned it on.

The cellar was immediately illuminated and she cried out with horror.

Bruno Pluvier was lying at her feet, at the bottom of the stairs.

His head was smashed open.

A few feet above him, drops of blood were visible on the corner of a metal shelf.

Thoughts whirled inside Nanesse's mind. Bruno must have slipped on the stairs and banged his head against the iron bar. He might just be unconscious. She crouched down next to the man's body and reached out to check his pulse, to make sure he was still alive . . .

Some shadows on the wall made her look up. Four legs had just appeared on the street beyond the basement window. They stood still, blurred by rain, cut off below the knee by the top of the window frame.

Nanesse's gaze swept along the brick wall of the cellar until it came to a wooden door. Did it lead outside? Could someone have come in through that door? Could someone have listened to their conversation? And waited for Bruno to come downstairs before killing him?

She rushed over to the door.

It was locked. And yet . . .

Nanesse froze with terror.

A series of still-wet footprints ran from the door to Bruno's body and back.

So someone *had* come in! And then, a few minutes—or seconds—ago, they had left, locking this door behind them.

Leaving her here . . . like a rat in a trap?

Nanesse looked up at the basement window and felt a thrill of dread. Now there was only one pair of legs outside the window. So, one man had stayed to stand guard, while the other . . .

Nanesse rushed across the cellar, stepped over Bruno's body, and started to run up the steps. But then she froze.

Somebody was standing at the top of the basement stairs!

Somebody holding the double-barreled shotgun. Slowly they lowered it.

Nanesse just had time to glimpse his face. A vision of horror: The man's skin was horribly burned, all except for his eyes, lips, and nose.

She had seen this man before. Four days ago, outside her home.

Nanesse took one step back, then another, terrified that at any moment two bullets would pierce her heart, and that she would die, without ever understanding why.

The last thing she saw was the sadistic smile of the man with the burned face.

Then everything went black.

# 10

## VICKY

***Hawkweed Guesthouse, Ruynes-en-Margeride***

Lola ran around the courtyard, frightening the hens and rabbits. In the distance, Rampion and Catsfoot trotted around their field, imitating the little girl.

"We're going to find Daddy!" sang Lola, dancing with Kasper. "We're going to find Daddy!"

After throwing the suitcases in the trunk of her Berlingo, Vicky looked up and said: "Lola, since you've got so much energy, please run over to see Florine's daddy and tell him that we're going away for a couple of days. Ask him if he can feed our animals for us, okay?"

Vicky often performed the same favor for her neighbors when they went on vacation, looking after their cats, goats, and two geese. Lola ran off along the path that led between the two farms. While she was gone, Vicky looked at the map, tracing the roads she would need to take to reach Florac. About seventy-five miles. They should be there in an hour and a half.

"Lola?"

Florine's farm was very close. Straight across the road, less than two hundred yards away, and there were no cars around here.

"Lola?" Vicky shouted.

Still no answer. Normally, her daughter would be back home in a few minutes. Vicky dropped her map and headed toward the neighbors' farm. She felt suddenly anxious. As she walked, she tried to reason with herself.

Nothing could have happened to Lola. There were no strangers around here.

Vicky quickened her pace.

But wasn't it reckless of her, letting her daughter wander around all the time on her own, as she did? She should be more careful. She—

Vicky stopped and sighed with relief.

She had been worrying over nothing.

Lola was standing on tiptoe in front of the hedge a few yards away.

"Mommy! We've got mail!" Lola sprinted proudly toward her mother and handed her a little rectangular card.

"A postcard! Can you read it to me? Who's it from?"

Intrigued, Vicky took the card from her daughter. It showed a Japanese puppet with a traditional appearance: red silk kimono, porcelain-white face, black wig, flower-shaped hairpins.

"Can I see, Mommy? Oh, that's funny—It looks like someone from *Totoro*."

"Yes, sweetie. It's a Japanese puppet."

"Did it come from Japan?"

Vicky turned the card over. There was no stamp or postmark. So someone had hand-delivered it to their mailbox?

But why would anyone come all the way up here just to give them a Japanese postcard?

"Yes, that's right," Vicky lied.

"Read it! What does it say?"

Vicky read the words on the card in silence. They were written in a jerky handwriting that she recognized instantly.

*My two little darlings,*

*I'm fine, don't worry. But please don't try to find me.*

*I can't explain anything right now, Vicky. All I can do is warn you that it would be too dangerous to go in search of me. I know you, my sweet stubborn girl. I know you'll find it hard to obey me, so I'm asking you for Lola's sake.*

*Don't come looking for me. Wait for me.*

*I love you both forever.*

*H*

"Is it from Daddy?"

"Yes."

Vicky's eyes filled with tears. She stared at the sunlight skimming the last flowers in the pasture until she was half blinded, then wiped her eyes with the back of her hand.

She mustn't cry in front of her daughter. She needed to decide. Quickly.

Should she get in the car with Lola and set off in search of clues to Hans's childhood . . .

. . . or stay here?

"Mommy? Will you read it to me? What does he say?"

"He says . . . that he loves us."

"You see? I knew he hadn't forgotten us."

Lola had already started running back toward their guesthouse, arms windmilling, sending hens flying in her wake. Vicky watched as her daughter climbed into the booster seat in the back of the Berlingo, right beside Kasper, and tried to put on her seat belt.

"Come on, Mommy. Quick, get in! Let's go find him."

Vicky hadn't moved. The words danced in her mind's eye.

*. . . don't try to find me.*

*. . . it would be too dangerous . . .*

*. . . I'm asking you for Lola's sake.*

Should she heed these warnings? What could they mean? Who could have brought the postcard here?

Hans?

How long had it been in the mailbox? Vicky hadn't checked her mail for the past three days. And why Japan? Because Hans wanted her to believe that he was far, far away? But in that case, who had delivered the card?

She thought she recognized his handwriting, but it would be easy enough to forge. Was Hans really the one who had written this?

*I know you, my sweet stubborn girl. I know you'll find it hard to obey me.*

Well, one thing was for sure: Whoever wrote this postcard knew Vicky!

*Don't come looking for me.*

But not well enough to convince her to just sit tight and wait.

Vicky was not the kind of person who could spend the rest of her life waiting. She was not the kind of mother who would disappoint her excited daughter. She was not the kind of woman who resigned herself to her fate.

Besides, what possible danger could there be in spending a weekend in Florac, by the Tarn River?

# 11

## Éléa

***Montmartre Cemetery, Paris***

Éléa was out of breath by the time she reached the entrance to Montmartre Cemetery. She had run all the way up Rue Lepic—and then along the wrought iron footbridge that stretches incongruously above the gravestones—in less than ten minutes. In the end she had decided to wear ballet shoes, a flared miniskirt, and a skintight top. The white sky was even more indecisive than Éléa herself, wavering between shy sunlight and hesitant rain.

The placement of Vaslav Nijinsky's grave, and the graves of a hundred or so other celebrities, was indicated on a map beside the front gates. Division 22. Éléa ran through the rows, tiptoeing between graves to save time. She reached Division 27 and went around a glass and marble mausoleum. After Division 26, she climbed a thirty-step staircase. And there it was . . .

Division 22.

She immediately spotted Petrushka's slender figure.

*I'm waiting for you.*

He was there, sitting on the grave, just as his message had promised.

"So what do you say to that, Brain? Have we reached a 100 percent chance that Pierre is alive?"

Brain didn't reply. Éléa had never met a cerebrum that was such a bad loser! She cautiously descended the steps toward her lover. The sun had finally burned a hole through the cloud cover and was blinding her. But Pierre was there, just ahead, waiting calmly on the marble gravestone, elbow leaning on his knee, palm open under his chin.

"Pierre, it's me!"

She kept moving forward until she stood in front of the grave.

She reached out her hand, but Petrushka didn't take it.

She put her fingertips to his cheek, but Petrushka's skin was cold.

Éléa's body froze with shock.

"Brain, tell me it's not true!"

Up above, the clouds had healed over the sun, and now, in this gloom more suitable to a solemn cemetery, Éléa could better see the surprising monument: not only one of the most famous in the cemetery but one of the most beautiful too. On Vaslav Nijinsky's grave sat a life-sized bronze statue of Petrushka dressed in a clown's ruff, a puff shirt, and a pair of fringed harlequin pants, with boots on his feet and a Russian cap on his head.

*It's a treasure hunt,* Éléa thought. *Pierre is having fun, making me run around like a headless chicken.* "Or maybe this is for you, Brain? He's created riddles for you to solve. It's his way of saying that he loves you as much as he loves the rose tattooed on my chest."

*How kind of him!*

Love was the only irrational thing that Éléa could accept. The only thing for which she didn't need her brain. Was Pierre inviting Brain to share in their intimacy?

"It's your move, Brain."

*Thank you. And what am I supposed to be looking for?*

"No idea. But surely it has some connection with this ballet."

Petrushka*?*

"No, *Swan Lake*!"

Brain didn't respond. Brain had no sense of humor and possessed a particular blind spot when it came to sarcasm.

"Come on, idiot, get on with it. Give me a summary."

Petrushka, Brain recited, *is a ballet by Igor Stravinsky—a Russian ballet, as they are known, but one created in France, at the Théâtre du Châtelet, in 1911. The story is astonishingly banal. During a carnival, in a village square, a sorcerer gives life to three puppets: Petrushka, the Moor, and the ballerina. Petrushka falls in love with the ballerina, but she prefers the Moor, who is stronger and more charming. In despair, Petrushka challenges his rival to a duel and is killed by the Moor's wooden saber. Only his spirit survives, and it pursues the sorcerer who gave it life.*

"Well, *I* think that's astonishingly beautiful. But I'm not going to let my Petrushka be transformed into a ghost. So let's get to work . . ."

She examined the sculpture more carefully, noting every fold in its shirt, every wrinkle in its face, every pattern on the stool on which it sat. Then she read the inscriptions on the oval headstone. *Vaslav Nijinsky. Born in Kyiv, 28 XII 1889, died in London 8 IV 1950.*

She lowered her gaze. A dozen dance shoes, filled with flowers and pink gravel, were arranged on the flat ledger stone. Éléa felt a stab of jealousy. Those shoes must have been left here by so many female dancers, no doubt younger and prettier than she herself, all of them in love with Petrushka.

She tried to reason with herself.

These ballerinas loved the bronze Petrushka, not hers. Now all she had to do was find him again . . .

"What's the matter, Brain? You're very quiet."

She looked again at the grave, the shoes, the marble, the flowers, searching for any possible message that Pierre might have left her. After an intensive examination, though, all that stood out to her was one minor detail. The vowels of the words engraved in the headstone had been lightly marked with a colored pencil.

*A, E, I, O, U.*

What could that mean? Was this a new code for her to decipher, or just another ballerina's discreet tribute to the dead Russian dancer?

"Any idea, Brain?"

*Nope.*

"You're not giving up, are you?"

Éléa never learned the answer to this question. Brain didn't have time to respond before her Precious buzzed on her finger. The ring turned pink.

A new message from her Petrushka!

The message was brief, Brian Molko's voice deep and soft.

*"Five vowels in the plural form the word that will guide you to me."*

# 12

## Nanesse

***Pont-à-Bar, Ardennes***

Nanesse held her breath.

*Don't move. Don't even breathe.*

Her fingertip was still touching the light switch. Her first instinct—when she saw the guy with the burned face aiming his double-barreled shotgun at her—had been to turn off the light. He must still be standing at the top of the staircase.

The darkness would buy her some time. But time for what?

She was trapped inside this cellar, with Bruno Pluvier's body lying at her feet. If the murderer came downstairs, he wouldn't have any trouble finding her. Slowly, cautiously, Nanesse turned her head.

*Can I find a hiding place? A weapon?*

*What if Pluvier has a gun on him? Should I search his corpse?*

Nanesse's heart was racing. The men who had killed Bruno Pluvier were professionals. There had been two of them, Nanesse felt sure, remembering the four legs she'd counted through the basement window. One had locked the cellar door from the outside, blocking all chance of escape, and the other had come into the house to flush her out. They had murdered Bruno without making a sound, entering the cellar and then waiting for him to go downstairs . . . Or maybe Bruno had found them there and they'd been forced to take him out of the picture.

But in the end, what difference did it make which one it had been? Now *she* was the one who needed to be taken out of the picture.

Footsteps . . . Footsteps on the stairs.

Terrified, Nanesse leaned forward and peered through the darkness. She could make out a man with a heavy build cautiously descending the steps, arms in front of his body, the gun aimed blindly into the gloom of the cellar. The shadow of the barrels stretched across the wall.

Oh God, she was going to die here, just as Renaud had died two days ago, without understanding why, without being able to defend herself, without—

"Agnès?"

The shadow spoke. And the figure on the stairs had a woman's voice. Not the most feminine voice Agnès had ever heard—a little deep and abrupt—but she felt sure it didn't belong to the man with the burned face.

"Agnès? Are you there?"

"Captain Marelle?"

All the nervous tension suddenly left Nanesse's body. She felt as if her legs could no longer support her, as if she was about to slide down the brick wall to the floor. She pressed her finger against the light switch and the cellar's only bulb came on again.

Everything was illuminated.

The boxes of files on the shelves, the dusty bottles of wine, the stacks of beer barrels, the tools hanging on the walls, Bruno Pluvier's body lying in a pool of blood, and Captain Katel Marelle, pistol in hand, whistling as she looked around.

She stared with distaste at Bruno's body, then at the blood-splattered corner of the metal shelf above him.

"Is this your witness?" asked the captain. "Poor guy took quite a tumble."

Nanesse was still shaking. She managed to stay upright on her wobbly legs, staggered a few feet forward, and sat on a beer barrel.

"It wasn't an accident, Captain. He was killed. By two men. Surely you saw them escape?"

Katel Marelle gave a little smile like a woman who had to consider all possibilities.

"I saw one of the killers," Nanesse went on. "His face was horribly burned. He had no forehead, no ears . . ."

Katel looked as if she was now being forced to consider the most far-fetched of possibilities.

"No ears?" Katel asked. "Well, then at least we know he wasn't here to spy on you."

"There were two of them."

"I believe you, Agnès. Calm down—we'll check it out."

The policewoman continued examining the cellar, careful not to come too close to Pluvier's corpse. Crime Scene 101, Nanesse assumed: Secure the perimeter and don't tamper with the evidence.

The cold metal of the beer barrel was freezing Nanesse's backside.

"How on earth did you come to be here, Captain?"

Katel scrutinized the locked door that led out to the canal.

"I'm just doing my job, aren't I? Protecting the good guys."

She turned around and stared at Nanesse.

"An hour ago, when we talked on the phone, you gave Mr. Pluvier's name and address, remember? I came as quickly as I could. I'm the cop. I'm the one who should do the questioning, not one of the suspects."

"I'm a suspect?"

Katel looked down at Bruno Pluvier's body.

"You could have pushed him down the stairs . . ."

Her gaze moved from the corpse to the wet footprints, easily visible on the dusty floor, that ran from the cellar's locked door to the victim and back.

"They came this way . . . Size twelve, by the looks of it. That exonerates you."

The captain took out her phone.

"Okay, here we go. Time to call the forensics team, the medical examiner, all those little geniuses with their new technologies . . ." She rolled her eyes.

Before pressing the call button, the captain looked at the neatly arranged boxes of archived files then turned to Nanesse.

"What was Mr. Pluvier looking for down here? Something to do with your husband?"

"Yes," said Nanesse. "He was looking for an old newspaper, from before Renaud was born."

Katel Marelle whistled.

"A Czech newspaper," Nanesse explained. "A local edition—Bruno couldn't remember the name of the town. But he kept a record of all his internet searches on hard disks, he said. Renaud had asked him to find this newspaper, you see, more than twenty-five years ago."

"Jeez . . . Digital archeology. The computer guys will love this."

The captain looked again at the dozens of dusty boxes arranged on the cellar's shelves.

"There's something else," Nanesse added. "The guy with no ears. I . . . I've seen him before."

"What?" Katel barked. "When?"

"Tuesday. He was walking on the sidewalk in front of my house. I saw his head poking above the hedge. We don't get many passersby, but even so, I probably wouldn't have paid him any notice if it wasn't for his . . . disability."

The policewoman frowned at her.

"Shit. If your version of events checks out, that means your husband really was murdered, that you're the only witness to a second crime, and that the killer knows where you live."

Nanesse said nothing.

"We're going to have to protect you, Agnès. I'm calling the cavalry now, and then we're going to take you home."

# 13

## Vicky

***Mayor's office, Florac, Lozère***

The drive to Florac was pure pleasure. An hour and a half of viewing beautiful landscapes, passing through valleys, and crossing the treeless plains of the Causses before descending toward another river. An hour and a half of *Whoa, look at those rocks, Mommy! They look like petrified trolls. And those waterfalls down there! And those sheep standing around the pond—do you think a wolf will attack them?* An hour and a half of stopping to take photographs at every lookout point, plus a longer stop at Point Sublime to eat their picnic lunch while gazing down into the void, feeling tiny as they sat there above the canyon that, according to legend, had been carved from the earth long ago by giants with axes.

After driving through cowboy country—*Oh, look, Mommy, miniature horses!*—they reached Florac in midafternoon, or Florac-Trois-Rivières to use the village's full name. Three rivers met there, joining forces at the impressive Gorges du Tarn.

Florac basked in the sun, between waterfalls and bridges, cobbled streets and empty terraces, high walls of schist, granite, and limestone. Time seemed to pass more slowly and more silently here.

Vicky's tires squealed as she pulled up a bit too eagerly and parked outside the mayor's office. The window ledges were all decorated with potted geraniums. A woman poked her head through the only open window and glared, her heavily mascaraed eyelashes batting angrily behind violet glasses. Vicky suspected the woman thought she was a Parisian and was about to give her a lecture about tranquil country life.

"I've just come from Ruynes-en-Margeride," Vicky announced, to disabuse her of this notion. "Sorry I was driving a little fast—I was worried your office might close before I got here." She flashed the woman a big smile in a bid to win her over.

"You should have taken your time—we're closed!"

Vicky stepped forward, leaving Lola to play with Kasper and her toy pony in the back seat of the Berlingo, and stared at the woman's face above the pink petals of the window boxes.

She decided to take a conciliatory approach. If the woman spent her Saturday afternoons racking up overtime, it must be because she liked her job and felt a responsibility to help people. All Vicky had to do was soften her up.

Vicky apologized profusely, made sure that the woman could see Lola in the back of her car, then launched into a long explanation that the employee, now sitting behind her computer again, appeared to ignore.

"I'm sorry, but it's quite a sensitive matter. I'm looking for a man who I think grew up here. Do you happen to have a register or some archives I could—"

"Come back on Monday! The secretary will be here then. I'm the treasurer."

The woman had not looked up as she said this.

"On Monday," Vicky said, "my daughter will be at school. I'm only here today and tomorrow."

Lola had gotten out of the car and come over to join her mother.

"Tomorrow is Sunday, so the office will be closed. Now, if you would kindly let me concentrate, I need to review the books . . ."

Vicky sympathized. She too often had to go through the account books for her guesthouse. But explaining that she shared the experience of hours spent calculating depreciation rates, social security contributions, and lump-sum allowances was unlikely to help her obtain the information she was seeking.

She was about ready to give up. After all, there was probably another person somewhere in Florac who was more disposed to be helpful. But then she felt Lola tugging at her sleeve. Vicky picked her daughter up and lifted her so that her face was visible through the open window.

"Ma'am?"

Lola gently moved aside the geranium flowers that were tickling her chin.

"We're looking for my daddy."

The woman sat very still, one fingertip touching her keyboard. Screen after screen of an Excel document flashed past without stopping.

"Your daddy?"

"Yes, he went to school here. His name is Hans Bernard."

"Have you . . . been looking for him for a long time?"

"Not really. He just sent us a postcard from Japan."

"Japan?"

Vicky held her breath. The woman's eyelashes were fluttering with a different emotion now.

"Yes. He's a truck driver. He often goes to Australia and China and places like that."

"Well, sweetie, I'm new here. I only arrived three months ago, so if your daddy went to school in Florac, I don't know him. But you could go to see Monsieur Mariotta. He's an old schoolteacher who has worked here for years and years. He would be bound to remember your daddy. Here, I'll give you his address and phone number."

"Thank you!"

Vicky could not believe it. In less than a minute, Lola had unearthed a witness who might have known Hans! Once the treasurer had handed over the precious piece of paper, she hunched over her keyboard again.

"Can you put me down, Mommy?"

Vicky put her daughter on the ground, but made no move to leave. The woman's eyelids batted irritably and she turned her unsmiling face toward the window. "Is there something else you need?"

"Yes. Could you recommend a place where we can stay the night?"

The campsite at the Pont du Tarn must be close to Lola's vision of heaven, thought Vicky as she watched her daughter run around the swimming pool with Kasper in her arms. Lola had not had many vacations. Summer was the busiest period at the guesthouse, so Lola spent July and August in Ruynes-en-Margeride, building cabins, catching grasshoppers, running after the rabbits, and feeding the ponies. She had never even heard of a waterslide before.

The treasurer at the mayor's office had directed them to this campsite before returning definitively to her accounts, and Vicky had managed to book a chalet for one night without any difficulty. According to Lola, the wooden cabin looked like a real-life doll's house. It had a view of the pebble beach, the river, and the chemical toilets.

The man at the reception office had never heard of Hans either, having only become manager of the campsite seven years before. So Vicky had sat down in one of the plastic chairs on her sunny little terrace and called Mathieu Mariotta, the retired teacher.

His wife had picked up after the first ring and whispered that her husband was taking a nap. And no, she couldn't wake him up—his nap was sacred, as was his postsnack walk to Quézac, and the game show he watched on TV every evening. But he would be awake tomorrow morning. He was a morning person—it was advisable to catch him before noon if you wanted him to be at his most alert, most able to recall old memories.

So, it was decided; tomorrow morning, Vicky would visit Mathieu Mariotta. If Hans really had grown up here, she thought, the teacher would surely remember him.

After hanging up, Vicky took the time to savor the warmth of the sun on her pale skin. She spent the summer outside, but she was always too busy running around to sunbathe. She was about to take the Japanese postcard from her bag and read it again when Lola came rushing over.

"Mommy, Mommy, can I go in the pool? I've made a friend!"

Already dressed in her bathing suit and her water wings, Lola ran off again. Vicky watched her attentively while periodically glancing at the postcard.

*I love you both forever.*

These words sounded like something Hans would say, but how could she be sure? Had Hans vanished to the other end of the world, or was he hiding somewhere nearby?

*Don't try to find me . . . It would be too dangerous.*

What was Hans afraid of? What did he want to protect them from?

Several times since their departure from Ruynes-en-Margeride, Vicky had gotten the feeling that they were being followed—a gray car, always the same one, shadowing the Berlingo from a few curves behind, never passing her, and remaining distant enough that she couldn't identify the vehicle with any certainty.

She had kept glancing at her rearview mirror, all the while cursing her own stupidity. Surely she wasn't about to start having paranoid fantasies about every car—gray, white, or black—that she spotted! Besides, what could possibly happen to them here, at a half-empty family campsite on a beautiful September weekend, lulled by the sound of pétanque bowls and Ping-Pong balls and the mouthwatering smell of barbecue smoke?

To stop herself from brooding endlessly over the same questions, Vicky took out her phone. Her intention was to use it to look up as much information about Florac as she possibly could, with the aim of identifying other potential witnesses from Hans's past: a mailman, a soccer coach, a baker . . .

"Mommy, Mommy!"

Lola was running toward her, accompanied by another girl of the same age, both of them wearing the same plastic sandals and the same water wings.

"Mommy, this is my friend. Her name is Manon!"

Manon gave a big smile that revealed all her baby teeth. She was clearly just as happy as Lola was to have found someone to play with.

"Hello, Manon."

"Look, Mommy. Manon is playing with Kasper's brother!"

The little girl nodded and held out her doll. Lola did the same. Two little mommies proud of their babies.

Vicky almost fell off her chair in surprise.

Manon's Kasper was identical to Lola's. They had the same celluloid face and pointed nose, the same Scottish costume, the same hat. Only the eyes were different: This other doll's were blue. Just like Kasper, Manon's toy was a hand-sewn, hand-painted puppet with a complex mechanism that no longer worked.

*How can this kid have the same doll?*

Vicky had always believed that her daughter's weird little doll was unique, a curio that Hans had found on his travels, probably in some remote European town . . .

Oblivious to such worries, Lola and Manon had already run off toward the wading pool. Vicky walked after them, trying to find Manon's parents. Eventually she reached the swimming area, where a dozen children were playing in the little pools, sliding down the waterslides, and scrambling up the inflatable towers.

Lola was bouncing atop a little unicorn on springs, but Vicky could see no trace of Manon.

"Isn't your friend here anymore, sweetie?"

"No, Mommy, her daddy came to pick her up. She's not on vacation—she lives here."

# 14

## ÉLÉA

***Montmartre Cemetery, Paris***

*"Five vowels in the plural form the word that will guide you to me."*

Éléa told her Precious to read the text again, and to turn up the volume. Her cell phone repeated the fourteen words in a deep voice. Around her, the cemetery was empty apart from a few elderly—and probably half-deaf—women who were visiting distant graves.

Éléa raised the ring to her lips.

"Read it again, my Precious."

*"Five vowels in the plural form the word that will guide you to me."*

What on earth was that supposed to mean? She wished her Petrushka wasn't quite so enigmatic.

Even so, she was happy to play along. This second text reassured her about one thing: Pierre was alive and he was having fun with her. He was waiting for her somewhere, and to find him all she had to do was solve his riddle.

She looked again at the statue of Vaslav Nijinsky, dressed as Petrushka, casually seated on the grave as though he, too, were thinking about the riddle. Or dreaming. She had been so afraid of the silence during the last eighty-five hours, afraid of the abyss opening up beneath her feet, the emptiness between her fingers, as she waited frantically for Pierre to write to her, trying to come up with possible explanations while at the same time pushing back the worst of them: that Pierre had met with a fatal accident.

Éléa looked up at the sky, which stretched out like a vast blank screen, neither menacing nor reassuring. So, Pierre wanted to play, did he? This was the moment to prove that she really was an autist. And to test out her most precious ally.

"This is a mission for you, Brain."

Éléa stood swaying lightly in front of the grave, gently buffeted by the wind, fully immersed in this conversation with herself.

"Are you ready, Brain? Give me a list of words made up of only five vowels."

*Impossible,* Brain replied confidently. *There is no word in the French language consisting of only five vowels. There has to be a consonant, and preferably more than one.*

"I don't care, Brain! My Petrushka only mentioned five vowels. In the plural! You want me to ask my Precious to list all the words containing an *A*, an *E*, an *I*, an *O*, and a *U*?"

*Don't be ridiculous. Your Precious would only repeat everything it found on the internet. The only one capable of thought here is me. Five vowels, in the plural . . . That might mean we need to add an* S.

"Wow," said Éléa sarcastically. "Thanks for that brilliant deduction, Sherlock!"

*You're welcome. Now we have the following letters:* A, E, I, O, U, *and* S.

"Five vowels and a consonant. Thanks, Brain! The internet can take care of the rest."

Éléa raised the ring to her lips again.

"My Precious, open an anagram dictionary and give me all the words that—"

*OISEAU!*

"What did you say, Brain?"

*The French word for* bird*—OISEAU. No need to do an internet search. Trust me, this is the only possible answer!*

She jumped up and down with excitement, as light on her feet as a sparrow that has just learned how to fly. She felt like kissing the bronze Petrushka.

"You're the best, Brain! *OISEAU*—yes, that must be it. So now what? 'The word that will guide you to me.' Um, should I follow a bird?"

She gazed all around the cemetery. Black shadows flew in all directions. Dozens of crows squabbled between gravestones, fleetingly making the sign of the cross with their wings before taking refuge in the highest branches of the trees that lined the aisle.

Was it possible her prankster lover was hiding in the treetops too?

Éléa peered at the maples and chestnuts and came to the conclusion that it would be impossible for a man to hide in their branches. Her Petrushka must mean another kind of OISEAU.

"I need you again, Brain. What other clues do we have, apart from those six letters?"

Brain thought about this but found nothing. Éléa felt a terrible emptiness inside her whenever her brain whirred in this circular way, as if its thoughts would loop around and around endlessly. She always got the odd sense that she was a computer that had been instructed to solve an equation with no solution, her circuits heating up until, one by one, they burned out.

Feeling suddenly dizzy, she searched for something that her gaze could cling to. The grave in front of her. The statue of Petrushka. The headstone, with its inscription . . .

"The colors, Brain!" she cried out. "Look, the vowels engraved in the stone have been colored with pencils. *A* is black, *E* is white, *I* is red, *U* is green, *O* is blue . . . like . . . like in that poem by Rimbaud."

*I was about to say that!* Brain said irritably.

"Sorry, I used my instant recall for that one. But what I'm asking you to do is much more difficult. Take Rimbaud, for example—what does he make you think of?"

*Hmm . . . Charleville-Mézières, Aden, Verlaine, arms dealing, the drunken boat, the sleeper in the valley, a season in hell . . .*

"Okay, Brain!" Éléa interrupted. "I'm looking for a bird, but not a parrot that will just recite Wikipedia for me. Focus!"

. . .

"Brain? Are you there?"

*Sorry, I've searched through all the Rimbaud poems I know. I've gone as far back through our memory as I can, back to when we were fifteen, but I can't find any trace of a bird.*

"It's okay, Brain, I'll just ask my Precious."

This time, Brain didn't protest. Éléa moved the ring to her lips and it shone blue before the voice of Courtney Love, her favorite singer—and the person she had chosen to read out Wikipedia pages—replied confidently:

"*Throughout his childhood, Arthur Rimbaud possessed an imaginary bird. A multicolored bird for which he wrote his first poems, at the age of fifteen. According to the novelist Sarah Cohen-Scali, it was this bird that persuaded him to flee the boredom that was suffocating him. Arthur Rimbaud called his bird Baou.*"

Baou?

Éléa collapsed onto the grave, almost into the lap of the bronze Petrushka.

Baou was the name of that bookstore in Alençon where she had gone when she was fifteen. The one where she had discovered the fanzine *I Wrote Silences*, named after another Rimbaud verse. That fanzine was where she had read Pierre's poems for the first time. And it was those words—Pierre's words—that had persuaded her to flee the boredom that was then suffocating her.

Was this what her Petrushka wanted? For her to go back to Alençon?

"My Precious," Éléa whispered, "could you give me the phone number for the Librairie Baou in Alençon?"

Her phone took longer than usual to respond, and when it did, Courtney Love said: "*There is no Librairie Baou in Alençon.*"

She sighed. Why had her Petrushka given her such a complicated clue?

"Okay, my Precious, search for a Librairie Baou anywhere in France."

This time, the result was instantaneous.

*"Librairie Baou, 3 Rue de Venise, Paris."*

She jumped up and down again.

"Let's go, Brain!"

Rue de Venise, in the fourth arrondissement of Paris, was only nine Metro stations from the cemetery.

# 15

## Nanesse and Katel

***Bourg-Fidèle, Ardennes***

Katel Marelle stood in front of the living room window and watched the rain fall onto the Duvals' yard. The hollows in the ground around the slides, dug there by an endless parade of children's feet, were now transformed into muddy ponds.

"Ugh, this weather!" she cursed. This was not the kind of weather that was usually conducive to murder. Any idiot who watched crime series on TV knew that there is no more dangerous witness than a soaked sidewalk, a driveway of damp gravel, or a wet door handle. It was even possible to detect a person's DNA from raindrops that had run down their nose. Or so she had heard . . .

Katel had accompanied Agnès Duval to her home and insisted on going inside with her. There was no question of leaving her there alone. Besides, she still had questions to ask her. A lot of questions.

Before driving back from Pont-à-Bar, they had waited for Lieutenant Jérémy Bonello to turn up with five other cops and investigate the crime scene. The initial analyses had confirmed Agnès's version of events. Two strangers had broken into the cellar through the outside door. They had probably hidden on the staircase leading up to the living room and listened to her conversation with Bruno Pluvier. Then they had hit him when he went downstairs. Had he simply caught them down there or had they been waiting there to kill him? There was no way to know for sure.

No weapon was discovered at the crime scene, but the medical examiner affirmed that Bruno Pluvier had been struck by a thin metal object. His face had collided with the corner of the shelf only after that, when he fell—or was pushed downstairs by the killer to make the murder look like an accident.

The crime scene investigation—the footprints on the floor, the absence of a weapon—exonerated Agnès, at least in theory. On the other hand, there had been no fingerprints that would have enabled the forensics team to identify the murderers. So, either they'd worn gloves or their fingertips had been as burned as the face of the man Agnès had seen.

She needed to go to the police station soon to help generate an Identi-Kit image of the suspect. But there were so many other things that also needed doing urgently: comparing the footprints in the cellar to those found at the lookout point; questioning Bruno's neighbors (even though, given the rain and the fog, it seemed unlikely that there would be many witnesses); and going through Bruno Pluvier's computer archives to find that old Czech newspaper. All of this would take several days, possibly even weeks.

"Wouldn't you be of more use at the crime scene?" Nanesse asked anxiously.

She had pushed aside Guignol and sat on his stool, and now she was looking at Pierrot and Columbine in their glass vase. She found it reassuring to be back in her familiar living room. Or slightly reassuring, at least.

"No, I'd just get in their way more than anything," said the captain, standing by the window. "Jérémy—I mean, Lieutenant Bonello—is young, and he loves all that stuff: taking samples, filling test tubes, dusting for prints. He's never been out of Charleville and he thinks he's some sort of crime-show hero. I don't want to take that away from him. Besides, with someone possibly prowling around your house, you need to be under police protection. Since we're short on manpower, it makes sense for me to protect you and question you at the same time."

"You're a strange kind of cop. Why is that?"

"Are you asking the questions now?"

"Sorry. Professional habit . . . I have to help create psychological reports on my foster kids—evaluations that get used by their teachers, judges, the child protection agency."

The captain was still staring through the window at the rain. The wooded plateau of the Ardennes climbed gently up toward Belgium. Nanesse's house looked like a raft lost in the middle of a brown ocean.

"So you're saying that we do the same job, essentially?"

Nanesse didn't say anything.

"True, I guess, although my job is to put people in prison. Whereas yours, Agnès, is to keep teenagers out of prison."

Still Nanesse remained silent. The policewoman seemed in a thoughtful mood, and she didn't want to interrupt her.

"That's the difference between you and me. I don't like anybody—professional habit. Whereas you like everybody."

"I'm not all that keen on people who hurt other people," Nanesse said.

"Are you sure? Your life consists of helping people with broken hearts, kids with problems. The same thing that makes you happy is caused by the suffering of others."

Nanesse was about to stand up and object, but Katel Marelle raised a hand.

"It's a compliment, Agnès. A genuine quality. I would have loved to be like you. To be able to find fulfillment in a shit heap. With all the horrible crap I've seen in my life, I'd be the happiest person on earth."

With an imperious flick of the wrist, the captain gestured for Agnès to let her continue talking.

"I've done my research on you, Agnès, as I'm sure you must have guessed. Everyone says the same thing about you. You're a saint. Oh yes, everybody talks about Nanesse, the Mother Teresa of the Ardennes. Always there to defend your foster kids, to help local charities and food banks, and always with a sweet smile on your face. So, yeah, you don't really have the profile of someone who kills her husband out of jealousy or hires assassins to eliminate witnesses . . . I could be wrong, of course, but in an investigation you have to keep moving forward, which means working on the basis of probability. You can't just leave question marks everywhere. So let's try to work together, okay, while the little geniuses play with the detective kits the government gave them for the start of the new school semester."

Katel fell backward into a chair.

"We could be here a long time. You wouldn't happen to have a little pick-me-up, would you?"

Nanesse had placed two bottles of Chimay Gold lager on the table, along with a bowl of salt-and-vinegar chips and some cured Ardennes ham. Katel had turned on her laptop.

"All right, here we go!" said the policewoman. "Let's start with our own little Tour de France, shall we? Charleville-Mézières, Paris, and Lozère . . . Your husband spent his childhood and adolescence in Charleville with his mother. We have enough evidence to be sure of that, and Bruno Pluvier confirmed it; he knew Renaud from Bayard Middle School. But according to what Monsieur Pluvier told you, Renaud also knew all the hiking paths in Lozère, and the museums, Metro stations, and streets of Paris, as if he'd grown up in those places too. Given that, according to the other driver's licenses, Hans Bernard was born in Lozère and Pierre Rousseau in Paris, it's hard to think that's a coincidence. Each of those places is at least one hundred fifty miles away from the other two. Agnès, do you have any idea what might connect them?"

Nanesse shook her head. She had been to Paris only three times in her life, and on the few occasions she had journeyed to the South of France, she had never left the highway before arriving at the Mediterranean shore.

"Maybe the answer is in that Czech newspaper that Renaud wanted?" she suggested. "The one from a town whose name reminded Monsieur Pluvier of a brand of beer."

Katel drank half her bottle of Chimay.

"Okay, Agnès, let's catch a plane to Bohemia! No, I'm just kidding. Did you know that there are more than ten thousand brands of beer in the world, and the Czechs are the biggest consumers on the planet? Yes, they drink even more than the Belgians—it's true, I checked! I'm going to put a Belgian intern in charge of that particular investigation—he should find it amusing. I doubt he'll find anything quickly, though. As for that newspaper, we don't have a date for it. Not even a year."

"It was from before Renaud was born."

"So, before 1977. Back in the days of the Iron Curtain. Czechoslovakia was one of the most secretive countries in the Eastern Bloc back then, so getting information isn't going to be easy . . ."

She examined the label on her beer bottle.

"Brewed about twelve miles from here! Why do things always have to be so complicated? I'm going to confess something, Agnès. When this investigation began, I really thought it was going to be a story of infidelity. I imagined your Renaud had fake identities to make it easier for him to keep mistresses. But the problem with that theory is that those licenses aren't fake. Plus your earless murderer doesn't really fit the profile of a typical jealous husband. So how can we explain the obvious fact that three different men all look exactly the same?"

Nanesse didn't know what to say. She had barely even sipped her beer. Almost reflexively, she glanced up at the ceiling, from which hung the ballerina, the male dancer, and the soldier with the saber.

"Admit the most obvious conclusion, Agnès—after all, you've thought about it as much as I have. Triplets! Two of them abandoned at birth by your mother-in-law, Milana Duval, like a litter of unwanted kittens. I'm talking about identical triplets, Agnès. The problem with that theory is that their documents say they were born in three different places. Beyond that, we have another problem. During my research I've discovered that true triplets—those that look so similar that they can't be told apart; monozygotic triplets, from a single egg, sharing the same placenta—are extremely rare. There are no more than three or four births of that kind each year in France, so it wasn't difficult to verify that none of the families who experienced this—three kids for the price of one—were your husband's family. We could extend the search beyond France, but frankly, I don't believe in this theory."

"Nor do I," said Nanesse. She hadn't had another sip of her beer. Katel stared enviously at the bottle; her own was already empty.

The captain tapped nervously on her computer mouse and said: "So what do we have? On one hand, we have proof that your husband lied to you, at least about one part of his professional life. He had one week a month to do whatever he wanted, including possibly transforming himself into Hans Bernard and Pierre Rousseau, two ghosts of whom we have, for the moment, found no trace. But on the other hand, there's the Renaud that you know—loving husband and father; an only child, devoted to his mother; someone who was born and grew up near here, like you . . . Tell me, Agnès, what secret was your husband hiding?"

Nanesse did not reply. She just looked in turn at each of the puppets around her, plus the one in her bedroom, visible through the bedroom doorway, her gaze coming to a halt on the red-haired Manicka on the nightstand, and the white wool fur of Manicka's dog, Zeryk. Was it possible that these silent witnesses—all these creatures Milana had created—knew more than she did?

The captain stood up. She was holding the charger for her laptop.

"Do you have a socket I could use?"

"Of course, but—"

"My battery's almost dead. I need to charge my laptop or it will die before tonight."

Surprised, Nanesse picked up her beer and raised it to her lips.

"You're staying here?"

"Yeah. Remote work—it's all the rage, didn't you know? There's no way I can concentrate at the station, with all those young cops running back and forth between the photocopier and the coffee machine all day long. They get on my nerves, and then they get upset when I yell at them. My being here is no problem; they know what they have to do, and they can contact me easily enough if they need me. And besides, like I told you, this way I don't have to call on another colleague to come and protect you. I feel comfortable being here with you, Agnès—it must be your Mother Teresa vibe."

"If you're going to stay here, you'll have to call me Nanesse, like everyone else."

"No, I don't think so."

"And call me *tu*, not *vous*."

"Absolutely not! How would you feel about us working together, Agnès?"

Nanesse didn't know what to say to that.

"It's not rocket science, you know. We can leave the tech genius stuff to Lieutenant Bonello, while you and I do things the old-fashioned way."

She took photocopies of the three driver's licenses from her bag.

*Renaud Duval*

*Hans Bernard*

*Pierre Rousseau*

"We've been looking for clues related to their addresses, but that hasn't yet produced any results. On the other hand, the local authorities in each place have confirmed that these three licenses really were issued on the dates in question, which would appear to indicate that Hans Bernard and Pierre Rousseau actually existed. So there's only one remaining piece of information we have to go on . . ."

Katel put her fingertip on one of the photocopies, between the first name and the address.

"The date and place of birth! We both know that the French government possesses a vast and efficient bureaucracy, right? So let's use it!"

Nanesse stared sadly at Pierrot and Columbine.

"Use it for what?"

"To find evidence that, while Hans and Pierre may have existed as adults, they didn't exist as babies. I don't want you to get your hopes up, though, Agnès: Your husband is dead. Even if he had multiple identities before his death, that doesn't mean we can bring him back to life. And Hans and Pierre must have died with him. You can't duplicate a life!"

# 16

## VICKY

***Pont du Tarn campsite, Florac***

"Mommy, I'm hungry!"

"Be patient, sweetie."

The Pont du Tarn campsite offered a range of take-out snacks, including pizza, sausages and fries, and sandwiches. Usually Vicky did not allow her daughter to eat this kind of junk food, because there was plenty of high-quality farm produce in Margeride. But just this once . . .

Vicky was clearly not the only parent to have made this calculation. There were about twenty adult campers waiting inside the snack bar, each of them holding a glass of rosé generously offered by the manager to make their wait time less onerous.

"Can I go and play, Mommy?"

"No, this won't take long."

"Oh, look!" Lola said this in a whisper, as if she was sharing a secret.

"What is it?"

"The two men over there, near the pizza oven . . . They look weird."

Vicky looked in the direction that Lola was pointing and immediately lowered her daughter's arm. She felt not only embarrassed but a little shaken too.

"Lola, it's rude to point!"

"But Mommy, they're . . ."

Vicky forced herself to look away. The faces of the two men waiting for their pizza were almost completely burned. The first man's nose, eyes, and lips were the only things that had been spared. The ears and the forehead of the second man were untouched, but the rest of his face was horribly scarred. Noticing the sunglasses he was wearing and the white cane he held, she guessed that his eyes were permanently closed.

"Yes, ma'am?" the pizza guy said to Vicky.

Relieved, she ordered two pizzas—one ham and mushroom, the other anchovy, with olives on both.

"There's no need to wait here in the smoke with your daughter. Give me your number and I'll text you when they're ready."

Vicky pulled Lola by the hand toward the exit. As soon as they were out of hearing, she crouched down in front of her daughter and spoke quietly.

"Those two men must have been in an accident. They must have suffered terribly. You know, sweetie, when someone is different, you shouldn't be scared of them. You should be nice to them."

Lola stood straight and proudly declared: "I'm not scared of them, Mommy."

# 17

## Éléa

***Librairie Baou, Rue de Venise, Paris***

Éléa opened the door to the bookstore, which was hidden away on a quiet cobbled street so narrow that only a thin line of sky was visible between the rooftops above. The dusty old spell books on display in the dark window were intriguing but somehow not inviting.

*It's gloomier than the store in Alençon,* thought Éléa. And yet her memory of those Russian, Chinese, and Japanese puppets that had hung between the books was as clear in her mind as if imprinted there by some trauma.

The bookseller stood behind the checkout desk, at the back of the store, wearing a smart brown Scottish blazer and a green velvet bow-tie. She recognized him instantly, even though he looked much older. The skin of his face was like wrinkled parchment, but the years had not altered the titmouse crest on his bald head, nor dulled his sharp, birdlike gaze.

"Hello, Éléa!" he said as soon as she entered the bookstore.

She was so surprised, she staggered backward a little. She almost grabbed hold of a Chinese dragon hanging close by, but in the end she steadied herself on a pile of old geography books.

"You remember me?"

"Of course. There aren't that many teenagers who read poetry, you know. Nor are there many as pretty as you."

Éléa felt herself blush. She hated blushing, especially in front of a smiling man who must be at least seventy years old. She blurted out a few idiotic words that she instantly regretted.

"It's strange, finding your bookstore here. In Paris, I mean, so close to where I live."

Baou smiled mysteriously.

"Perhaps you entered a *bookstore of requirement*? Like the Room of Requirement in Hogwarts. You dreamed of a book, and I appeared to help you find it."

"I'm not a teenager anymore, you know. I don't believe in spell books, or in talking creatures."

She gestured dismissively at the beautiful Japanese doll suspended in front of her.

"Really?" the bookseller said, raising one mocking eyebrow.

Suddenly Éléa seemed to see the doll's lips twitching, her arms starting to move.

"Don't be scared," Baou said soothingly. "It's a *karakuri ningyō*—a mechanical puppet from Japan, a traditional art that can be traced back to the seventeenth century. These sophisticated automatons could walk and serve tea. The word *ningyō* means both doll and puppet, which are synonymous in many other languages. Did you know that the Italian word for puppet is *pupi*?"

*He's hiding something,* Brain whispered. *All this talk is just a distraction.*

"No, I didn't," said Éléa. "But could you please stop playing games and answer my question. What are you doing here? In Paris?"

The bookseller stared at her with a calm intensity in his pale eyes. They were somewhere between blue and pearl-gray.

"I moved here a few years ago. It's every bookseller's dream to set up shop in Paris, isn't it? There are more readers in each arrondissement of this city than in any department in the rest of France."

Éléa walked slowly toward the checkout. The farther she moved into the store, the darker it grew. Why would anyone build such a long store on such a narrow street? The sunlight could barely pierce this deeply into the room.

She spotted the fanzine *I Wrote Silences* on a display stand.

This edition had a cover different from the one she had looked through so many times as a teenager. So this old madman was still publishing it, after all these years?

She tried to think as quickly as possible, but Brain didn't want to get involved.

The bookseller must certainly be aware of the treasure hunt that her Petrushka had organized, she told herself. They must be in on it together. No doubt he was about to hand her an envelope containing a clue or a puzzle that would lead her to the next stage. *But when does your game end, Pierre? It's your arms I want, not your brainteasers.*

"Are you looking for something, Éléa?"

"Yes. My friend, Pierre Rousseau. Do you know him?"

The bookseller smiled sadly. "Perhaps. I don't recognize that name, but I do see a lot of customers."

*Yep,* said Brain, *he's definitely hiding something.*

"He was the one who sent me here," Éléa told the bookseller.

"That doesn't surprise me. Few people come in here by chance."

*Bastard!*

She had no choice now but to silence her brain and play along.

"I'm sure you would remember him," she said, forcing herself to remain polite. "He's tall, slim, always very elegant. He moves like a graceful robot. And he has startling gray eyes, similar to the color of your own eyes."

"At my age, you know, one doesn't really look at boys anymore. And very rarely at girls."

Éléa had never been the most patient of people, and she hated it when conversations went on too long.

"Stop bullshitting me! You published Pierre's poems in your fanzine. You even delivered a letter to him for me."

"Really? And did he reply?"

"Yes."

*Eight thousand seven hundred and fifty-nine times, to be precise,* said Brain.

"I'm very happy for you," the bookseller said with a smile. "As you can see, my little magazine still exists. Please, take a copy."

Éléa hesitated, then raised her voice.

"All right, that's enough. Tell me the truth! Why did you know Pierre's address? Why did you publish his poems?"

She pointed up at the karakuri ningyō above her head.

"Why do you have all these puppets hanging all over your store when Pierre's greatest role is a puppet—Petrushka?"

The bookseller remained completely calm and unruffled. He replied in a soft voice, while touching the crest of hair on his head with his fingers.

"Pure coincidence, I assure you. But a happy coincidence. The art of puppetry is a synthesis of all the other arts. Literature, dance, sculpture, drawing, theater, and—of course—poetry. Please take this fanzine, Éléa, I beg you."

Éléa understood what was going on. The bookseller had been given certain instructions. Say nothing and hand the magazine to Éléa. But why would her Petrushka play such a cruel game?

"No, I'm begging *you*!" Éléa shouted. "At least tell me if Pierre is alive!"

The bookseller didn't blink.

"Tell me where he is! If he's okay. If I can write to him. If he'll reply. Please, I'm begging you, tell me."

The old man picked up the poetry fanzine and forced Éléa to take it.

"I'm sorry, that's all I can tell you. But take this, take it."

Éléa's fingers tightened around the magazine. They were trembling. Little by little, though, as if the paper had some soothing quality, they relaxed. She calmed down. The bookseller wasn't going to tell her anything. A feeling of resignation came over her.

She headed toward the white light of Rue de Venise, but before she opened the door she turned back one last time.

"When I go outside, will your bookstore magically disappear?"

The bookseller gave her his most disturbing smile.

"Perhaps. As I said, you entered a bookstore of requirement. Everything depends on you now."

Éléa walked hurriedly, angrily along the street, the fanzine rolled up in her hand.

*Ugh, that bookseller! Who does he think he is, with his silly crest and his Merlin-like mysteriousness and his patched-up puppets hanging all around his store like fake spiderwebs on Halloween?*

Obviously the bookseller was part of Petrushka's plot. And the next stage in this stupid treasure hunt would be found . . . in this fanzine.

The last stage?

Without even being aware of it, she had walked toward the closest park. She opened the gate and sat down on the first vacant bench. A few mothers were watching their children; two lovers were kissing on the grass; some Asian tourists were waiting to climb up the gothic tower so they could enjoy the panoramic view over Paris. She remembered going up there with Pierre one summer.

The evident happiness of the people around her left Éléa feeling panicky and sad. She took the pair of earbuds from her pocket and inserted them into her ears so that anyone looking at her would assume she was listening to something on her phone. This way, she could chat quietly with Brain without everyone thinking she was a lunatic. In fact, Éléa felt pretty sure that most of the people she saw speaking into their cell phones, their clip-on microphones, their earpieces, were actually talking to themselves.

"So, Brain, what do you think?"

*Well, obviously the bookseller knew Pierre. The question is whether Pierre is just a customer he knows from publishing his poetry, or . . .*

"Or?"

*Or they have a more . . . intimate connection.*

"Like what?"

*You know what I mean. You saw his gray eyes, didn't you?*

"Yes. And my Petrushka never told me anything about his father. So, Baou would be my . . . father-in-law, more or less?"

*Why not? Maybe Pierre was trying to find an original way of introducing you to his family . . . So what will be the next stage? Your mother-in-law? His elder sister? His younger brother? Come on, open that magazine. Let's take a look at the next riddle . . .*

The fanzine was only twelve pages long. Éléa flipped through it and it fell open to the right page, as if—once again—everything had been premeditated. Pierre's poem covered the entire central two-page spread.

"To Music," a poem by Arthur Rimbaud

Suggested by Pierre Rousseau

*Place de la Gare, in Charleville.*
*In the square, with all its tiny little lawns,*
*This park where all is neat, the trees and flowers,*
*On Thursdays gather all the bourgeois bores,*
*With their petty little jealousies, their suffocating hours.*

*On green benches, retired grocers with walking sticks*
*Stare gravely at the sand where pigeons feed*
*And discuss the latest news, the price of bricks,*
*Clear their throats and mutter: "Indeed, indeed!"*

She surrendered to the flow of images, the rhymes. Those neat little lawns, those green benches, those bourgeois bores with walking sticks appeared before her as if onstage. She felt what Rimbaud must have felt: that distance from the world; that way of observing the busyness of cities like a scientist looking down at a colony of ants; that certainty that she was right even though nobody else seemed to think about things the same way.

*I wonder if Rimbaud was on the spectrum too,* Brain suggested.

Éléa nodded unenthusiastically. "Stay focused, Brain. Why did Pierre choose this poem, 'To Music'? Why mention the square near the train station in Charleville? Does he want us to go there?"

Éléa read and reread the nine lines, then lingered on the single image in the fanzine that illustrated the poem—a photograph of a strange-looking church with an entrance resembling that of a Greek temple: two Doric columns supporting a triangular pediment.

"What about this church? Is it the one in Charleville?"

*I seriously doubt it. There's no connection between the neoclassical style of that church and the architecture of the Ardennes.*

Éléa smiled. Brain always managed to impress her. He possessed an incredible capacity for storing information.

"One thing's for sure," said Éléa. "Pierre knew that when he sent me to Librairie Baou, I would see this fanzine, and the bookseller would give me a copy. So it's possible that Baou himself isn't in on the plot. Perhaps my Petrushka is even more Machiavellian than I imagined."

She rapidly flicked through the fanzine until she noticed the date it was published. *Friday, September 15.* Yesterday!

"You see!" she said jubilantly. "Yet more proof that Pierre is alive!"

*Not necessarily. He could have sent that poem to the bookseller last week. Or even a year ago.*

"I hate you! Don't forget that he sent me two texts. Just find the location of that church, will you, instead of trying to make me miserable?"

*How am I supposed to do that? I don't know all the churches in France.*

"Then what use are you?"

She raised her hand, as if to kiss her ring.

"My Precious, can you scan the photograph of this church and download it to LocateThis?"

The phone's camera scanned, Brain sulked, and the app—especially useful for locating where vacation photographs were taken, years after the event—began its work. A few seconds later, a name appeared, accompanied by an address, the geographic coordinates, and the distance between Éléa's current location and that of the church.

*Église Saint-Martin, Florac*

*Distance: 412 miles*

*Fastest journey time: 6 hrs. 12 mins.*

"Shit!" hissed Éléa. "Florac? In Lozère? In the middle of nowhere? *That*'s where I'm supposed to find Petrushka?"

*Your Pierre must be dreaming if he thinks we're going all the way down there. How are we supposed to get there, for a start? You don't have a car. You don't even have a driver's license. So unless you don't mind being stuck on a train for ten hours . . .*

As always, Brain was right. It would be completely crazy to set off on such a long journey merely on the basis of a single photograph. Éléa looked around at the park from where she sat, pushing away the uncomfortable suspicion that she was being watched. Maybe she felt that way simply because of those tourists at the top of the Tour Saint-Jacques, a hundred and fifty feet above her?

"My Precious," she said suddenly. "Could you tell me how long it would take to get from Paris to Florac by BlaBlaCar? Leaving as soon as possible."

*BlaBlaCar? The rideshare?*

The stone in Éléa's ring turned ruby, then sapphire, before proudly announcing:

*Next departure tomorrow at 5:00 a.m.*

*Porte Dorée Metro station.*

*Arriving in Florac at 11 a.m.*

*Nonstop. 25 euros.*

"Pack your bags, Brain!" Éléa said triumphantly. "We're going on vacation!"

*What nonsense!*

"Are you jealous of my Precious?"

*Jealous of a machine? Are you kidding?*

"So what's your problem, then?"

*Did you know that BlaBlaCar was invented for people who get bored when they travel on their own? People who like to spend the whole trip chatting? People who love making new friends? They're the exact opposite of you, my little autist.*

# 18

## Nanesse and Katel

***Bourg-Fidèle, Ardennes***

Captain Katel Marelle hung up after the phone at the office had rung for the sixth time.

"Shit! Surely not all of them have left work?"

Nanesse gave her a kindly look. "At half past five on a Saturday afternoon? It seems pretty likely."

"And here I was vaunting the merits of our government's bureaucracy! Is there seriously no way in this country of checking a birth register when the local mayor's office is closed?" Annoyed, Katel stood up and ogled Nanesse's bottle of Chimay Gold. "Aren't you going to finish that?"

"I've barely started it."

A lock of hair fell over Katel's left eye. She began pacing around the room, first watching the rain that continued to stream down the windows, then the slight swaying of the puppets that hung from the ceiling, as if they too were staring at the horizon. Were the killer with the burned face and his accomplice hiding outside somewhere in that storm?

"I can't wait until Monday," muttered Katel. "Not with two murderers at large. I need confirmation that Renaud really was born in

Charleville, and that the birth dates and places for Pierre Rousseau and Hans Bernard are fake."

Nanesse appeared not to be listening. She looked at her watch and then opened the drawers of the sideboard, visibly preoccupied with something she found more important than the fugitive assassins.

"Fuck it, I'm going to order the cavalry charge! I'll call my colleagues in Mende and the eighteenth arrondissement of Paris. They'll find a way to make one of the local government employees help them search the archives at the mayor's office. In Charleville, I'll ask Officer Vigneules—he has an uncle on the local council. That should save us some time."

She swallowed a mouthful of Nanesse's Chimay, then unlocked the service phone that gave her access to the direct line of every police station in France. She was working her way through the various security checks when Nanesse tugged at her sleeve.

"Captain, would it bother you if I made dinner while you're busy on the phone?"

"Sorry?"

"I'd planned to cook a *cacasse à cul nu* tonight. But I need to let it simmer, so . . ."

Katel Marelle stared at her incredulously. "Hang on, Agnès . . . You told me that your foster kids had been placed elsewhere temporarily, and that your own children have already flown the nest. And obviously your husband is, um . . . well . . . what I mean is, you're on your own, and yet . . . you want to *cook*?"

Now it was Nanesse's turn to look amazed. "Yes. Cooking always soothes me. And helps me think. What does it matter if you're on your own or with your whole extended family?"

The captain put down her beer.

"What does it matter? I just open a can or defrost something. It's sad enough eating on your own, without going to all the trouble of following a recipe every day. What is a 'bare-assed' cacasse, anyway?"

"It's a local specialty. Potatoes and onions, cooked in a Dutch oven."

"And you have to cook it without wearing underwear? Even if you're single?"

Nanesse smiled and a brief titter escaped her mouth—the first time Katel had seen her laugh in two days.

"No." She explained that it was called *cul nu*—bare-assed—simply because it was a poor man's dish. "It really just means *without meat*, because meat was too expensive then. These days, though, it's usually cooked with bacon or smoked sausage."

Katel stared into space for a moment—her thoughts drifting from the prospect of the local potato dish back to the sadness experienced by the solitary diner—before nodding to Nanesse and refocusing on her cell phone. She spent the next fifteen minutes trying to contact the police stations in Mende, the eighteenth arrondissement of Paris, and Charleville-Mézières. When she got through, she gave precise orders, often becoming irritated—*Yes, tonight, Lieutenant! This is urgent. I already have two corpses on my hands*—and sometimes negotiating—*Tomorrow morning at the latest? You promise? I'll buy the mayor croissants if I have to, as long as he cooperates.*

At last she hung up. Nanesse was now wearing an apron.

"Mathias—I mean, Officer Vigneules—is going to call his uncle tonight. The other cops have promised they'll make the mayor's offices open tomorrow morning. It's a pain in the ass that we can't sort this whole birth certificate thing out today, but . . . oh well. I'm sorry."

Agnès was crying. She waved Katel's concern away with a knife, indicating she was crying not from sadness, but because the diced onions were stinging her eyes.

"Don't be sorry," she said. "People should have the right to some time off work, so they can be with their family. Do you have family, Captain?"

She had asked the question with a naturalness that Katel found disconcerting. "Ugh, no, thank God!"

Nanesse gazed tenderly at Pierrot and Columbine in their glass vase.

"Will you stay for dinner?"

"Huh?"

"There's enough cacasse for two. Or even for three."

Katel smiled—her own first real smile in two days. "That's kind of you, Agnès. You're a very caring person. But I do have to get home. It's not really legal for me to work remotely from here. Bring me some leftovers tomorrow, though, okay? You'll have to come to the police station anyway, for the deposition and the Identi-Kit and all that jazz."

"Captain, can you promise me something?"

"No, probably not."

Nanesse wiped her hands on the apron and gave Katel a look of tender concern.

"When you get home, try to cook something. If you like, I know some excellent pâté recipes . . ."

Katel smiled again. Two smiles in less than a minute—a new record for her. She watched as Nanesse went back into the kitchen. Agnès Duval was one of those women who go with the flow of daily life, floating like a cork on the sea of existence—children, meals, gardening—always busy with something, days and nights following one another as tirelessly and relentlessly as the tides.

"I tried, Agnès," the captain confessed. "Family life, I mean. Being part of a couple, making nice meals, taking naps together."

Katel had no idea why she was saying all this to someone she hardly knew, someone who was also a witness in an unresolved criminal case.

"I tried men, Agnès. Several of them. With and without children. Experienced men and inexperienced men. I think I must be misandric, or misanthropic, or whatever the word is to describe women who can't stand men. I tried women too, though, and I hated them just as much. So I'm a misandrist *and* a misogynist—an equal opportunity hater. I'm not that crazy about dogs either. Right now, I'm trying out cats. I started with a white Persian, but he's already getting on my nerves. I should have insisted on a trial period first. I think I was duped by all those kitten videos on social media. Now I'm stuck with this one for at least ten years. Ugh . . . At least when it's over with a guy, you can tell him to stop turning up and expecting to be stroked and fed."

Nanesse turned and leaned over her Dutch oven. She was crying again. And not because of the onions this time. Katel realized how insensitive she had been. Nanesse's guy would never turn up again, to be stroked or fed.

"I'm an idiot, Agnès. I'm sorry."

They shared a moment of intimate solitude. The silence was threatening to last a long time when it was broken by the ringtone of the policewoman's cell phone.

"Probably Vigneules—he must have talked to his uncle by now. Hello, Mathias?"

"No, sorry to disappoint you, Captain, it's Jérémy. Everyone at the station is looking for you."

"I'm working remotely! See—you call me, I answer. Simple. So, do you have any news?"

"Yes! You're going to be proud of your little geniuses. We're making great progress. About those size twelve shoe prints . . . the ones we found in Bruno Pluvier's cellar don't match the ones at the Four Sons of Aymon. So, if Renaud Duval was murdered, it wasn't by the same guy who killed Bruno Pluvier."

"Unless the murderer just changed his shoes."

"Huh, that's true. We didn't think of that."

Katel sighed.

Jérémy Bonello went on: "On the other hand, we compared the tire tracks from the vehicles parked at the lot near the lookout point on the night Renaud Duval was killed with those of the car parked beside the Ardennes Canal, near Bruno Pluvier's home, and . . . bingo! Same tires. Which means, Captain—"

"That we have two killers at large," Katel interjected. "One killer with a burned face and the other not yet identified, since Agnès Duval saw only his feet. She'll be at the police station first thing tomorrow. Have a good evening, Jérémy."

She was about to hang up when Lieutenant Bonello said: "Captain, wait, there's something else."

"Yes?"

"Our colleagues have continued searching the first crime scene. They went down into that pit in the middle of the meadow—the wool hole—but didn't find anything. Then they rappelled down from the lookout point to the Meuse River, and guess what they found in some brambles?"

From the silence that followed, Jérémy must have surmised that the captain wasn't in the mood for guessing games, because he went on.

"A pistol! And not just any pistol—a CZ 75. One of the most popular handguns in the world. According to the ballistics guys, only one shot was fired. If it was aimed at Renaud Duval, the person obviously wasn't a very good shot, because there were no bullet wounds on his body."

"Maybe he jumped off the edge of the lookout to escape the shooter . . . Or maybe it was his gun."

"The fingerprints on the butt and the trigger aren't his, though. They belong to someone else, unidentified for now. But I bet whoever it is wears size twelve shoes!"

"Okay, Jérémy. Good work."

"There is one strange coincidence, though." The lieutenant paused for dramatic effect.

Katel sighed. "Spit it out, Jérémy!"

"Um, yes, sorry," Bonello stammered. "Well, the CZ 75 is a Czech gun. Developed in Czechoslovakia during the Cold War. And you remember what Agnès Duval told us? Bruno Pluvier went down to his cellar to find a Czech newspaper."

"Good point, Jérémy."

"So, I went out on a limb, Captain. You know how Pluvier said that the only clue to the name of the town where the newspaper was printed was a brand of beer? Well, I consulted . . . an expert, let's say. To be perfectly honest, he's a neighbor of mine, but he knows his beers, believe me. You should see his cellar—he's got more lagers and ales than the Belgian embassy!"

"Get to the point."

"Oh, yeah. Anyway, he suggested a name. *Pilsen.*"

"Pilsen?" Katel repeated.

"That's it!" cried a voice from the kitchen.

Katel looked up in surprise.

"You did say 'Pilsen'?" Nanesse asked, walking toward her. "That must be it! I often heard Renaud and Milana talking about that city."

"What's so special about Pilsen?" Katel demanded. "Apart from the beer."

Nanesse looked in turn at Guignol, Pinocchio, the puppets on the ceiling, and the heads in the vase.

"It can't be a coincidence," she replied. "Pilsen is the world capital of puppetry."

Katel Marelle stood there speechless, the phone still glued to her ear.

This was their first breakthrough!

Two pieces of this damned puzzle finally fitted together.

"Okay, Jérémy, go through all the local newspapers you can find from Pilsen and run them through Google Translate. I'll be there right away!"

There was a brief silence.

"It's just that . . ."

"Just that what, Jérémy? It's Saturday evening—is that what you were going to say? You had plans with your wife and children? Well, cancel them! And send two men here, to Bourg-Fidèle, to guard Agnès Duval's house. I don't want to leave her here alone; the two killers know where she lives. If we get a third murder, you'll be working Sundays too."

"I suppose I could send Will and Mehdi, but they're not going to like it."

"Tell them they'll get to taste a cacasse à cul nu—that should cheer them up."

# I THINK I'M IN HELL, THEREFORE I AM

*A Season in Hell* by Arthur Rimbaud

# MINA'S STORY

## The Spring of Petrushka

***August 1968***

My name is Mina. I was born in 1956, in Czechoslovakia, a country that no longer exists. A country that young people these days probably believe never existed. A country with a name that some people can't pronounce. So I prefer to say I was born in Bohemia—the name of the largest historical region of my homeland.

In France it is called *Bohême.* But it is not the same bohemia that French people love—the *bohème* of starving artists in Parisian garrets, of absinthe nights and doomed poets, of Rimbaud and Aznavour—which is written with a grave accent: that little line slanting northwest to southeast over the *e.*

The *e* in my Bohemia wears a little hat. Bohême.

Not that I knew any of this in 1956, when I was born, in the Vyšehrad neighborhood of Prague.

My father was a drawing teacher at the UMPRUM, the School of Applied Arts in Prague. My mother was a French teacher at Václav Hanka High School.

They were privileged intellectuals. We lived in a large apartment on Celetná Street. My parents played Smetana and Dvořák records at full volume; you could hear the violins from *The Moldau* or *The New World*

*Symphony* all the way down to the Mánes Bridge. They read Čapek and Kafka, and a great deal of French literature too, of course. Apparently, my mother even hung a portrait of Arthur Rimbaud above my cradle and recited his poems to me.

I had a happy childhood, listening to musicians on the Charles Bridge and—as soon as I was old enough—watching the puppet shows at the Spejbl and Hurvínek Theater. My father was friends with Josef Skupa, the greatest puppeteer in the world. He designed sets for him. I even had a photograph in my room of me sitting in Skupa's lap—taken a few months after I was born, a few months before he died. Perhaps my love of puppets can be traced back to that picture? Was it Josef Skupa, playing with my chubby little arms as if they belonged to a cloth puppet, who inspired me to take up that vocation?

My life was a fairy tale. A bohemian life in Bohemia. Prague was simply a vast stage on which I acted. I spoke my parts in French, most of the time. I was practically bilingual by the age of ten, eleven, twelve . . .

It was springtime. I had never seen my parents looking so happy. Every evening, they would invite their friends to our apartment to drink French wine and speak of things I knew nothing about: socialism with a human face, the Prague Spring, Alexander Dubček.

Late one night, I fell asleep in my mother's arms. The last memories that I took with me into my dreams were of adult laughter, cigarette smoke floating over from women chatting on the balcony, the warmth of the night, notes played on the piano, shivering as my father's mustache rubbed against my cheeks, shivering one last time when he kissed me good night, when Mama tucked me in with my puppets, the ones given to me by Skupa himself: Hurvínek, his red-haired girlfriend Manicka, her dog Zeryk, and—above all—my favorite of them all, the one I hugged to my chest in bed every night, Petrushka.

The next morning, when I woke, the earth was shaking.

I just had time to grab Petrushka.

A moment later, the apartment exploded. When I woke up again, I was covered in rubble and dust. Of the art nouveau walls that my father's architect friends talked about so proudly, nothing remained but the ruins of a façade. Everywhere I looked, people were yelling, running, fleeing. Who? What? Where were my parents?

I was twelve years old back then and I didn't know anything.

I didn't know that half a million foreign troops, six thousand tanks, and almost a thousand airplanes had just invaded Czechoslovakia and were now attacking Prague. I didn't know that families who laughed, sang, read books, and smoked on balconies would be crushed by military might. I didn't know that the human face of socialism that my parents had dreamed of would be stamped on by the Russian boots of Operation Danube.

Where were Mama and Papa?

I cried out. I called for them. And I ran. I saw hundreds of parachutists falling from the sky. I saw thousands of protesters blindfolding statues as a symbol of protest, moving road signs to point the wrong way. Were they hoping that would be enough to keep away the Russian tanks? I wandered for hours through the streets of Prague before collapsing at the foot of the Charles Bridge, close to a boy about three years older than me who was playing a violin to drown out the noise of machine gun fire.

I was alone, with Petrushka.

Where were Mama and Papa?

I never found out the answer to that question. Were they killed in the bombardment of our apartment on Celetná Street? Imprisoned, like most politically engaged intellectuals when Prague was taken? Murdered by the conservatives who had opened the country's borders?

I didn't know it yet, but I was only one of thousands of little children abandoned to a life on the streets, punished because their parents had believed in a utopia.

You must smash the dreams of children before they start to truly believe them. Otherwise you will be forced to kill them once they grow up.

When I woke under the Charles Bridge, the boy with the violin had left. Petrushka was still asleep in my arms.

"Hello," said a voice. "What is your name?"

When I looked up, the Moor was standing beside me. His mouth opened and closed in time with the words he spoke. His arms and legs moved like real limbs. They were slender and muscular. He rose into the air for a few seconds, then fell back to the ground with the lightness of a crow's feather. In the morning sunlight, the silver threads were almost invisible.

Not once did I feel an urge to look up, to see what the puppeteer looked like, the man who was giving the Moor life.

I picked up my cloth doll and I made him move too. I was the best puppeteer at Skupa's theater school.

"Everyone calls me Petrushka."

"Are you lost?"

"I think so, yes."

"You're good at that. You're very talented."

I started dancing around him.

"Thank you!"

The Moor smiled, flickered his eyelids, and nodded his head, exactly as a shy boy would. Never before had I seen a puppeteer imbue his marionette with such realistic expressions.

"If you're lost, do you want to come and spend some time with me?"

I looked at the corpses scattered over the riverbank, the tanks lined up alongside the Vltava and on the lawns of the Kampa Park, the flowers of flame and columns of smoke rising all over the city.

And I said yes.

Libor Slavik was just twenty-five years old. Professionally, he went by the name Louka.

Even if I was too young at the time to have an informed opinion on the matter, I do think he was a very good puppeteer. With his horse-drawn caravan, he had been touring Czechoslovakia and beyond, through all the Warsaw Pact countries—for several years.

Libor was handsome, with the grace of a fairground strongman who can also dance like a ballerina. The magnetism of a magician at the border of reality. The joyous charm of a street peddler. And he had a pair of smoldering gray eyes that grew darker whenever he looked at you.

Libor was handsome, yes. He was also married with two children—boys aged four and three, named Kristof and Amos. He roamed, free and elusive, along the roads of Bohemia and central Europe, with his sons and his wife, Zuzana.

Whenever they parked their caravan in a village square, the puppets would perform *Petrushka.* Zuzana would manipulate the ballerina while Libor played the parts of Petrushka and the Moor.

Libor also performed magic tricks, juggled, and breathed fire. Zuzana had a rare talent for fortune-telling. All across Bohemia, Moravia, and Silesia, the villagers would listen to her with fear and respect. I must admit, Zuzana fascinated me.

Libor and Zuzana took me far, far away. Toward the Austrian border. They were obsessed with the idea of distancing themselves from Prague. Escaping from cities and heading to places where artists were not persecuted. I followed them unquestioningly. What else could I have done?

I grew up on the road, sleeping in barns, eating as I walked, making thousands of Czechs laugh when I made Petrushka waltz with the dancing bear, and making them cry when Petrushka died in agony, his heart pierced by the Moor's wooden saber.

Petrushka was my favorite role. I cut my hair very short and dressed like a boy, wrapping a scarf around my breasts to flatten them. I looked like my puppet: young, pretty, light on his feet. Libor played the Moor as violent and strong, while Zuzana was a manipulative, jealous, beautiful ballerina.

Kristof and Amos grew up on the road too. I spent a lot of time taking care of them—more than Zuzana did, in truth. I often wondered if that was why their parents took me in.

Kristof was not afraid of anything. He was pulling the ears of our mare, Kinsky, and trying to breathe fire like his father, before he could even read or count. Amos was calmer, sweeter; he liked to listen to and tell stories. In northern Bohemia, he would spend hours watching the sun set over the Giant Mountains, then reproduce the colors with pencils that a teacher—fascinated by the chalk sketches that he had made on the concrete school wall—had given him.

I was their mama, their nanny, their big sister. I woke beside them, ate beside them, slept beside them.

Or at least I tried.

I tried to never be alone.

With Libor.

The first time he raped me, I was thirteen. It happened in a field near Pilsen, during the puppet festival, less than a year after the horrors of the Prague Spring.

After that, he kept doing it, more and more often, almost every night, while Zuzana slept in the caravan.

I moved my mattress out under the stars. I waited, eyes wide open, knowing that he would come.

I should have run away, but I had nowhere to go.

I should have run away, but Libor gave me a roof, a family, a job.

I should have run away, but I was afraid. Afraid of defending myself. Even afraid of hating him.

I should have run away, but I loved playing the role of Petrushka. And what would have become of him without me? What would have become of me without him?

Maybe I would have ended up accepting that life, if it hadn't been for the accident.

Was it sent to punish me or to save me?

A blessing or a curse?

I don't know the answer to that even now.

# 19

## Vicky

***Sunday, September 17, 2023***
***The banks of the Tarn, Florac, Lozère***

Nicole and Mathieu Mariotta lived in a small, traditional house built of Cévennes stone, in a hamlet by the banks of the Tarn, a few hundred yards from the village, as if the old schoolteacher had deliberately chosen to settle in a place where he could keep an eye on his former students without having to bump into them every time he left home.

Vicky had bought a dozen *petits choux*, and Lola handed them, with disarming politeness, to the woman who opened the door.

"For you, ma'am."

Nicole Mariotta was dried up and wrinkled, like an apple that had spent too long in the sun. A sour-tasting apple. She barely even glanced at the paper bag, simply ushering them inside and leaving the bag of cream-filled pastries on a table in the entrance hall, to the dismay of Lola, who had been dreaming of those light Viennese treats ever since they left the bakery.

"I should warn you ahead of time," said Nicole Mariotta in a whisper, "my husband doesn't remember much at all anymore. The doctors have told me that it's not Alzheimer's—that his brain is working fine, just slower than before—but, well, they're not the ones who have to live with him." She concluded this warning by giving Vicky a conspiratorial smile.

Mathieu Mariotta was sitting in a large armchair, turned toward the patio door. Sunlight poured through the glass, which offered a view of the river flowing past the end of their yard. All Vicky could see of the former schoolteacher was a tuft of gray hair at the top of the chair.

"Your daughter can play outside," said Nicole. "There are lots of bird feeders in the yard, so that should keep her entertained."

Vicky looked out at the birdhouses she could see in various trees, and then at the white water of the passing Tarn a hundred feet away.

Tight-lipped, Nicole Mariotta added: "There's a fence. Nobody has ever drowned in the river here."

Lola thrust Kasper into her mother's hands and ran out to chase blue tits around the sunny yard. Vicky watched her for a few seconds, then sat down beside Mathieu Mariotta, keeping half an eye on Lola while looking back at him. His face, in contrast to his wife's, was as round and red as an apple.

"Sir," Vicky began, "I don't want to take too much of your time, so I'll come straight to the point. I'm looking for a man, Hans Bernard. I believe he went to the school in Florac. Do you remember him?"

"Hans? Hans Bernard? Yes, of course! What happened to him?"

The certainty of the old man's tone made Vicky's heart leap. She didn't know where to focus her attention: on Lola, outside in the yard; on Mathieu Mariotta, to assess the credibility of his testimony; or on Nicole, who stood behind her husband, shrugging and rolling her eyes as if to suggest that he was soft in the head.

"Are you . . . are you sure, Monsieur Mariotta?"

Mathieu leaned forward and smiled. "Of course I'm sure! I could never forget any of my students. Least of all little Hans . . ."

Taken aback, Vicky said: "Why Hans least of all?"

"Well, he was my student for a long time. For the whole of his time in school. And he was such a sweet boy."

Behind him, Nicole Mariotta made circling motions with her finger next to her temple.

"Um, what was he like?" Vicky stammered. "Physically, I mean."

The man sat up straight. "What, you don't believe me? You think I'm losing my marbles? Hang on, I'll fetch you some proof. I kept all the documents."

Mathieu Mariotta stood up slowly and shuffled across the floor in his slippers to the adjoining room. As soon as he disappeared into what Vicky assumed must be his study, Nicole hissed: "Don't believe anything he says! You could ask him if he remembered Napoleon Bonaparte and he'd swear that he taught the man to read and write."

Mathieu quickly returned with a thick folder under his arm. He skated over the smooth waxed floorboards, polishing them with his slippers. As he sat down in the chair again, Vicky looked out at the yard and then around the room. Lola was playing near some bird feeders that hung from the low branches of a weeping willow, while Nicole Mariotta continued to roll her eyes to the corners of the ceiling, where spiderwebs glistened.

Mathieu opened the folder, took out a sheet of paper, and passed it to Vicky.

"Read that, ma'am. My eyes aren't sharp enough anymore."

Vicky looked down at a list of names. Presumably these were all the children Mathieu Mariotta had taught, arranged in alphabetical order. She skimmed through them, her finger tracing the page.

*Jérôme Avril*

*Isabelle Baron*

*Selim Belkacem*

*Sylvie Béranger*

And just like that, there it was.

*Hans Bernard*

Lola was trying to play with the birds, but it wasn't much fun. No sooner did she step toward one than it would fly off out of reach. These birds were nothing like Rampion and Catsfoot, her beloved ponies who did everything she told them. Lola would have liked to climb over the fence and run to the river, where she could climb on the rocks, maybe find a dragonfly or a toad . . . But she wasn't allowed. And besides, the fence was too high, and Mommy was keeping an eye on her, and . . .

Lola froze.

On the other side of the fence, two men were watching her.

They smiled, and she forced herself to smile back.

Mommy had told her yesterday: *When someone is different, you shouldn't be scared of them. You should be nice to them.*

Lola walked toward them. She would try her best to be very nice, because the two men behind the fence were really very different.

"Look," said the man wearing sunglasses. "Do you recognize him?"

The other man—the one without ears—was holding out a puppet.

*Another doll just like Kasper!* Although this one was painted black and was carrying a wooden sword.

Intrigued, Lola kept walking toward them.

*I'm not scared, Mommy,* she whispered in her head. *I mustn't be afraid of them.*

Although the truth was, deep down, she was very scared.

Because she had never seen such frightening men before.

But it wasn't their fault, and she should make an effort to smile at them and talk to them.

And to not look disgusted by their burned faces.

# 20

## Éléa

***A71 highway, Allier***

Samuel Galet was making less and less effort to conceal his irritation as he drove his Renault Captur SUV. He had fantasized about this journey from Paris to Florac, even though he was going simply to perform another hygiene inspection of some cheese factories in the Cévennes, a trip no different from the regular tours of dairy cooperatives that he undertook three times a month. There was no possibility of taking the train for such inspections: There were no stations in the tiny villages he visited, and he had a hundred pounds of official equipment in his trunk.

But he had started fantasizing about this particular Paris–Florac trip as soon as his passenger signed up on BlaBlaCar. Éléa Simon. Young and very cute, to judge by the photos of her on social media. It certainly made a change from his usual passengers—couples who spent the whole journey smooching in the back seat, or gangs of students who would jabber away to each other, paying attention to him only when they wanted to ask if they could open their packs of chips and cans of beer in his car.

When she'd gotten in his Captur at five in the morning, Samuel had thought she was even cuter in real life, with her kohl-darkened eyes, her flared pink miniskirt and fancy pantyhose, and her tattooed shoulders bared by a strappy Lycra top.

And so began their six-hour trip.

Not that Samuel wanted anything to happen with this girl. He wasn't about to put his hand on her knee or let his eyes wander over her thighs—she was about twenty years younger than him, after all. But just as it is more enjoyable to drive through a landscape of hills and vineyards rather than just endless flat plains, it is also more enjoyable to sit beside a pretty, smiling girl and have a nice chat than to share the car with a less pleasant passenger.

Well, she certainly smiled a lot. But she didn't chat at all.

The girl had kept her eyes glued to the screen of her smartphone throughout the four-hundred-mile journey, with one of those stupid smart rings flickering on her finger. Samuel had tried to start a conversation with her at least a dozen times—in vain. And yet whenever he managed to catch a sideways glimpse of her, he could see her lips moving, as if she was talking to her ring, or her phone, or herself . . .

*All this technology is driving people crazy!* thought Samuel. *Even this BlaBlaCar app, which is supposed to be all about helping and sharing. Before, all you had to do was stand with your thumb up by the side of the road and a car would stop for you.*

He saw a sign indicating that Florac was only twenty-three miles away.

He would drop this girl in the square near the church, as she had requested, then he'd get his twenty-five euros and that would be it. Next time he'd choose a man—even some big hairy guy with legs so fat that Samuel wouldn't be able to change gears would be preferable to this.

At least then they'd be able to talk about soccer, cars, and chicks.

# 21

## Nanesse and Katel

***Police station, Avenue Charles-de-Gaulle, Charleville-Mézières***

Sergeant Will Walcourt parked the blue Mégane outside the police station, just behind Agnès Duval's Clio. He and Mehdi had accompanied the car all the way from Bourg-Fidèle to Charleville. Before he cut the engine, he checked the dashboard clock.

11:15 a.m.

The boss was probably still going to be in a foul mood. She had left him at least five messages on his phone already: *Where are you? We're waiting for you! What the hell are you doing?*

But it was hardly William's fault that this Nanesse Duval—whose safety they had been ordered to ensure—had insisted on making them a huge breakfast this morning, flipping pancakes before proceeding to get out the Ardennes butter and Mirabelle plum jam. Even if it meant getting bawled out by the captain, William had not been about to refuse such a feast, offered by such a kind, lovely woman. Besides, he deserved some compensation for the forty-eight-hour shift he had worked and the night spent in the Mégane, with Mehdi snoring beside him.

He wolfed down one of the chocolate cookies that Nanesse had practically forced into his pocket—*for your children, William*—then wiped his fingers on his uniform. He would finish the rest on his way home. Well, he didn't want his kids to end up as fat as him, did he?

Captain Katel Marelle was waiting for them outside the front door of the station, arms crossed, a lock of her black hair covering her left eye: the bad one! At the police station in Charleville, legend had it that the captain was in a good mood whenever her hair fell over her right eye. William could not remember that ever happening. He held out a greasy hand, but she didn't shake it.

"Will and Mehdi, go to Place Ducale. We need as many officers there as possible."

Both cops sighed, then obeyed. Will knew that they would barely have time to go home and see their wives and children over the next nine days. The biggest event of the year was opening this weekend in Charleville-Mézières: the World Festival of Puppet Theaters. For nine days, their town would become the center of the puppet world. Artists would come here from all over the planet, as would four hundred thousand other visitors, and every public square in Charleville would be transformed into an open-air stage. For the duration of the festival, an ambiance of joy and family fun would reign as the townspeople found themselves surrounded by the strangest, most spectacular creatures. That was the job of the police: making sure the atmosphere remained one of joy and family fun.

For everybody, that is, except them.

That Sunday morning, the Charleville police station—located on the edge of town, amid car dealerships and discount stores—appeared strangely empty. Only three police officers remained to man the fort: Fatoumata, who worked at the reception desk, Lieutenant Jérémy Bonello, and Captain Katel Marelle.

"Did you sleep well, Agnès?" the captain asked as she opened the door to her office. "I trust Will and Mehdi didn't keep you awake all night by playing on the swings in your yard? Lieutenant Bonello here is going to help you create an Identi-Kit image of the guy with the burned face—the one you saw outside your house and in Bruno Pluvier's cellar. Then we'll let Jérémy go, and the two of us will keep working together, okay?"

Lieutenant Bonello led Nanesse into the office and wearily pulled out two chairs. He looked at her with dark-ringed eyes: He appeared not to have gotten much sleep last night, and not only that but—unlike Will and Mehdi—he had not been lucky enough to partake of her enormous breakfast this morning. They sat in front of a computer screen, and Bonello opened an app that looked like a primitive version of Photoshop.

Dozens of chins, mouths, noses, and foreheads flashed past, but Nanesse had to admit that she could remember nothing of the killer's face other than the fact that the skin had been burned. She had no idea what shape his face was, nor what the color of his eyes or even his hair was. Pale chestnut? Dark blond? She didn't know. As for his accomplice, all she had seen were his feet, through a basement windowpane streaming with rain.

All the same, the lieutenant managed to draw up an approximate portrait, even if it did look like a cross between Frankenstein's monster and a caricature gangster. He saved it, then slapped his own cheeks.

"Are you tired, Lieutenant?" Nanesse asked with concern.

"Katel and I spent the whole night on the internet," he explained. "We began by researching Pilsen: 175,000 inhabitants; European Capital of Culture in 2015; gateway to Bohemia. It's also the birthplace of Czech engineer Emil Škoda, the soccer goalkeeper Petr Čech, and the physicist Peter Grünberg, the latter of whom—to be perfectly honest with you—I'd never actually heard of before. I guess that means I must know more about cars and soccer than I do about quantum physics. But most importantly, Pilsen is the world capital of puppetry, thanks to another local star, Josef Skupa. Before the Second World War, this guy was the most famous creator of puppets on the planet. Unfortunately, we haven't yet been able to find any trace of the newspaper article that

Renaud Duval was searching for and that, presumably, cost Bruno Pluvier his life. But don't worry, we'll get there in the end!"

Captain Marelle came over and stood behind them.

"Yes, and we'll also capture those two killers. But, while they remain at large, Agnès, I'm afraid you can't go anywhere without a police guard, so you'll have two cops trailing you all day. I know that might seem excessive to you, but those men are clearly on a mission to eliminate any inconvenient witnesses. And—apart from a facial composite that looks like an ogre drawn by Picasso, some fingerprints taken from a Czech pistol found on the ground near your husband's body, and tracks left by four Michelin CrossClimate tires used by most midrange SUVs—we have nothing on them for the moment."

Lieutenant Bonello yawned.

"Would you please let me go home, Katel? I've been working non-stop since Wednesday. Just give me a chance to chill out a little bit? I promised Anne-So and the kids that I'd take them to see the Vietnamese water puppets."

"Okay," said Katel. "You can go."

"Hang on," said Nanesse.

She took a small Tupperware box from her bag and handed it to the lieutenant.

"Cacasse à cul nu. I hope you'll accept this small thank-you gift. Will and Mehdi ate two bowls each last night and they haven't been poisoned!"

"Can I keep you with me for a while, Agnès?"

It wasn't exactly an order, but Nanesse knew she wasn't really being given a choice. The two women were now alone in the largest room in the police station, where under normal circumstances there would probably be a crowd of uniformed men and women running in all directions.

"Come on, I have something to show you. Something I think you'll find reassuring."

# 22

## Vicky

***The banks of the Tarn, Florac***

*Hans Bernard.*

Vicky was still holding the list of former students that Mathieu Mariotta had given her, reading and rereading the name of the man she loved.

Hans was on the list!

So he hadn't lied to her. He really had spent his childhood in Florac. Hans was not a ghost, just a little kid from around here.

Her breathing slowed down as she felt relief flood through her.

"Mathieu," she said in a gentle voice, "could you tell me about him? About the little boy you thought was so sweet?"

"Oh," said the old man. "It was a long, long time ago . . ."

*It wasn't* that *long,* thought Vicky. But lovers' internal clocks probably tick faster than retired schoolteachers'. Mathieu scratched his head, in search of an elusive memory. As Nicole continued her mime performance behind his back, Vicky began to have her doubts.

"Mathieu . . . do you . . . have any photographs of him?"

"Of course! I'll go and fetch them."

The old schoolteacher climbed to his feet. His slippers began their slow shuffle across the floor. As soon as he had disappeared into his study again, his wife whistled.

"I told you he didn't actually remember that name. You were hoping he'd be on that list, weren't you? So now you have your answer. As for the rest, don't get your hopes up. He's just making it up—he's lost it."

Mathieu returned with a thick photo album then sat down and started carefully turning the pages. Old pictures of students, yellowed with age. Hundreds of faces. Mathieu was right, after all. It was all so long ago.

Finally he came to a stop and placed the open album in Vicky's lap while he looked for his glasses. She gazed down at a double-page spread containing photographs of about twenty students, all wearing serious, well-behaved expressions, each staring directly into the lens.

She felt an electric shock run through her.

She felt sure she recognized Hans! *There, on the third line, already looking a little bit dreamy, his head in the clouds . . .*

This was the perfect opportunity to test Mathieu Mariotta's memory.

"Mathieu," she said innocently, "could you point out Hans to me?"

The teacher pointed unhesitatingly at the copper-blond boy with daydreamer's eyes.

"That's him."

Vicky felt heat suffuse her face.

Mathieu Mariotta had not lost his marbles at all. He remembered this delicate little boy—her Hans—perfectly.

The old man picked up the album and looked up at Vicky, with a smile.

"That was a test, wasn't it? The same kind of test those stupid doctors are always giving me; those charlatans that my better half forces me to see."

Nicole Mariotta, still standing behind her husband's armchair, grimaced. Her fingers, Vicky noticed, were writhing strangely, like those of a witch clumsily casting spells.

"Not at all," Vicky said, blushing. "It was just that I—"

"Hans had beautiful gray eyes," the teacher went on. "When he looked at you angrily, his irises were like two pencil leads, ready to write the worst words on you. Then the next instant, his gaze would grow soft, as if he'd just erased all those bad words. He moved with a strange sort of grace too, like a wading bird with long, straight legs and heavy wings. But when he spread those wings . . ."

*He flew,* thought Vicky. What the old man was describing—that look, that gait—it was Hans, without a doubt. She must have blushed again, because Mathieu gave her a tender look.

"You love him, don't you? He's lucky to have such a pretty, young fiancée."

The witch behind his back looked like she was about to cast another evil spell . . . against Vicky this time. Mathieu Mariotta addressed his wife without even turning to look at her.

"Would you fetch me my tramadol tablets, dear?"

Nicole grumbled but apparently knew she had no choice. As soon as she went into the kitchen, Mathieu put his hand on Vicky's knee.

"I have other memories, you know. I remember Hans's mother too. My wife didn't like her . . . Well, she didn't like most of the women in Florac. But Hans's mother was—how can I put this?—a little too artistic."

The old schoolteacher pronounced this last word, *artistic*, with a reverence bordering on religious devotion.

"What kind of artist was she?"

"A little of everything, to be honest. Dance, singing, theater, drawing . . . But all these disciplines were used in the service of a single art. She was a puppeteer."

Vicky squeezed Kasper's chubby arms. Her daughter's broken toy was still sitting in her lap.

"Hans's mother used to come to all the local schools," Mathieu continued. "She would bring her little puppet theater to the classroom and put on a performance, for Christmas or for children's birthdays."

"Her puppets, did she . . . make them herself?"

"Oh yes. She had her own little studio. She gave her creations to all the children in the town. I think most of the families around here probably still have one. Mothers pass them down to their daughters, or their daughters-in-law."

"Puppets like this one?"

Mathieu put his glasses back on and examined Kasper.

"Yes, I'm sure of it. That is one of Marion's creations."

"Marion?" echoed a voice behind him.

Nicole Mariotta was holding the white pill and a glass of water in front of her husband's face.

"You can't remember your children's birthdays, or mine, but you still recall the name of that crazy woman?"

Mathieu flashed Vicky the quick, resigned smile of a prisoner whose time in the visiting room is about to end. She clutched Kasper to her chest. For a second, she thought about standing up, walking to the patio door, and looking for her daughter, but her desire to find out more about Hans overcame her.

"Do you remember any other details?"

Nicole Mariotta moved the glass closer to her husband's lips, her fingers threatening to shove the pill into his mouth the moment he opened it.

"A few," the old man muttered, almost without moving his lips. "Hans was rather a fragile child, often unwell. His mother would sometimes go away on tour, but she always came back. She never forgot to perform his favorite show at the Florac fete. She did it for free, and very discreetly, because she didn't even want the local newspapers to write about it. But Marion was so talented . . ."

This time, Mathieu looked as if he had disappeared into his own past: eyes staring, mouth hanging open. His wife pushed the tablet inside and knocked the glass against his teeth, and he promptly closed his lips over it.

"Swallow it! And stop talking nonsense. Have no illusions, ma'am: What my husband is making out to be some magnificent opera was actually just a shabby little puppet theater made by a bohemian woman who cleared out years ago."

Mariotta kept his mouth firmly shut, biting the rim of the glass so hard that Vicky feared he might break it.

"He mixes up everything," insisted Nicole. "The kids, the mothers, the years . . . I said swallow!"

Once again, Vicky thought about going out to the yard and calling Lola, but she decided to ask one last question first.

"Mathieu, do you remember the name of that show?"

He hesitated, then suddenly opened his mouth; the water poured down his throat, along with the pill. He coughed so hard Vicky thought he was going to choke, before he breathlessly declared: "How could I forget? It was the most beautiful thing I have ever seen here. If you knew how much I miss it now . . . We used to wait for it all year long. The Moor, the ballerina, . . . and, of course, Petrushka!"

Lola stood in front of the gate as the two men with burned faces stood on the other side. At first, she had tried to focus her gaze on the black puppet the earless man held out, and only on the puppet—Kasper's brother—but after a while she grew used to the men's strange faces and managed to look at them without flinching. *Mommy was right,* she thought. *People are all different. Just because someone is ugly, it doesn't mean he is a bad person. Often, in fact, the opposite is true.*

She stared at the man in sunglasses.

"You can't see, can you?"

The blind man turned his face in the direction of the voice, then raised his black glasses. His eyes were as white and blank as those of a dead fish.

"That's right."

Startled, Lola turned to the man with no ears.

"And your friend, he can see me but he can't hear me?"

The earless man was watching every movement of her lips.

"That's right," said the blind man. "My brother is deaf and dumb."

Lola stood there a moment looking from one burned face to the other, trying to understand how these two men were able to cope with the challenges of everyday life.

"So you can't leave each other?" Lola asked. "You need him to see, because he is your eyes. And he needs you to hear, because you are his ears. Is that right?"

"Exactly!" the blind man said. "You're very bright for a five-year-old."

He smiled at her, but Lola frowned. "If you're blind and you can't see me, how do you know how old I am?"

"My brother told me."

"But your brother can't talk!"

"No, but he can write down everything he sees."

To prove this, the blind man showed her the cell phone he was holding. The screen was bigger than a normal phone. Lola hesitated, then took a step closer to the gate. The blind man felt with his hands for Lola's hand.

"Touch the tablet, and you'll understand."

Without letting the blind man grab her hand, Lola touched the screen.

She jumped. The screen wasn't smooth. She could feel hundreds of bumps and hollows under her fingertips, like her arm when she had gooseflesh.

"It tickles my fingers," said Lola.

"It's braille," the blind man explained. "With training, you can learn to write and read it even more quickly than you can with ordinary letters. Do you understand now? My brother has the same kind of tablet—it's called an insideONE. He writes to me about everything he sees and I write to him about everything I hear."

Curious, Lola turned toward the earless man. It was true: He too was holding a phone with a giant screen in one hand, while his other hand lifted up Kasper's black twin above the fence. The blind man's fingers continued to dance across the screen.

"What are you writing now?" Lola asked him.

"That you have a pretty voice."

"And what does he say to that?"

"That you have a pretty face."

Lola jumped back, like a frightened cat. From a safe distance, she eyed the blind man warily.

"You can't even know what that means—pretty. You can't see!"

"No, but I remember."

The little girl bit her lips. She hadn't thought of that.

"So you used to see?"

"Yes."

"And you . . . had an accident?"

"Yes. But I prefer not to talk about it . . . Come closer—Kristof has something to show you."

Lola remained where she was.

"Your brother's name is Kristof? What's yours?"

"Amos. Come closer. You're not scared of us, are you?"

Lola immediately became defensive. "No! Mommy told me I mustn't be afraid."

"And Mommy didn't say you couldn't play with the doll, did she?"

Kristof made Kasper's twin dance above the gate. The puppet spun around and around. Lola wasn't a baby anymore; she knew that it was Kristof's invisible hand making the puppet move, but he was so gifted that she could almost have sworn that the toy was alive, that he was actually swinging his sword. Oh, how she would have loved it if . . .

"Take it," Amos said. "It's for you."

Lola reached out her hand, but Kristof was holding the puppet too far away, too high up, and she had to step forward, until she was almost touching the gate.

"What's he called?" Lola asked. "Mine is Kasper, but he's broken. Daddy promised to fix him."

"You know, Lola, if your daddy can't fix him, I have lots of other puppets I can show you. Girls and boys. I have enough for all the children in the village. They're in my car. Do you want to come and choose one?"

"I'm not allowed!" Lola said confidently.

"You're allowed to come and look at least."

As if by magic, the gate opened. Lola took a step forward—just one step. She could see a silver-colored car a little farther away, parked beside the riverbank.

Mommy had always told her not to talk to strangers, but she had also told her to be nice to people who were different: disabled people, elderly people . . .

Suddenly Lola stopped thinking, stopped moving. On the other side of the fence, Amos continued to smile while staring into space and leaning on a cane.

A white cane. But not just white.

White and red.

*Stained with blood.*

Lola wanted to cry out, to run, to escape, but a big, hairy hand covered her mouth and lifted her up. She could smell sweat. She was powerless to fight back: She couldn't use her teeth to bite, or her nails to scratch, or her legs to run. All she could use were her eyes, to weep. When she heard Amos's voice, sounding as harsh now as it had sounded soft before, the tears started to pour down her cheeks.

"Let's get out of here. We'll go to the gorges. There'll be nobody there to stop us from doing what we have to do."

But Kristof couldn't hear him! So was the blind man talking to her?

Lola screamed, but the sound was stifled by the man's hand.

# 23

## Nanesse and Katel

***Police station, Charleville-Mézières***

*Come on, I have something to show you,* Katel had said.

The captain went over to a computer. There was a printed page set next to the keyboard.

*Something I think you'll find reassuring,* she had promised.

But Nanesse did not feel reassured. She was trembling.

"Officer Vigneules just sent me this," the captain explained. "His uncle opened the mayor's office early this morning."

Nanesse looked down and read.

*Mayor's office, Charleville-Mézières*

*Birth certificate*

*Surname: Duval*

*First and middle names: Renaud Richard Alain*

*Born: January 29, 1977, in Charleville-Mézières*

The birth certificate was signed and stamped. You could even make out the name of the official who had certified it—a certain Marie-Cécile Friedrich.

"I'm still waiting to hear from Mende and Paris. They promised they'd get back to me before noon. That way, we'll know for sure."

Automatically, Nanesse looked up at the red Ducati clock that hung on the wall of the police station.

11:38 a.m.

"Know what for sure?"

"Well, that Hans Bernard and Pierre Rousseau never existed. That they were just identities that your husband used. Agnès, do you know how a birth register works?"

"Um . . ."

11:39 a.m.

"I looked into it. The process is extremely rigorous. A birth certificate is a legal document. The bureaucrats call it an *authenticated* certificate. The objective is to have official proof that the child has been born. So the official in charge has to make sure that, first of all, the child wasn't stolen or illegally adopted, and second, that the child was alive at birth. Generally, that means requesting a medical certificate, but legally the official has the right to go to the labor ward and see the child for himself."

"Surely that never happens!"

11:41 a.m.

"It's less common nowadays," Katel admitted. "But before he can stamp the birth certificate, he must receive a declaration of birth, in other words an official confirmation from the midwife or the doctor who was present at the birth, plus verify the identity of the person who declared the child's birth at the mayor's office—usually the mother or the father. Go ahead, Agnès, read the rest of your husband's birth certificate. It's a gold mine of information!"

*Mother's surname: Duval*

*Mother's first and middle names: Milana*

*Born: September 29, 1956, in Charleville-Mézières (Ardennes)*

*Father's name: unknown*

*Identity of declarant: the child's mother, who today acknowledges the child as her own and declares that she is aware that the parental relationship thus established is independent from that of the father*

Nanesse skimmed over the document, then looked up wearily.

"Great. So my mother-in-law's name is Milana Duval. I already knew that."

"But that is precisely why I want to make sure that there is no birth certificate for Hans Bernard or Pierre Rousseau. Because this document contains information about the parents, and Milana cannot possibly have given birth on January 29, 1977, in three different places."

11:47 a.m.

The captain pushed two chairs on wheels over to the computer screen.

"In both Mende and Paris," she went on, "they should have finished going through the dusty archives of the mayor's offices by now. They should call any minute. In the meantime, Agnès, what do you say we visit the Czech Republic? The city of Pilsen, for example? Jérémy and I targeted five local newspapers there. We subscribed to their databases, which gave us access to seventy years of information, before and since the end of the Soviet Union. We began by copying and pasting the articles with the most intriguing photographs into Google Translate . . . I'm pretty fluent in Czech now! So come on. *Hýbeme zadkem!* That means: Let's move our asses!"

# 24

## VICKY

***The banks of the Tarn, Florac***

"Lola?"

She wasn't in the yard.

Vicky rushed over to the gate and opened it. She walked along the riverbank.

"Lola?"

She wasn't on the riverbank either.

Vicky came out into the hamlet and looked at the road that ran alongside the riverbank, south toward the center of Florac, and north toward the Gorges du Tarn.

"Lola? Lola?"

Lola would never have wandered off alone in a strange village.

Vicky turned around. Nicole and Mathieu Mariotta stood speechless beside the bird feeders.

"Lola?"

Lola would never have left without Kasper. Lola would never have gone near that river without asking permission.

Vicky was yelling now. One by one, worried neighbors came out of their houses.

"Lola? Lola! *Lola!*"

# 25

## Éléa

***Route Nationale 106, Tarn Valley, Lozère***

FLORAC—7 MILES.

Samuel Galet had calmed down. The trip was almost over, and the breathtaking beauty of the landscape had helped to relieve his irritation. The Gorges du Tarn opened up before him as the road rose more and more steeply. He savored the panoramic view of the cliffs, the trees clinging to every crevice, and—at the bottom of the plunging valley, after he'd rounded a curve a bit quickly—the sparkling scales of the river.

Samuel always preferred visiting dairy cooperatives in places like the Cévennes, Auvergne, and the Pyrenees rather than regions like Beauce or the Vendée, whose landscapes were as flat as a pancake.

"Stop here!" Éléa suddenly shouted.

The driver, startled, almost crashed at a bend. He hurriedly parked by the roadside, raising a cloud of dust, the side of his car nearly touching a metal barrier that separated them from a sheer precipice.

Samuel was a kind man, without a bitter bone in his body. In fact, that got him into trouble at work, because he always ended up being talked out of punishing the farmers who were out of compliance with safety standards.

"The church in Florac is seven miles away. I'm not going to drop you off at a bend in this road. It's narrow, and the canyon is very steep. It's too dangerous to get out here."

But his passenger wasn't listening. She had already opened the door of the Captur. As she slipped through the narrow gap between the car door and the metal barrier, Samuel caught a glimpse of the violet gleam from her smart ring, and of the photograph on the screen of her phone.

Samuel's fingers tensed around the steering wheel.

The photograph showed the landscape right in front of them.

It was identical, in every detail. The same bend in the river, the same sandbanks slowing the current, the same chaos of rocks on either bank. The same stone bridge spanning the Tarn a little farther downstream.

Éléa stepped over the safety barrier. She paused for a moment at the edge of the chasm, to compare the view with her photograph, and then she vanished.

Samuel hesitated.

Should he set off again? Or go after the girl? But if he did that, then what?

She was younger and faster than him, and more determined too. He checked that nobody was coming, then maneuvered his car onto the road. The silence inside the Captur was the same as it had been before he had dropped the girl off, but he couldn't help feeling disturbed by it. Before entering the next curve, he glanced in his rearview mirror again, hoping to see Éléa. He felt like that girl was going to haunt his memory for quite some time, because she was so pretty . . . and completely crazy.

*You're completely crazy!*

"Shut up, Brain. Not now."

Éléa looked down at the steep slope that led into the valley, searching for a way to descend to the river.

*Have you seen how steep it is?* Brain persisted. *It's a fifty-five degree slope, and well over three hundred feet to the bottom. And what about those brambles? And those rocks? You really think you're equipped for this kind of descent, in your miniskirt and your ballet shoes?*

"And did you see the photograph that Pierre just sent me? It's the next part of the treasure hunt! That bridge, this bend in the river, this valley. He wants me to stop here."

Éléa began to climb down the hillside. Her ballet shoes slipped from under her, and at the last second she managed to grab hold of a rowan branch, which tore her palm.

*What if it's not your Petrushka who's sending you those messages?* Brain demanded. *He usually prefers words to photographs. Someone could have stolen his phone to send you on a wild goose chase. Or worse . . .*

Éléa let go of the branch, skidded downhill about ten feet, then clung to another tree.

"Mute yourself, Brain. I need to focus here."

Éléa spotted a less steep passage to her right: a rocky platform beyond which the stones formed a sort of staircase. It would be possible to climb down them, like a ladder. She stuffed her ballet shoes in her bag and kept moving, trying to slow the pounding of her heart.

"Don't say a word, Brain! I mean it—not a word!"

With the greatest difficulty, she crawled down the hillside. Her tights were ripped, her knees grazed, her feet bruised, her hands bloodied. At last the slope grew a little shallower. Now she was less than two hundred feet from the stone bridge at the center of the photograph that Pierre had sent her.

*Do you really think your Petrushka is waiting for you under this bridge?*

"Oh yes, Brain!"

Suddenly, amid the deserted landscape of rocks and rushing water, she saw a shadow move. Her heart leapt.

"Petrushka?"

A moment later, her heart stopped beating altogether.

It wasn't him.

There were three of them. Two hulking men and a little girl. The girl couldn't have been more than five years old.

Éléa's eyes widened as she took in the scene before her.

The little girl was struggling, hitting and kicking at the man who held her above the waters of the Tarn.

"Shit, what are they doing?"

*You can see what's going on as well as I can: It's just a father trying to calm down his hysterical daughter.*

"Don't be such a pathetic coward, Brain. Look at them—they're trying to drown her."

The two men appeared as solid as the blocks of granite that Éléa had just climbed down. Even if she tried to intervene, she would be easily overpowered . . .

*The rational thing would be to stay calm and to—*

"Do something useful, Brain—find me a weapon of some kind!"

Without waiting for Brain to react, Éléa bent down to pick up the first rock she could find—a piece of flint with a vaguely sharpened edge—then started running downhill, her bare feet kicking up a cloud of dust. She yelled at the top of her voice, trying to scare the two men, hoping this would be enough to make them run away.

Instead, they simply turned around. Toward her.

Once again, Éléa's heart stopped beating.

Their faces! What had happened to them? They looked like extras in a war movie or a horror film, the kind that require hours in the makeup room . . .

But this was not a movie, and they were not wearing makeup.

*Hide!* Brain shouted.

Near the Tarn, the earless monster had taken out a gun and was aiming it at her.

*Too late,* Éléa thought, in a flash.

Too late to listen to her brain, to analyze the situation, to react rationally. She was being pulled onward by gravity, by her momentum, and by the hope she saw in the little girl's eyes. Éléa was like one of those sacrificial soldiers sent charging in the vanguard to impale themselves on the bayonets of the enemy.

What could she do, besides yell even louder?

"Leave her alone! Get away from her!"

The two men did not appear inclined to move. Brain was right: It had been madness to launch herself at them like this, alone, without a second's thought. Brain was always right. And she was wrong—for what she suddenly understood would be the last time.

The pistol's barrel gleamed.

She screamed with all her might before the bullet could pierce her heart.

"Let her go!"

The sound of her voice echoed through the narrow canyon.

*"Let her go!"*

The words echoed back strangely.

*"Lo—la—lo!"*

Éléa realized that the monster hadn't fired.

"La . . . Lo . . . La! Lola! Lola!"

It wasn't an echo of her voice. Someone else was yelling.

Someone down in the valley was yelling with fear, yelling for the little girl . . . who was surely the Lola in question, because she looked up and appeared shocked as soon as she heard that name.

Lola?

And then she struggled with a new determination.

Everything went very fast after that.

Éléa spotted a dirt path ahead that led to the stone bridge. A gray SUV was parked close by. The two burned men let go of the kid, and the earless man grabbed his partner's arm and they ran toward the car. A few seconds later, the vehicle sped off.

The little girl stood trembling by the riverside.

Éléa walked toward her. The danger was over. She even reached out with her arms to reassure her, but by then Lola had already turned around. She was staring at the path that ran alongside the Tarn, in the direction from which the other voice had come a few seconds before.

"Lola?"

The girl suddenly started running, almost flying as she leapt from one stone to another on the rock-and-sand riverbank, unafraid of the rushing water beside her.

"Mommy!"

# 26

## Katel and Nanesse

***Police station, Charleville-Mézières***

Katel stared at the hands of the clock, grumbling at each passing second.

"They promised me they would call before noon! I was only asking them to get into a couple of mayor's offices, not the Elysée Palace!"

Nanesse said nothing. She was concentrating on the computer screen, divided into two panels: on the left, the text from the Czech newspapers, and on the right, the AI translation. She was reading paragraph after paragraph of completely useless information, including the meanings of the titles of those local newspapers: *The Friend of the Czech People, The Truth of Bohemia, The Pilsen News, The Socialist Word, The Pilsen Gazette . . .*

"What the hell are they doing? I'm going to—"

Katel's phone rang just before she could threaten violence. A name appeared—*Barjac*. Her contact in Mende, whose number she had put into her address book. She answered.

"Barjac, what's the news?"

A loud beeping sound was the only answer. Had that idiot Barjac set off the fire alarm in the mayor's office? Katel instinctively glanced down at her phone screen and saw the cause of the sound.

She had another call coming in!

She looked down at the number and saw it was a call from Paris. That had to be Lagrange, from the eighteenth arrondissement!

This time, Katel cursed her own stupidity. Why had she given them both the same deadline?

"Hang on, Barjac, I've got a call on the other line."

She clicked over.

"Lagrange? Can you hold for a second?"

She switched back to the first call.

"Barjac? Go ahead. Please tell me you haven't found any record of Hans Bernard in the cellar of the Mende mayor's office!"

"Actually, I have, Captain."

"What?"

"I have the birth certificate in front of me now. Hans Bernard was born in Mende on January 29, 1977. It's all in order—the day, the place, the time, the official's stamp and signature, the declarant's signature. The child was born here, alive and kicking, forty-six years ago."

"Damn it . . ."

She told Barjac not to hang up and switched calls again.

"Lagrange? Can you hear me? Please tell me you haven't—"

"I found him, Captain! Pierre Rousseau. Born on January 29, 1977, at the Bichat Hospital, in the eighteenth arrondissement. Certified, verified, authenticated—it's all official. Shall I scan it all and send it by email?"

Katel was speechless. She moved the phone away from her ear. She needed time to think about this, to write it all down. Nanesse, still focused on the translations of the Czech articles, turned distractedly toward her.

"Is there a problem, Captain?"

Katel continued to mull over the unsolvable equation in her head.

Three people, all with the same face, born on the same day, in three different places.

"No, Agnès, there's no problem. I was just wrong about something."

She said nothing for a moment before she added the rest.

"Your husband really did manage to duplicate his life."

# 27

## Vicky and Éléa

***Pont du Tarn campsite, Florac***

Vicky had put Lola to bed. Though the little girl rarely took a nap anymore, she had allowed her mother to hold her in her arms for more than an hour as she shook, cried, and made excuses—*It wasn't my fault, Mommy, it was because of Kasper's brother, and they seemed so nice, Mommy.* Slowly Lola's fear had visibly receded and her heart had, it seemed, gradually stopped racing before she had finally fallen asleep in her little bedroom at the chalet.

Vicky tiptoed out of the room. Éléa was waiting for her, sitting in one of the two plastic chairs on the terrace.

"I'm going to grab a beer," Vicky told her. "Do you want one?"

"No, thanks. I never drink alcohol."

The sun was at its zenith, beating down on the cloth awning that shaded the front of the wooden bungalow. The Tarn's lapping waters, a few dozen feet away, created the illusion of coolness. It had been a day of contradictory feelings, paradoxical emotions.

Vicky opened the fridge and picked up a bottle, a bottle opener, and a glass while her mind flashed with images from the past hour: Lola's disappearance, her panic, the neighbors running to help, the search—frantic at first, then more organized. *She can't have gone far. She might have gotten lost. Don't worry, ma'am, she hasn't been kidnapped—everybody knows everybody around here.* Their quick march along the Tarn, since Lola had been nowhere to be seen in the village. *She must have followed the river. Maybe she was running after birds, or fish, or doodlebugs . . .* And the locals' growing wariness toward her. *Are you sure she wasn't upset about something?*

Vicky hadn't replied to them. She had saved her voice for calling out Lola's name. And then the miracle had occurred when they reached the Fayet Bridge: Lola was there!

Alive and well. She had thrown herself into her mother's arms. The locals had gone home, relieved and a little annoyed. She could tell what they were thinking. *Can't she keep control of her kid? What if she'd drowned?*

Only the three of them had been left: Vicky, Lola, and this stranger who had showed Vicky and the others the way to Lola, arriving there just before they had.

Where had she come from? Who was she? A guardian angel?

Not that she looked very angelic, with her kohl-rimmed eyes, her tattooed shoulders, her ripped tights, her filthy bare feet, and that weird high-tech ring she was wearing on her finger.

Vicky pulled up a chair and sat in front of Éléa. The shadow of the chalet divided the terrace in two. Vicky chose to sit in the sun, while Éléa remained in the shade. The solar blonde and the lunar brunette.

Vicky exhaled and gave a big smile.

"Thank you! Without you, I don't know what would have happened. Lola confirmed everything you told me. She described those two men with the burned faces. They didn't hurt her, but they did threaten her. Apparently they wanted her to tell them about her daddy—well, her adoptive father, Hans. And about Hans's mother too. Lola told them she never knew her, but they didn't seem to believe her. I'll talk to the police as soon as Lola wakes up. I think she needs some rest first. It's . . . it's like a miracle, that you were there and that you had the guts to scare off those men."

Éléa drank half her glass of water.

"Yeah . . . Sometimes I think too much, and occasionally I don't think enough."

Vicky smiled understandingly. For a while they sat in silence, until Vicky said: "Don't worry, I'm not going to start interrogating you, asking you why you were there and all that. But if you don't have anywhere to eat, or sleep, or if you need anything at all, I'd like to help."

"Thanks, but I'll be fine."

"I gather you're not the talkative type?"

"Well, I'm more used to talking to myself."

"I understand that. I run a guesthouse in Ruynes-en-Margeride. I think I'm a pretty good judge of when I need to shut up and when I need to talk for two."

*Then shut up!* thought Éléa.

She needed to talk things over with Brain, to figure out why Pierre had sent her that photograph at the precise moment and in the precise spot where that kid had been kidnapped. Was Petrushka watching over her?

"What do you think, Brain?"

*I can't think at the moment, sorry. You know how lost I am when things get irrational.*

"What do you know about those two men with the burned faces?"

*All I can tell you is that the SUV they were driving is a Skoda Karoq. A fairly old model. Apart from that . . .*

Éléa sighed, and pretended to sip her glass of water so that Vicky wouldn't see her lips moving. This woman was her polar opposite, Éléa sensed. Someone who didn't paralyze herself with endless questions but simply moved forward, built things; someone who must love children as much as Éléa feared them; someone who enjoyed change as much as Éléa loathed it; who relished the conviviality of the countryside as much as Éléa preferred the shared solitude of big cities; who lived in reality to the same extent that Éléa lived in her dreams; who was as blond as she was dark. They were as different, as the phrase went, as night and day . . .

And yet she also sensed that they were united by something bigger than all their differences. That their meeting was not the result of pure chance.

*Maybe I'm lost,* said Brain, *but you're really losing it!*

Éléa ignored her cerebrum and continued to reason without it. What if Pierre had wanted her to save that little girl at that precise moment? What if he had wanted her to meet this Vicky? What if this was the next part of the treasure hunt? Petrushka's new challenge: for her to trust this woman?

Éléa took a long drink of water before speaking.

"So you don't want to interrogate me, but you do want to know what I'm doing here?"

"Well, I could probably guess," replied Vicky.

"Oh, really? So you think you're a psychologist?"

"You tell me . . . My bet is that you're in love, but things aren't going well. Or something like that."

Éléa shrugged and scowled. In the end, she replied sourly: "Mmm. Something like that."

The sunlight illuminated Vicky's blond hair, making her look even more radiant.

"Things will work out, don't worry. You're so pretty. And original. Men love that."

"No . . . Men hate that. With a few rare exceptions. So when you find one who accepts you the way you are . . ."

"I understand."

"I don't think you do!"

*You don't have to be so aggressive,* Brain told her.

"I'm going to tell you a secret, Éléa," said Vicky. "I came here in search of a man too."

"That Hans guy, you mean? Lola's adoptive father? The one those two weirdos were looking for?"

*That's better,* said Brain. *You're showing that you're interested.*

"Exactly." Vicky lifted her blond beer to her lips. The bottle gleamed in the sun. "Are you sure you don't want something to drink?"

"Just more water."

Vicky started to stand, but Éléa raised her palm.

"Don't worry, I'll get it."

Vicky heard the chalet's floorboards creaking under Éléa's bare feet; she heard the cupboard door open and close; she heard water running from the faucet, running endlessly, for far too long . . . The glass must have been full a long time ago. Then she heard nothing for several long seconds.

Until the glass exploded.

Vicky rushed inside, crushing fragments of broken glass under the soles of her shoes and almost slipping in the puddle of water.

Éléa was standing in the kitchen, petrified, in front of a photograph of Hans that Vicky had stuck to the fridge door by a magnet. To aid her in her search for him, she had chosen one of the most recent pictures she had of her lover, taken in front of a wide, steep-sided valley where a bend in the river formed an almost perfect loop.

Hearing the crunch of glass behind her, Éléa spun around, as fast as a tiger. She was still gripping a shard of bloody glass between her thumb and her index finger. She pointed it at Vicky's throat.

"Who are you? How the hell did you get this photograph?"

Vicky stayed calm. There was no need to panic. This girl was just disoriented; whatever heartache she had suffered was making her delirious. Vicky had seen the same thing in others; she knew how to handle it.

"Take it easy, Éléa. Put down the piece of glass. That man is Hans. Hans Bernard. I live with him. He's Lola's adoptive father."

"Liar!"

The shard of glass moved closer to Vicky's jugular.

"His name is Pierre. Pierre Rousseau. And he's the man I'm here searching for. My Petrushka, the love of my life!"

# 28

## Katel and Nanesse

***Police station, Charleville-Mézières***

Captain Marelle's tone of voice had changed. Both Inspector Lagrange and Lieutenant Barjac had noticed it immediately. Her timbre had abruptly altered from a general sounding the charge to a private begging for leave. Some aspect of the news they had delivered to her had completely stunned her.

Neither one had tried to find out why. The policewoman from the Ardennes had been harassing them ever since yesterday, and they were relieved to be done with her. Both men simply scanned the birth certificates and emailed them to the captain.

As soon as she received them, less than three minutes later, Katel printed out the birth certificates. She was trying to stay calm, trying not to look at Nanesse. She put the printouts on the largest table in the police station, next to Renaud Duval's birth certificate.

*Renaud Duval*

*Born: January 29, 1977, in Charleville-Mézières*

*Mother's surname: Duval*

*Mother's first and middle names: Milana*

*Born: September 29, 1956, in Charleville-Mézières (Ardennes)*

*Father's name: unknown*

*Hans Bernard*

*Born: January 29, 1977, in Mende*

*Mother's surname: Bernard*

*Mother's first and middle names: Marion*

*Born: October 13, 1956, in Mende (Lozère)*

*Father's name: unknown*

*Pierre Rousseau*

*Born: January 29, 1977, in Paris (18th arrondissement)*

*Mother's surname: Rousseau*

*Mother's first and middle names: Judith*

*Born: May 20, 1956, in Paris (5th arrondissement)*

*Father's name: unknown*

Katel arranged the three driver's licenses, each above its corresponding birth certificate, then turned back to Nanesse.

"So, Agnès? What do you make of all this?"

Nanesse stood up. She looked at the documents for a moment, then turned her teary eyes to the captain.

"It makes me think that Renaud was just an ordinary husband. No secrets or scandals. A loving but not very imaginative husband. A solid but rather dull father. Which is exactly what I'd thought, what I'd felt, all these years, until you told me he'd died."

"Dull?" repeated Katel. "Not very imaginative? Hmm, I suppose it's possible. Maybe he didn't know about the existence of these two clones . . . Even though he was driving around with their licenses in his glove box."

Nanesse forced herself to look at the three photographs again. To examine in turn the three identical smiles, the three identical pairs of gray eyes.

"What about you, Captain? What do you think?"

Katel walked across the room and stopped in front of a whiteboard hanging on the wall.

"Do you really want to know?" she asked, picking up a marker. "If you think about it, this is basically just an equation featuring three unknown men. Or, to be more precise, two equations, one featuring three unknown men and the other featuring three unknown women."

She drew three crosses and three circles on the whiteboard, then a line connecting each cross to a different circle.

"First we need to imagine three women giving birth on the same day, all of them single. Each woman declares the birth of their baby in the place where he is born: Paris, Charleville, and Mende. By some unknown miracle, those three children are identical."

"Well, they are if we trust the photographs on their licenses," Nanesse pointed out.

"Our experts are prepared to swear that these documents are genuine, that the photographs haven't been torn out and replaced."

"Your experts? Hmm . . ."

"Okay, but the theory is the same, whether the IDs are fake or not. Three different women, three different babies."

Nanesse was still staring at the whiteboard.

"I see what you mean. And what are your other ideas?"

"Mathematically, there are only three other possibilities."

Beneath the first sketch, Katel drew one cross with three circles, then traced lines connecting them.

"One woman, using three different identities, declares the birth of three different children. Three children who look strangely alike. Maybe her children, if we accept the possibility that they could be triplets."

Nanesse nodded. "So, Judith Rousseau, Marion Bernard, and Milana Duval would all be the same woman? That seems logical. According to the birth certificates, they were all born the same year. And this woman had three children? That would mean that the woman with three children was Milana, my mother-in-law. And your theory is that she faked the other two identities to conceal the existence of Renaud's brothers? Well, I knew Milana, and I can assure you that—"

"You can't assure me of anything," Katel interrupted her. "She could easily have lied to you. But in any case, this theory doesn't solve the problem of the birth dates."

Katel quickly scrawled another diagram. This one had one cross, one circle, and one line connecting them.

"Another possibility. One woman uses three different identities to declare the birth of her only child under three different identities. Why? How? What would be the point of these three identities? It's a total mystery. But this theory is at least more plausible than the final one."

She drew three crosses and one circle.

"Three women, on the same day and in three different places, somehow give birth to the same child."

"Whoa!" said a voice behind them. "That's completely crazy, but I love the idea!"

Startled, Katel turned around. Officer Mathias Vigneules, a young policeman with the body of an athlete, had just entered the police station, accompanied by a woman old enough to be his grandmother.

"You're going to be proud of me," Vigneules added. "I've found a witness!"

Katel Marelle stared at the new arrival. She was at least sixty. If she'd been a puppet, she would have been made of wood, not cloth. A bourgeois marionette with shiny rings in her ears, gold bands and a single diamond ring on her finger, perhaps to distract people from the ugly red wart under her right nostril. She shook hands firmly with Katel.

"Marie-Cécile Friedrich. I was the one who opened the mayor's office for your policeman. I have been in charge of the registry office in Charleville-Mézières for the past thirty years."

Katel did the calculations in her head. Thirty years? Not enough! Marie-Cécile Friedrich would not have been in situ back in 1977. And even if she had been, how could she possibly remember a declaration of birth dating back more than four decades?

"But I started at the very bottom of the ladder," Marie-Cécile said, staring haughtily at Katel and Nanesse. "I was a Category C employee, to be exact. I passed my registry official exam in January 1977. My internship took place in Charleville, and I signed my first contract there. And I'm still there now." She paused. Then, sounding regretful, she added: "For three more months."

Katel exchanged an excited look with Nanesse. Was it possible that this woman actually remembered . . . ?

"Your colleague explained the situation to me," Marie-Cécile went on. "And, while I may with some accuracy claim that I have a good memory, I certainly don't remember all the twenty-odd-thousand birth certificates I've stamped. But, as it happens, you're in luck . . ."

"You remember Milana?" Nanesse blurted out excitedly.

At last Marie-Cécile allowed herself to smile, almost as triumphantly as Officer Vigneules, who stood beside her, basking in her glory.

"Milana Duval? Yes, I remember her quite clearly. I'd only been in the job a few weeks at the time, I think. You always remember your first customers or your first students, don't you? And then there was the fact that I found her . . . How can I put this, so many years later? I found her a little disturbing."

"Disturbing?" Katel echoed.

"She came in person, which is rare. Generally, it's the fathers who declare the newborn, because the mother is still in the hospital. She came with her baby, which is even rarer still, as I'm sure you can imagine. And, lastly, there was this look in her eyes—an expression of distress, of urgency—that disappeared the moment I stamped the paper.

"Later, I learned to recognize and understand the origin of that distress. I saw it almost every time in the faces of immigrants, whether their papers were in order or not. They were all haunted by the fear that the French state wouldn't recognize their child. As if they couldn't quite believe that all it took to obtain French nationality was to be born in this country; that this would allow them to walk out of the mayor's office with official documents proving their child's Frenchness."

Katel, surprised, turned to Nanesse.

"Your mother-in-law, Milana . . . she wasn't French?"

"She was. Of course she was. At least, I never had any reason to think otherwise." She frowned. "Although . . ."

"Although what?" Katel pressed.

"Well, she spoke perfect French, but sometimes—very occasionally—she would have a slight accent. It was almost imperceptible, but—"

"How would you describe that accent?"

"I don't know. Eastern European, maybe. Slavic . . . Or Germanic, perhaps."

"Czech?" suggested Katel.

Nanesse didn't have time to reply, because Marie-Cécile was waving her diamond ring around, visibly annoyed that they had interrupted her.

"Captain, I haven't finished! I haven't told you the most important part of the story yet. I saw Milana Duval again, once. I think that's why I remember her. Particularly now."

"You mean, because I asked you to look back at this birth register?"

"No, that's not why. And please stop constantly interrupting me, Captain. It's very annoying."

Katel felt like she might explode, but she kept her expression under control.

"It was the World Festival of Puppet Theaters that reminded me," Marie-Cécile said. "The traffic in Charleville this morning! An entire town brought to a standstill by a Pierrot and three Guignols—it's ridiculous, frankly. But anyway, as I was saying, I saw Milana Duval again in 2017, at the festival . . ."

*A few months before she died,* calculated Katel, although she knew better by now than to say anything about it.

"My grandchildren had dragged me to Place Ducale. And I recognized her immediately because she was up on the stage! Alone. And, using only her ten fingers, she was animating three puppets at once. I must admit I'm not really a fan of that kind of thing, but Milana's show was quite breathtaking. The mayor's office spent a small fortune bringing puppeteers with far less talent from all over the world."

Katel silently cursed. This woman still hadn't given her any new information. Nanesse had already told her that Milana had given one last performance—for her own grandchildren—even as she was suffering from the cancer that killed her.

"Her show was about Petrushka," Marie-Cécile continued. "Admittedly, it wasn't quite as spectacular as Stravinsky's ballet performed in an opera house, but then Charleville isn't exactly Milan or Sydney, is it?"

This time, Katel could not swallow her irritation.

"I'm going to be honest, Madame Friedrich. Our time is precious, and we already know about all this. So I'm going to bring this conversation to an end, unless you have anything substantial and new to communicate . . ."

Marie-Cécile glared at Katel.

"While he drove me here, your colleague told me about your investigation. Two killers at large. One of the men with a burned face . . ."

Katel, in turn, glared at Mathias Vigneules, whose proud, muscular body appeared to deflate.

"Don't blame him," said Marie-Cécile with triumphant disdain. "As representatives of authority, we're on the same side, aren't we? Anyway, I don't think there are many men around with a face like that burned fellow, and so I'm quite confident when I say that I saw two men with burned faces standing a few feet away from me, back in 2017. They were in the audience for Milana's show about Petrushka, you see. And, believe me, they never took their eyes off her."

# 29

## Vicky and Éléa

***Pont du Tarn campsite, Florac***

Night had fallen over Florac and the Pont du Tarn campsite. Only a few lights still flickered on the terraces of the chalets: a glowing cell phone screen, a reading lamp, a scented candle . . . and the last fireflies of this Cévennes summer, the air so mild that people were filled with the desire to stay outside even as the days grew ever shorter.

Lola had slept for two hours that afternoon before waking with Kasper clutched to her chest. But she had not said anything, had only smiled, as if her kidnapping had been nothing but a bad dream. Vicky hadn't had the heart to make her relive that nightmare by asking her about the men with burned faces. She had decided that she would talk to Lola about it later and they could safely postpone their visit to the police station until tomorrow—Lola had been through enough trauma already today.

She had let her daughter play outside the bungalow—*don't wander off, sweetie*—while she quickly cooked a meal for three: Pasta, eggs, and cream all went into something vaguely resembling a carbonara. Lola, the poor exhausted thing, had fallen asleep again before the sun had even set.

Vicky poured a few drops of eglantine liqueur into her tiny glass. Éléa was sitting with her on the terrace, under the single light bulb. The crowds of tourists and mosquitoes had gone, leaving only this late-summer warmth.

"As a general rule," Éléa said out of nowhere, "I don't really like children. But Lola is okay."

"Should I take that as a compliment?" asked Vicky.

"Oh yes, absolutely!"

Éléa stared at Vicky while she sucked the dried blood from her fingertips. A few hours before, she had dropped the shard of glass pointed at Vicky's jugular the moment Brain yelled inside her head: *Stop, Éléa, stop!*

But Éléa had continued to stare defiantly into the other woman's eyes, firm in her conviction that she was a liar.

This woman, Éléa believed, was trying to trap her. Either that or Vicky was mistaken about what she believed. Not that it really mattered which was true. In any case, Éléa knew that the man in the photograph on the wall of the bungalow—that slender, gray-eyed man—was Pierre. Pierre who danced all over the world, wrote beautiful poems, showered her with words of love, and never let more than three hours pass without sending her a message . . . Or at least all of that had been true until four days ago.

Vicky, too, had refused to back down. Both women had defended their version of reality. But, deep inside, Éléa had also brooded over the meaning of it all, and she suspected Vicky had too.

*What if . . . ?*

"I think I will try some of your eglantine thingy."

Vicky looked up in surprise. Éléa had told her more than once already that she didn't drink. But Vicky poured her a glass without asking questions.

*You shouldn't,* Brain warned her.

*Oh, but I should!* Éléa replied, without moving her lips. *Because I want to get you drunk, Brain, so you won't keep lecturing me.*

Vicky had put the photo on the table of the terrace, halfway between their two chairs. They hadn't mentioned it again while Lola was awake, tacitly agreeing to a truce while each of them prepared their arguments.

Vicky was the first to advance a pawn.

"Maybe your Pierre and my Hans are identical twins?"

Éléa sipped her drink. It felt like molten lava was trickling down her throat before setting fire to the contents of her skull.

*Take that, Brain!*

"Pierre was an only child," replied Éléa. "And I feel sure that your Hans was too."

Vicky nodded. "He said so, yes. But maybe he didn't know? They could have been separated at birth. These things happen . . ."

Éléa took another sip, and felt another eruption. Burning all her thoughts: Wasn't that the best solution?

"No, these things don't happen. Real life is always simpler than that."

Vicky grimaced, then downed the rest of her drink. It appeared to have no effect on her at all. She leaned forward to rummage around inside her bag.

"Well, it's easy enough to check."

She took out a large red diary, which she opened in front of Éléa.

"Shall we put our cards on the table? I keep a record in here of every week Hans has spent with me—generally about one in four. I'm pretty sure you keep a record of every time you see Pierre too. All we need to do is figure out if he was ever in two places at once."

Éléa hesitated. Did she really want to know the truth?

*What are you scared of?* Brain taunted.

Éléa blitzed him with another mouthful of alcohol. Her whole body trembled as it entered her bloodstream. She looked down at her ring.

"My Precious," she whispered shakily, "can you tell me all the days this year when Pierre came to visit me?"

It was all in her electronic diary: every memory, down to the precise minute.

They compared their timelines.

That year, Vicky had seen Hans thirteen times, spending a total of eighty-eight days with him. Éléa had seen Pierre only six times, for a total of eighteen nights and twenty-three days together.

There was no overlap at all.

When Hans spent the week with Vicky, Éléa was never with Pierre, and when Pierre went to Paris to see Éléa, Hans was never with Vicky.

"So, technically," Vicky admitted, sounding disillusioned, "Hans and Pierre could be the same man. Well, it would have been pretty easy for him to lead a double life . . . Actually, can you even call that a double life? I mean, he only goes to see you about once every three months."

Éléa hated the mischievous smile that crept across Vicky's face.

"And when he went away for three weeks," she said, "how often did you hear from him? One brief text every night, maybe? *Give Lola a kiss from me. I miss you. I love you.* But Pierre and I were in continual contact. I don't know if you can even imagine how close we were. Nothing ever came between us. Our love was pure, eternally new. We weren't worn down by the boredom of routine or the worries of daily life."

"Yes, I see . . . Well, it's very practical, keeping all your feelings virtual like that."

Éléa smiled, sure of her superiority. "Let me fill in the details for you, Vicky," she said. "I have a feeling you're not going to like it, but what can I do? Even when he was with you, Pierre still spent his time writing to me. I was the one inside his head, not you."

Vicky poured herself another glass of eglantine.

Éléa didn't have time to say more, nor to take another sip of her drink, because Vicky was already on the attack again. "I think Hans went to you because he was looking for something a little exotic. A bit out of the ordinary, you know? A quick dose of adrenaline, like eating a spicy meal from time to time, or getting a little too drunk, or ending up in bed with someone else just to prove to yourself that you're still free. But we were his family. Me and Lola."

Éléa laughed. The effects of the alcohol, presumably. She felt a sort of desperate euphoria. The kind of lightness you might feel as you were approaching death and your soul was floating out of your body.

"Oh yeah, Vicky! That's it! A family! It was Lola who trapped Pierre, not you. He kept going back to you out of a sense of duty, because he didn't want to disappoint that little girl. With me, he came back . . . out of passion!"

Vicky, in turn, burst out laughing. Her eyes shone. Was she drunk too? Éléa wondered. Maybe Vicky didn't handle alcohol as well as she'd imagined? Maybe she was feeling the same kind of desperate euphoria as Éléa?

"Out of passion? Dear God, Éléa, don't you know *anything* about men?" She laughed again, a little too loud. "Your . . . what did you call him? . . . your *Petrushka* . . . What was it he told you? Oh yeah, that he was a famous dancer! Ha ha, why not an astronaut? Or a big-game hunter in Bengal? Didn't you even think of checking him out online? I'm pretty sure there's not a trace on the internet of your famous dancer, Pierre Rousseau!"

*Definitely not as dumb as she looks,* Brain said helpfully.

*Keep out of this,* Éléa grumbled at her cerebrum.

She drank another mouthful of eglantine, hoping to drown Brain's thoughts, but all this did was accelerate her downward spiral.

"Go on, Éléa," Vicky said cruelly. "You live in a virtual world anyway. Show me! Find a single example of a show that Pierre has performed. Anything at all . . ."

Of course, Éléa had already done this search, years ago, and found nothing.

"He lied!" Vicky shouted triumphantly.

"No!" Éléa replied fiercely. "He danced under a pseudonym. His artist name. I never asked him for it, though, out of respect . . ."

Éléa felt like she was being swept away by a whirlwind of jealousy.

"I'll be blunt with you too, Vicky," she said. "The man we shared . . . How exactly did he have fun when he was with you? By cutting up plasterboard? Sanding your beams? Replacing the tiles on your roof? And in the evenings, after such a full day of work, I bet he just collapsed on the couch in front of the TV, right? God, he must have been so bored! A man as refined and sensitive as him, I don't know how he could stand it . . ."

For a second, Éléa felt like she was going to fall off her chair. But she regained her balance and continued: "Frankly, Vicky, everything you've told me sounds like a joke. I want to believe it all, but the idea that my Petrushka was a . . . a truck driver!"

"What's wrong with being a truck driver?"

"Oh, nothing . . . But go ahead, you're so superorganized. Why don't you show me some of his pay stubs, some receipts for work he had done on his truck, a few bills for driving on toll roads . . . No? What about the name of his boss? His colleagues?"

"He was self-employed."

"Really? How convenient."

# 30

## Katel and Nanesse

***Police station, Charleville-Mézières***

After Officer Vigneules had taken Marie-Cécile's statement, the captain had sent him to Churchill Park, where a battle between South American puppets was taking place. She didn't really know what a puppet battle entailed, but she thought that maybe it would help him unwind.

What she really wanted, though, was to be alone with Agnès Duval, without anyone to disturb them. Not that she achieved this by sending the officer away, since cops kept coming and going all the time, as their shifts ended or began. They kept banging the door too hard, complaining too loudly about the endless rain . . . and, worst of all, complaining about their boss.

"Jeez, Mehdi," sighed Sergeant Will Walcourt, as he followed the other man to the door. "Finally we can go home! Seventy-two hours without a break—you can tell Marelle doesn't have kids!"

"Have a good weekend, Will."

"Thanks! You too . . . Oh, is that you, Captain? Sorry, I, um . . . I didn't notice you there."

Will Walcourt straightened his too-tight uniform, then rushed outside without taking the time to open his umbrella.

"Shut the fucking door!"

"Sorry, boss, I'll do it now. See you tomorrow . . . And, um, have a good evening."

Alone at last!

Katel felt like barricading the door and unplugging the phone. All she asked for was an hour or two without being bothered. A police investigation was not a car chase, like in those ridiculous American movies; nor was it a puzzle to be slowly, elegantly solved, like in those boring French movies. No, an investigation often boiled down to sitting in a chair and doing nothing but thinking. It had more in common with a math exam than any cop movie she'd ever seen. *You have three hours to solve the problem. Please remain seated and silent. Your time starts now . . .*

Night had fallen over Charleville. Most of the town's inhabitants had gone home or were out enjoying the last of the evening's attractions. Police officers were patrolling the streets. Barring a catastrophe, Katel figured, they should be left in peace for the rest of the evening. They had ordered some burgers from the fast food restaurant next door, but Nanesse had barely touched hers.

"Sorry, Agnès, no cul nu while we're working!"

"So you're still not going to call me Nanesse? Or stop saying *vous* to me?"

Katel didn't answer, she just threw the greasy remnants of her burger into the closest trash can.

"Ready to get back to work?"

They sat in front of the screen, still divided into two panels: Czech newspapers to the left, translations to the right.

"Agnès, you need to tell me more about your mother-in-law. Everything you remember. You heard what Marie-Cécile Friedrich said about those men with burned faces. Milana is the key."

Nanesse stared at the lines of incomprehensible Czech words on the left-hand side of the screen.

"Everything I remember? That could take a while! I mean, I knew Milana my whole life. Well, at least from when I met Renaud until her death six years ago."

"Uterine cancer, right?"

"Yes. But don't go looking for some kind of trick there. I accompanied my mother-in-law to the oncologist's office. I could give you her whole medical history, if you want. It was a long battle, as they say; at least a year and a half . . . That's plenty of time to prepare yourself for the afterlife."

"So the two of you were close?"

"Yes. Very. Milana lived with us toward the end, when she became too weak to be left at home alone, in either her Charleville apartment or in her railcar workshop. She also took care of her grandchildren when they were young and I was busy with the foster kids . . ."

"And while Renaud was running around with his three driver's licenses!"

Nanesse refrained from commenting on that.

"She was a remarkable woman, Captain. An extremely discreet person. Maybe that was why she hid behind her puppets? Puppeteers are usually shy geniuses. And, even if she was too modest to admit it, Milana was a highly gifted artist."

"Tell me more."

"You remember the puppets you saw at my house, don't you? Milana had an impressive array of talents. She could sculpt, and of course she could paint and sew, but she also had a solid understanding of mechanics. She was skilled at all sorts of precision arts, like building music boxes and *rayoks*—you know, those old boxes like little theaters a person could look into to see a show of pictures? I even saw her dismantle clocks so she could fix them. And she passed on this passion to her son. If it wasn't for her, Renaud would never have been interested in microrobotics."

Katel was concentrating hard, recording all this information in her head.

"So she was an unusually talented woman," she said, "but someone who kept her art within the family. Who refused to demonstrate her gifts in public. Didn't that ever strike you as strange?"

"It's true for most women, isn't it?"

This time, Katel couldn't help smiling. "Very true! But Milana did perform onstage, at least once."

"Only once!" Nanesse said. "At the World Festival of Puppet Theaters, a few months before her death, when she knew that she didn't have long to live."

"Her swan song, performed in front of those two burned men. I'm sorry, Agnès, but with all due respect for your mother-in-law, I have a feeling that she was keeping a big secret from you . . . And that this secret can be traced back to the pretty old town of Pilsen, in Bohemia."

# 31

## Vicky and Éléa

***Pont du Tarn campsite, Florac***

Vicky and Éléa took a brief pause, as if a bell had been rung. The campsite echoed with a few bursts of adolescent laughter from the playground for under-tens. The moans and sighs of lovers, half concealed beneath the hiss of the river, could be heard coming from the pebble beach. Vicky listened distractedly to these sounds. As she prepared for the next round of their bout, she poured herself another glass of eglantine, managing not to spill any this time. Éléa was looking through the diary in front of her.

*Eighty-eight plus twenty-three,* Brain calculated. *Time with Vicky and time with you. That left your beloved another 254 days of freedom during the year.*

Éléa didn't bother replying to this. She didn't need Brain to do simple math like that.

And she had no desire to confront the evident truth.

Vicky, too, was staring at the red-circled weeks with a look of dawning comprehension.

"It looks like we were both right. Or both wrong. I get the impression that he was able to transform himself into whoever we wanted him to be. The man we were hoping for, the man of our dreams. A chameleon, changing color to match the bed in which he slept. Hans, Pierre . . . How many other names do you think he has? How many other jobs? How many other personalities?"

Éléa had calmed down too. She pushed away her glass. She'd drunk enough; Brain was well and truly drowned. She looked at the photograph on the table, at Pierre's smile, at those gray eyes that had no doubt charmed Vicky too. She thought about his sweetness, his body . . . She had loved him so much. She still loved him so much.

Vicky snapped. "For fuck's sake, Éléa! Who the hell is this guy? Why did he do this to us? Why was he okay with this? Two such completely different lives! Is it . . . is it our fault?"

Éléa looked up. "What?"

"The perfect sailor's wife," Vicky muttered. "Maybe he needed two women because we didn't love him enough."

Not enough? Éléa felt like screaming. But Vicky was already backtracking.

"No, that's not what I meant. Maybe he needed two women because neither of us wanted him with us all the time. Because we didn't behave like most women do: jealousy, possessiveness, all that shit."

"Is that what you meant by the perfect sailor's wife?"

"Something like that, yeah."

Éléa smiled, surprised by the closeness that was growing between them. They had both started calling each other *tu* without even realizing it.

"That's the only way I know how to love," she said.

"Me too," said Vicky. "So that's what we have in common? We're selfish. We want love, but not at the cost of our freedom? Not if it means entrapping the person we love. Not if we—"

"There's something else we have in common," Éléa said suddenly. She looked Vicky in the eye. She had just understood something that, until then, had apparently escaped them both. "Pierre and Hans knew each other!"

"Well, obviously," Vicky replied wearily. "They shared the same body."

*You're making things worse,* Brain murmured.

"That's not what I meant," Éléa explained. "What I meant was, I'm starting to realize that Hans and Pierre's lives weren't completely separate. There are bridges—or tunnels, or whatever—between them. First of all, Pierre sent me here, to Florac, to this village where Hans spent his childhood. Why?"

Vicky nodded slowly. "You're right," she said. "I found out this morning that Hans's mother was an artist, who specialized in puppets, and that she put on a little performance every year for the children at the school here."

"So that's the connection? Puppets? Do you think the treasure hunt will continue? Do you think we'll find him? Or find *them* . . . So what—and where—will the next stage be?"

"Do you think they're alive?" Vicky asked. "I mean . . . do you think *he*'s alive?"

"Oh yes!" Éléa said confidently. "Don't you?"

"I hope so. For . . . for Lola's sake."

Éléa gave her a strange look, but she overcame the urge to restart their argument over who had the better relationship. She realized that she had not had such a long, in-depth conversation with anyone other than Pierre for years. Prior to this evening, discounting her recent interrogation of the bookseller, her record was probably a dozen phrases exchanged with the owner of a patisserie seven months ago, when she had ordered a tropical fruit tart for Pierre's birthday. Well, at least he'd celebrated that day with her, and not with some other woman . . . Unless he had as many different birthdays as he did lovers!

Vicky had pushed away the bottle of eglantine, presumably hoping that this simple gesture would help her to sober up.

"Hans sent me—or, rather, hand delivered—a postcard from Japan," she said. "That suggests he's alive, doesn't it?"

"Do you have proof that he delivered it himself?"

"No, but then you don't have any proof that your Pierre is the one sending you those texts, right?"

*Aaand . . . it's a tie!* Brain declared, waking up. *Take it easy now, girls. You were better off when you were on the same side.*

"You want to know something amazing?" Éléa asked suddenly. "Look at this photo of Pierre. Or of Hans, if you prefer. I received the same photo a week ago! So that's something else we have in common. And maybe a clue."

"Go on."

"Look at the background: a bend in a river, making an almost complete loop, so that the land in the middle is practically an island."

"What's your point? That could be any steep-sided river. The Tarn, the Dordogne, the Ardèche . . . Any of them, really, except for the Seine."

*Take that, you pampered Parisian!* Brain laughed.

"My Precious," said Éléa, sounding sure of herself, "show me the photograph Petrushka-221 in the folder September 2023 and scan it on LocateThis."

Vicky's eyes widened. The ring flickered. Brain went back to sleep, too drunk to bother with feeling jealous.

A few seconds later, the response appeared on her phone.

*The photograph was taken at Bogny-sur-Meuse, next to the statue of the Four Sons of Aymon, in the Ardennes.*

"Shit," said Vicky, "that's not exactly Japan!"

Éléa had already clicked on her cell phone's GPS.

"The statue is located almost on the Belgian border, in a place known as Givet's Finger."

She spoke the following words, delivered to her phone by her Precious: "Givet's Finger is a territory fifteen miles long by six miles wide that sticks like a finger into the Belgian Ardennes. If you look at a map of France, it is easily visible, looking like a mistake by the cartographer, as if he slipped while tracing the border. The finger roughly follows the contours of the Meuse Valley, and just beside it is—"

Éléa abruptly stopped speaking.

"Beside it is what?" Vicky asked.

"The town of Charleville-Mézières."

"So?"

"So? I met Pierre because of a line by Rimbaud—'I wrote silences.' Rimbaud was born in Charleville. And to send me here, to Florac, Pierre used another Rimbaud poem, 'To Music,' which describes the park near the train station in Charleville."

"It could just be a coincidence," Vicky said, while typing on her own phone so that she could see images of this northern French town. "He liked that poet, and he wanted to visit the house where Rimbaud was born, or his grave, and—" Abruptly, she froze. "Shit! You were right, Éléa!"

"About what?"

"That's where we have to go! To Charleville-Mézières! I've just found the answer on the internet."

*See?* said Brain. *You don't need your Precious for that . . .*

Vicky pushed her phone across the table to Éléa.

On the local government website for the Ardennes, a huge headline covered the welcome page.

*September 16–24, 2023, in Charleville-Mézières: the World Festival of Puppet Theaters.*

# 32

## Katel and Nanesse

***Police station, Charleville-Mézières***

Katel's finger hovered in the air just above the Return key.

"Are you ready, Agnès? Ready to visit Bohemia?"

Nanesse nodded.

"I typed five words in French and in Czech," Katel explained. "Keywords for our investigation."

The screen read:

*Pilsen or Plzeň*

*Puppet or loutka*

*Petrushka or Petruška*

*January 29, 1977 or ledna 29, 1977*

*Milana and Renaud Duval*

"Let's throw these words into the cooking pot of the internet and see what the soup tastes like!"

Katel pressed the key, and immediately groaned with frustration.

Nothing!

She was going around in circles. Her computer screen was still showing the same articles from Czech newspapers, whose names she was starting to know by heart: *The Truth of Bohemia, The Pilsen News, The Pilsen Gazette . . .*

They had already been through dozens of pages, with no results.

"What if," suggested Nanesse, "we put in something about the burned men?"

"With all due respect, Agnès, that was the first line of inquiry we investigated. Jérémy researched the main criminal cases in the Czech Republic, going back decades. We got a list of all the cold cases, the wanted criminals, the serial killers . . . But we didn't find anything there either. What else do you want me to search for—*Man without ears*?"

"No, just something simple like *fire*. We're looking for a news story, but not necessarily a crime. It could just have been an accident . . ."

The captain gave Nanesse a smile that mingled embarrassment and admiration. Of course—it was so obvious! Why hadn't she thought of that?

She feverishly typed in the words *fire or požár* and *accident or nehoda*, then swallowed a curse word.

An image appeared on the screen, below a headline that read:

Tragicky požár v Plzeň, červen 03 1976

The article from *The Pilsen Gazette* was brief. With two clicks, Katel copied it onto the translation site.

Tragic fire accident in Pilsen, June 3, 1976

The inhabitants of the Pilsen region, especially parents and their children, will be well aware of the puppeteer Libor Slavik, better known as Louka. For more than fifteen years, following in the footsteps of his grandparents and parents before him, he has moved his famous caravan from village to village all over Bohemia. As soon as he pulls up at a village square, or stops in a meadow, all the children and parents come running, more eager than the pigeons in Wenceslas Square. Libor Slavik and his little traveling troupe even played in Marienbad a year ago, for Gustáv Husák and several other members of the Central Committee of the Czechoslovak Communist Party.

Yesterday, as on every other day of the year, Louka and his troupe performed their most famous show, Petrushka, before closing up their puppet theater.

How could anyone have guessed that this would be their last ever performance?

We do not yet know the cause, but we do know that, in the middle of the night, their caravan caught fire, trapping the sleeping occupants inside: Libor Slavik, his wife, Zuzana, and their two children, Kristof and Amos.

Early evidence suggests the fire was accidental. The police wish to speak with anyone who was in the vicinity at the time. Any witness statements would be welcomed, even though Libor—who, miraculously, suffered only a few minor burns—assured police that he saw and heard nothing.

# LIFE IS THE FARCE WE MUST ALL PERFORM

*A Season in Hell* by Arthur Rimbaud

# MINA'S STORY

## The Crime

***June 1976***

So that was how I grew up, on the roads of Bohemia. I didn't run away. Maybe I got used to that nomadic life: a new village every day, a new camp, the laughter of new children. A life of freedom, so Libor said, in a country—Czechoslovakia—where freedom was in short supply. But what freedom did I enjoy? Every night, Libor came to see me. I was alone with my secret.

Well, not completely alone.

Zuzana knew.

She claimed to be a clairvoyant, a tarot reader, a fortune teller. She would sometimes extort enormous sums of money from gullible villagers who, unable to burn candles in churches under the Czechoslovak Communist regime, instead entrusted their hopes and dreams to passing charlatans.

Zuzana knew that Libor came to have sex with me under the stars. How could she not know, when he got up every night before returning to sleep beside her and snore until dawn?

Zuzana knew, but she didn't say anything.

Libor was not the kind of man you could accuse of anything, and he was not the kind of man to ever apologize. Embarrassment, shame, bitterness, fear . . . they were not emotions he experienced. He was the absolutist ruler of his miserable, wandering kingdom of two children, two women, and one horse.

Zuzana never said anything, never reproached Libor at all. After he came inside me and went back to the caravan to lie beside her, she probably clung to him out of fear that she would lose him, that I would steal away her husband. And then, the next day, she would take her revenge.

In August 1968, when Libor had saved me from the streets, Zuzana had treated me with detached indifference; now, she treated me as a rival, as someone to be punished, dominated, humiliated at every opportunity. I was the one she sent to draw water from the well, to dig latrines in the frozen earth, to gather firewood until nightfall.

I was her slave during the day, and his at night.

Zuzana's bad moods had an effect on Libor's moods. Maybe she refused to make love to him anymore—I never knew—but, with me, Libor became more and more violent. He would hit me, bite me, even whip me, if he could find a rope or a branch. Sometimes he would cut me, if a bottle of absinthe had been emptied then broken near the campfire. Sometimes he would burn me with the embers from the fire.

I let him do it, the stars the only witness to my suffering.

I was nineteen. The two boys were ten and eleven. I took care of their education, speaking a little French to them. Every day, Kristof became more like his father—strong, happy, tyrannical—while Amos became as secretive, silent, and submissive as his mother.

One morning, near the German border, while Libor was off on a journey to trade with smugglers from the West, in the Bavarian forest—something he did increasingly often—I summoned the courage to talk to Zuzana. The two of us were washing ourselves, more or less naked, in a stream known as the Devil's Water.

"I don't want to steal your husband, you know. I don't love him. I reject him as much as I can. You and I would be stronger if we joined together, if there was peace between us."

Zuzana looked at my breasts, my hips, the pubic hair visible through my drenched underwear. I think I was desirable; I sensed it in the way she looked at me, and in the way the men of the villages we visited looked at me too. I no longer looked like a boy. Onstage, the children would all watch Petrushka, but the husbands watched me instead.

"Witch!" Zuzana spat. "You have cast a spell over my husband! It's because of you that he drinks. It's because of you that he steals. It's because of you that he lets Louka die."

I knew what she meant.

Louka, the famous puppeteer who roamed Bohemia in his caravan, was now merely an alcoholic with trembling fingers. The articulated hands of the Moor could barely hold his wooden saber straight, and if the crowds still gathered in the village squares as soon as we arrived with our puppet theater, it was now to see Petrushka dance.

My art, my talent, was my life preserver and my cross to bear. Never would Libor and Zuzana set me free. Because, without me, they had no show.

And without the show, who was I?

I lived for nothing but those performances, one hour every day when I could escape by pulling the strings of a fate that wasn't mine.

"If it's all because of me," I said to Zuzana as I sank neck deep in the river, "then let me leave."

"Just try it, my beauty! If you run away, we'll track you down. And we'll kill you!"

I wanted to drown myself in the Devil's Water that morning, in water that could not have been more than sixty degrees. I had realized that I was a prisoner; that Libor and Zuzana were my torturers.

I had realized that Zuzana didn't care if Libor lusted after me, slept with me, raped me.

I was her lightning rod. If I left, Zuzana was the one Libor would hit.

We spent more and more time visiting the villages on the Austrian and Bavarian borders. Libor took advantage of his status as a traveling artist. Puppetry was one of the few means of expression allowed by the Communist regime. The Central Committee believed in maintaining the ancient tradition of rayoks, folk tales, and street theaters as a way of distracting the uneducated masses in remote, rural Bohemia.

The colorful caravan; Petrushka's Russian arabesques; Amos and Kristof running around the horse in our camp . . . this entire façade formed a picturesque, bucolic illusion. Our nomadic family was the ideal cover for what was really going on.

It took me a while to understand why we kept moving farther away from the Iron Curtain. And why Libor was now earning so much money. It certainly wasn't the meager pile of coins that the villagers dropped in the cap in front of the puppet theater that was making us rich.

Gradually, as I overheard snatches of conversation between Libor and members of the StB—the Czechoslovakian version of the KGB—I understood that he was a smuggler. He had various ploys for importing contraband goods from the West—cigarettes, whisky, perfume, records, jeans, chewing gum—and selling them for a fortune. He was paid in Czech korunas, Russian rubles, German marks, even in American dollars sometimes. He kept his loot in a bag, hidden under the caravan's roof.

Libor, the brilliant puppeteer who had saved me that morning in August 1968, under the Charles Bridge in Prague, was now nothing more than a small-time smuggler, profiting from the Normalization—those miserable years when the Czechoslovak Socialist Republic became one of the poorest and most docile countries in the Eastern Bloc. Scavenging the carcass of his homeland during the dark days of its history.

The accident happened one morning in spring 1976.

Three months earlier, Libor had replaced old Kinsky, who pulled our caravan from village to village, with a two-hundred-horsepower Kirovets tractor. We had parked by the banks of the Radbuza, a few miles from Pilsen. We visited the world capital of puppetry every year, even if Libor was ever less keen on such big gatherings.

A blessing, a curse . . . What should I call it?

I don't know.

I was pregnant. With Libor's child, of course. I was not yet twenty years old.

Zuzana had known before I did.

Even before my period stopped; even before my first bout of morning sickness; even before Libor called a doctor from Pilsen, who examined me and confirmed it.

That night in June 1976, the sweltering temperatures did not abate with the sunset. A leaden heat was pressing down on central Europe, drying up the fields and rivers.

Kristof was playing naked in the Radbuza River with some local teenagers. He was growing increasingly handsome and increasingly arrogant. Intoxicated by the passions of the world, he liked to show off his muscles and his thuggish good looks to the older village girls. Amos watched them from the riverbank, mesmerized more by the glimmers of dusk on the rushing river than by the transparent shirts and underwear of the laughing girls. The colors of the world fascinated him.

Did Kristof have time to kiss one of the village girls that day?

Could Amos have known that it would be the last time he would ever admire the golden gleam of the gloaming, the silver shimmers of the river, the diamond sparkle of the stars?

Libor had already been drinking for a while when Zuzana summoned us to the campfire, where the goulash had finished simmering.

"You can't keep the kid," she told me bluntly.

"Why not?" Libor belched.

I didn't say anything; I just wrapped my arms protectively around my belly.

"I'll take care of it," Zuzana said. "Any decent-sized needle should work."

I wasn't naive. I knew how babies were disposed of, and I knew the risks too. Libor was drunk, but he saw the mute fear in my eyes. Maybe he cared about me, deep down? Maybe he would never let his wife hurt me?

"Why shouldn't we keep the kid?" he asked, looking in turn at Zuzana, me, then the boys on the riverbank. "I mean, we're a family, aren't we?"

Zuzana glared at him. She was determined to stand up to him, for once in her life.

"Why? I'll show you why!"

In front of us, she threw down the tarot cards that she used to impress the villagers, then picked up the one that had fallen between me and Libor. The thirteenth Major Arcana card. The Card with No Name, the Grim Reaper . . . Death, in other words.

"Why?" repeated Zuzana, waving the card threateningly. "Because it is written. Because I see it. This kid, Libor—*your* kid—he will kill you!"

Libor laughed mockingly and drank the rest of his absinthe, but he was sweating more than ever. He was frightened. I realized in that instant that Zuzana was the dominant partner in their marriage; that she had gotten the upper hand over him and her two sons; that she was gradually constructing her revenge; and that she would never let my child live. And when she killed my child, she would not be able to resist killing me too . . .

When Libor looked at me one last time, as if to ask me what I thought of this, I lowered my eyes, to signify that I was resigned to my fate, that I accepted it, that I trusted them, that I didn't care about this creature growing inside my belly. Zuzana called the boys over. She even helped me wash the dishes, which she never did. Libor collapsed after drinking another bottle, then everyone went to bed.

After that, everything happened quite naturally. My movements came one after another, almost automatically, as if I had no choice in the matter, as if it was all inevitable.

First, I took the money from under the caravan's roof.

I was owed compensation, I thought. And it would be a useful bargaining chip if everything went wrong.

We always kept some cans of gas in the back of the caravan, and every morning we would use them to fill up the tank of the Kirovets. Occasionally Libor would use them for his fire-eating too. I emptied two cans in a perfect circle around the caravan, then I set light to it.

Drawing a curtain: That was what came to my mind. Building a wall between them and me; a wall of flame. Burning the wheels of the caravan, the way you might slash a car's tires to give yourself time to flee.

The tall, dry grass instantly caught fire. The circle of flames rose higher, surrounding the caravan with an insurmountable barrier.

I ran. Into the wind, where the fire could not find me. Into the shade of a willow, on the edge of the forest. For several minutes, I could not see anything because of the thick smoke. Then, when all the grass had been consumed, only the wooden caravan remained, and it went up in a gigantic torch.

*My God,* I thought, *what have I done?*

I climbed up into the densest branches of the willow, so that I could see without being seen.

And I saw.

I saw Libor burst through the wall of flames, then pour a bucket of water over the blanket in which he had covered himself, before returning to confront the blaze.

I saw the roof of the caravan collapse.

I saw a human torch, Zuzana, emerge from the fire, pushing her two children ahead of her, both of them burned alive.

I saw the torch shrivel and die, becoming an inert, black mass.

I saw the boys' bodies shaking. I saw Libor cover them with the wet blanket.

I heard their cries—*I can't see, Papa! Papa, I can't hear!*

For the first time in my life, I saw Libor weep. He wept over his wife's corpse, over what remained of the faces of his sons.

I heard Libor howling up at the stars, at the infinite night.

"I'll find you, Mina. Wherever you are! I'll hunt you down and I'll kill you, just like you killed Zuzana. And before I kill you, I'll hurt your child, and your child's future children, the way you hurt mine."

# 33

## Vicky and Éléa

***Monday, September 18, 2023***
***A31 highway, Langres Plateau, Haute-Marne***

"What does 'ASD' stand for?" Lola asked.

The little girl was sitting with Kasper in her booster seat in the back of the Berlingo. For the first few miles, she'd been kept amused by the rising and falling roads. Vicky had pointed out Les Sucs, those extinct volcanoes that looked like giant molehills, and then the red statue of the Virgin and Child perched on a high rock as they passed the town of Le Puy.

But after that, the journey became more monotonous as the highway skirted around various big cities: Saint-Étienne, Lyon, Dijon. After leaving behind the vineyards of Burgundy, they drove for almost an hour on the treeless Langres Plateau. There were still another two hundred miles to go before they reached Charleville, according to the GPS. They had left at five that morning—too early to stop at the police station.

Vicky, the only driver, had drunk sixteen ounces of coffee at the first service station they spotted. Around seven, she had called Florine, her neighbor, asking her to inform the school that Lola would be absent that day, and to feed the rabbits, hens, and ponies. Lola had opened her eyes about eight o'clock. But she must have opened her ears sometime before that.

"What does 'ASD' stand for?" she repeated.

But Éléa simply could not stop talking. In less than forty-eight hours, she had crisscrossed France, first from north to south, and then from south to east, after hardly even sitting in a car during the five previous years—with the exception of a few brief taxi rides with Pierre, on rainy days in Paris. In contrast to her silence in Samuel Galet's passenger seat, Éléa was positively chatty now. She told Vicky everything: how she had first discovered Pierre's poems in Librairie Baou; their passionate escapades in Paris; the treasure hunt that had led her to Florac.

*I never knew you were so talkative,* Brain noted ironically inside her head.

*Neither did I,* admitted Éléa.

Why did she feel such an urge to confess her secrets to this stranger? Because it was important that Vicky understood who she was? That Vicky understood why Pierre loved her. That she understood why Éléa's relationship with Pierre was exclusive, that Éléa was bound by an unbreakable connection to her Petrushka.

"What did you say, sweetie?"

Vicky had finally heard her daughter. Lola quickly asked her question for the third time.

"What does 'ASD' stand for? Lea kept saying that she was 'diagnosed with ASD.'"

Éléa turned back to face the little girl.

"Oh, you're awake? Don't you want to watch a cartoon or something?"

In the back seat of the Berlingo, Lola had all the modern equipment necessary for long car trips: iPad, 4G connection, earbuds . . .

"I'd rather listen to you and Mommy!"

Éléa grimaced. She felt sure that today's children were easier to raise than they had been in the past. A screen, a tablet, a phone, a joystick, and they should leave you in peace for hours. That was progress! These days there was no need to keep them entertained. You just had to fight for their attention now and again to get them to eat a meal or take a bath. But this little brat clearly preferred adult conversation to Pokémon or Minions. Éléa tried to ask Brain about the best way to deal with this situation.

*Sorry, my dear, but I don't understand kids either. Their brains haven't yet reached their definitive weight. Hers isn't even three pounds yet. It's like trying to work out how a robot functions when it's only half built.*

"So?" Lola asked again. "What *does* 'ASD' stand for?"

"It stands for 'autism spectrum disorder,'" Vicky finally answered, her eyes never leaving the road. "But it would take too long to explain what—"

"Oh, I know about autism!" Lola interrupted. "Enora, in my class, is autistic. She only has to talk to other people when she feels like it. It's cool!"

"Well, there's no risk of that with you," Éléa remarked. "Don't you ever pipe down?"

"Why do you say that, Lea?"

"My name is Éléa, not Lea!"

"That's what I said."

"No, it's not . . ."

"Yes, it is!"

For the first time that day, Vicky burst out laughing.

"Stop bickering, you two!"

"Tell me, Lea," Lola insisted. "What's it like being autistic?"

"Oh, leave me in peace!" Éléa shouted. There was an uncomfortable silence. She took a deep breath, then said in a calmer voice: "Sorry, I was feeling overwhelmed. Would you please leave me in peace, Lola? Maybe you could just look at your iPad instead."

At last Lola looked down at the screen in her lap. Vicky was fully focused on the road ahead, passing endless lines of trucks.

*Nicely done,* applauded Brain. *So we are alone at last, just the two of us. Now what do you want to talk about?*

"Nothing! I want you to leave me in peace too. All I want to do is think about Pierre. I haven't had a single message from him since I arrived in Florac yesterday. So now I'm afraid for my Petrushka again . . ."

A little voice piped up behind her.

"My teacher says that even if Enora doesn't talk to us, she's supersmart. Are you supersmart too?"

Brain leapt at this opportunity.

*Go on, brag about me! It would be nice to be flattered for a change.*

Éléa said nothing. Vicky had finally managed to get back in the righthand lane. The next truck was still a good two hundred yards ahead.

"Yes, sweetie," Vicky said with a big smile. "Éléa's brain doesn't work quite the same way as ours. For example, she can't cook noodles, or do simple things like that, but if you were to empty out a box of toothpicks, she'd be capable of counting them all in three seconds, or of remembering all the cards that had been played in a game of UNO. You see?"

"Wow!"

Lola looked through the window for something to count.

"Lea, can you tell me how many telegraph poles there are before the next sign over there?"

Ignoring her, Éléa looked at Vicky.

"Why did you tell her that? It's stupid and mean. And discriminatory. And it's not even true!"

"Oh, are you chickening out, Lea?" Lola taunted her. "Nobody can beat me at UNO! I'll play you any time you want, autism or not."

Éléa gave another long sigh.

"Well, why don't you explain it to her then?" Vicky said to Éléa. "Explain it truthfully."

Éléa rolled her eyes, then turned to face the back seat.

"The main thing about having autism is that I can't stand hypocrisy. Or lies. My brain isn't all twisted, like the brains of most adult humans."

*Thank you!*

"So if I give someone my love," Éléa continued, "I do it for life. And I'm sorry to tell you this, Lola, but the man I gave my love to is the man you call Daddy."

Lola's eyes widened with surprise, then narrowed with anger, but she appeared unable to think of a response to this, and in the end she just shoved her iPad earbuds into her ears.

"It's stupid and mean to tell her that," Vicky protested in a cold voice. "And it's not even true!"

For a long time they sat in silence. The highway ran through the Orient Forest. Oaks and hornbeams flashed past endlessly.

*If you want to defend my reputation,* Brain suggested after a while, *I don't mind playing a game of UNO.*

# 34

## Katel and Nanesse

***Police station, Charleville-Mézières***

At eight in the morning, the station in Charleville was once again transformed into a hive of activity. Dozens of police officers came and went through the corridors, looking happy and relaxed, talking in loud voices, drinking coffee, munching pastries. They had a big week ahead of them. On a large map of the town, hung in the main room, the festival's various events were noted with colored thumbtacks, each color representing the team responsible for that event's safety. The rain had grown less intense during the night, finally stopping in the early morning. The weather forecast promised a dry day.

Today's events, mostly performed for schoolchildren, would take place in every neighborhood, making it complicated from an organizational point of view . . . But Captain Marelle had other priorities.

"Jérémy," Katel said, "I need you."

"But . . . it's just that—"

"Listen, Jérémy, the logistical teams have been working on the festival's safety plan for months. If those bureaucrats in local government know one thing, it's how to open an umbrella. There'll be more uniforms than kids on the streets of Charleville: police officers, riot squads, even the army reserve. So let them get on with it. If they need us, they'll call."

"But—"

Katel waved away his protests. She quickly summarized the latest developments in the investigation: the three different birth certificates from Charleville, Mende, and Paris, plus that news article in *The Pilsen Gazette*—the traveling puppeteers' caravan that caught on fire, supposedly by accident.

"What does that have to do with our case?"

"Listen to this. 'Their caravan caught fire, trapping the sleeping occupants inside: Libor Slavik, his wife, Zuzana, and their two children, Kristof and Amos.' Say those kids had been about ten years old in 1976 and they'd survived . . . They'd be more than fifty now. Two men with burned faces? Ring any bells? That could match Agnès Duval's Identi-Kit . . ."

"Has Nanesse gone home?" Jérémy asked.

Katel frowned. Apparently the whole brigade was calling Agnès Duval *Nanesse*. All except for her . . .

"Yes, I told her to get some sleep, surrounded by her mother-in-law's puppets. And I ordered Will and Mehdi to keep an eye on her until morning. They grumbled about it. Said they didn't fancy spending another night in the Mégane."

"Yeah, the accommodation's terrible," Jérémy agreed. "But the food's really good."

"You're right—what the hell are they complaining about? Anyway, they're supposed to come back to the station before noon. Until then . . ."

"Yes?" the lieutenant said.

"Until then, I want you to find out everything you can about Hans Bernard and Pierre Rousseau. Now we have their mothers' names, it should be easier. Take Fatou and Mathias with you, and call me with updates as often as you can. And don't look like that—I've got to deal with Interpol!"

# 35

## Vicky and Éléa

***Service station, A4 highway, Marne***

The old Berlingo struggled up the hillsides of the Seine Valley and the Aube Valley before entering Champagne. For almost an hour, Vicky had vaguely noticed that they were being followed by a gray Skoda. A gray Skoda that made no attempt to pass them.

They stopped for a sandwich at a service station. The bright summer weather they'd enjoyed in Florac had gradually given way to a damp autumnal gloom.

Lola, who had never traveled this far north before, didn't seem to care about the weather. When they'd entered, she had stood on tiptoes to grab a flyer from a display case of local tourist attractions designed to lure drivers away from the highway.

While Vicky ordered another coffee and Éléa left to search desperately for a store that sold pantyhose so that she could cover her bare legs (having neglected to bring a change of clothes with her from Paris), Lola waved the leaflet in front of her doll.

"You see, Kasper? That's where we're going! To the puppet festival! You're going to meet so many friends there . . ."

Ever since Vicky had announced the name of their destination, and Éléa had agreed to show her some photographs of the festival on her cell phone, Lola had been able to think about nothing else. Her little mind was filled with images of giant teddy bears, frightening creatures, and living dolls.

Finally, in the car later, Lola calmed down. The last part of the trip threatened to be long and boring; she began to yawn, and her eyelids drooped. She forced them open and—as if the previous conversation had just come back to her—declared to Éléa, "Anyway, you and Mommy can keep arguing as much as you like. I don't care! Daddy only loves me!"

Lola fell asleep as they were passing Reims. There was still an hour to go. Vicky had been driving for seven hours but did not feel tired. She regularly checked her rearview mirror, but the gray Skoda was no longer there. An old beige Volkswagen Golf seemed to have taken over, driving behind them for several dozen miles without ever passing them, staying far enough behind that it was impossible for her to make out the faces of its occupants.

She imagined that it was Hans who was chasing her, then immediately told herself to stop being so stupid. It was ridiculous enough to imagine that she was being followed by men who were capable of changing cars mid-journey, let alone that it might be the very man she was looking for!

She was torn from her thoughts by the voice of Éléa, who had waited until Lola was asleep before continuing their discussion.

"Vicky, did you hear your daughter? 'Daddy only loves me!' That's exactly why I don't want children."

"You're very talkative for someone with autism," Vicky replied tersely.

"Don't try to change the subject! Children are vampires who suck the blood-red passion from their parents' veins. Loving a man and wanting a child with him is like . . . I don't know, drinking a glass of vintage champagne and sweetening it with crème de cassis."

*Nice metaphor!* Brain congratulated her.

"It's a shame that you have so much to say," Vicky remarked, "but that what comes out of your mouth is often so stupid."

Thirty miles later, they saw a huge banner flying above the road.

**22ND WORLD FESTIVAL OF PUPPET THEATERS**

By the roadside, a sign indicated:

**YOU ARE ENTERING ARDENNE MÉTROPOLE**

Vicky and Éléa fell silent, both of them secretly terrorized by the same anxiety.

Was it here that Hans/Pierre had come to hide? And, if so, what terrible truth was he trying to conceal?

# 36

## Katel and Nanesse

***Police station, Charleville-Mézières***

Three hours had passed before Jérémy Bonello, Katel Marelle, and Agnès Duval found themselves together in the captain's office. Before that, Katel had bolted the door and given an order not to be disturbed unless a group of terrorists was threatening to blow up the mayor's office in Charleville's main square.

In theory, her office communicated with the rest of the police station through enormous windows that enabled her to keep an eye on everything that was happening. But to preserve her privacy she had put some very big posters for *The Godfather* movies on the windows. Her officers did not need to be constantly supervised, and she felt no desire to transform herself into Big Sister.

"Okay, let's start with me," said Katel. "This shouldn't take long. I spent the morning being bounced between various departments of Interpol, explaining over and over again that I was seeking information on an accident from almost half a century ago. In the Czech Republic! I ended up speaking to a certain Jan Horák, a moron who is supposedly the coordinator for all the police forces in eastern Europe. He thought fit to remind me that, at the time, the Czech Republic did not exist—*it was called Czechoslovakia, ma'am*—and that, less than ten years after Prague was invaded by Russian tanks, the local atmosphere was not necessarily conducive to sharing information with Western democracies. The 'police' mentioned in the article is in fact the old secret service, better known as the StB—the Czechoslovak equivalent of the Stasi in East Germany or the Securitate in Romania: the most feared machine for spying, torture, and assassination in the entire Eastern Bloc. Horák promised to look into the matter, to find out what happened to Libor Slavik and whether there are any records of those burned men over there, and to call me back."

Jérémy didn't bother hiding his skepticism. "Yeah, but . . . I mean, it was fifty years ago . . . in Pilsen . . ."

"All right, your turn," Katel said sourly. "I hope you found out more than I did."

"Well, Fatou and Mathias did a great job manning the phone lines. If they ever get fired from the police, I think they'll have a career ahead of them selling new roofs or heat pumps. Let's start with Hans Bernard: son of Marion Bernard, born January 29, 1977. We tracked down traces of his past pretty easily, first to Mende, and then to Florac. He spent the whole of elementary school in Lozère. The mayor of the village even sent me scans of class photographs from back then: school outings, village fetes, and so on—you can see little Hans in each one. The mayor of Florac is ten years older than Hans, but she remembers him quite clearly. According to her, Hans left school as soon as he could, and since then, there's been no news of him or his mother. Nothing surprising about that: Most people from Lozère get out of there at the first opportunity. All she remembers is that his mother was an artist, or something like that, and that from time to time she would organize performances at the school, although she has no memory of what they were like. She was in high school when Hans was in elementary school."

Nanesse was listening attentively, and Katel noticed her jump when she heard the words *artist* and *performances*.

"As for Pierre Rousseau," Jérémy went on, "he was even easier to track down. He always lived at the same address—his mother's house at 17 Rue de Sofia in the eighteenth arrondissement. It's a pretty safe neighborhood, the kind of place that's home to rich lefties. The locals even have a charity called PhiloSofia! You can imagine what it's like there: aperitif evenings where they pair Chilean tapas with Australian wines, communal picnics on their balconies, welcoming parties for new arrivals in the neighborhood. Long story short, their charity has a hundred and fifty years of archives! All the progress reports from the local school; the list of everyone belonging to local organizations; files on the customers of all the local shopkeepers and artisans . . .

"And, no doubt about it: Pierre Rousseau grew up there. His school reports are excellent. He borrowed books regularly from the local library. And he was a highly gifted dancer, according to the president of the Dance Time 18 Club, who remembers him vividly. A very handsome boy who had a quirky way of moving his body. And an unforgettable pair of gray eyes that made all the girls in the neighborhood swoon. Apparently young Pierrot took full advantage of his charms! In this case, too, he disappeared along with his mother—a discreet, even secretive woman—around the time he was eighteen or twenty years old. Since then, not a word . . . But, as the members of PhiloSofia often lament, it is sadly far from rare, in a big city like Paris, for people to move away once they grow up and never keep in touch with their old friends."

While Jérémy was delivering this speech, Nanesse had been leaning against the wall of the office, staring at the black *Godfather* posters.

What she had heard from Lieutenant Bonello's mouth made no sense to her. It was true that, physically speaking, Hans and Pierre resembled her Renaud, and they had all been raised by single mothers. But in every other way, those three children seemed so different. She recalled Bruno Pluvier's words—*The other soldiers called us Nono the Sniper and Renaud the Chameleon.* Pluvier had mentioned Renaud's in-depth knowledge of Paris and Lozère. Obviously there was some connection between these three boys, but what was it? Could they have swapped identities at some point, like twins who enjoy sitting in each other's places in the classroom just to drive their teacher crazy?

But why? How? When? Was it possible that Renaud was . . . alive?

Katel Marelle apparently deciphered the glimmer of hope in Nanesse's eyes.

"Calm down, Agnès. The one thing we know for sure in all of this is that your husband is dead. We have plenty of proof of that fact. Anyway . . . good work, Jérémy."

Jérémy was not used to receiving compliments from his boss, and the look on his face showed that he savored them. Lost in her thoughts, Nanesse continued to stare at the posters. There was one detail that bothered her, something she hadn't even noticed until now: The same symbol featured on every poster, between the faces of Marlon Brando and Al Pacino. A fist gripping a cross, from which hung six white strings. A puppet controller, held by an anonymous hand.

*More puppets . . .*

"Milana is the key to all this," she said suddenly.

The captain and the lieutenant turned to her, surprised.

"I don't know anything about my mother-in-law's childhood. I know nothing about her life before I met Renaud. All I know about her is her passion for puppets, and the fact that she had a very slight Slavic accent. There has to be a link between Milana and that fire in Pilsen. Maybe she was the wife of that guy, Libor Slavik."

Katel raised a dubious eyebrow.

"Which would mean that her children—Amos and Kristof—were your husband's brothers? In that case, maybe the man with the burned face you saw outside your home in Bourg-Fidèle wasn't trying to kill you after all. Maybe he was just trying to get in touch with his sister-in-law."

Nanesse couldn't decide whether to smile or scowl. Katel's dark sense of humor when it came to Renaud's death made her feel physically sick.

"Then again, the article in that Czech newspaper doesn't say if Libor Slavik's wife was killed in the caravan fire," Lieutenant Bonello pointed out.

Katel appeared to consider this. Nanesse stood up, determined.

"There's no time to lose. We should go there now!"

"Go where?" the two police officers asked at nearly the same time.

"Into Milana's past."

"But where?" Katel repeated, alone this time.

"Where her ashes were scattered: outside her railcar workshop. It must still be where it was six years ago, at the end of an abandoned railway line, close to the French-Belgian border, in Givet's Finger. Milana's apartment in Charleville was sold after her death, but Renaud refused to let go of the workshop. Besides, who would have wanted to buy such a rusty old wreck? Renaud would go back there occasionally, to lay flowers beside it. A street performer's grave, he called it, with wheels but no coffin."

Givet was only thirty miles from Charleville. They could be there in three quarters of an hour.

"Let's go!" Katel said. She was already putting on her jacket.

Just then, she heard somebody knocking on the glass wall in front of her, between the posters for *The Godfather* and *The Godfather Part II*.

The face of Officer Vigneules appeared, his nose practically touching the glass. From behind her sweep of black hair, Katel glared at him.

"I gave orders not to be disturbed under any circumstances!" she growled.

But Mathias Vigneules had already run around the office and opened the door, his face distorted by panic.

"Unless a group of terrorists was threatening to blow up Place Ducale—that's what you said."

"I know that," the captain barked. "So?"

The policeman's whole body was shaking. "We just received an anonymous phone call, saying there's a bomb in one of the recycling bins between Rue de la République and Place Ducale."

The police station emptied out amid a blue streak of squealing sirens. In less than a minute, Nanesse was left alone, with only Fatoumata, the receptionist, to keep her company.

"That's an order!" Katel had bellowed at her before diving into one of the police cars. "You stay here and you don't move! I don't want you taking any risks, Nanesse!"

*You stay here and you don't move!*

Nanesse looked through the window at her Clio in the police station parking lot.

*I don't want you taking any risks, Nanesse!*

The captain was making progress. Katel had called her Nanesse. Soon she would be saying *tu* instead of *vous* . . . As with Nanesse's shyest foster kids, it was just a question of time before she was tamed.

*A question of time . . .*

Over the past forty-eight hours, Nanesse had not moved a single muscle without at least one police officer watching her. She had been terrified, down in Bruno Pluvier's cellar, when she spotted that armed man at the top of the stairs, but her fear had faded in the past two days.

Now in its place was an ardent curiosity. And the certainty that she couldn't leave it only to the police to investigate this case, however motivated Captain Katel appeared.

Nanesse herself needed to find answers to all these maddening questions. This wasn't just a police investigation, it was a personal quest.

From the corner of her eye, she observed Fatoumata, who was peering at her computer screen. The receptionist was not paying her any attention at all. And surely Libor, Amos, and Kristof Slavik were not standing outside the police station, waiting for her.

Nobody was following her.

She felt sure that the truth would only be found there.

In Milana's railcar workshop.

# 37

## Vicky and Éléa

***Boulevard Gambetta, Charleville-Mézières***

Vicky waited patiently behind the wheel of her Berlingo for the traffic light to turn green. Every time they stopped at a junction like this, Éléa argued with the GPS's directions, which clearly had not been updated to include recent modifications in the flow of traffic around Charleville and kept insisting that they go the wrong way down one-way streets or break through the barricades that kept certain streets pedestrianized during the festival.

*Boulevard Gambetta, Rue de l'Arquebuse, Avenue de Montjoly . . .*

Having realized she would never reach the center of town by following the car's computer, Vicky was now desperately searching for a parking lot on the periphery. With all the U-turns and sudden changes of direction she was making, she would have known immediately if they were still being followed by a gray Skoda or a beige Golf.

Suddenly, Lola cried out: "Look!" She was pointing at a building by the side of the road. There was nothing unusual about the three-story house . . . except for a gigantic mural painted on one of its windowless outer walls.

"It's beautiful!" Lola cooed, staring at the painting. It was at least fifteen feet high and ten feet wide, and it showed a multicolored bird trying to take off, but tied with strings of fire to a golden star.

As they waited for the traffic light to change, they had time to read the handwritten letters beneath the enormous picture.

*I have stretched ropes from belltower to belltower;*

*garlands from window to window;*

*chains of gold from star to star,*

*and I dance.*

*Rimbaud's* Illuminations, whispered Brain, and Éléa repeated what he told her out loud:

"One of the great poet's most beautiful texts. Not only is the town celebrating him in his childhood home—an apartment building known as the House of Elsewhere—but there are a dozen murals in the streets illustrating his most famous quotations."

As they continued to drive randomly through the town, searching for somewhere to park, they passed several other giant paintings, all of them stunning: a glade-green Sleeper in the Valley; a sun-blue Drunken Boat; a candy-orange Childhood; a viscera-gray Tortured Heart; a ghost-pink Ophelia.

*And yet Arthur Rimbaud's sole desire was to leave Charleville!* Brain pointed out. *He left at sixteen and didn't return until twenty years later, when the remains of his body—racked by cancer, one leg amputated—were . . .*

"Okay, okay, I can read," Éléa said wearily. "Let's just dream and focus on the murals."

At last, after a long, labyrinthine detour, they found themselves by some miracle only a few streets from Place Ducale. And, even more miraculously, they spotted an empty space in an underground parking garage. They wandered for a while through its dark, dirty, subterranean corridors, past walls bereft of poetry, then climbed three flights of moldy stairs before emerging into Place Ducale.

And there they stood, stunned.

A vast crowd had invaded the stern-looking square, as if a movie director had decided to use thousands of extras to shoot the wildest fantasy epic ever made. Hundreds of children ran, laughing, to escape the clutches of the monstrous animals that pursued them: talking spiders, flying ostriches, thousand-legged sheep harassed by a three-headed sheepdog. Fluorescent angels and giant ladybugs patrolled the skies, casting their oversized shadows onto the buildings' ocher and brick-red façades. In the middle of the square, an elf was playing the violin. Nine dwarves danced under archways.

Lola seemed unsure of where to look. She held Kasper tight to her chest like an anxious mother.

It was all so enthralling.

Vicky gripped her daughter's hand firmly in her own and turned to Éléa.

"I feel like we've stepped into the fifth dimension. What does your Precious have to say about all this?"

The smart ring blinked.

*"The World Festival of Puppet Theaters has taken place every two or three years, in September, for the past sixty years. It lasts nine days and draws hundreds of thousands of spectators, who flock here from all over the world to enjoy more than a hundred and fifty official shows, plus many more unofficial street performances."*

"That's great," admitted Vicky. "Lola will be thrilled. But what are *we* looking for?"

"Petrushka!" said Éléa.

They searched everywhere, among all the stalls and performances. The artists were clearly trying to surpass each other with their creations, some ultrarealistic and others wildly imaginative, but Éléa saw very few classic puppets: hardly any Guignols or Polichinelles, and even fewer Petrushkas . . .

At last, she came to a stop in front of a strange-looking building between the International Institute of Puppetry and the Museum of the Ardennes. A crowd of spectators was gathered in front of a window.

"The Clock of the Great Puppeteer!" Éléa muttered.

Vicky and Lola stared at the window, which was surrounded by a green frame topped with a green clock. It looked like something out of *Alice in Wonderland*.

"According to my Precious, that's what it's called, this theater of automata. It's the big local attraction. It starts up every hour, twelve times a day, and shows twelve scenes from the most famous local legend: the Four Sons of Aymon."

A wooden shutter slowly opened, accompanied by a medieval-sounding song, revealing two large golden hands with articulated fingers attached to four silver threads, which animated a simple tale of gallant knights.

"The same four sons as in the statue at the lookout point in Bogny-sur-Meuse?" Vicky asked.

"Yes!" Éléa replied. "Apparently, the legend was born here. It was the four giant rocks on the cliffs above the Meuse that inspired the legend. The four sons of Aymon were Charlemagne's sworn enemies, and they were helped by the enchanter Maugis and by Bayard the—"

*Over there!* Brain suddenly shouted.

A golden horse had just appeared in the window.

*No, the other way!* Brain told her. *Stop staring at your Precious and look at what's happening around you.*

Éléa turned. In the square, a brilliant artist had attached puppet heads to both of his arms, each one a perfect simulacrum of the artist himself, creating the illusion of identical triplets.

"Does that guy have three heads?" asked Éléa.

*Not there! In the crowd behind him. There's a man in a long gray coat.*

Flustered, Éléa tried to follow her brain's directions. Brain was always vigilant, even when she was fully focused on something else. She stared at the three-headed puppeteer, then at the dense crowd that formed a semicircle around the improvised stage.

*A man? In a long gray coat?* Her eyes flicked from figure to figure, then suddenly her legs almost gave way beneath her.

She had just spotted Pierre!

Already, the crowd was closing in around him, and the man in the gray coat vanished from her field of vision.

Her eyes grew wide.

Could that really have been her Petrushka?

Well, of course it was him—why else would Brain have alerted her? Suddenly, Éléa felt convinced. Pierre was here, very close, even if there were dozens of tourists, strangers, and whining children separating her from him.

"Did you see something?" Vicky asked.

"I don't know. I thought I . . ."

Éléa was about to dive through the crowd to find her Petrushka—because it had to be him: Nobody could possibly imitate his awkward, puppetlike grace—when a voice behind her froze her to the spot.

"Hello, Éléa."

# 38

## Nanesse

***Milana's railcar workshop, Givet's Finger***

Nanesse drove as far as it was possible for her to drive.

She exited the departmental road to follow the Meuse all the way to Belgium, then turned onto a paved path that led to the Rond Tienne forest. The asphalt of the narrow path soon gave way to gravel, then to dirt. It became more and more difficult to progress along this path, which finally became overgrown with weeds, at which point Nanesse was forced to park her car and continue on foot.

At least it was impossible to get lost here: All she had to do was follow the tracks of an old railway line that ran between the young trees.

When she had left the police station less than an hour ago, nobody had tried to stop her. The receptionist had barely even looked up.

Now, ahead of her, two parallel lines of rusted metal invited her to enter the forest.

Nanesse remembered. She had been here once before, with Renaud.

One week after Milana's death.

She kept walking. She hadn't expected to have to hike so far, and the flat-soled ankle boots she was wearing were not ideal for this kind of terrain. The thin trunks of chestnuts, not even twenty years old, grew through the gaps between crossties that had been abandoned almost a century ago. Back in the old days of prosperity in the Ardennes, trains used to run all over the area, transporting coal, iron, and wood between the hills and the winding river. Now, nobody ever stopped in this border region, and Givet's Finger was no longer the strategic, fortified corridor it once had been.

Nanesse approached the tunnel into which the railway line disappeared. She could see nothing but the brick archway and darkness beyond.

Nanesse had never gone any farther than this. Six years ago, Renaud had asked her to wait for him outside the entrance. She had watched as he'd disappeared into the black hole, carrying his mother's ashes. He had reemerged an hour later, the empty urn in his hands and his eyes full of tears.

But Renaud wasn't here anymore to ask her to wait for him.

Without a moment's hesitation, she went into the tunnel. Daylight filtered through the far end, a hundred yards in the distance, softening the darkness with a dim glow. The air smelled of juniper berries, beer, and urine. The teenagers who came here to drink and make out had presumably marked their territory like dogs. The vaulted ceiling that led toward Milana's mausoleum looked like something from a cathedral, but the place lacked that religious solemnity.

All in all, Nanesse preferred it this way.

Beer and urine were better than holy water and incense.

That was always what she had liked about Renaud and his mother. Their independence of mind. Their refusal to belong to any particular side. Their determination to live always in accordance with their feelings and beliefs. Not to follow the rules.

Milana especially had always jealously guarded her independence. She had been impeccably polite, loving her son and her grandchildren with a self-effacement that seemed almost excessive. Milana was available whenever you asked to see her, and alone the rest of the time. As happy, apparently, to read in her apartment on Rue de Wailly as she was to create puppets in her workshop.

Nanesse spotted the first green glimmers of the clearing. She advanced toward the light, her thoughts focused on her mother-in-law.

Milana had never asked for anything, never seemed to need anything. One question, which Nanesse's mind had never even posed before, haunted her now. Milana had appeared to be an aged artist who had taken an early retirement, one who preferred to devote herself to her art purely for the pleasure and beauty of it. But if that was true, then who had paid the rent on her (admittedly modest) apartment in the center of Charleville? Who had paid for this railcar workshop?

Where had her money come from?

Nanesse had never seen Milana work. And she had certainly never seen her beg.

The tunnel came to an end. The rusted tracks continued on, leading Nanesse into the clearing that opened up in front of her, astonishingly sunny and radiant after the gloom from which she had emerged.

Suddenly, the railcar appeared.

*It must have been so beautiful, once . . .*

Decorated with bright colors and elaborate graffiti, it was like something from a cartoon. One of those old freight wagons made entirely of wood, with no windows—the kind used to transport circus animals, or perhaps even clowns and trapeze artists. A burst of laughter washed up in the middle of a forest. The rusted carcass of a poem.

Nanesse stood still for a few moments, staring at the strange vehicle bathed in light. Up above she saw overhead power lines, remnants of the old railway. So Milana must have been able to hook up her workshop to an electric current. The tracks continued into the distance, between oaks and hazel trees, the otherwise straight line twisted by their roots, as if the forest—beyond this tiny clearing—had taken its revenge on the intruder.

Nanesse kept thinking about Renaud. Her husband used to come here occasionally, four or five times a year, to this place where he had scattered his mother's ashes. To think. To leave flowers. To . . .

Nanesse's heart leapt. A bouquet of anemones had been placed below the step that led to the railcar's door. The flowers were freshly cut.

How long had they been here? One day? Two? Even longer, perhaps? She took a step forward and examined the petals, the leaves. She could swear that these flowers had been placed here only yesterday . . .

But that was impossible. Who could have come to leave flowers? It had been four days since Renaud fell to his death from the lookout point. He was the only one to visit the workshop regularly. Who else could have made the same pilgrimage? And why?

Nanesse opened the door of the railcar and stepped inside.

# 39

## Vicky and Éléa

***Place Ducale, Charleville-Mézières***

"Hello, Éléa," repeated the voice.

The simple fact of hearing her name had paralyzed her, as if a burning blade had been driven into the back of her neck.

That wasn't her Petrushka's voice.

She didn't know anyone but him. She had no friends in Paris, let alone here. Who could have followed her to this square, among this cheering crowd? Who could have recognized her? Spoken her name?

She turned around automatically. The closest stall was unremarkable: a tent, no different from dozens of others that had been put up in Place Ducale. All selling the same supposedly artisanal junk: puppets made in Taiwan or Korea, masks, puppet costumes, puppet theaters, records, and books . . .

The stall a few feet away looked like all the others, but it had an unusual name.

*Librairie Baou.*

"You?" Éléa stammered. "So you're not in Paris anymore?"

The bookseller, standing at the back of his stall, still had that little birdlike crest sticking up from his head, and still looked as elegant as ever in his Scottish tweed suit.

"Oh, I am, I am," he said with a big smile. "But you might have noticed that my bookstore is a tribute to my two greatest passions: Arthur Rimbaud and puppets. I don't think I've missed a single Charleville festival in forty years. A significant portion of my turnover is made here, in fact, so I leave my Parisian bookstore in the hands of an intern and I move down here for the duration of the festival."

*He's hiding something again,* Brain told her.

Éléa no longer knew what to think. She looked at the puppets displayed in the stall: Japanese, Chinese, Hindu, Russian . . . Baou grinned, happy as a child.

A few feet away from them, Lola was still staring admiringly at the golden hands of the Great Puppeteer, which were moving the swords of the four knights. Vicky had also come over to the stall.

"Look around you, Éléa," Baou went on. "Observe the artists' imagination, the tourists' fascination. You have to understand: Men have always dreamed of giving life to figures in their own image, of making them move, making them speak. Ever since . . . well, since the day the daughter of a Cro-Magnon man played with her first doll! Man's desire to create figures that he can animate and manipulate is, essentially, the desire to become a god. Immortal." He gestured at the Japanese puppets. "Do you remember these karakuri ningyōs? These seventeenth-century automata? Did you know that the first talking doll was invented by Edison, almost a hundred and fifty years ago? A simple miniature phonograph hidden inside a porcelain body, which could be activated manually, and—"

"Please stop!" Éléa burst out, unable to stand it anymore. "Stop this cruel game! If you know where Pierre is, tell me!"

The bookseller looked confused. Or was that all part of his act?

"We just want to know for sure that Pierre is still alive," Éléa begged him.

"And that Hans is still alive!" added Vicky behind them. "We'd like to ask him some questions about his double life . . . and maybe beat the crap out of him!"

Baou was still smiling. He appeared to have no idea who Hans was, to know Pierre only from the poems he had published in his fanzine, and to be completely ignorant of the two women's quest.

The Great Puppeteer's show came to an end. One of the four knights had fallen. The shutters closed. A few customers came over to admire the old books in Baou's tent.

*Well, maybe he's telling the truth after all,* suggested Brain. *Maybe you're the one that keeps following him rather than the other way around. Maybe his store truly is a bookstore of requirement and—*

Brain never finished his sentence. He was torn from his own thoughts by Vicky's yell.

"Liar!"

Vicky took a step forward, glaring at Baou, and shoved aside all the books and weird objects laid out on his stand, with no regard for the damage she was causing or the shocked expressions of the other customers. She grabbed the bookseller by his jacket lapels.

"These automata aren't from China or Japan!"

She pointed at the ancient celluloid dolls displayed alongside some art books.

"No," said Baou, choking. "But—"

With her free hand—the one she wasn't using to strangle the bookseller—Vicky picked up an automaton, the identical twin of Kasper.

"Where did this come from?"

"I . . . I don't know."

Éléa had finally understood what was happening.

*You were a bit slow on the uptake this time, Brain . . .*

Vicky had been faster than her, but Éléa's euphoria soon got the better of her jealousy. She stepped closer to Baou too.

"You know Petrushka! That's why you're here!"

The bookseller gasped for breath as the two furies assailed him.

"It was Hans's mother who made these dolls!" Vicky said. "In Florac. So what the hell are they doing in your stall?"

"We'll destroy all your crap if you don't tell us the truth!" Éléa threatened.

"We're not going to warn you again," Vicky added.

This time, Baou panicked. As soon as Vicky released her grip on his lapels, he walked away from his stall, signaling for the two women to follow him toward the archways of Rue du Théâtre. Vicky looked over her shoulder to check on Lola: She was sitting down, delightedly watching a ventriloquist's act that had just started.

"All right, I'll tell you everything," Baou said.

His mask of mystery, like something from a Tim Burton film, was abruptly removed, and he stammered like a prankster caught red-handed.

"I don't know anything about your Petrushka, or your Hans, or whatever you want to call them. On the other hand, I did know the woman who made these puppets . . . Milana."

"Milana?" Vicky repeated, in shock. "I thought Hans's mother was called Marion?"

The bookseller did not reply to this, but his eyes seemed to gleam with a melancholy light.

"Milana was a remarkable artist," he continued. "I was lucky enough to meet her . . . many years ago. She had already stopped performing, back then, but I had the privilege of visiting her workshop, her 'railcar' as she called it. It was . . . like a cross between Ali Baba's cave and Geppetto's studio. That was where she made automata like this one . . ." Here, he gestured at Kasper's twin. "And fascinating copies of Japanese karakuri, kathputli from Rajasthan, Bozo heads from Mali, Karagöz from Turkey, and of course her masterpiece, the work to which she devoted her life . . . her rayok."

"Her what?" said Vicky.

*If you ask your Precious about this,* whispered Brain to Éléa, *I'll go on strike for a month.*

"Her rayok," Baou repeated. "The traditional traveling puppet theater of eastern Europe. A sort of barrel organ in which the perforated card is replaced by cutout figures. You look inside through magnifying glasses while the puppeteer unfurls a strip of paper that tells the story. It's like an ancestor of the television. Milana's rayok was the most sophisticated one I've ever seen . . ."

"Okay," Vicky interrupted, "you can tell us the technical details later. Where can we find this amazing woman of yours?"

"Oh, Milana was never *mine*," Baou said defensively.

"Whatever," said Éléa. "Just give us her address."

"Well, that would be difficult."

"Why?"

He looked up at the overcast sky. After four days of almost ceaseless rain, the clouds looked exhausted. And yet one drop did roll through the deep wrinkles around his eye.

"Because she's dead. She passed away six years ago. She wanted to be cremated. So her address . . . I suppose it's wherever the wind has blown her."

Éléa and Vicky hesitated for an instant, shared a glance, and nodded at each other without even speaking a word. Éléa was certain that the other woman was feeling the same thing she was: Baou wasn't telling them the whole truth.

The relationship he'd had with this Milana—their mother-in-law?—was far more intimate than that between a little-known artist and her admirer. And they were not going to leave him in peace until he had told them everything!

It was at precisely this moment that the epic fantasy film someone seemingly had been shooting in the square suddenly turned into a horror movie. Men and women in uniform came running from every direction. Police officers, some of them dressed in riot gear, started shoving people and yelling: "Get back! Get back!" With stunning speed, they established a security perimeter around a few isolated tents, three empty benches, and a row of recycling bins. "Keep back!" they bellowed. "Keep back!"

From every corner of Place Ducale there came screams of panic, followed by the calm, clear orders of schoolteachers taking control of their classes. The crowd moved back. Vans pulled up, and soldiers leapt out of them.

Baou was the quickest to react. With surprising agility, the old bookseller ran over to Lola and picked her up. He whispered a few words of reassurance into her ear as he carried her, then placed her into her mother's arms.

"Thank you," said Vicky. "If it wasn't for you—"

"Get out of here!" Baou hissed.

Patrols of armed men were everywhere. A police captain brushed past them, walkie-talkie in hand, glaring at the crowds around him.

"You need to get away now," Baou told the two women. "If someone's reported a possible terrorist attack, they might seal off the whole neighborhood."

But Éléa wasn't ready to leave without learning more.

"We're not going anywhere until you—"

"Go to Givet's Finger," Baou blurted out. "The old abandoned railway line. Just follow the tracks as far as you can, and you'll find Milana's railcar workshop."

# 40

## Nanesse

***Milana's railcar workshop, Givet's Finger***

As soon as she entered the workshop, Nanesse breathed a sigh of relief.

She had been expecting the worst. The railcar had been abandoned for six years, so there was every chance that the young beer-drinkers from the tunnel, or some other visitors, had come here.

She examined the long, rectangular room.

Nothing had been vandalized. Milana's lair had been left untouched, as if it was some sacred mausoleum. In the middle of the space was a long and narrow sewing table. Arranged around it in dozens of polished wooden boxes were accessories in every imaginable shape, made of every imaginable material: mother-of-pearl buttons, scraps of felt, paper streamers, cotton balls, glass beads, balls of wool, gold and silver threads . . . Watching from the shadows were puppets of all ages and from all places, some of them ancient, their colors faded, others still unfinished, their eyes not yet painted, their hair half unstuck.

Milana had continued giving life to her little cloth children until her final day.

Nanesse's gaze came to rest in one of the corners of the railcar. Her attention had been caught by a strange, colored box, the shape and size of a large doghouse, resting on two trestles. One of the box's angled planes was made entirely of glass.

Was this the famous rayok? The paper theater to which Milana had devoted her life?

Was it still in working order? Would it be a violation of Milana and Renaud's memory if she tried to start it up?

Nanesse stepped forward, continuing to look around the workshop. So nobody had come here to pillage this treasure in all the time that had passed since Milana's death? Why? Because the place was so remote, so hard to find? Because nobody was really that interested in a bunch of old dolls and rusted automata? Or because Renaud had, until four days ago, guarded it vigilantly?

*Until four days ago,* Nanesse repeated to herself.

Certain details took her by surprise. Even beyond the flowers left outside the door, she felt sure that somebody had come inside, not too long ago. She could see footprints ahead of her own feet: Muddy soles had left their mark on the old floorboards.

Size 12?

She also spotted gaps in the layer of dust. Certain objects had been moved: scissors, reels of thread, cans of paint . . . Recently.

*Before or after Renaud's death?*

But who could have come here since then?

Those men with burned faces?

Had she taken a big risk in coming here alone, to such a remote spot, without telling anyone? Without even leaving a note or sending a message to Katel?

Nanesse closed the door of the railcar. She could now hear no sound from outside, and very little light filtered in. The only openings in the car—long, narrow ventilation gaps—were mostly hidden behind piles of various objects: cloths, boards, cardboard boxes. Nanesse moved toward the nearest opening, to clear the pile of junk out of the way and let some light in. She started to push away some fabric, some old papers, and then suddenly she froze.

In a picture frame nearby was a large photograph that Nanesse instantly recognized.

In the image, Renaud was posing beside his mother, in front of an immaculate white curtain. It was their favorite portrait, taken years ago, in honor of Milana's fiftieth birthday. This was the picture that Renaud had placed in front of his mother's coffin during the ceremony at the crematorium. She hadn't seen it since. Apparently, he'd brought it here.

But, before leaving the photograph in the railcar, her husband had added a few handwritten words . . .

*For you, Mom. Eternally.*

*I love you*

*I love you*

*I love you*

. . . and he had signed it, three times:

*Renaud*

*Hans*

*Pierre*

Shocked, Nanesse stumbled backward, unconsciously seeking out the stability of the wall or the table or the door . . . anything at all.

*Renaud had signed it three times . . .*

She didn't hear the railcar door open behind her.

She didn't see the two figures approaching.

In the end, all she heard was what sounded like a gasp, or a sob.

And she turned around.

# 41

## KATEL

***Place Ducale, Charleville-Mézières***

Place Ducale was sealed off by police tape, held up every five yards by an officer. The spectators were packed outside it: a surreal crowd of adults and children, dwarves and giants, fantastical monsters and extraterrestrial creatures.

Within the tape, the square was empty, except for a team of ten bomb disposal experts, hidden behind a wall of shields, who were advancing cautiously toward the three recycling bins.

"These really are crazy times we're living in," Katel remarked.

She was standing at the line between the crowd and the empty square, next to her assistant.

"Any joker can force everyone to stop what they're doing," she said, "and all it takes is one phone call. In fact, whoever did this might be in the crowd right now, watching us and laughing his head off."

In front of them, the safety team had been deployed, its number growing constantly. Six riot vans blocked Rue de la République. Squads of police from Sedan and Reims had been called in as backup. Flashing lights painted the walls of the surrounding buildings a flickering blue, just like in one of those American crime shows.

"I think it's impressive," said Jérémy. "Kind of moving, actually. Seeing all these forces mobilized at the same time."

The captain observed the twenty or so cops holding up the tape around the sealed-off zone.

"Give me a break! The antiterrorist squad is in charge now. We're just a bunch of extras. Look at Mehdi, Mathias, and Will . . . I mean, they may not be Sherlock Holmes, but surely they deserve better than just standing there like fence posts."

For once, Jérémy did not back down from a confrontation with his boss.

"But that's the idea, Katel. We each have our part to play. It's great, don't you think, this cooperation between different services? Police, army, CRS . . ."

"Yeah, it's just like being at a riot!"

Katel checked her watch. Place Ducale had been sealed off for almost an hour already. The bomb squad appeared to be advancing, behind their shields, at about one centimeter per minute. The lock of black hair fell over her left eye.

"For fuck's sake," she muttered. "I've got things to do, you know! I need to investigate this case and—"

Lieutenant Bonello cut in: "No, Katel! You can't leave now. Not in the middle of the Reinforced Security Level of Operation Vigipirate. We may not be playing the lead role here, but . . ."

Katel was preparing to reassure Jérémy. After all, she wasn't completely insane! She was in charge of the entire brigade. If a bomb really had been planted in that bin and it exploded, the panic would be indescribable, and her men would need to intervene immediately. Even if her intuition told her that this alert was nothing but a hoax and . . .

As she was thinking this, her cell phone buzzed inside her pocket.

A message from Jan Horák.

It took Katel a moment to remember that this was the name of her contact for the eastern European zone of Interpol. Jan sounded pretty pleased with himself. He told her he had been through the entire legal file for that fire in Pilsen in June 1976.

Jan had emailed Katel the scanned documents, but he wanted to give her the most important news by text: Libor Slavik's wife, Zuzana, had been killed in the fire. The documents were categorical on that point: Her corpse had been recovered and identified.

The Slavik boys, on the other hand, had survived. They had been badly disfigured, but they were alive. Back then, on the eastern side of the Iron Curtain, plastic surgery had not been an option. The boys had spent a long time sheltering in a military hospital in Prague before returning to their father's address in Pilsen, at which point all trace of them was lost.

*All trace of them was lost,* Katel read again.

*Well, I've found them, Jan, forty-seven years later.*

*They threw one man down a mountainside, then murdered another man in his cellar . . .*

*And they're still at large now!*

# 42

## Nanesse, Vicky, and Éléa

***Milana's railcar workshop, Givet's Finger***

Two women.

Two women had entered the railcar and were standing behind her.

One of them blond, the other dark haired.

For a moment, Nanesse wondered who they were, where they had come from, what obscure motivation could have driven them to follow that abandoned railway line, to go through that tunnel, to penetrate this clearing, climb onto the step of the railcar, and open the door to this workshop.

Then she followed their gaze.

The two women were staring, as if hypnotized, at the framed photograph of Renaud and Milana, and at the three signatures scrawled beneath it.

*I love you*

*I love you*

*I love you*

*Renaud*

*Hans*

*Pierre*

Instantly, Nanesse understood.

These two women must be the wives of Hans Bernard and Pierre Rousseau, just as she was the wife of Renaud Duval.

Three men, three women.

Which one loved Hans, and which one Pierre?

The blond woman was holding hands with a little girl. Pierre's daughter, or Hans's? This woman was pretty in her own way; her face was a little severe looking, but she gave off a sort of raw animal energy, and Nanesse could see how that might have aroused the hunting instinct in a man.

The brunette was more beautiful; she had a doll-like body, with black brambles tattooed on her arms, a strange electronic ring on her finger, slender shivering legs, and a sort of bewitching absence in her eyes. Her beauty was like a suit of armor, and Nanesse imagined that she kept her heart locked up in a strongbox, protected from hopeful knights.

They were young too. As she held her breath, Nanesse prayed that Hans Bernard and Pierre Rousseau actually existed, that they were not merely identities used by Renaud to cheat on her with these two women, ravishing the heart of one while starting a family with the other.

The blonde must have been ten years younger than Nanesse, which meant she was ten years younger than Renaud too. The brunette wasn't even thirty yet; maybe as young as twenty-five . . . Was it possible that Renaud could have had a relationship with someone that young?

No!

No!

No!

*I love you*

*I love you*

*I love you*

And yet all three of them had signed the same portrait.

*Renaud*

*Hans*

*Pierre*

Was she going crazy?

"Whoa!" exclaimed the little girl as she looked around the workshop. "It's really cool in here! There are Kaspers everywhere."

She moved through the railcar like an explorer, going into ecstasies over each new puppet she encountered. For a moment the three women just stood there looking at each other, a nervous smile on their lips.

Nanesse was the first to break the strange solemnity of the scene.

"My name is Agnès Duval," she said, holding out a trembling hand to the other two. "Until just now, I thought that this railcar was my mother-in-law's workshop and that only my husband, Renaud Duval, knew about its existence."

"Yeah, well, nothing's quite the way it seems," replied the blonde. "That's certainly how it's been for me recently. Until a few days ago, I thought that handsome, gray-eyed man in the photograph was my lover and the adoptive father of my daughter. My name is Vicky Malzieu."

They shook hands hesitantly.

"And you?" Nanesse asked.

The dark-haired girl moved her lips but no sound came out of her mouth. She was like a mute ventriloquist without a dummy. Vicky put an arm around her shoulder and gave her an encouraging look. At last the young brunette spoke.

"Éléa. Éléa Simon. And I have always known that that gray-eyed man is the one true love of my life."

Nanesse put a hand on the long sewing table to keep herself from falling.

"And," she said, forcing a smile, "was the mother of your, um . . . Hans"—here, Vicky gave a quick nod—"and your . . . Pierre"—Éléa's lips twitched—"also an artist? Someone with a gift for acting, painting, sewing . . . ?"

Vicky nodded again, unless she was just shaking. Nanesse turned to look again at the three names.

*I love you*

*I love you*

*I love you*

*Renaud*

*Hans*

*Pierre*

"Renaud is dead," she murmured in a soft, almost motherly voice. "I sincerely hope for your sakes that Hans and Pierre are alive."

The brightness in the two women's eyes was enough to convince her that each felt absolutely certain that her man still lived. And yet a voice inside Nanesse's head kept telling her that three different men could not look so similar.

As cruel as this might appear in the face of the women's hopes, Nanesse knew that Renaud, Hans, and Pierre were one and the same man. And that, consequently, all three of them were dead.

They were startled by the sound of chimes breaking the silence, like a musical box forgotten in an attic, its handle turned by a ghost. Three notes on a xylophone. A festive, memorable melody.

Vicky looked at her daughter. "Lola, what did you touch?"

The little girl had put Kasper down near the strange doghouse that looked like a prehistoric television.

"Nothing, Mommy. Well, only this."

Lola pointed to the angled glass pane that she couldn't touch, even when she stood on tiptoes, and to the buttons beside it, which were within her reach.

The chimes sped up. Lola's eyes shone. No doubt she believed that all the puppets in the railcar were about to stand up and start dancing. That this workshop was magical, a fairy grotto.

Inside the rayok, a glow lit up the angled glass.

"Lola!" Vicky said menacingly. "What did you do now?"

A bluish light filled the car. Éléa stood staring, her mouth agape.

*Some new technological wonder? Your Precious will turn green with envy!*

"Shush!" Nanesse hissed. "Listen!"

The chimes slowed down, becoming less intense, before fading to silence. A second later, they heard a voice.

"Hello."

Nanesse immediately recognized the voice of her mother-in-law.

"Welcome," continued the voice. "Although I have no way of knowing this for sure, I think you are all here. So now we can begin. I have a story—a very old story—to tell you."

My name is Mina. I was born in 1956, in Czechoslovakia, a country that no longer exists. A country that young people these days probably believe never existed. A country with a name that some people can't pronounce. So I prefer to say I was born in Bohemia—the name of the largest historical region of my homeland.

In France it is called Bohême. But . . .

# 43

## Amos and Kristof

***Milana's railcar workshop, Givet's Finger***

*"They're inside,"* Amos wrote. *"I can hear them. They're talking."*

Kristof, enclosed in his perpetual silence, looked at the railcar. He could make out only vague shadows behind the narrow gaps in the boards of the railcar's walls. He watched them for a moment, then his gaze scanned the clearing around them. Nothing moved, apart from the branches of hazel trees silently shaken by the wind.

From his observation post, crouching in the ferns and tall grass, with one eye on the tunnel entrance and the other on the railcar, Kristof could see everything. He typed another message for his brother. The tactile screen of the insideONE tablet vibrated.

*"What are they saying?"*

Trying to hear better, Amos raised his head and shoulders above the rampart of ferns. Kristof grabbed him by the sleeve, then wrote.

*"Stay under cover!"*

It was an automatic reflex for him, watching over his brother like this. He was Amos's eyes, just as Amos was his ears. They trusted each other, always, a blind (and deaf) trust, like that of two trapeze artists swinging above the void. If there was a noise, Amos would inform him in a matter of seconds. And Kristof described to Amos everything of interest that he saw. Naturally, these vital senses of vision and hearing connected less rapidly via a tablet than they would have through the neurons of a single brain. But each of their senses was far sharper than any normal person's.

The proof lay in the fact that they had been able to follow Agnès Duval to Bruno Pluvier's house. Amos had listened to their conversation. After that, a few phone calls to the least densely populated department of France had been enough for them to discover that a certain Marion Bernard had, for years, given the schoolchildren of Florac . . . a performance of *Petrushka*.

Eight hours of driving later, when they reached the banks of the Tarn, they'd found Vicky Malzieu and her daughter asking all the villagers to help them find Hans Bernard. The woman and the little girl had practically fallen into their arms. Kristof and Amos hadn't lost sight of them since then, although it was hardly a surprise that their final destination should be Mina's workshop.

A new message tickled Kristof's fingertips.

*"I need to get closer to hear what they're saying."*

Kristof assessed the risks. The railcar door was closed, and the openings were too narrow to betray them, but the three women could easily come outside at any moment.

*"Is the kid with them?"*

*"Yes,"* wrote Amos. *"I heard her. Her mother just told her off."*

*"Why?"*

*"I don't know."*

Kristof watched Amos's hand. It was trembling. His head leaned down lower, like an animal concentrating on a distant sound. Kristof knew that Amos would have liked to spare the little girl, to sacrifice only the three women; Amos was far weaker and less determined than he was.

*"Tough shit,"* typed Kristof. *"You didn't hesitate yesterday, when you were holding her above the Tarn."*

*"We never talked about killing her. We kidnapped her so we could scare her into telling us where her father was hiding."*

Kristof cracked his knuckles, a habit that became harder to resist whenever he was nervous. Inside the railcar, nothing moved. The tactile screen vibrated as he typed his response.

*"True, little brother, but things have changed since yesterday. Fate has brought those three women together in the same remote spot. We'll never get a better chance to keep our promise."*

Bitter tears welled in Amos's sightless eyes.

*"We never promised to kill a child. Papa wouldn't have wanted that."*

His little brother's sentimentality annoyed Kristof. It had annoyed him ever since he could remember. He stared imperiously at Amos, even though he knew perfectly well that it would have no effect on his blind brother. Surrounded by total silence, Kristof looked at the black tunnel, then at the railcar, before typing:

*"If you cut a branch, the fruit dies too."*

# PART TWO

## Mina

# MY INN AT THE SIGN OF THE GREAT BEAR

"My Bohemia" by Arthur Rimbaud

# MINA'S STORY

## THE OTHER SIDE OF THE CURTAIN

***June 1976***

Now you know my crime, and you know the circumstances. Do you consider them extenuating? My experiences during the Prague Spring when I was eleven; the Russian invasion, one night in August 1968; the meeting of the Moor and Petrushka, and my meeting with Libor; our years spent traveling around Bohemia; being raped every night; the child growing inside my womb; the caravan fire. Now I can tell you what happened next. Now I can tell you how I got away.

The flames were still dancing when I ran into the forest, fleeing Libor's threats and the vile images of the three burned bodies. I could still make out the blaze behind me—a red ball on the horizon, hours before dawn, like a premature sunrise.

I found refuge in Pilsen with a troupe of amateur puppeteers whom I had met quite often during the previous five years. They agreed to let me stay with them for a few nights. Like all Czech artists, they were starving and frightened. I knew they wouldn't denounce me to the StB, but I also knew they wouldn't be prepared to die for me if Libor ever found me.

And he would find me. It was just a question of time, of days. As soon as he had buried Zuzana, as soon as Amos and Kristof were out of the hospital, he would hunt me down and make me pay.

We were playing a game of hide-and-seek . . . to the death.

The small town of Pilsen was famous for three things. Its beer, the most famous in the country; its car factories, created by its native son Emil Škoda; and, of course, its puppets. Even during the Cold War, Pilsen remained the capital of puppetry. For centuries, traveling Czech artists had elevated the manipulation of wooden marionettes into the realm of pure art, making puppetry a source of national pride. The Czech authorities used puppetry as a tool of diplomacy and propaganda at festivals all over the world dedicated to international peace.

That summer, a small French delegation stayed in Pilsen. It had been sent by the cultural arm of the French embassy in Prague to recruit artists, with a special eye to the World Festival of Puppet Theaters in Charleville. Since the creation of the festival in 1961, artists from the East had performed there every year.

The head of the French delegation was a man named Baptiste Marou, who preferred to go by the nickname of Baou. The first time I met him, I thought him ugly, pretentious, and distant. He looked like all those western Communists who came to visit us from time to time, who looked at us the way people look at zoo animals, careful only to see what conformed to their ideals and to close their eyes to the rest.

I explained to him that I wanted to join the team of puppeteers who would travel to France to perform, and that I was ready to do anything to achieve my ambition, even if it meant giving him all that remained of my honor and my money.

Baou didn't ask for either of those things. Against all my expectations, he agreed to add my name to the festival's schedule, to place me under the protection of the French embassy, and to reserve a seat for me on the delegation's official coach, which would leave the next day from Pilsen to the Ardennes.

Possibly he was surprised by the quality of my spoken French.

Probably he was genuinely impressed by my talent as a puppeteer.

Almost certainly he was astonished that I was able to recite several poems by Rimbaud—his favorite poet—in their entirety.

And no doubt, too, he was touched by the story of a little orphan of the Prague Spring. I told him everything. The rapes I had suffered since the age of thirteen. The beatings. My pregnancy. My escape. The only detail I omitted was the crime I had committed.

I could tell from the way he looked at me that I had bewitched him, even if he never touched me.

Baou saved me, taking advantage of his spheres of influence and of the thawing political climate at the time: one year after the Helsinki Accords, which marked a pause in the Cold War, and one year before the Charter 77 manifesto, signed by more than two hundred Czech intellectuals, to defy the Communist government.

I moved to the West in an almost surreal moment of euphoria, leaving behind a country still jubilant over the historic events of June 20, 1976, when a miraculous penalty kick by the new national hero, Antonín Panenka, made the Czechoslovakian soccer team the champions of Europe.

On the final day of the World Festival of Puppet Theaters, in Place Ducale, as twenty-odd Czechoslovak puppeteers and an equal number of StB agents piled into the coach for the return trip to Pilsen, Baou came to see me in my hotel room.

"Mina, you're not planning to go back, are you?"

"I'll get you in trouble if I don't."

"You'll get in a lot more trouble yourself if you do."

Baou looked out the window at the waiting coach, then turned to me.

"Libor and his sons have left the hospital. He's enlisted the aid of the first secretary of the Czechoslovak Communist Party, Gustáv

Husák, to track you down. The official version—the one that's printed in the newspapers—is that it was an accident. As you can imagine, they don't want any scandals. But the StB has you on their wanted list as a murderer."

I realized that Baou must have known the whole story all along.

"You'll need new ID papers. Libor won't find it easy to get out of Czechoslovakia, but it's a possibility we have to take into account. As is the possibility that, one day, the Iron Curtain will no longer exist and people will be able to travel freely all across Europe."

Despite the seriousness of the situation, I couldn't help smiling at the absurdity of such a utopian idea.

"I have money," I told him. "I can pay for the fake papers."

"I know a lot of people," he said. "I could help you."

I moved closer to Baou. I still found him ugly, but I had come to understand that his pretentiousness was a form of self-protection, his remoteness a form of modesty. I wanted to kiss him, not out of desire, but simply to thank him. He was the first man who had ever shown me the slightest affection.

He gently pushed me away.

"You need to escape, Mina. Don't waste time. The StB agents will start worrying soon. They'll come and look for you."

I felt oddly perplexed. Until then, my personal laws of survival could be summed up by two simple rules: Men used their strength, and women used their charms. Why was Baou helping me if he didn't want anything in exchange?

"I'm a strange animal," Baou explained shyly. "A Communist, a poet . . . and a homosexual. Now listen, Mina: You should make as many new identities as you can. You and your child will need protection from Libor, because he will never stop seeking revenge."

I did what he told me. I escaped. The agents of the StB might enjoy absolute power in Czechoslovakia, but in France all they could do was wait in the hotel lobby and hope that I showed up.

# 44

***Milana's railcar workshop, Givet's Finger***

The cardboard-and-felt figures in the rayok moved past while Milana's voice kept speaking. The drawings were beautifully simple. A small caravan remained in the center while the backgrounds behind it changed. The plains, villages, and mountains of Bohemia, magnified by the alternating play of light as days became nights became days . . . During each day, spectators gathered to applaud the artists as they emerged from the caravan, dressed for their performance.

*"We achieved great success at the International Puppet Festival in Pilsen, which brought together artists from the whole world, even from the West."*

At night, all that remained were a few stars winking in the black sky, and Milana's voice.

*"I lay down every night and counted the constellations, waiting for my torturer to fall asleep."*

Agnès, Vicky, and Éléa leaned close to the glass screen, watching and listening attentively, fascinated by this paper cinema. At first Lola had insisted on being allowed to watch too, but since she was too short she had to be held up, and she had soon grown bored. She didn't understand anything about all these tales of tanks and parachutists, and she found the succession of sketched images too slow. Why should she waste her time on an old machine like that when she had hundreds of cartoons to watch on her tablet?

Or a cavern full of dolls! She sat down in a corner of the railcar and had fun dressing Kasper with all those amazing costumes of pirates, policemen, princes, ninjas . . .

*Hans had gray eyes,* thought Vicky. Just like Libor Slavik. Was it also from his father that Hans had inherited his love of traveling, that nomadic lifestyle? Had he ever known his father? Had he known what his father was—a rapist?

*Petrushka,* thought Éléa. Always Petrushka. Libor Slavik had had the grace of a fairground strongman who could transform himself into a ballerina. Was it from him that Pierre had inherited his talent as a dancer? Had Pierre known his father? What had happened to him?

*Just listen to the story,* Brain advised her. *Don't think about anything else—leave that to me. I'm recording it all, analyzing it. The Prague Spring, the cities of Bohemia, the art of Czech puppetry . . .*

*So Milana was born in Czechoslovakia,* thought Nanesse. She had managed to hide it, all those years, because she'd been practically bilingual by the age of ten. And a gifted puppeteer. And Renaud? When would Renaud appear in Milana's story?

*"Can you hear them?"* wrote Kristof.

The two brothers had moved closer to the railcar. Kristof was still watching their surroundings, his eyes switching from the tunnel entrance to the trees of the clearing, while Amos, his ear pressed to the gap between two planks in the workshop door, listened intently.

*"What are they saying?"* Kristof demanded.

*"Nothing."*

*"What do you mean, nothing? Can you hear them or not?"*

*"They're not the ones speaking. It's Milana."*

*"Milana?"*

If Kristof had not been mute, he might well have cried out so loudly that the others would have heard him.

*"MILANA?"* he wrote several times. *"MI-la-NA."*

The insideONE tablet included some incredible tools that had helped to revolutionize the lives of blind people: autocorrection, copy-and-paste keys, capital letters, 3D emoji.

*"She left them a message,"* Amos explained. *"A long story."*

*"And what's she saying?"*

*"That you used to pull the ears of our horse Kinsky, and that I drew sunsets . . . I'd forgotten all that."*

Kristof, too, was plunged into the past for an instant. Kinsky. He hadn't thought about that horse in years. As for Amos's drawings . . . Yes, his brother had been genuinely talented. He could have become a great artist. That painful memory only reinforced his steely determination.

*"Perfect. If she's going to tell them her life story, that gives us time."*

*"Time for what?"*

Kristof noticed the sweat trickling off Amos's fingers, onto the keyboard of his screen. He watched his brother pressing his ear to the door, his face showing all the emotions provoked by the story he was hearing, then angrily typed:

*"To keep our promise! To make them suffer as much as Mama suffered."*

# 45

***Place Ducale, Charleville-Mézières***

Captain Saint-Hilaire, Lieutenant Massigue, and Sergeant Dargonne were the three most experienced members of the Grand Est Bomb Disposal Unit. The three of them had defused several thousand bombs between Verdun and the Chemin des Dames. They had encountered bombs of all calibers and all weights, left there by various armies.

And yet, despite their being protected by ten CRS officers, each one of them holding up a riot shield, when the remote-controlled robot began to cut open the third recycling bin at the junction of Place Ducale and Rue de la République—the one in which the bomb had supposedly been left—the three men's hearts simultaneously skipped a beat.

There really was a bomb in there.

As soon as the lid of the recycling bin went flying, everything was out of their control.

They had just looked the devil in the eye.

# MINA'S STORY

## The Ghost Army

***January 1977***

I chose the name Milana Duval—an unusual first name and a very common surname—and four months later, I gave birth, at the Manchester Hospital in Charleville, to a little boy. *Renaud.* He was a healthy child who took to my breast easily, so the nurses let me leave after only two days.

I went to declare his birth myself. In the mayor's office, I held Renaud in my lap. I was hoping that the bureaucrat would be charmed by this, but I ended up with some young woman who seemed to believe that she had been granted a divine mission. She had a diamond ring on her finger and a red wart under her nose, and she was zealous. She was intrigued by my accent, which I later managed to erase. Perhaps she was intrigued by my fear too. But I had paid enough for my fake ID papers that they appeared completely legitimate, and—after interrogating me for what felt like hours—she finally stamped the birth certificate.

*Renaud Duval, born January 29, 1977.*

*You should make as many new identities as you can,* Baou had told me. I spent the whole of that night thinking about his advice.

*You and your child will need protection from Libor, because he will never stop seeking revenge.*

At five in the morning, I was breastfeeding Renaud in my apartment on Rue de Wailly. All the documents I had ordered from the counterfeiter were spread out on the table. I had several identities, but my baby had only one. As a single mother, I realized how vulnerable my child would be if Libor ever found him, in a year, in ten years, even in thirty years.

So I wrapped Renaud up in a blanket, gathered a few belongings, and set off for the train station in Charleville. My train reached the Gare de l'Est in Paris at noon. One hour later, I was sitting in the mayor's office in the eighteenth arrondissement, at counter number four, facing a bureaucrat who seemed absolutely charmed by my son's little smile.

I gave him my second ID card, in the name of Judith Rousseau, along with a birth certificate, stained by curdled breast milk, and an embarrassed smile. "Sorry for the mess!" I had simply replaced the name of the Manchester Hospital in Charleville with that of the Bichat Hospital in Paris. A crude forgery that I had put together and then photocopied at a print store near the station. I had gambled on the idea that the mayor's office employee would have no reason to doubt the document's authenticity. Who bothers falsifying the name of a maternity hospital?

Certainly not a tired but radiant mother who walks in with the baby in her arms!

The man stamped the birth certificate without posing a single question, then congratulated me on the name I had chosen, which he said was timeless.

*Pierre Rousseau, born January 29, 1977.*

According to French law, parents have three days after the birth to declare their child's existence. I arrived in Mende on the afternoon of the last day, following a long trip by train and then bus. I chose Lozère more or less at random. I wanted somewhere a long way from

Charleville and the eastern border, and the farthest possible distance from a big city. If Libor tracked me down, or if he paid someone else to do it, I wanted to be able to change my life overnight. To vanish into a new identity, leaving behind only the shell of the old one, with nothing to connect the two. Like someone in a witness protection scheme, I thought.

This might seem crazy or impossible, but it all went according to plan with almost disconcerting ease. In Mende, a smiling, gray-haired woman barely even glanced at the birth certificate from the Lozère Hospital, which had, this time, been stained with vomit. "Sorry about the mess!" Her attention was fully focused on Renaud, or Pierre, who appeared to be mesmerized by the gleaming, heart-shaped pendant that hung from the woman's neck.

"What a cutie pie!" she gushed. "And look how awake he is! Oh, I can't wait to be a grandmother . . . And his name is Hans, is that right? Hans Bernard?"

A second later, she stamped the paper in front of her, and Hans was officially a person.

*Hans Bernard, born January 29, 1977.*

As far as the French state was concerned, he really existed, as did Pierre Rousseau and Renaud Duval.

One baby, with three lives—real, official, certified lives.

I understood then that, in the eyes of the French state, a single baby could be officially declared dozens of times, if only his parents thought it worth their while. A life is more than a piece of paper, signed by some bureaucrat who saw the child for only a few minutes. Perhaps there are—in France, and elsewhere—armies of ghosts, virtual citizens living fictitious lives, backup identities, paper twins or triplets, who have been declared born, then married, then deceased, without ever having taken a breath.

I left the mayor's office in Mende with my baby clasped to my chest and wrapped in a large knotted scarf. It was an unseasonably warm winter day, the kind of early spring that sometimes descends on the South of France and makes you regret having to travel north again. I crossed the Lot River back to the train station, looking up at the black pines on Mount Mimat. The Causses and the Cévennes were nearby, and I was attracted to the idea of staying there. But Charleville—or Paris—awaited us.

My son was trying to find my breast.

"Hang on, little one," I whispered. "Just wait, my angel. My darling. My—"

And for the first time, I asked myself the question I had not had the courage to anticipate.

*My Renaud?*

*My Pierre?*

*My Hans?*

What was I—his mother—going to call him?

# 46

***Milana's railcar workshop, Givet's Finger***

"Will Daddy be here soon?"

Lola shouted the question, to make herself heard over Milana's voice. Vicky touched the button that controlled the paper figurines, and they all froze instantly. The rayok's screen darkened. A strange silence fell, broken only by a few sounds from outside. The sigh of the wind, the crack of a branch—nothing sinister.

"Will Daddy be here soon?" Lola repeated.

The little girl had apparently not been listening to the rayok's story; she'd been too busy dressing up Kasper as a knight. Presumably it was the sound of the name Hans, spoken several times by this exquisite machine, that had popped the bubble of imagination in which she had taken refuge.

Nobody answered her. The silence that followed seemed even heavier.

"Will Daddy be—"

"Yes," Vicky said at last, in a shaky voice. "Yes, sweetie, you'll see Daddy again soon. I . . . I promise."

Éléa bit her lip.

Nanesse lowered her head.

Lola started playing with her knight again, soothed by this news and happy in the certainty that her doll would soon come to life again and talk to her, because now she knew his secret. The old bookseller had whispered it into her ear earlier, at the puppet festival.

She just had to wait for Daddy to come back and fix Kasper!

Amos, his head leaning against the railcar's door, quickly typed a few words on his tactile tablet.

*"They're not talking anymore. Where are you?"*

Kristof had moved away. While Mina was speaking, he had walked back to the Skoda Karoq, hidden near the parking lot, and opened the trunk, intending to return as quickly as he could. He received his brother's message as he was exiting the tunnel.

*"It's okay,"* Kristof wrote. *"I'm almost there."*

The blind man listened even more intently through the thin gap in the wooden door. What else could he do, lost in the dark as he was, without Kristof to hold his hand? His heart was pounding now. He imagined the women in the railcar could hear it as clearly as if someone was hammering on the door.

If the door opened now, he would be caught.

Automatically, he touched the bag of cremation ashes tucked in the front pocket of his coat. Then he heard a new voice from inside the railcar.

"Perfect, Vicky," said Éléa. "Now that your sweetie has been reassured, could you please press the button on the paper television again?"

No answer. No sound at all, until Vicky spoke anxiously.

"Agnès, are you okay? Do you want us to keep listening?"

Mina's story, Amos realized, must have been like a punch in the face for Agnès Duval. How could she ever have imagined that her kind mother-in-law—that gentle and solitary artist who was such a loving grandmother—could be a murderer?

The blind man savored the moment: This was it, when the masks fell away, and the bad guys became the good guys, and vice versa. The ashes, inside the bag, weighed heavy on his heart; he wanted to get this over with. He could distinctly hear his brother's footsteps coming toward him. They sounded more labored than usual. His senses on high alert, he could also hear a barely perceptible lapping sound, could smell the discreet odor of gasoline. So Kristof must be coming over, carrying the two jerry cans of gas they had put in the trunk of the Skoda.

Nothing would make him back down now.

Inside his head, Amos repeated the words his father had said to Mina at the fire: the words that Mina had just spoken, and which had haunted him since he was eleven years old.

*I'll hurt your child, and your child's future children.*

His father's anger had subsided the last time they'd spoken, five days ago, beside the statue of the Four Sons of Aymon.

Amos had not been able to stop thinking about it since.

# 47

## Five Days Ago

***Wednesday, September 13, 2023***
***Statue of the Four Sons of Aymon, Bogny-sur-Meuse***

Libor, Kristof, and Amos all sat in the Skoda in the parking lot close to the lookout point. Amid the darkness of night, all they could see were the distant glimmers of the villages in the valley below; the monumental statue of the Four Sons of Aymon, lit up by a single lamp; and the pale shape of Renaud Duval's car, parked a little farther off, under the low branches of an oak tree.

Well, Libor and Kristof could see it, at least. They had watched the headlights coming toward them, the white 307 stopping beside the tree, then Renaud Duval getting out of the car and walking quickly toward the steps that led up to the lookout point.

Sitting behind the wheel, Libor turned on his phone light, making it as dim as possible so that it wouldn't be visible from the outside, then turned to his two sons in the back seat.

He placed his five fingers on his mouth and said: "Thank you!"

That way, both his sons understood, Kristof by watching and Amos by listening.

Libor had spent two years learning sign language, at the Jakobson Institute in Prague, between 1977 and 1979. Since then, he had gotten into the habit of expressing himself with words and hand signals at the same time. Throughout Kristof's and Amos's adolescence, long before the invention of the insideONE tablet, their father had been their sole connection, the only way they could communicate with each other. When Amos wanted to talk to Kristof, he had only one option: to ask his father to translate his question into sign language. And the same was true for his brother's response.

Had their father always been a trustworthy translator? Amos wondered. Neutral? Impartial? He'd held absolute sway over his two sons.

"Thank you," Libor repeated, moving his hands. "Without the two of you, after all these years, I would never have tracked down Mina and Renaud Duval. You both played your roles perfectly. But now, I need to go and meet your brother on my own."

Amos heard the clicking sound made by the safety on a pistol being released. He had learned to identify the sounds made by different guns, and this, he knew, was a CZ 75 semiautomatic, his father's weapon of choice, and the StB's weapon of choice too.

"I'm sure your brother won't be armed," added Libor.

Amos hated it when his father used those words for Renaud Duval: "your brother." This man was, at most, their half brother, responsible—simply by virtue of his existence—for their mother's death. Sometimes, Amos imagined that Libor preferred this third brother to his other two—with their burned faces, their battered brains—and that he had searched so tirelessly for Mina and Renaud not out of hate but out of love. No matter how many times he told himself that he was being paranoid, the doubts kept returning, more and more frequently.

"Listen, Amos," he heard his father say. "I trust you more than your big brother. You were always the more reasonable one. You're the thinker, whereas Kristof is all action. You were always the one who made the best decisions, even before you lost your sight and your brother lost his hearing."

Amos didn't know how Kristof was reacting to this; he just heard his breathing grow faster, heard him crack his knuckles.

"I'm going up to the lookout point, alone and armed, to meet your brother. Whatever happens, I want you and Kristof to stay here in this car and not move. Amos, you'll open the window and listen. If I don't come back and you hear a gunshot—just one—then you must pursue our vengeance. That will mean the prophecy has been fulfilled, that Renaud has killed me, just as Zuzana predicted. That will mean there is no reconciliation possible, and that you must hurt Renaud Duval, his children, and his children's children—everyone that shares his blood."

Though Amos's older brother would only be able to tell him about this later, Kristof immediately joined his hands together, then raised his right hand while placing the left over his heart. These gestures meant *I promise* in sign language.

"And you?" Libor insisted.

Amos swallowed. Never had the darkness in which he had wandered for four decades seemed quite this black to him. He coughed, then breathed deeply while his heartbeat slowed down again. And then, at last, he said: "I promise."

What else could he say?

"Thank you," murmured Libor. "Now listen very carefully, Amos, this is really important. As I told you, if you hear only one gunshot, you and your brother must pursue our vengeance. But if you hear two gunshots, that will mean that the vengeance is complete."

"Complete?" repeated Amos incredulously.

He could sense Kristof's agitation from the sound of his cracking knuckles. Was he also asking questions, with his fingers, to which Libor was not replying?

"Who . . . who would the second bullet be for?" Amos asked.

"For your brother, if one bullet isn't enough to kill him. For the sky, if one bullet is enough. Or . . ."

"Or?" Amos repeated, hoping this time that his father would not respond.

"Or for me," said their father. "If I kill him, and then myself, then it's all over. And you are free."

As soon as he'd said this, Libor opened the door, cutting short all further questions. Amos heard the click of the CZ 75's safety again, then the thud of the car door slamming shut. The lookout point was too far away: Kristof would not be able to see what was happening up there. So Amos would be the only witness. A blind witness.

To whom could he confess afterward what he had thought, as he listened to his father's footsteps recede in the night?

Amos had hoped that he would not hear any gunshots at all, that his father and his half brother would both return alive.

Amos had listened intently. No sound could have escaped his hearing.

And that night, he could have sworn that he heard only one gunshot.

There were two dead bodies, but only one gunshot.

So the vengeance would continue, whether he liked it or not.

The tablet vibrated, tearing Amos from his memories. Kristof must have put down the two cans of gas to write him a message. Amos read it with trembling fingers.

"Everything is ready, little brother! All you have to do is break the handle on the railcar door and they'll be locked inside. Trapped, just like we were. Like Mama was. We are going to keep our promise. Our father will be proud of us. The fire will devour them just like it devoured us."

# 48

***Place Ducale, Charleville-Mézières***

Along with everyone else gathered in Place Ducale, Captain Saint-Hilaire, Lieutenant Massigue, and Sergeant Dargonne watched the devil fly up.

After half a second of terror, the three bomb-disposal experts were shaken by nervous laughter.

The devil was on a spring!

A demon made of felt and crepe paper: two yellow horns protruding from its forehead, a fork in its hand, a prankster's grin. The moment the bin's lid burst open, the devil had leapt ten feet above the cobblestones of Place Ducale . . . before slowly falling back to earth.

Some comedian must have thought it would be funny to take advantage of all the noise and agitation of the festival to hide this little demon in a garbage can before making that anonymous phone call. Maybe he'd even filmed the scene? Maybe he would claim this was performance art? He wouldn't think it was so funny, thought the three officers, when he was caught and sentenced to two years in prison and a thirty-thousand-euro fine.

Captain Katel Marelle had witnessed the scene, along with hundreds of others. She, too, had caught her breath when she saw the devil jump up, before giving a long sigh.

She turned to Lieutenant Bonello, who was still standing beside her.

"All right, Jérémy, the fun is over. Let's get out of here."

Lieutenant Bonello didn't move an inch.

"Um, boss . . . I think we might be stuck here for a while longer, you know. These bomb-disposal guys don't leave anything to chance. There'll be doing fingerprinting, DNA searches, and all that jazz. Worse than a crime scene. They're going to want to catch whichever bastard did this."

"I get it—they're embarrassed and angry. But what does that have to do with us?"

"We're here as backup. For security. You know as well as I do, Captain—we can't just leave in the middle of an operation. It's procedure."

"Okay," said Katel. "Seeing as you're such a big fan of procedure, you can be my representative here." She shot one last look at the police officers holding up the tape. "Go be a fence post like Will and Mehdi if you want. I've got better things to do!"

Lieutenant Bonello was used to his boss not always following the rules, but it was clear that this was too much. He stared at her, wide eyed in shock.

"Better things?"

"I got a text from Interpol. Zuzana Slavik really did die in that caravan fire in Pilsen. But they confirmed that the two burned men are still at large, and personally I wouldn't be surprised if their brains got fried along with their faces."

Jérémy, looking at his colleagues holding up the police tape, started to object. But the captain was already walking away, her cell phone pressed to her ear.

"Hello, Fatou? It's Katel. Tell Agnès Duval I'm on my way back to the station. I'll be there in five minutes."

The line remained silent.

"Is there a problem?"

"Um . . . She's not here anymore."

The captain stopped dead.

"What do you mean she's not there?"

"I'm looking through the window and I can't see her car in the parking lot anymore either. So I suppose she must have, you know . . ."

"Are you fucking kidding me? You were supposed to keep an eye on her!"

"Whoa, Captain, calm down! I may only be a receptionist, but I still deserve respect. This is a police station, not a prison. And I didn't see you putting handcuffs on your witness. So, to me, it seemed reasonable to assume that—"

Katel hung up. She would deal with that insolent idiot later. She walked more quickly toward the archways in Place Ducale, where the police cars were parked. While she walked, she made several calls to the house in Bourg-Fidèle, but nobody answered.

So Nanesse hadn't gone home . . .

It wasn't too difficult to guess where she had gone.

The captain thought about what Agnès Duval had said just before the bomb alert had sent all the police officers running from the station.

*We should go . . . into Milana's past. Where her ashes were scattered: outside her railcar workshop . . . at the end of an abandoned railway line, close to the French-Belgian border, in Givet's Finger.*

Agnès must have gone straight there, the fool.

With nobody to protect her.

# MINA'S STORY

## EXPLORER, DANCER, ENGINEER

***March 1977***

During the first few months after my son's birth, the fear didn't leave me. I felt certain that Libor would find me, that he had contacts in the West, that he would pay men to track me down. I lived in Charleville for three years, shut away with my child in the little apartment I was renting with some of the money I'd stolen in Pilsen.

I saved the rest, but I knew it wouldn't be enough. I had only one skill—my puppetry—but I knew it would be too dangerous to perform onstage, even if I was concealed behind a little puppet theater.

How could I survive while remaining in hiding? Baou came up with the solution. He was always my sole support, the only one to send gifts—books or toys—to my son. He even agreed to be the boy's godfather.

"Why don't you make puppets?" he suggested. "I could sell them in my bookstore."

Baou had moved to Alençon, in Normandy, with his new partner. He was right. My creations—automata inspired by Japanese karakuri ningyō, or Edison's speaking dolls—proved a big success. Baou bought them from me at a good price. Thanks to him, they were sold by a whole network of specialized stores, while I didn't have to take any risk because, officially, there was nothing that connected me to the puppets.

And yet the danger was always there, a looming menace. Several times, I felt convinced that my neighbors were spying on me. That a woman sitting next to us in a tram was staring a little too attentively at my son's gray eyes. That a man was smoking a cigarette on the sidewalk opposite my apartment for too long, as if waiting for me to come out.

Once my son turned three and he had to go to school, I decided to use my three identities. With some money that Baou lent me, I bought a used car and rented two other small apartments, one in Paris and one in Florac.

A leap into the unknown . . .

I didn't know how long I would be on the run like this. I didn't know if my son would be able to bear it. I didn't know if I was even capable of living three lives in one, each of them fragmented.

It might seem impossible. I mean, it's already hard enough living just one life!

But, at the risk of sounding immodest, I have to admit that living three lives turned out to be disconcertingly easy.

A leap into the unknown? Sure, but all lives are like that.

At least I was given three attempts to get it right.

I decided to split my life in three: one third in Charleville, one third in Florac, and one third in Paris.

With all of his teachers, I played up my role as a nomadic artist, bohemian with a lower-case *b*. I requested for my son the privilege granted to the children of fairground workers—enrollment in several successive schools, following the movement of the fairgrounds.

When it came to persuading them I deserved such favorable treatment, I had quite a few things on my side: I was charming; I was a brave single mother, fully devoted to my son; and Renaud/Hans/Pierre was a good student—calm, discreet, and highly intelligent, despite his somewhat fragile health. I used this medical issue to justify his long absences.

Everyone was eager to help my son, to help me. The teachers sent him his homework in the mail. My son had to do three sets of homework, take three sets of exams; he complained about this sometimes, of course, but I laughed it off, helped him out, and we got through it all. None of my son's school reports ever mentioned his absences; I made sure of that.

When, on two or three occasions, some of the more finicky teachers took offense at his long, repeated stretches of nonattendance, I played my trump card: His absentee father was dangerous, forcing me to move away from the place where I had lived, for the safety of my child. *But he will be back at school soon,* I promised. And I kept that promise. Renaud, Hans, and Pierre would always return to the classroom after a few weeks, and none of them were ever tardy.

The most difficult teacher to convince, through all those years, was the headmaster of the school in Florac, Mathieu Mariotta. The only solution, offered to dissuade him from reporting the matter to the board of education, was to teach the village children how to make puppets and to perform a show every year for the village fete. A form of bribery? Sure, but as long as the strings attached were invisible, I didn't see a problem with that.

I suspect you must be growing anxious at this point in the story. Anxious to know the answer to the ultimate question: How did Renaud—or Hans, or Pierre—cope with this unusual situation?

What can I tell you? Simply that everything I did—all the moving around, all the deception—was to protect him, to keep him safe. And our situation wasn't that uncommon, after all: divorced parents with shared custody, children shuttled from one house to another, one school to another, one family to another . . . He was far from the only one to live like that.

At least my son only had one family.

And three names!

It started off as a game. I would call him—successively, or randomly—by each of those three names, like one of those bilingual parents who jump from language to language so that their children get used to juggling multiple nationalities. Renaud/Hans/Pierre was even quite proud of it.

It was his secret, his little mystery.

In Charleville he was called Renaud; in Florac, he was Hans; and in Paris, he was Pierre.

I told him part of the truth: His father was a bad man, and he was searching for us. To stay away from him, we had to keep moving. We must never say anything to betray our secret, must never make a mistake over his name.

I also pointed out all the benefits of the situation, like one of those parents who try to soften the trauma of a divorce by explaining to their children that they will now have two houses, two bedrooms, twice as many presents and friends.

When we were in Charleville, Renaud was calm and composed. He spent lots of time with me, making his dolls, improving them, transforming them into articulated automata. Renaud had a gift for manual activities; he was blessed with great patience and creativity.

When we were in Paris, Renaud became Pierre; his hands were used mainly for writing and the rest of his body for dancing. At the age of seven, he started dragging me from museum to museum. He insisted on joining a dance school—Temps'Danse18, on Rue de Panama, and he turned out to be just as talented as all the students who practiced year round. He read a lot in Paris, whereas he never opened a book in Charleville or Florac. He wrote poems, which—once he had gained enough confidence—he sent to his godfather, Baou, who published them in his fanzine *I Wrote Silences*. He was so proud of that!

When we were in Florac, his hands were no use at all, except for hanging from a tree branch occasionally, or catching a grasshopper. As soon as Pierre became Hans, he could no longer stand being indoors. Rainy days drove him to distraction; he would pace around like a dog waiting to be walked. And once he did get outside, he would walk for hours alongside the Tarn or to the caves of the Causse Méjean. Sometimes we wouldn't see anyone else at all during our hikes, and when we reached the mountaintops—the Pic de Finiels or the observatory on Mount Aigoual—Hans would look out at the horizon and tell me that this was what he wanted: to get his driver's license—for a car, a motorcycle, or a boat—and set off far into the distance, to explore the vastness of the world, all its deserts, forests, and oceans.

And I would weep.

I would weep because my son could never be all these things at once: explorer, dancer, engineer. I would weep because I felt as if I were living with three different children, each one so lovely, but every time we moved, I gave all my attention to one of them, and the other two died. I had enough love in my heart for all three, but only one body to hug tight to my chest. I had only one child, and—month by month—I was driving him crazy.

When Renaud/Hans/Pierre was eleven, I had a choice to make. And I have to admit that it came as a big relief.

It was impossible for him to continue his education in three different middle schools.

This was 1988. My fear had faded with the years. I felt less and less menaced by the idea that my life was being monitored by an insidious mafia of spies. In fact, I had almost come to forget Libor, to convince myself that the life I'd led before 1976—the nights under the stars, the caravan fire, the death threats—was nothing but a nightmare, from which I had woken up for good.

I enrolled Renaud at Bayard Middle School in Charleville-Mézières. Renaud the engineer had won out over his rivals, but I promised that, during the holidays, we would visit Pierre the poet-dancer and Hans the explorer-hiker as often as we could. How could I deprive Renaud of his two other identities, even if I no longer feared for his safety?

Until he was twelve years old.

Until November 9, 1989.

Until all the newspaper headlines told the story of the fall of the Berlin Wall and the disappearance of the Iron Curtain from Estonia to Bulgaria. Suddenly, Europe's borders dissolved. If Libor, Amos, and Kristof were still alive, there was now no barrier to keep them away from me.

But they had to find me first!

I clung to that hope. I had not made any mistakes, in all those years. I had gone to extreme lengths to cover my tracks. Libor and his sons had no way of knowing where or under what name I was living.

This is what happened . . .

Czechoslovakia went through its Velvet Revolution, its division into the two separate countries of the Czech Republic and Slovakia, its entry into the European Union, and nothing changed.

Renaud enjoyed a normal education at Bayard Middle School, and then at Monge High School, and no strangers approached him.

As Pierre, he wrote dozens of poems for Baou's fanzine; he danced in *The Firebird*, *The Rite of Spring*, and even *Petrushka* at the little Théâtre du Funambule in Montmartre, and none of the spectators had burned faces.

As Hans, he mountain-biked across the Causse Noir and the Cévennes without ever encountering any scary men.

I was proud of him. I felt like I had won. My child was living happily. And he was growing up.

He got his driver's license as soon as he turned eighteen. I insisted on him taking the test in three different places: Charleville, Mende, and Paris. It was just a formality: At Hans's request, I had been teaching him to drive in Lozère since he was sixteen. Those three licenses were our last guarantees. In the eyes of the French state, they are official identification papers, so my son could now decide to change his name and his life whenever he wanted.

After passing his baccalaureate exam in the summer of 1995, he hesitated for a long time.

Renaud planned to take a degree in mechanical engineering at a school that specialized in microrobotics; Pierre envisaged a career as a professional dancer; and Hans wanted to explore the world behind the wheel of a truck, if he could find an employer to fund his travels.

This time, I thought, it would be his choice to make.

But, once again, life decided for him.

He met Agnès in Place Ducale on the last day of summer.

I knew instantly from the look in his eyes that his wandering days, his three identities, the whole of that eccentric existence, were over.

Hans and Pierre would be erased.

Renaud would remain in Charleville with this nineteen-year-old girl, Agnès, who asked only one thing: that we should call her Nanesse.

Nanesse, who was so full of tenderness and caresses. Nanesse, who had a heart big enough for three. Nanesse, who loved me as if I were her own mother.

Renaud was in love. Without hesitation, he amputated two-thirds of his life. Without remorse, he strangled the dreams of Hans and Pierre. Without regrets, he gave up his freedom for a prison of love and his beautiful jailer.

Or so I hoped, at least.

I wanted to believe that Renaud would not seek to escape.

# 49

***Milana's railcar workshop, Givet's Finger***

Vicky turned off the rayok. She couldn't bear to listen anymore. The weight of these revelations had suddenly grown too heavy. Instantly the parade of figurines came to a halt. Mina's voice fell silent and the blue glow that had illuminated the workshop vanished, leaving only a weak, pale, cold light.

Nanesse collapsed onto a chair.

Mina's story was far beyond anything she could have imagined.

*One baby . . . with three official, certified lives.*

*Renaud, Pierre, and Hans.*

The workshop seemed to spin around her, with its surreal décor, that cluttered chair where she had put her handbag, those multicolored fabrics spread over the sewing table, and all those hands, arms, faces of cloth, porcelain, cardboard . . .

And those faces of flesh too, Éléa's and Vicky's, frozen with horror.

Nanesse watched them. Was it possible to divide misery into three equal parts?

Éléa appeared paralyzed, her mouth open, eyes bulging, as if her brain had frozen and refused to talk to her, leaving her alone with her distress, this unacceptable truth.

Vicky remained standing, her eyes filled with tears, staring by turns at the silent rayok and at her daughter's delicate gestures—the only thing moving in this petrified mausoleum.

Lola was playing, silently, seriously, unaffected by the complicated story that she hadn't listened to. She focused her gaze on Kasper, her broken doll, which she dressed and undressed, dressed and undressed, this automaton that her daddy had promised he would fix when he returned.

*Poor little thing,* thought Nanesse.

When they killed Renaud, those murderers had also killed Pierre and Hans.

One murder, but three crimes.

One death, but three women with broken hearts. Three shattered families. Three . . .

Nanesse's gaze took in the whole interior of the railcar.

She cursed her own empathy.

Was she stupid enough to feel more sorry for these women than she was for herself? These rivals who had stolen her husband? These women with whom Renaud had betrayed her, all those years . . .

But, having heard Mina's story, was it really that simple? Who had betrayed whom?

One man, but three official lives.

Who among the three women in that railcar could truly say that she had been the most loved? Who could claim to be the most important? Who could swear she had received the sincerest love letters?

The woman who loved Renaud, or Hans, or Pierre?

The wife, the coparent, the lover?

Nanesse was forced to admit that Vicky genuinely loved Hans, her secretive and solitary truck driver.

Just as Éléa passionately loved Pierre, her radiant poet and dancer.

Just as she had loved Renaud, her discreet and caring husband, for the twenty-eight years of their marriage.

Nanesse was shaking, and so was the rickety chair beneath her, swaying on the loose floorboards. Mina's confession had descended upon the three of them like a guillotine blade, cutting off, she realized, the hope to which Vicky and Éléa had been clinging.

Hans and Pierre, alive . . .

An illusion that Mina had just trampled.

# 50

The tactile tablet vibrated inside Kristof's pocket. He slid a hand inside to read his brother's words with his fingertips.

*"They're not talking anymore. They've stopped the rayok."*

He looked up. Amos was still crouched in front of the railcar, his ear pressed to the door. Kristof tapped the braille signs as quickly as he could to reply.

*"So let's get on with it! If that viper's story is over, they'll be coming out soon."*

The two cans of gas were lying under the railcar. All Kristof had to do now was remove the lid and light a match, and the whole workshop would go up in flames.

Kristof watched as his brother's hand reached out toward him. Moved by a surge of pity, he took a step forward and gripped Amos's hand in his own.

With his free hand, Amos typed:

*"No, they're just taking a break to digest what they've heard. The story isn't over."*

*"So they won't get to hear the end. Tough shit."*

Kristof only had to reach out to touch the lid on the first jerry can. But suddenly, Amos's hand grabbed hold of his. Kristof grew irritated again.

*"Let go! I have to do it. We owe them."*

*"Stop! And don't move!"*

All Kristof knew was that his brother no longer had his ear pressed to the door, but had turned, like a suddenly alerted guard dog, toward the tunnel entrance.

*"Stop,"* Amos wrote again. *"Someone's coming."*

Captain Katel Marelle advanced cautiously through the darkness. Her feet followed the train tracks, but her eyes never left the archway of light ahead of her. The end of the tunnel . . .

Even on her own like this, she couldn't stop herself from grumbling.

Why had Milana Duval chosen such a remote spot to make her puppets? What was so special about this place? Why hadn't Renaud and Nanesse Duval packed up all the old woman's belongings in cardboard boxes one Sunday afternoon? Why had Nanesse rushed over here, alone, rather than waiting for an hour in the police station? Why wasn't she answering her phone? Had she turned the ringer off and left it at the bottom of her handbag?

The captain stopped moving. She listened intently.

Because she knew Nanesse was here. She had seen her Clio, parked in the precise spot where the paved path ended, next to a red Citroën Berlingo. Katel had not had any trouble locating the abandoned railcar. *Givet's Finger, French-Belgian border, abandoned railway line.* An old map had been enough; no need to waste time typing approximate addresses into Google Maps.

Katel could just make out, behind the curtain of light, the trees at the near edge of the clearing. Instinctively, she removed her SIG Sauer from its holster. There was one detail that simultaneously troubled and reassured her.

She could see several footprints in the mud ahead of her. At least six different sets. None of them appeared big enough to match the size 12s they had found before, but one of them was small enough to belong to a young child—between three and eight years old, she guessed.

Was this some family reunion? Or had the burned men brought two accomplices to trap Agnès? Two accomplices and a kid? That made no sense . . .

The captain knew only one thing for sure: There were a bunch of people at the end of the tunnel, and she wasn't about to announce her arrival.

As Katel approached the end of the tunnel, she spotted one corner of the workshop under some tree branches. It was a railcar from a freight train, an old wooden model, with no windows. The leaves of the oaks and hazel trees shaded the rusted train tracks almost completely. Katel listened to the silence, trying to hear through the rustle of leaves in the wind any other sounds.

She realized she was acting just as stupidly as Nanesse had. She hadn't told anyone she was heading this way, not even Jérémy or Fatou the receptionist. The most reasonable procedure would have been to order a few agents to go with her, but that would have meant waiting until the incident in Place Ducale was declared over, or negotiating with the local authorities for her men's early release: Either way, the day would have been wasted. All because some joker had hidden a devil on springs inside a recycling bin! Because of a simple phone call. A prank that anyone could have . . .

For an instant, Katel imagined the worst. What if that call had not been a prank, but a diversion tactic, designed to trap the captain and her officers at Place Ducale? To separate Agnès from her police guard? To lure them here: first Nanesse, and then Katel. Each of them alone . . .

One phone call—it had been so easy.

Katel tightened her grip on the butt of her SIG Sauer.

At last she emerged from the tunnel. A frail light filtered through the canopy of trees, bathing the clearing in a soft glow.

Everything seemed calm.

She glanced down at the six sets of footprints.

*Too calm.*

Katel held her breath, all her senses on alert.

Vision first. She scanned every detail of the clearing. A "green hollow," as Rimbaud once put it. She hoped she would not end up with a red hollow in her chest.

Half hidden amid this golden greenery, the railcar workshop looked like something straight from a fairy tale. The train tracks invited Katel to keep moving forward, into the witch's lair. The tunnel from which she had just emerged seemed to be a border between the real world and an imaginary world.

Imaginary?

The captain pushed a lock of hair out of her eyes and squeezed the pistol's grip. She mustn't let herself get sidetracked by the strangeness of this investigation: those killers with burned faces, that parade of puppets . . . The murders of Renaud Duval and Bruno Pluvier were real, not some Disney illusion.

The footprints continued on through the mud and the trampled grass to the door of the railcar, coming to a stop before the step.

So all six of them were inside the workshop? Five adults and a child?

Suddenly Katel smelled something that made her look more closely.

Two jerry cans of gasoline were lying under the railcar. Each one looked like it could hold eight gallons. Enough gas to send the whole car up in flames within seconds . . . Immediately, Katel's detective brain started fitting together the pieces of the puzzle at her disposal, asking questions and attempting to answer them.

*Who could have brought those jerry cans here?*

Katel remembered the article from the Czech newspaper: an accident forty-seven years ago, a traveling artists' caravan that went up in flames, leaving one person dead and two severely burned . . .

*Is someone trying to bring the past to life? The Slavik father and his two sons, seeking vengeance?*

Katel aimed her pistol straight ahead, then pivoted and swept the space to the side of her. They had to be here, somewhere, close by. She must have stumbled in on them as they were about to commit a crime.

While she continued to scan her surroundings, Katel listened for the slightest rustle, crack, breath. All she could hear, though, was a vague humming sound, coming from inside the railcar. A muffled conversation. So Nanesse was inside? But with whom?

Again Katel looked around at the tunnel, the tracks, the trees, refusing to lower her guard.

Nothing moved.

Were the two burned men still here? Had they run away?

The captain slowly backed up toward the railcar, making sure that nobody was coming up behind her, then waited for several seconds. She needed to stay focused, despite her racing thoughts.

Milana's cancer; her cremation; the ashes scattered here by her son . . .

Katel too wanted to be cremated after she was dead. Who would bother bringing flowers to her grave? Not her cat, that was for sure! Nobody would miss her once she was gone . . . But wasn't that the most elegant way to live? Not to love anyone, so that nobody was grief-stricken when you passed away . . .

A rustling sound interrupted these morbid meanderings. The soft crunch of a flower bed trampled underfoot. The sounds were coming from the shadowy parts of the forest, where the train tracks disappeared. Katel's trigger finger tensed.

Someone was moving in the undergrowth.

Someone who wasn't looking at her, even though he was facing her directly. She advanced toward the woods, her pistol aimed straight ahead. At last, Katel caught sight of the burned man. The killer was groping his way through the trees, like a blindfolded child.

*The blind man . . .*

*So where's the other one—the one with no ears?*

Pain engulfed the captain's skull.

She caught a glimpse of the white metal cane after it hit her in the temple. As she fell, she let go of her gun.

*That bastard was hiding behind me,* she had time to think. *The jerry cans and the blind man were just there to bait me.* A second blow caught her in the back of the neck.

A third blow, and the pain made all thought impossible.

Katel lost consciousness after the fourth blow.

Kristof hit her three more times, before Amos caught his arm.

*"Stop!"* he typed frantically.

Kristof saw the blood trickling down his cane; the captain's smashed face; her curled-up body. Ever since the fire in Pilsen, he had been unable to control his violent rages. One blow would have been enough to neutralize this cop. Instead . . .

Amos crouched down beside the motionless body. He pressed his ear to the policewoman's chest and knelt in that pose for a long time, as if praying. Kristof knew that his brother was capable of perceiving even a tiny five-decibel sound, with almost as much precision as a high-caliber stethoscope. So if her heart was still beating, even faintly, he would hear it.

After a long time, Amos finally looked up at him.

*"She's dead."*

# MINA'S STORY

## THE POISON OF SECRETS

***September 1995***

For the first time in my life, I was truly happy. For the first time in my life, my son and I could lead a normal life. We could put the horrors of the past behind us.

Renaud was in love with a nice girl. A local girl who knew nothing about his triple identity, for whom Renaud was ready to forget his other two lives. Agnès had the peculiar energy of someone who loves without judgment, who welcomes others unquestioningly, who trusts first and suspects later, who risks everything for love, friendship, solidarity. And she was modest too. Nanesse hated it when we talked about her personal qualities; she often repeated her belief that her optimism and generosity must have been stolen from some poor person who then had to go without, as if the virtues of one individual caused the vices of another.

Renaud and Agnès married quickly; they were barely even twenty years old. Did he do it to ward off the past? To give Hans and Pierre no opportunity to come back and haunt him? Were those dreams of exploring the world and dancing in front of crowds truly forgotten?

I hoped so.

Renaud and Agnès soon became parents. My two grandchildren, Axel and Robin, changed my life. Could I ever have imagined when I was young that one day I—the orphan under the Charles Bridge—would become a grandmother?

A grandmother who often looked after the little ones, since Renaud worked constantly and Agnès was also devoted to her foster children.

Not that I was complaining. In the eyes of Axel and Robin, I was a fun, young granny. And maybe I really was. They were the only ones I allowed in my railcar workshop, to help me cut and sew and create.

They sorted through buttons for the eyes of my karakuri or my Bozo heads; chose the colors of their dresses or pants; gave them names. They called me Mamina or Granny Petrushka, after their favorite story; they adored the beautiful ballerina, and hated the evil Moor. If they had only known what that story meant to me . . .

The years flew by so quickly. A happy year goes by faster than a painful day.

Nanesse welcomed all those foster children into her home. I could hardly criticize her for offering a second chance to these poor, unfortunate kids.

Axel and Robin grew up while I grew old. Renaud had become a well-regarded microrobotics engineer, working on increasingly sophisticated automaton projects. How ridiculous my own amateur puppets seemed to me, in comparison. The son had surpassed his mother, though that achievement meant that he spent long stretches of time traveling. Too long.

I never dared question him about this, but I always feared that Hans and Pierre had returned to haunt him. Renaud possessed two other birth certificates, two other identity cards, two other driver's licenses, and two other boxes of childhood souvenirs: schoolbooks, report cards, medical histories, photograph albums. I often thought that if Renaud ever wanted to cheat on Nanesse, to live a double or triple life, I had provided him with the perfect alibi.

After all he had been through, could my son really be content with only one home? Only one family? Did he love Nanesse enough for that?

I never knew the answer to that question.

It was his secret to keep, just as I kept mine.

Is it ever a good idea to try to pierce another person's mysteries? Life is so short, and it takes so much time to bury our secrets under shovelfuls of happy smiles and joyful memories, to make life grow again from that fertile soil . . . Why tear up all the flowers and plants, just to find what's buried underneath? Out of pride? An obsessive desire to know the truth?

That's what I believed, all those years.

I didn't realize that secrets can rot. That they can poison the earth in which the new flowers are growing. That they would gnaw at my roots, devour me.

I didn't understand this until I was sixty years old and I went to see my gynecologist for a routine examination. She diagnosed cancer of the uterus.

It was terminal. I had less than two years to live.

That was a year and a half ago.

I never guessed that danger might arrive in that way, in such a commonplace manner. Once you've escaped the clutches of an ogre like Libor; once you've survived a thousand threats; once you've covered the tracks of your every footstep . . . you don't imagine that death might be lying in wait inside you; that it had been there all along, in the form of a microscopic malign tumor, and that even if you went into hiding on the moon or in another galaxy, you would never be able to escape your fate.

This time, I decided not to hide anything.

Besides, chemotherapy would soon reveal the truth.

Nanesse was strong. Strong enough for two, or three, or four people. Renaud was devastated. Did Pierre and Hans weep for me too? Axel and Robin searched through the wigs in my workshop for the one they wanted me to wear—an old Mary Poppins number—and I didn't have the heart to refuse them. And every time they came to visit, they begged me to keep my promise, the one I had always delayed.

"Mamina, when will you perform your show for us?"

I was a puppeteer whom they had never seen onstage. A retired artist. And what they asked for, year after year, birthday after birthday, never changed.

"Mamina, we want to see you perform!"

"One day, children. One day."

In the spring of 2017, I knew I had only a few months left to live. One last Christmas, at best. Libor and his two sons were now far from my thoughts. Robin and Axel were so insistent. In more than forty years, I had never made the slightest mistake, had never done anything that might betray me. What did I have to fear after all this time?

And I have to acknowledge, even if this lowering of my guard put me in danger, that it was something I wanted to do.

I wanted to play Petrushka again. I wanted him to waltz with the dancing bear, to seduce the ballerina, to evade the Moor's saber, one last time.

The World Festival of Puppet Theaters was taking place in a few weeks. Every two years, since their birth, I had taken Axel and Robin to watch the shows on Place Ducale. Some of them were mediocre, some brilliant, but they all made my heart ache at the thought that I was no longer the one manipulating the strings behind the puppet theater.

This time—one last time—I would be the queen of the festival! Or one of the hundred and fifty little queens, at least; I didn't harbor any illusions about my aging talents. Baou still sat on the organizing committee, and the two of us were still friends: We met up every two years, when he was in town for the festival. It was no trouble for him to schedule a performance for me.

I played Petrushka under the archways of Place Ducale. That moment has a prominent place in my memory. If I were allowed to bring only three or four treasured memories with me to heaven, that would be one of them.

Baou was there. So were Nanesse, Renaud, Axel, and Robin. In the wonder-struck eyes of my son, as Petrushka danced in front of the little theater, I saw again Pierre's arabesques, Hans's dreams of elsewhere. I performed for him, for the three children he had been, and for the grandchildren he had given me.

There were only about fifty people in the audience; there must have been a dozen other shows happening at the same time, some of them far more impressive than the swan song of a dying artist with trembling hands.

Yes, I would soon be dead, and yet I had never felt more alive than when the meager crowd rose to applaud me, one last time. When Axel and Robin rushed onto the stage to hug me.

Then the audience, including my own family, moved away, looking for the next source of entertainment. Only three people remained.

An old man with tears in his eyes, and two others, younger than him, with horribly burned faces.

# 51

*"Help me!"*

As soon as he had typed those words, Kristof dropped the inside-ONE tablet into his pocket and began dragging the policewoman's corpse by the feet. Amos didn't move. His face remained frozen. His eyes seemed lost in darkness. His fingers continued to move, though, typing messages that his brother didn't read.

*"Why, Kristof?*

*"There was no need to kill her.*

*"She wasn't part of our vengeance.*

*"All we had to do was neutralize her."*

Kristof, on his own, managed to drag Katel's body to the edge of the forest and hide it in some ferns. He checked that the body couldn't be seen from the tunnel or the clearing, then finally he looked at his messages. He suppressed the roar of rage that he could feel swelling inside his chest. Since becoming deaf, he had unlearned to speak; now, when he felt an urge to express himself, he would growl or bellow like a bear, incapable of controlling his voice. But now was not the time to attract attention. He would scream with anger in the Skoda later, when this was all over.

*"She would have reported us!"* Kristof typed with two fingers. *"Go back to the door and listen to them while I get the bonfire ready."*

Amos didn't argue. Kristof knew he would obey him.

His blind brother walked slowly but unhesitatingly toward the railcar. In addition to his extraordinarily sensitive hearing, Amos had also developed an impressive sense of direction, and he tracked the sounds and memorized the dimensions, the obstacles and safe passages, in each new place he encountered.

*"Watch out!"* Kristof typed. He had seen the door handle twisting. *"Someone's coming. Hide!"*

He immediately lay down under the trees.

Amos had no choice but to flatten himself against the railcar wall, to the left of the door. It would hide him when it opened, but he would be discovered as soon as someone came out.

The blind man held his breath again. First he heard footsteps, too light to be an adult's, jumping down onto the first step.

"No, don't take Kasper with you. And don't wander off too far, sweetie."

Amos recognized Vicky's voice.

"Don't go into the forest or the tunnel, okay? And come back as soon as you've peed."

"Yes, Mommy!"

Lola jumped onto the muddy ground. Amos heard her run across the clearing to the trees directly opposite. She did not turn around.

If she had, she would have seen him—and he would have heard her scream.

The door did not fall shut. Amos guessed that Vicky was watching her daughter from inside the railcar, checking that she wasn't in any danger. He held his breath a few seconds longer, and then the hinges creaked softly as the door closed.

Vicky must think her daughter was safe. Why would she doubt it, after all? And she was no doubt eager to hear the end of Mina's story. As soon as Amos heard the door click shut, he exhaled and typed furiously:

*"Don't touch the kid!"*

Amos hated the silence that followed.

He imagined the worst. Was it possible Kristof would beat a five-year-old girl with the same ferocity he had shown that cop? His desire for vengeance was driving him insane. Sometimes Amos imagined that vengeance was just an excuse, something his father had invented to give Kristof a channel for his hate. But it was too late now: Kristof's hatred had burst through the dam. It was uncontainable.

Amos heard Kristof's heavy footsteps, a muffled cry, the sound of crushed leaves, followed by an interminable silence, then the cracking of knuckles.

"Kristof?"

There was no reply.

*"KRISTOF?"*

*"It's done."*

*"What do you mean?"*

*"The kid is tied up and gagged. Like a prettily wrapped gift. Be happy—fate sent her to us."*

Amos had thought Kristof was coming toward him, but his brother must have abruptly changed direction. From the soft scraping sound of his brother's jacket against his pants, he realized that Kristof was crouching down by the two jerry cans that lay under the railcar.

*"I don't understand,"* Amos typed feverishly. *"Why* fate*?"*

His nostrils flared. He was trying not to sneeze. His sense of smell—every bit as sensitive as his hearing—had just detected the unbearable odor of gasoline.

*"You wanted to save the fruit, remember? Well, it just fell into our hands. Now we can cut the branch!"*

# MINA'S STORY

## We, Poor Puppets

***November 2017***

"Come in. What are you afraid of?"

Renaud had brought a bouquet of flowers. Anemones—my favorites. He remained standing outside the door of my hospital room, like a guilty child. In that moment, I saw in his eyes Pierre's sensitivity, Hans's yearning for independence.

"Come closer. Sit down. I have things to tell you."

Renaud closed the door behind him. He was holding an envelope, and I knew he'd just been in discussion with the doctor. He was doing a beautiful job of playing his role as the thoughtful, reassuring only son, looking after his mother in her final moments.

"We're not going to lie to ourselves by talking about the future, okay? You promise? There's no point looking at the clock when you know that the bell is about to ring."

I hadn't seen Renaud cry that much since he started first grade in three different schools.

"I haven't always been a good mother, as you probably realize."

Renaud was about to protest, but I managed to raise my hand, despite all the plastic tubes attached to my arm, and he fell silent again.

"We haven't talked about it in years. Not since you met Nanesse, since Axel and Robin were born . . ."

"That's all in the past, Mom," Renaud said hurriedly.

I could tell from the look in his eyes that the ghosts of Pierre and Hans still haunted him.

"I'm not who you think I am, Renaud. I kept part of my past hidden from you."

I looked down at the IV drips hanging from my arms and had the thought that, this time, I was the puppet, my strings in the hands of the Great Puppeteer in the sky, the one who created us all, who waltzes us once around the dance floor then tosses us aside. My prayer was simply that he would give me a little more time, that he wouldn't cut the silver strings quite yet.

"Listen to me, Renaud. A long time ago, to save my life, I had to put yours in danger."

I told him about everything: the Prague Spring, Libor's caravan, Petrushka and the villages of Bohemia, nights under the stars, Zuzana's jealousy, the childhood of Amos and Kristof, his own forced conception, that tiny embryo, and what happened afterward . . . My crime. My unforgivable crime, and my escape. "I'm sorry, son. Please forgive me."

With infinite gentleness, Renaud took my hand.

"There's nothing to forgive, Mom. All you did was defend yourself. And defend me."

I felt a desperate urge to tear the tubes from my arms. I couldn't stand being one of the puppets: the strings attached, the absence of freedom. I couldn't stand being unable to hug my son to my chest.

"I did everything I could, Renaud. I asked so much of you. And I didn't make a single mistake, during all those years. Not one. More than forty years of constant vigilance. Until last week . . . Until that performance in Place Ducale."

I saw again Libor's crazed look and the ugly smiles on Amos's and Kristof's unrecognizable faces.

"They tracked me down. They know who I am. And it won't take them long to find out who you are . . ."

An expression of panic crossed Renaud's face before he forced himself to smile reassuringly again.

"You need to leave," I told him. "Protect yourself, Renaud. And that will protect Nanesse, Axel, and Robin too. You need to hide. You need to change your identity."

"I can't."

"Of course you can! Don't forget, this was the whole reason why Pierre and Hans existed. They've been waiting for this moment, all these years. Two sleeper agents—that's what they call them in spy movies. Even the StB couldn't have fabricated a better fake identity. Hans and Pierre already have a legal existence, official ID papers, childhood memories, living witnesses who could swear that they had met them years ago . . . Libor and his two sons have no way of connecting the dots from this life to those lives. The only link is you—and me."

Renaud stared at me in horror.

"Mom, it's impossible. I can't leave Nanesse. Or Axel and Robin. I can't just run away. What if Libor takes out his vengeance on them?"

"It's you he's looking for. Only you."

"Why? Why does he want revenge on me?"

"It's not revenge he's after. It's . . . to protect himself. Libor was always superstitious. He always believed in magic, in sorcery. And so, naturally, he believed the prophecy."

Renaud's hand tightened around mine.

"What prophecy?"

That was the only detail of my life in Czechoslovakia that I hadn't dared mention.

"When Zuzana found out that I was pregnant, to convince Libor that I shouldn't be allowed to keep you, she told him the child I was carrying was going to kill him."

Renaud sat in silence. He had finally understood the danger he was in; why Libor would never leave him in peace. At least, I hoped he had understood this.

"You'll find all the archives for Pierre's and Hans's lives in my workshop. Official documents, photographs, lists of people who knew you, diaries describing everything we did in Florac and Paris . . . I wrote a journal entry every day, so that you would be able to fill the holes in your memory. Now you just have to choose: Do you want to be Hans or Pierre?"

I saw something light up in Renaud's eyes every time I said those names: Hans and Pierre. Seeing that, I felt as if the three of them were hiding something from me, like a conspiracy of brothers. Renaud was still holding the envelope in his left hand—the bad news hand. Presumably the envelope had been given to him by a surgeon and it contained a letter that, beneath the scientific words—*carcinoma, neoplasia, hysterectomy*—was essentially the announcement of the date of my death. How long did I have? A few weeks? A few days?

I smiled with all the strength I had left.

"I have two favors to ask you, Renaud. First, when this is all over, I want you to scatter my ashes in the clearing, outside my workshop."

Renaud opened his mouth to object, but I waved my puppet arms to make him understand that there was nothing else to say on the matter. And then, once again, I smiled.

I wasn't putting on an act. I really did accept the end of my life philosophically. It had given me so much more than I'd ever hoped for. It could easily have come to an end much earlier—on the cobblestones of Wenceslas Square in August 1968; drowned in the Radbuza, near Pilsen; shot as I was crossing the Iron Curtain. So many human beings are born upon this earth and leave it again in a flash, barely granted the time to grow up, dying without ever knowing happiness. Zuzana's life had been one of those . . . Mine could have been the same.

"So . . . ," Renaud asked, shyly interrupting my thoughts. "What's the second favor?"

Suddenly I felt exhausted. I made an effort to speak clearly.

"After you've scattered my ashes, go into the railcar. In there, you'll find my old rayok. I fixed it years ago. It works perfectly now. The characters and the backgrounds are all ready. Now I just have to finish dictating the story. I'll leave it all on a thumb drive. The nurses will give it to you, along with the rest of my belongings. You will be the guardian of my past. You know, Renaud, each of us comes up with a way to leave a trace of our passage here on earth, before we fall silent forever. Some write it in a notebook, others sing it, or film it, or whisper it to a trusted friend. But what choice do I have? I will tell my story through little felt figurines."

Renaud nodded, and we continued talking, I don't recall about what—just everyday stuff; a precious return to normality—before a nurse came in and ruined it all by telling Renaud it was time to leave. Which he did, the envelope of death still in his hand.

Tonight, which might well be my last, I am recording these final words. This damned disease is devouring my body, but at least it has spared my brain until now. I would have hated to leave the stage without first saying goodbye to the people I love. My small but faithful audience.

What will you think of my story, my dear listeners?

Is it the story of a little girl who loved to play, sew, draw, and dance? The story of a criminal on the run? An immigrant? A loving mother? A madwoman obsessed by a paranoiac fear? All of these?

What will you think of us, once our lives are over?

We, poor puppets, are merely beings of cloth and paper. One day we move, we think we live, we think we are free, and we turn a blind eye to the nylon strings, the cardboard background, because we are so afraid that the show will come to an end, that the curtain will fall like a guillotine blade, that we will be once again what we have always been: a toy, tossed around by invisible forces, during a single dance in the light, before being dumped in a drawer once more, lying motionless in the darkness.

# 52

***Milana's railcar workshop, Givet's Finger***

This time, the rayok stopped without anyone touching it.

The screen slowly went dark, before turning off completely. Mina's story was over.

Nanesse turned to look at the glass eyes on the sewing table, avoiding the gazes of Vicky and Éléa. She thought again about the days that had followed her mother-in-law's death. She remembered Renaud's tears, as well as her children's, but she also recalled her husband's haste.

*We need to leave the house in Charleville,* he told her the day after the cremation. *I need to find another job, and we need to find another school for Axel and Robin.*

Nanesse had interpreted this sudden desire for change as a part of Renaud's grieving process, an urge to break with the painful past. Although, if she was honest with herself now, she hadn't really analyzed his behavior at all at the time, preferring simply to support her husband during that difficult moment.

Deep down, she had actually been quite happy to move from Charleville to the Ardennes, to swap their little town house for a much bigger one in Bourg-Fidèle. She was proud that Renaud had started thinking about his career by applying to be an engineer in Belgium. Her only regret was the abrupt departure of Axel and Robin, who in a matter of weeks were packed off on a foreign exchange program, Axel to Hungary and Robin to Spain.

Now, Nanesse understood.

Renaud had not been able to leave her. He had disobeyed his mother, refusing to follow the plan she had laid out for him. He had thought that relocating and changing jobs would be enough. It had taken Libor and his sons six years, but in the end they had tracked him down . . . and killed him.

Now, Nanesse realized: This was partly her fault too. She remembered all the times Renaud had talked about his desire to move farther away, to the south or the west of France, maybe even abroad, to distance themselves from Charleville by more than the thirty miles they had. But she'd been unable to bear the thought of losing contact with her protégés. Oh God, why hadn't Renaud explained the situation to her? She would have followed him to the ends of the earth if she'd known he was in danger.

Nanesse looked up through her tear-filled eyes at the blurred faces of Vicky and Éléa.

*And what about them?* she wondered. *What is their role in this story?* If Renaud had not obeyed his mother, if he hadn't left her entirely to take on another identity, it was for a reason that was as cruel as it was banal: Hans, Pierre, and Renaud had already been reunited years before. All three of them had been enjoying themselves. Hans with Vicky, helping to renovate her farm, revitalizing himself amid the vast open spaces, and being a daddy to a little girl . . . Pierre with Éléa, a woman who was so much younger than him, so much prettier than Nanesse; a woman who must have gazed at him with a smoldering desire that Nanesse herself, despite all her love for him, simply hadn't felt anymore.

Milana's plan had been for her son to replace one life with another—like a man who owned three suits, and three pairs of shoes—in case something went wrong. But how could a man resist the temptation to try on those three suits, to wear them all?

Nanesse's throat was tight and there was an acidic taste in her mouth. She lowered her eyes as soon as she felt Vicky and Éléa looking at her.

"I . . . I'm sorry," she whispered. "I failed. I couldn't protect him."

"It's not your fault at all," Vicky reassured her. "Your husband loved you. He would never have left you."

Nanesse grimaced. But Renaud *had* left her, for one week every month, to go and stay with this woman, who showed no shame about it whatsoever.

"And I know that Hans is alive," Vicky added.

Nanesse almost choked.

*Alive? Hadn't she been listening to the story?*

"I know it," Vicky went on, "because I don't want to believe that Lola could grow up without her daddy. Because he promised her he would come back and fix Kasper. Because he promised me he would come back too. And Hans was someone who kept his promises. I know it because . . . I just can't imagine my future without him."

"But still . . . you have to face facts!" Nanesse practically shouted. "He's dead."

"No," a voice said softly behind her.

Éléa had walked up to the sewing table and placed her hands on a papier-mâché puppet head.

"No," repeated Éléa. "If Pierre was dead, I would know. I would feel it."

She shook her head as if trying to silence a voice inside it, then nervously tore strips of varnished newspaper from the head.

"There are some things that cannot be explained by reason," she said. "Sometimes you shouldn't listen to your brain, just trust in your feelings. And my feelings tell me that, even if someone showed me Pierre's corpse, even if they gave me an envelope containing his DNA analysis or his dental records, I would still swear that he was alive."

Nanesse slowly shook her head. She wished she was crazy enough to ignore the facts in this way. But she had recognized Renaud's body, and the police had officially identified him, leaving her no hope at all. Lost in her thoughts, she barely noticed Vicky moving past her.

"I'm going to see what Lola's doing."

Vicky twisted the door handle.

It came off in her hand.

"Shit!"

She studied the broken handle in her hand and then tried to put it back, to turn the bolt, but the lock refused to give. She banged her shoulder against the wooden door next, then kicked it as hard as she could.

The door did not move.

"Shit!" Vicky repeated.

"They found us," Nanesse said, realization dawning on her face.

*You should have listened to me,* said Brain.

"Oh, shut up!" yelled Éléa.

# 53

Kristof reverently scraped the red head against the side of the matchbox. He had chosen a long one, the kind used to light an altar candle. He held the match for an instant before his eyes. The frail flame flickered, wavered, curled up on itself for a moment, becoming nothing but an incandescent red ball, before leaping up again, prouder than ever.

Kristof held it up between his hands and admired it, like someone staring at the light while they pray. The tactile tablet vibrated in his pocket. Amos was still in the undergrowth with the kid. He could send a thousand messages for all Kristof cared. He wasn't going to let his little brother's qualms and worries spoil the solemnity of this moment.

Had Amos forgotten?

Had he forgotten waking up in the middle of the night, at eleven years old? The sudden heat inside their bedroom, their beds. The bedroom door opening and the human torch that rushed toward them. Barely having time to recognize their mother before she shoved them, burned them, as they screamed; who threw herself into the flames to save them; who sacrificed herself, dying so that they could live.

And the pain. The unbearable pain of a face devastated by burns. And the terror, when that butcher at the socialist hospital in Pilsen performed emergency surgery on them, using hardly any anesthetic at all. And the horror, when Kristof discovered that monster in the mirror, woke up in a world of silence. When that monster followed him, morning after morning. The horror, in the looks of disgust on the faces of the people he passed; in the looks of pity on the faces of the girls he paid; in the stern looks his father gave him, as if he were now nothing more than a dog to be trained. Trained to kill.

Amos had never seen that monster in the mirror. Amos had never seen the vicious faces of those who stared at them, had never glimpsed their expressions of vile pity. Kristof had had to face up to the world for both of them.

He waited until the match had almost burned itself out, until it stung his fingers, before he dropped the match.

The flame fell slowly, like a butterfly of fire. The blaze spread instantly. The gallons of gas all went up at the same time, a hot yellow cloud that swallowed the worm-eaten wood. Some of the planks collapsed.

Éléa and Nanesse just had time to run back toward the rayok before the costumes, the planks, the cardboard boxes, the wooden arms and legs, the backgrounds, and the papier-mâché heads all burst into flame. The railcar was transformed into a tinderbox as the fire rose all around them, climbing up the walls, licking the roof, preventing any possibility of escape through the door, which was locked anyway.

Three-fourths of the railcar was consumed within seconds. Their lungs filled with smoke, the three women could only curl up together in the one corner that was not yet on fire. They felt as if their skin was melting. It was only a matter of seconds before they would meet the same fate as the Czech puppets, the African heads, the Japanese karakuri, and be turned into ashes.

"Lola!" Vicky managed to yell, gripping Kasper to her chest.

Her daughter had given her the doll to look after. Her daddy would never come back to fix it.

"I'm sorry," Nanesse repeated. "I'm so sorry."

She thought about cutting short her suffering, about stepping forward into the wall of flames. Vicky held her back, in one last desperate gesture.

"Pierre!" shouted Éléa. "You can't let me die like this!"

*Farewell, Éléa,* murmured Brain. *Once the temperature reaches two hundred degrees Fahrenheit, I will no longer be able to function . . .*

"Pierre!" screamed Éléa. "Pierre, I need you!"

Then Pierre appeared.

With Hans beside him.

The two men had smashed down the railcar door with their shoulders. They threw blankets over the flames, clearing a temporary path through the blaze, and rushed inside.

"Come on! Come on!"

"Hans," whispered Vicky. "Is that really you?"

She recognized his gray eyes when he looked at her, his brute strength when he picked her up and carried her toward the open doorway.

It *was* him!

"I'm here, Éléa!"

Pierre, too, had approached, dancing through the fire. He lifted Éléa up like a twig blown from a hearth and threw her far away from the fire. Suddenly she felt as if she was flying, passing through the sun, before landing in the muddy grass of the clearing beside Vicky.

Their two saviors had already disappeared again. Together, they pulled Nanesse out of the blaze, a few seconds before the railcar roof collapsed in an explosion of sparks.

The three women wept. They laughed.

Hans kissed Vicky, who was still in a state of shock, her face blackened, her eyebrows singed.

Pierre kissed Éléa and held her against his slender torso, his skin showing red under the tatters of burned fabric.

Nanesse was sitting in a puddle of mud, ash, and soot, coughing up black mucus.

Vicky's head cleared and she began looking around for Lola, her eyes frantically searching the edge of the forest.

Éléa, still trembling, clung to Pierre as if he were a piece of driftwood in the middle of the ocean.

*Fuck,* groaned Brain. *You're going to have to explain to me what just happened.*

# PART THREE

## Renaud

# AND THIS IS STILL LIFE! WHAT IF DAMNATION IS ETERNAL?

*A Season in Hell* by Arthur Rimbaud

# RENAUD'S STORY

## The Most Wonderful Gift of All

*January 1977*

I was born on January 29, 1977. You who are listening to this, discovering my story, will perhaps find it hard to believe. It begins like a fairy tale. When I was born, my mother gave me the most wonderful gift of all: She gave me three lives.

For as long as I can remember, I have always been able to move from one life to the next, as easily as a child of divorced parents swaps one family for another. In Charleville, I was Renaud; in Paris, I was Pierre; and in Florac, I was Hans.

I changed my name the way most men change their pants: naturally, like someone putting on warmer clothes when he travels from Lozère to the Ardennes, or more fashionable clothes when he goes to Paris. I had always known this strange form of gymnastics; I had learned to divide my brain into three equal parts, never to betray myself. I felt very proud about this. I was like one of those heroes with superpowers in the comics that I read.

When I started middle school, when Mom told me I would have to spend less time with Hans and Pierre, seeing them only during holidays, I felt as if my brothers were being taken away from me, as if I were being sent to a boarding school where my existence would become sad and stale. And that's pretty much what happened.

Part of me couldn't stand being kept away from Paris, with its poetry and museums, and another part missed the Tarn River, the hills of the Cévennes, the wind on the Causses. If my friends at that time had been able to read my mind, they would have thought I was crazy. But I found myself wondering how they could bear it, having only one life. To me, they were prisoners, unaware of the bars that surrounded them, while I roamed free.

But I didn't really have superpowers. During my years in middle school, Hans and Pierre grew more distant, like old friends whose faces are slowly erased in your memory. High school shrank my horizon even more. And then Agnès arrived.

For Agnès, I was only Renaud, and I had only ever been Renaud. For her sake, I turned my back permanently on Hans and Pierre, with as little regret as someone leaving behind their best friends as soon as they fall in love for the first time. Nanesse never knew about my past, about those two other identities. I kept my childhood a secret, perhaps out of some self-protective instinct.

Nanesse, my love, I hope you are one of the people listening to these words. Wherever I am now, wherever you are now, believe me when I tell you this . . .

I was never tempted to use those other two identities to cheat on you.

I never felt the urge to rediscover Hans or Pierre.

I never felt any regret at having abandoned my triple life. I was happy with the one life I had, divided in two with you.

You made me realize that one life was enough, that one family was enough.

I imagine you have already listened to Milana's story, my love. So you have heard her confession. Her last words, recorded in her hospital room. Her terror when she realized that Libor, Amos, and Kristof had tracked her down. The advice she gave me to protect myself, to protect you, to change my identity. But there was one thing that Milana didn't know. The envelope that I was holding that day had not been given to me by a doctor. It did not contain the latest analyses of her cancer. The envelope had been left at the hospital's reception desk, with a short, scrawled note: *For the son of Milana Duval.* When I entered my mom's room, I took care that she didn't read those words. That she didn't see that handwriting.

Because she would have recognized it instantly.

The note was written by Libor Slavik.

My father.

And what he wrote changed everything that I had ever believed.

# 54

***Milana's railcar workshop, Givet's Finger***

The last ashes fluttered away. The plume of smoke dispersed, letting more light into the clearing, along with the foul smell of burned gasoline. The stink was mingled with horror. The flames had reached the branches of the closest hazel and oak trees, but the blaze had not spread through the forest. The endless autumn rain that had fallen on the Ardennes for the past four days had been enough to save the trees.

Nanesse walked a few feet away from the smoldering remains of the railcar, her cell phone glued to her ear.

"Pick up, Katel! Please pick up!"

The police captain had called her, but not left a message, less than an hour ago, and there had been nothing since. Nanesse cursed as the phone call was diverted to Katel's voicemail.

"Call me back! Please. It's urgent."

The others—Hans and Vicky, Pierre and Éléa—were already heading toward the tunnel. Before following them, Nanesse took one last look at the ruins of the railcar, the soot-covered embers, the blackened scraps of wool and silk, and all that remained of the puppets: glass eyes, plastic buttons, a pipe, a pair of glasses, like so many melted snowmen. So many melted fates.

Wasn't this what Milana had wanted? Everything reduced to ashes and dust?

As she walked, Nanesse called the policewoman again, then grumbled when it went to voicemail for the second time. But what was that strange echo she had heard, as if the captain's phone had been ringing somewhere close by?

She told herself to stop being silly. Katel Marelle was busy in Place Ducale and had no idea where Nanesse had gone. Besides, if she could have guessed it, there would already be three police vans in the clearing.

She was about to hang up, then call her for a third time, just to make absolutely sure, when Vicky's voice broke the silence.

"What the hell are you doing? Come on! We've got no time to lose!"

Their eyes met. Vicky had only one obsession now.

To find Lola.

She had called her daughter's name until her voice cracked and she coughed up all the smoke she had inhaled. She had frantically searched the woods around the clearing, without finding any trace of Lola. After a while, she seemed to surrender to the inevitable conclusion. The same conclusion that Nanesse guessed they must all have come to: Those burned men, Kristof and Amos, had kidnapped her before setting fire to the railcar. Perhaps accompanied by their father, Libor, those two men must have followed them here, before trapping them.

Regretfully, Nanesse walked more quickly to catch up to the two couples who were entering the tunnel.

Nobody spoke. Nobody asked any questions. They were all focused on not stumbling over the train tracks in the darkness. Hans was supporting Vicky, who refused to let go of Kasper. *Mommy, look after him for me,* Lola had said. *I'll be back soon.*

Ten feet behind Vicky and Hans, Pierre was holding hands with Éléa. Éléa didn't mind the silence. Only one thing mattered to her: that she had found her Petrushka's strong hand, his feline movements, his puppet-dancer gestures, and that he was leading her through the tunnel's pale night. She really wished that, for once, her brain would leave her in peace.

*Please pick up a branch and hit yourself on the head with it!* Brain advised her. *I just want to be sure that I'm not dreaming. Don't you understand, Éléa? We're walking behind another Pierre. Well, either that or his doppelgänger!*

Éléa had to admit this was true. Hans had exactly the same gray eyes as Pierre, the same slender build and long muscles. If she'd met Hans in the streets of Paris, she would have felt certain that he was her lover. Only a closer examination enabled her to spot the differences between this man and her Petrushka: Hans's hands were less manicured than Pierre's, his hair was slightly longer, his skin a little darker . . . Tiny differences, but enough to reassure her.

"No, Brain, not a doppelgänger. My Petrushka is unique."

And she tightened her grip on her lover's hand.

*Your Petrushka should be dead,* Brain said. *And so should we, for that matter.*

They had already reached the end of the tunnel. Nanesse, still bringing up the rear, watched daylight swallow the four silhouettes. Four black, backlit shadows. A strange emotion—a mix of anger and relief—gnawed at her. When Hans and Pierre had come out of the flames to save their lives, Nanesse had finally understood.

She had understood why Vicky and Éléa had never doubted that their lovers were alive. She had understood what it was in Mina's story that had rubbed her the wrong way, nagged at her as she listened to her mother-in-law's story, without ever quite managing to grasp the unbelievable truth.

As Nanesse emerged from the tunnel, she saw her Clio waiting patiently for her on the grass, beside a red Berlingo.

Vicky's car?

She took another step forward and almost collapsed with shock. She had to grab hold of the tunnel's brick wall to stay on her feet.

*A police car was parked next to the other two vehicles. Katel Marelle's car.*

A hundred thoughts rushed suddenly through Nanesse's head. If the captain's car was here, that meant that Katel had gone into the tunnel to try to save them. But if the two burned men had managed to set fire to the railcar, that meant that Katel had failed. So where was she? With Lola?

"Get in!" called Vicky. The Berlingo's headlights flashed. She handed Kasper to Hans, then opened the door. "Come on, I said get in," she shouted again. "My daughter's in danger."

Éléa and Pierre stood waiting, looking unsure about what to do.

"And where are you planning to go?" asked Nanesse. "The first thing we should do is call the police, which is what I've been trying to do. This car belongs to Captain Katel Marelle. There's something we don't know and—"

"I need to find my daughter," yelled Vicky. "And we don't have a second to lose."

Pierre walked over to Vicky and, in a calm, almost singsong voice, said: "She's right. Those two men could have taken your daughter anywhere. They must have parked somewhere around here too, but I'm guessing their car was hidden. Otherwise we'd have seen them. We don't have a choice. If the captain isn't answering, we have to call the police."

Pierre took out his cell phone. Éléa was gazing at him in admiration. Vicky was shaking, clearly in shock. Hans seemed oddly detached from the scene. He was sitting on a fallen tree trunk nearby, using a pocketknife to perform open-heart surgery on Kasper.

"Katel's still not answering," Nanesse confirmed in an exasperated voice.

"I'm calling the cops," Pierre said decisively.

"No!" Vicky shouted. "No!"

Her phone had just beeped. Two notes, indicating that she had received a message with a photo or a video.

Lola's terrified face appeared on the screen.

# 55

***Bogny-sur-Meuse, Ardennes***

The Skoda slowed down as it approached the sign indicating that they were entering the town. The center of Bogny-sur-Meuse opened up in front of them, on the other side of the imposing steel bridge, built around the bend in the Meuse River. Kristof was used to not being able to hear the rumble of their car's engine, or the sound of any other traffic. Whenever an emergency arose, and the air was pierced by the siren of a police car or ambulance, Amos—now sitting in the back seat with the girl—would always warn him.

Before crossing the river, they stopped in front of a group of children who were walking along the towpath that ran from their school to the sports field. When Kristof and Amos had bought their Skoda Karoq, they had chosen a model with privacy glass, so they wouldn't be ogled by pedestrians and other drivers. Unfortunately the windshield was not tinted. The kids crossing the road ahead of them went very slowly, staring with wide-eyed curiosity, as if Kristof were a monstrous goldfish trapped inside a bowl.

Kristof resisted the urge to drive into them.

These violent urges came over him more and more often these days, and they were increasingly hard to control. He felt as if he were gradually being transformed into the wild beast that people saw whenever they looked at him. That was their fault—the world's fault. It had been like this ever since the fire. People stared at him as if he were a leper, avoided him as if his burns might be contagious, seemed to believe that his outward ugliness made him monstrous inside as well as out. It was their fault if that belief had, ultimately, become true.

It took them a few minutes to emerge from the labyrinthine streets of Bogny-sur-Meuse and begin driving along the hairpin bends that led up to the statue of the Four Sons of Aymon. They didn't pass any other vehicles on their way. In such gray weather, who would want to climb all the way to the top?

The landscape appeared caught between the clouds that skimmed the wooded hilltops and a sauna-like mist that was rising from the Meuse. No doubt all the tourists had migrated toward Charleville-Mézières. The police must have found the devil inside the recycling bin by now, and Place Ducale must have been cleared . . . Too late! Their diversion tactic had worked perfectly. By a stroke of luck, they'd even managed to get rid of that nosy policewoman.

Still driving one-handed, Kristof typed on the tactile screen that hung above the dashboard.

*"You can remove her gag."*

Kristof had been afraid that the girl would cry for help in the village. Now she could scream as loud as she liked and nobody would hear her. Anyway, he certainly wouldn't!

In the rearview mirror, he saw Amos cautiously reach out and touch the girl's hair, then her nose and her cheeks, before tearing off the bandage that had covered her mouth. Seeing the girl's mouth open wide, Kristof smiled at the thought that she had presumably just howled at the top of her voice, and yet for him the car remained perfectly silent.

So there were occasional benefits to being deaf, after all. If some operation existed that would give him back his hearing, would Kristof be able to stand the shrill squealing of children anymore? The barking of dogs? The interminable conversations? For a long time, Kristof had thought of a person's mouth as being no different from a cow's, bellowing the same nonsense inspired by a fear of the void.

*"What are we going to do with her?"* asked Amos.

Kristof didn't reply. He drove across the empty parking lot, into the undergrowth below the trees. From here, they had an unobstructed view of the four schist summits and the statue on the lookout point, although a thin veil of fog prevented him from seeing beyond that.

He turned off the engine and looked over his shoulder. Lola was contorting her body on the back seat, desperately trying to open the door. Amos was trying and failing to control her, the little girl having worked out how to take advantage of a blind, middle-aged kidnapper who had only one free hand.

*"She won't calm down,"* wrote Amos. *"She says she wants to see her mommy. And that her daddy is going to kill us."*

Kristof smiled, despite himself.

*"You'll figure it out. Just tell her a story or something."*

*"What?"*

*"That'll calm her down. Kids love stories."*

He laughed silently to himself as he watched the girl punch his brother with all the strength in her little body. She was a real fury, this one! Amos had to push her away so he could write a response.

*"What story?"*

Kristof checked his watch. It had been almost half an hour since they left the clearing. Twenty-seven minutes exactly since they had emerged from the tunnel and gotten into the Skoda, which they'd hidden along a narrow path that ran perpendicular to the asphalt road through the woods. Twenty-six since they'd seen the two gray-eyed saviors jump out of the taxi before running along the abandoned train tracks.

Had those two arrived in time to rescue the women from the blaze?

Probably.

Could Kristof and Amos have stopped them if they'd stayed?

No, it would not have been a fair fight. Kristof was acutely aware that they could not have physically overpowered those two men. But he also knew that wasn't what mattered.

What mattered was that they had finally lured those two ghosts from their hiding places. After being hunted for so many years, they had finally taken the bait. Now he and Amos just needed to entice them onto more favorable terrain before finishing them off.

And, as it happened, Kristof had just had an excellent idea . . .

*"Tell her the story of the wool hole,"* he replied at last.

*"The wool hole? Why?"*

*"You'll see."*

Kristof observed his brother and the little girl in the rearview mirror. The more his brother's lips moved, the less frequently Lola's fists and feet rained down on him. With each passing second, the girl's violent movements slowed and lost their intensity, finally stopping altogether. As far back as Kristof could remember, Amos had always been a wonderful storyteller. His brother's voice was gentle, soothing, almost mesmerizing. The last time Kristof had heard it had been more than forty years ago, on the banks of the Radbuza River, in a field near Pilsen.

"You see, Lola," Amos explained, without letting go of the girl, "beyond the parking lot, there's a big meadow, and at the end of that, there's a stairway that leads up to an enormous sculpture: the statue of four knights and their horse, Bayard. Around it there's a barrier to keep people from falling off the cliff that slopes down to the river. But in the middle of that plain ahead of us, even if we can't see it from here, there's a big hole that's even more dangerous than the cliff. Actually, it's a kind of cave. Do you know what a cave is?"

"Yes," Lola said quietly.

"That cave is known as the wool hole. Do you know why?"

"No." Quietly again.

"The story is that, a long time ago, in the Middle Ages—back when there were princesses and knights and all that stuff—some robbers used to steal a lamb from the flocks that grazed on these mountainsides. Just one lamb, a very young sheep, preferably a girl sheep. After that, they would tie the lamb to a stake, at the edge of the hole. Do you know what the lamb would do, finding itself tied up like that, all alone?"

For a moment, Lola was silent.

"Cry out for her mommy?" she finally said.

"Exactly! You're a very intelligent little girl. The lamb would call for its mommy. Lambs can bleat very loudly, and their mommies are capable of recognizing their bleats among a hundred others, at a distance of several miles. So the mommy sheep—the ewe—would come running to rescue her daughter. She would rush down the hillside, and the whole flock would follow her, because there's nothing more stupid than a sheep. When one runs off somewhere, all the others follow . . ."

"Like boys at recess?"

"Sure, if you like. So, as I was saying, the whole flock would run down the hillside, with the mommy sheep in front. Sometimes there would be several hundred sheep in the flock, and when a lamb calls for its mommy, there isn't a sheepdog in the world that could stop the ewe from finding its child and saving it. So the mommy was always the first sheep to reach the edge of the hole, but the rest of the flock would continue running behind her and they weren't able to stop so easily. The ones at the back would bump into the ones in front, and the ones in front would have to move forward a little bit more, and it was all rather chaotic, like being in a big, noisy crowd, if you know what that feels like. And in the end, most of the sheep would get pushed and jostled until they fell down into the hole."

"Poor sheep." Lola sounded shaken by this.

"Like I said, a flock of sheep is very stupid," Amos went on. "So the robbers, who were watching all this from a distance, would come running too, and they would go down into the hole with ropes and knives, and they would cut all the flesh from the sheep, because it's really tasty when you cook it. That way, they could steal the meat of dozens of animals without having to run up the mountainsides after them. All they had to do was capture one little lamb. The robbers left the remains of the sheep down there in the hole: their bones, their fat, and their wool, because it wasn't worth as much money and it was too heavy to carry. And that's why the cave is, even today, called the wool hole."

"Is . . . is there still some down there?"

"What, wool? I don't know. It was a long time ago."

"Poor sheep," Lola said again. "And poor lamb too. The robbers were bad people for eating the sheep. And for pushing them into a hole."

Amos tried to think of an ending for his story. A less sad ending. Maybe the wool at the bottom of the hole could offer a soft landing, and the next flock of sheep that fell down there would bounce back up, as if they'd jumped onto a fluffy mattress . . . He felt his tablet vibrate under his right hand.

*"Tell her that since she's been a good girl, we're going to let her call her mommy."*

Amos tensed, immediately suspicious.

*"Why?"*

*"If Vicky Malzieu made it out of that blaze alive, the first thing she'll do is come looking for her daughter, and then she'll call the cops. The first cop she'll call is Captain Marelle, but I have a feeling she won't pick up . . ."*

Kristof grabbed his cell phone from the dashboard.

*"Before she has time to call any other cops, we need to reassure her by sending her a video. Don't you think that Lola will make a perfect little lamb?"*

# 56

***Path near the abandoned railway line, Givet's Finger***

Nanesse, Éléa, Hans, and Pierre all circled around Vicky. She stood frozen, the phone screen held in front of her eyes. Frozen with fear, as she watched Lola's distorted face.

"It's . . . it's a video."

With one trembling finger, she clicked on the triangle in the middle of the still image. Lola came instantly to life.

"Don't worry, Mommy, I'm okay."

Her daughter's frightened, bulging eyes belied these words. It was obvious that she was trying to be brave, but suddenly it was all too much and she burst into tears.

"Mommy, I'm scared! Come and find me. These men are scary. I want Daddy to save me."

Lola suddenly vanished from the screen, her face replaced by that of the earless burned man. At the same time, Vicky heard another man's voice—the blind man, she presumed—speaking threateningly.

"Whatever you do, don't call the police. You're the ones we want, not your daughter."

That was all. The whole video had been no more than thirty seconds long.

The others stood with Vicky in front of the screen, heads pressed together, like a group of friends taking a selfie.

"How did they get your number?" Éléa asked.

Vicky thought about this.

"At the Pont du Tarn campsite. When I ordered pizzas with Lola, I had to give the owner my cell number. They were standing right behind me."

"Play it again," Nanesse said.

On Vicky's phone screen, Lola put on her brave face again. *"Don't worry, Mommy, I'm okay."* Then started to sob.

"Stop!" shouted Nanesse.

Vicky paused the video.

"There!" said Nanesse. "Look at the background, behind Lola."

None of the others seemed to recognize anything.

"The four rocks," said Nanesse, using her finger and thumb to zoom in. "It's the Four Sons of Aymon. That's where Lola is."

"Take me there," Vicky begged her. "Is it far?"

"Ten miles."

Hans picked up Kasper and said sternly: "We need to call the police."

Vicky glared at him. "Absolutely not. You heard him—we're the ones they want, not Lola." Cutting the discussion short, she opened the door of the Berlingo and sat down behind the wheel.

"Nanesse, quick, get in. I want you to navigate."

Nanesse sat in the passenger seat, and the other three all squeezed into the back seat. Hans, still armed with his pocketknife, laid Kasper on his knees so he could continue the operation.

"I promised Lola," he said defensively when he saw Vicky staring daggers at him in the rearview mirror.

She shrugged, then put the car into gear and stepped on the gas.

"Keep going straight until we reach the Meuse," Nanesse told her.

*Did you hear that? The four sons of Aymon.*

Éléa remained silent.

*We're heading straight into the wolf's mouth,* whispered Brain. *It's a trap. And they're using little Lola as bait.*

"Well, then," said Pierre out loud. "We'll go up to the Four Sons of Aymon and rescue her from the hook."

Hans nodded. Éléa shuddered.

Hans and Pierre could apparently read her mind. It was as if they could hear everything Brain said to her. Were they living inside her skull too?

"We don't have a choice," said Nanesse. "Renaud died up there. I need to understand why."

# RENAUD'S STORY

## The Letter

***November 2017***

I had just left my mother's room, where she had confided her last wishes to me: that I should scatter her ashes by the railcar and fix her old rayok. After wandering through hospital corridors like a robot, I sat down on a chair in some specialist's waiting room and exhaled.

I understood that the letter in my hand was from my father. Libor Slavik. A few hours earlier, I hadn't known anything about him: his name, his crimes, his determination to find my mother; I hadn't known about Amos or Kristof either, my two terrible half brothers . . .

My mom had spent her whole life protecting me. So, now what?

I slowly tore open the envelope, then read the letter. Several times.

> *My son,*
>
> *Don't worry. I don't know your name or your face. I hung around in the hospital lobby, trying to recognize you, to spot some resemblance that would allow me to find you, something in the way you walked or the look on your face, but all I saw was a lot of busy strangers. So I decided to leave you this letter.*

*I have been searching for Mina for more than forty years. It didn't take me long to realize that she had escaped to the West, so in the fall of 1989 I began to search for her more intensely.*

*I was groping around in the dark, with no clues. Mina could have taken any name whatsoever. She could have called you anything she liked. I know your mother well: She was always willful, cunning, capable of incredible stratagems. She would be hard to find.*

*But I never gave up.*

*I don't know if your mother ever told you about me. If she did, I suspect you must think that I am a terrible man. Libor Slavik, a man who bore no resemblance to Louka, the gifted puppeteer. Libor Slavik, a pitiful petty criminal, in cahoots with the most corrupt members of the StB. A pathetic profiteer of the socialist Normalization, a failed artist, an alcoholic, a rapist.*

*It's all true. I can't pretend that Mina blackened an innocent man's name. But I suspect she didn't mention the mitigating circumstances.*

*Did she tell you that, without me, she would probably have ended up in a Prague orphanage, or been drowned in the Vltava by drunken Russian soldiers?*

*Did she tell you that I taught her everything she knew? It's true that she was talented, but she was only twelve when I saved her from the streets. I passed on my art to her, and the more she learned, the more she eluded me.*

*Did she tell you how much I loved her, during all those nights under the stars?*

*Did she tell you that I wanted to spend the rest of my life with her, not with Zuzana? Did she tell you that she was the only light, the only source of beauty, that remained in my life?*

*Did she tell you that I wanted a son with her, not with Zuzana? Did she tell you that I would have loved you more than Amos and Kristof, those children who had been raised like thugs? Did she tell you that I never, ever could have killed you, my own son? That I would never have let Zuzana abort you, and that I would certainly never have let your mother risk her life?*

*Did she tell you that I never believed in the prophecy invented by that witch Zuzana*—your son will kill you—*which I knew was just some ridiculous lie she made up because she had no other cards to play? Zuzana was never able to predict the future; all she did was make fools of some gullible villagers. But I was never gullible.*

*I don't know if you'll be able to believe this, my son, but I never wanted to hurt you. All these years, I have been searching for you not because I wanted vengeance, but because I want to protect you.*

*I am not the danger, believe me. I am just an old man now, bereft of both hate and happiness. I can admit this to you: Even Zuzana's death didn't affect me. If you knew the number of times I wanted to abandon her by the roadside, leave her behind, under the stars, and invite your mother to share my caravan . . .*

*The danger comes from Amos and Kristof. My sons. Your half brothers. To be fair, they do have genuine grievances against you and your mother. She killed their mother and ruined their lives. She transformed them into beings who are completely dependent on each other. But they had talent too. Amos could have been a great artist, and Kristof would undoubtedly have taken advantage of the fall of the Iron Curtain to climb the greasy pole of capitalism.*

*No doubt you understand why they have never given up hunting you. They were the ones who found Mina. Your brothers have been to every puppet festival in Charleville since 1989, hoping that Mina would finally crack, that she would give in to the temptation to perform in public again. They never doubted, never weakened. They had only one clue—Petrushka. But that was enough.*

*Don't worry, Amos and Kristof don't know your name or your face either.*

*They know Mina's face—or at least Kristof does. They also know that her name is now Milana. They have found out that she has an incurable disease, because she said so when she was thanking her audience at the festival. And, of course, they know the faces of your children, the only ones who went up onstage with Mina.*

*I know what you're thinking. I have no doubt that your mother told you that I cursed her—and cursed you too—after the fire. That I swore to kill you both. Who wouldn't have reacted like that? But the years have gone by, more than forty of them, and my desire for vengeance has gradually faded, while for Amos and especially for Kristof, it has grown bigger and stronger over time. Perhaps I passed on all my anger to them, just as I passed on my art to your mother?*

*Kristof is like a wild beast, caged inside the bars of a silent world. Amos is devoted to him. His blindness has robbed him of all independence. Will he ever dare to disobey his brother?*

*For a long time I felt convinced that my sons would never renounce their quest for vengeance, even if I asked them to. But everything has changed now, since that Petrushka show in Place Ducale. You must be reading this letter somewhere in the corridors of the hospital where Milana is dying. My greatest regret will always be that I never had a chance to talk to her again, but I will spare her that ordeal. I saw her again at the festival, playing Petrushka with the same grace and talent that she showed at twenty, and that unexpected joy will be enough for me.*

*Amos and Kristof will not be able to take revenge on Milana. Once she isn't with us anymore, once you have scattered her ashes, maybe their hate will be scattered too. After all, you, your children, your wife . . . none of you did anything to my sons.*

*This is the gamble I am offering you. This is the challenge I am laying down.*

*Here is my email address and my phone number:*

*LoukaSK@yahoo.fr. 07 11 26 36 31*

*This is not a trap. It is a hand that I am holding out to you. The somewhat shaky hand of your elderly father, who wants to finally put an end to this war.*

*Libor, aka Louka*

# 57

***Parking lot near the Four Sons of Aymon statue, Bogny-sur-Meuse***

Kristof looked at Lola's terrified face on the screen of his phone, then at the girl's identical face in the back seat of the car. Ever since he'd sent the video to Vicky Malzieu, the kid hadn't stopped silently screaming.

For a moment he looked away from the rearview mirror to examine his surroundings. He still had a little time to prepare for the arrival of the flock. He had parked in the perfect position. From his observation point, overlooking the Meuse, it would be impossible for him to miss Agnès Duval's Clio or Vicky Malzieu's Berlingo as it climbed up through the bends in the road.

A new message from Amos vibrated under his fingertips.

*"What if they call the cops?"*

Kristof typed irritably:

*"When the lamb bleats, its mother doesn't call the shepherd—she comes running."*

Amos did not appear convinced by this. *"What makes you think they'll behave like sheep?"* he objected. *"Thanks to that video, they know where we are, and—"*

Kristof's message appeared before Amos had finished writing his own.

*"We warned them not to call the cops! They won't take that risk. The message was clear*—You're the ones we want, not your daughter. *They think we're not going to harm the kid."*

Amos flinched, as if the tablet had just electrocuted him.

*"What do you mean, 'they think'?"*

*"You know our father's orders as well as I do. We must eliminate Mina's children. And her children's children."*

Lola was now clinging to Amos's right arm. His left hand was shaking so hard, he was incapable of typing a single word.

*"Don't forget,"* Kristof reminded him, *"five days ago, here in the parking lot, how many gunshots did you hear?"*

One finger was enough to type a number.

*"1"*

*"So justice must be done. You promised! Watch the kid while I find something to tie her up."*

Kristof saw Amos lean over the girl, nearly crushing her underneath his body. He gave a satisfied smile: His brother, too, was as docile as a sheep . . .

But then his smile was transformed into a grimace of rage.

Amos's hand was reaching out for the door handle.

*"What the hell are you doing?"* Kristof typed nervously.

Amos was lying on top of Lola now, his right hand groping at thin air.

When his brother's fingers finally tightened around the door handle, Kristof bellowed like a beast. The blind man pushed at the door with all his strength, then sat up and shoved the little girl toward the open doorway.

Amos's lips moved, and Kristof read the words he yelled: "Run, Lola!"

Kristof contorted his body between the two front seats and reached out with one hand, but his fist closed on nothing.

The girl had gone. She was running for her life.

She went in a straight line, her legs disappearing in the long grass, leaping with the desperate agility of a panicked hare.

She ran straight for the statue, straight for the lookout point.

She could not know that just ahead of her, on the dirt path, gaped the vast open mouth of the wool hole.

# 58

***The banks of the Meuse, Givet's Finger***

"Come on, faster!" Vicky mumbled, urging the car on.

At the wheel of the Berlingo beside Nanesse, Vicky cursed at every junction, every speed bump, every hesitant cyclist, every bend . . . The road followed the river for the most part, but took shortcuts whenever the Meuse meandered too exaggeratedly, before rejoining it at every bridge or factory or group of houses in the valley.

Nanesse was navigating. Once or twice she had pressed the green call button on her cell phone. Trying to get hold of Katel, she told herself, was not exactly the same as calling the police . . .

The other three were still squeezed in the back. Hans was still leaning over Kasper, performing surgery with his pocketknife, as if the idea of bringing the doll back to life was more important than saving Lola.

Éléa was clinging to Pierre, but staring in astonishment at the tangle of electronic components under the puppet's chest.

*Promise me you'll never let anyone cut me up like that,* said Brain.

"Even when you're old, rusty, and going haywire?"

*I'm haywire already!*

Éléa smiled. Brain was right. The mere fact that she talked to her own cerebrum was proof in itself that her brain wasn't functioning normally. She gazed at Hans for a long time before pressing herself against Pierre's long, muscular arm, to convince herself that the two men were actually real, that Brain hadn't just invented these two saviors, that she wasn't dreaming.

Vicky drove past an empty campsite, past a deserted river port, before the road ran parallel to a long stretch of canal. Whenever the narrow road straightened out, she had been speeding up, and she accelerated again now . . . before braking suddenly when a pedestrian stepped out onto a crosswalk.

*Shit!*

The seat belt caught Nanesse at the throat. Éléa gripped tightly to her dancer's arm. Vicky cursed, resisting the urge to honk her horn at the bent-backed old man carrying a baguette. As soon as he was halfway across the street, she got ready to step on the gas again.

"Wait!" Hans had almost shouted. "Vicky, wait. I think I've fixed Kasper." He sat the puppet in his lap. "You just have to press his heart to send him to sleep or bring him back to life."

He put his palm flat on the doll's chest. At first Kasper just gently nodded his head. Then his legs and arms slowly started to move, as if the doll were waking after a long, long slumber. His gray eyes lit up and his lips began to move.

*"I was born on January 29, 1977. You who are listening to this, discovering my story, will perhaps find it hard to believe . . ."*

*Am I dreaming,* asked Brain, *or did that doll just start talking?*

"You're not dreaming!" Éléa snapped. "Now shut up."

*"It begins like a fairy tale. For my very first birthday, my mother gave me the most wonderful gift of all: She gave me three lives."*

The puppet's mouth opened and closed without any real coordination with the words it was speaking.

*"For as long as I can remember, I have always been able to move from one life to the next, as easily as a child of divorced parents swaps one family for another . . ."*

# 59

***Parking lot near the Four Sons of Aymon statue, Bogny-sur-Meuse***

*"Idiot!"* typed Kristof.

He was trying to stay as calm as possible. He watched Lola run toward a dead end, a long esplanade that ended at a steep cliff face—or, if she turned away from that, led up to the four mountain peaks, unscalable by a five-year-old girl. She wouldn't get far. She was trapped.

*"That kid has nothing to do with any of this,"* wrote Amos. *"She's not even related to Mina."*

Kristof did not reply. He got out of the car, forcing himself to move slowly, to close the door quietly, so as not to give Amos any audible clues to his state of agitation.

*"She's faster than us,"* Amos added, still sitting in the back of the Skoda. *"You won't catch her."*

Kristof opened the trunk. He took his time laying the plastic case on the rear windshield before unzipping it with calculated slowness. He wanted his brother to hear the crackle of each individual tooth as it opened, like an alligator grinding its teeth. Once the case was open, he put his right hand on the butt of the assault rifle.

*"She may be faster than us. But she's not faster than a VZ 58."*

Kristof savored the grimace of shock and outrage on his brother's face. The VZ 58 had been a gift from their father. It was their inheritance. The Czechoslovak Socialist Republic had been the only country in the Eastern Bloc not to use the Kalashnikov, preferring to produce its own assault rifle.

The Czech VZ 58 and its variants had become prized possessions for guerrilla fighters around the world, but Libor's was an authentic original model, acquired when a high-ranking StB official exchanged it for a complete collection of James Bond videocassettes that Libor had managed to smuggle over the border from Austria.

Kristof weighed the assault rifle in his hand, appreciating its balance and easy handling, before strapping it over his shoulder and typing one last message.

*"Want to come hunting?"*

# 60

***The banks of the Meuse, Givet's Finger***

While the Berlingo moved alongside the Meuse, all five of them listened intently to Renaud's story. His triple childhood, meeting Nanesse, his last conversation with Milana in the hospital room, the letter from Libor Slavik . . .

Vicky kept driving, calmly. Hans, behind her, held the puppet in his lap. Éléa, nestled against Pierre, appeared hypnotized by the movement of Kasper's celluloid lips.

Nanesse was crying. She realized that Renaud had confessed his secrets to this talking doll just as his mother had confessed hers to the rayok. Now the puppet was speaking to her, in her husband's voice.

"Give him to me," she said suddenly to Hans.

Renaud had just finished reading Libor's letter, but she wanted to rewind the story. She wanted to hear the beginning again. To hear the lines . . .

*Nanesse, my love . . . I was never tempted to use those other two identities to cheat on you.*

Hans picked up the puppet like a newborn baby and passed him between the two front seats. Nanesse carefully took Kasper from him.

*I never felt any regret at having abandoned my triple life. I was happy with the one life I had, divided in two with you . . .*

It should be possible, thought Nanesse, to have a conversation with this automaton. Renaud had been a specialist in microrobotics, artificial intelligence systems, and virtual assistance programs. It should not have been more difficult for him to design such a robot than to develop a vacuum cleaner, pressure cooker, or refrigerator that could converse with a human.

*You made me realize that one life was enough, that one family was enough.*

Nanesse sat Kasper in her lap and examined the strange doll dressed as a knight. He seemed to actually look at her. Shyly, like a mistrustful animal waiting for the first words to coax it into tameness. Once she'd managed to catch her breath between sobs, she leaned down until her eyes were staring directly into the puppet's glass eyes. His troubling pale gray eyes . . .

"Hello, Renaud."

*"Hello, Nanesse,"* the automaton replied.

Nanesse's eyes immediately filled with tears.

"I love you, Renaud," she whispered.

*"I love you, Nanesse,"* replied the doll.

*Brilliantly designed,* remarked Brain.

"You're so heartless," snapped Éléa, snuggling against Pierre.

They drove through the town of Revin and across its double bridge over the Meuse, almost without slowing down. Straight ahead, rocky peaks rose up from the line of hills. The statue of the Four Sons of Aymon, on the lookout point where Renaud had lost his life, sat atop one of them. Nanesse again looked down tearily at the puppet-knight.

"I need to know, Renaud. Why did you go up there?"

The automaton sat motionless and silent in her lap.

"Promise me, Renaud," Nanesse insisted, "that you didn't believe what your father told you in that letter. Promise me you didn't walk into such an obvious trap. Promise me that you didn't trust him, that you didn't respond to him."

No answer.

"Try asking a less complicated question," suggested Éléa.

Kasper waited, watching Nanesse with his wide pale gray eyes.

*Brilliantly designed . . . but not brilliant enough.*

Éléa tried to keep her mouth shut. She had the feeling that the others could hear every inappropriate remark that her brain whispered to her. Nanesse appeared about to reformulate her question, to come up with a new method for restarting this strange conversation. But Vicky, her eyes still focused on the road, exploded:

"For God's sake, don't you realize you're talking to a puppet? Wouldn't it have been easier just to leave us a letter? What the hell is wrong with this family? Why do they all have to communicate through these weird, old-fashioned machines?"

Nanesse wrapped her arms around Kasper, as if to shield him.

"Renaud is dead," she replied calmly. "And this automaton is his testament. To me it's worth as much as any official documents in a notary's office."

Hans and Pierre seemed content to listen, like two mute ghosts. They had not spoken a single word since Kasper had come to life.

They entered Bogny-sur-Meuse, and Vicky slammed on the brakes. A class of ten-year-old schoolchildren were crossing the road in front of the bridge, returning from the sports field to the school.

Nanesse held the doll's legs in place and wondered whether to continue questioning him. Even if Kasper hadn't answered any of her questions, his story still allowed her to reconstruct part of the truth. Six years had passed since Renaud had read Libor's letter. So obviously he hadn't been that naive. He hadn't contacted his father, at least not right after receiving that letter.

She observed the widening river, the town stretched out along its banks, the wooded hill overlooking it, punctuated by the four peaks . . . Then she stared at Hans and Pierre in the rearview mirror. They were silent again now, and she wondered if their faces, their hands, their bodies were going to disappear along with their voices.

*And yet Renaud went to the Four Sons of Aymon lookout point five days ago,* Nanesse reminded herself, *to meet his father.*

*And his father had been waiting for him there, armed with a CZ 75, so he could force Renaud to jump. Had the poison injected by Libor finally done its job, all these months and years—six years—later?*

The Berlingo flashed through Bogny-sur-Meuse and began climbing through the lower curves of the road that led up to the lookout point, with Vicky clipping the edges of each bend, braking at the last possible moment, accelerating as soon as she could. Nanesse placed a friendly hand on her thigh.

"Don't worry. We'll be there in a few minutes. Lola is bound to be there. And they said they wouldn't touch her."

She looked down at the automaton. Éléa tugged gently at her sleeve.

"I think Kasper only understands a few programmed words. He was designed to recite phrases from a recorded file."

*Like a tape recorder. With a head and arms.*

Nanesse still hesitated, staring at the puppet as if he were a child stubbornly refusing to answer a question, then put her hand against his cold heart.

"Okay, Renaud. Tell us the rest of your story."

# 61

***The wool hole, near the Four Sons of Aymon statue, Bogny-sur-Meuse***

Lola ran as fast as she could, but the grass was too high. She couldn't see her feet, or even her knees. It was like walking in a swimming pool, with the water weighing down her legs.

And it's impossible to run in a swimming pool!

But it is possible to run through grass. Besides, she didn't have a choice. She had to get as far away as possible. She simply hoped that the grass didn't get any higher, that she wouldn't end up out of her depth. Some of the stalks were already up to her face, and she had to avoid them, without complaining or crying, and especially without screaming. She had understood the story that the man with white eyes had told her: The lamb had been kept a prisoner so it would call its mother to the trap, where they killed her.

So she mustn't call for her mother. She must run away instead.

Or find a good hiding place.

Or—

Suddenly she stopped.

A few inches from the edge of the hole.

She had seen it at the last moment, when she pushed away the blades of grass in front of her eyes, like someone pushing a lock of hair to the side of her face. One more step and she would have fallen.

The hole was surrounded by grass, trees, and rocks. It looked deep, but Lola didn't want to find out how deep it actually was. She stood on tiptoes and turned around, but she couldn't see a thing. The two kidnappers were too far away. But the earless man would come after her—she felt sure of that. She had to keep going, to reach the other side of the hole, to escape.

She wished Kasper was with her. She could have confessed her fears to him, or just had a conversation.

Lola thought she heard a noise coming from behind her. She couldn't stay here. She needed to keep going, around the edge of the abyss.

She grabbed hold of the nearest branch, which moved too much, and began—step by step—to walk the precipice. Her heart was pounding.

It reminded her of climbing across the footbridge on the yellow route of the Margeride Adventure Park, the one for over-fives. She'd had to keep hold of a rope until she reached the slide. Holding on to these branches wasn't any harder than that. It was just that the drop below was a lot deeper.

She needed to concentrate on walking along these rocks. On watching where she was putting her feet. On not—

The rock on which she stood toppled to the side. Her foot slipped.

Her hands gripped the branch as tightly as possible, but Lola wasn't strong enough to hold on. She could feel the hole sucking her in like Coca-Cola bubbles through a giant straw. She was just a little bubble, leaving behind the safety of the ground, falling into the black mouth of a toothless ogre.

# RENAUD'S STORY

## Disappearing

***November 2017***

I sat in that hospital waiting room for a long time, reading Libor's letter over and over again. And each time I read it, I felt more sure of one thing: I had no reason to trust this father I had never even seen.

He had given me his email address and phone number, but that didn't mean I had to contact him.

I had known for years about what happened to my mother, ever since I read that Czech article in *The Pilsen Gazette*, which Bruno Pluvier had found for me. My mother hadn't organized my triple identity for all those years only for me to ruin everything with my naivety.

Libor's letter was an admission of weakness on his part. He didn't know my face or my name. He might have guessed that I was using my mother's surname, Duval, but that was such a common name. I'd checked: There were a hundred and thirty-eight Duvals in the Ardennes alone. But, to make sure that Libor and his two lost souls had no chance of finding me, I decided I ought to move, to find another job, to disappear, cutting the few ties that bound me to Charleville.

Nanesse had always loved the idea of living in a remote village in the Ardennes; she dreamed of having a bigger yard for her foster children. But I couldn't convince her to leave the region. Everything would have been so much simpler if I'd managed that.

Moving to a different place protected Nanesse and me, but it didn't solve all our problems. I thought again about the threat Libor had made after the fire: *I'll find you, Mina. Wherever you are! I'll hunt you down and I'll kill you, just like you killed Zuzana. And before I kill you, I'll hurt your child, and your child's future children, the way you hurt mine.*

Libor and his sons weren't only after Milana and me; they wanted vengeance on my children. I couldn't stop thinking about this line from Libor's letter: *They know the faces of your children, the only ones who went up onstage with Mina.*

My sons were in danger, even more than I was. The killers knew their faces. It would not take them long to track down Axel and Robin.

Nanesse gave a cry of distress and turned off the puppet's voice with a blow to his heart. She whispered questions, almost inaudibly, to the doll gripped between her thighs.

"What would have been simpler, Renaud, if we had moved to a different region? Why didn't you tell me the truth, during all those years? Why didn't you warn me about the danger we were in? Why didn't you tell me about the danger our children were in?"

Nanesse was shaking; she could hardly breathe. In a single movement, Hans and Pierre moved toward her, reaching out to hold her hands. She gripped their fingers tightly in hers.

"Are you okay, Mom?"

# 62

***The wool hole, near the Four Sons of Aymon statue, Bogny-sur-Meuse***

Amos stopped. He had been walking through the meadow, very carefully, for about fifty yards. In the tall grass, he struggled to assess the obstacles in front of him with his white cane.

*"I heard a sound,"* he wrote.

Kristof advanced ahead of his blind brother. He, too, came to a halt, rifle barrel raised.

*"What sound?"*

*"Like a body falling into a pit."*

Kristof turned and stared at his brother. He had learned to read Amos's emotions from the movements of his face, as easily as if they too were written on the tactile tablet. Lost in his eternal night, Amos had no awareness of what he revealed with each smile, grimace, or frown. He must have thought that his facial expressions were as indecipherable as his thoughts.

*"She fell into the wool hole,"* added Amos.

He wasn't lying—Kristof felt certain of that. The terror in his brother's features could not have been faked. He really had heard the child's body tumbling into the void.

*"She's playing a trick on us,"* Kristof typed. *"She probably just threw a rock into the cave."*

*"She's too young to come up with a trick like that."*

Too young? Was that true? Is a five-year-old girl more cunning than a simple hunted animal? Kristof had no idea.

He held out his VZ 58 and started moving forward again. A few yards later, he stopped at the edge of the wool hole. He lowered his gaze to the abyss, cursing inwardly. Had the kid really fallen, or was she hiding somewhere nearby? There were plenty of trees and ferns around the hole where she could easily be concealed.

*"Listen!"* Kristof typed nervously. *"If she's hiding, you'll hear her."*

Lola held her breath.

*One, two, three . . .*

A moment before, when the rock toppled under her foot, she had thought she was going to fall. She had grabbed a branch at the last second as the rock tumbled down toward the hole.

*Nine, ten, eleven . . .*

Lola had slipped onto her backside a few inches from the precipice, while the rock had been swallowed up by the dark void.

*Plop.*

When it hit the bottom of the cave, it made the soft sound of something falling into mud. Far from an explosion, but enough to get the attention of Eyeless and Earless. Eyeless heard everything, and Earless saw everything.

*Fourteen, fifteen, sixteen . . .*

Lola had quickly climbed away from the edge and hidden under a tree with low, dense branches that sheltered her like a hut. It was small, like a doll's hut, but she knew she could make it inside if she wasn't afraid of being scratched, of bleeding.

*Eighteen, nineteen . . .*

She hadn't been scared. Not scared of scratching her elbows or knees, anyway.

The two men were coming closer. She could see them. Earless looked down into the hole. Eyeless had stopped behind him, presumably because he was afraid of falling in.

*Twenty!*

At last Lola let herself breathe—one long, silent exhalation and one long, silent inhalation, like someone drinking a single mouthful of water because their flask is almost empty. Then she shut her mouth and pinched her nose and held her breath again.

*One, two, three . . .*

# RENAUD'S STORY

## Invisible Strings

*November 2017*

Axel and Robin were in danger.

That was my sole preoccupation: Protecting my sons.

Their entire education had taken place in Charleville. Axel had practiced gymnastics and dance at the Citadelle gymnasium, while Robin had skateboarded, go-karted, and played soccer for years. They were still walking around town, meeting up with their friends, sitting outside cafés, and going to concerts, unaware of the risk they were running. If Amos and Kristof did even a little digging, they would have no trouble identifying them. A pair of twins in their early twenties, both with that telltale puppetlike gait. Both with the same unforgettable gray eyes as their father and grandfather. A few days, and their hunters would track them down. Axel and Robin had to get away. As quickly as possible.

They were old enough to understand. They were old enough to know the truth.

The idea—the crazy idea—took hold of me almost instantly. No doubt because I had no other choice. Axel and Robin needed to create two new identities. Axel and Robin looked eerily like me; we joked about it as a family whenever we looked through old photographs. I realized that my plan could actually work when I spread out some papers in the back seat of my car: all the archives detailing the lives of Hans Bernard and Pierre Rousseau, which Milana had kept in her workshop.

Maybe, in the end, this was the reason Milana had forged those three identities? One for me, and one each for my sons. That was her inheritance. The division of my life.

It was so simple. I looked at those birth certificates, those ID cards, those driver's licenses, those school reports, those old class photos: an entire childhood, officially documented. Anyone would have sworn that it was Robin and Axel in those photographs. Only the date of birth on their papers betrayed them. Twenty years too early.

On some of the documents—handwritten, typed, photocopied—it wasn't too difficult to transform 1977 into 1997, 1979 into 1999, 2000 into 2020 . . . For the more official ones, I simply declared them lost and asked for replacements. If that didn't work, or if there was a delay in receiving the necessary documents, and they were stopped by the police, all they had to do was smile broadly and say that the bureaucrats had made a mistake, got their figures the wrong way around. It was pretty funny when you thought about it. I mean, Hans and Pierre were clearly not forty years old. *Right, officer?*

Axel and Robin came with me to Mina's railcar. We turned on the rayok, the paper theater that they had helped to renovate throughout their childhood, and they listened to their grandmother's story. They were moved to tears by her tragic fate. Then they discovered the two ghosts inside those dusty cardboard storage boxes: Hans and Pierre. And they realized how closely they resembled them.

Not only physically. The physical similarity was a given, but there was all the rest too . . . Axel had so much in common with Pierre: poet, dancer, dreamer, full of ambitions. Whereas Robin was much more like Hans, with his love of escape, wide open spaces, extreme sports . . .

There is no such thing as coincidence. After all, every father tries to pass on his passions to his children, doesn't he? To share the secret elements of his childhood with them? How else can he bring back to life what has, for him, vanished into the past? How else can he turn his failures into successes, heal the wounds of regret?

That was all I did, I think. I simply tried to teach my sons about the things I loved most. I was lucky that I had one for each of them. This way there was no need for jealousy, no hint of favoritism. Just two invisible strings.

Axel and Robin agreed to take on my two old identities, on one condition: that it should be temporary. An emergency operation, to distance themselves from the men who wanted to kill them. As soon as the police had Amos and Kristof in custody, they would throw those old forgeries away.

I added another condition: This should all be kept secret from Nanesse. Axel and Robin were twenty years old; it would be easy enough to come up with an excuse for their disappearance. A foreign exchange program, a girlfriend living abroad . . . They could even say they'd fallen out with me. They could write to her as often as they liked, and come home occasionally, discreetly, once we had moved to our new house. In other words, they would each have the kind of independent existence that is normal for a young adult. But if we'd told Nanesse, she would have been in danger too.

Forgive me, Nanesse. Forgive me for lying to you all these years. But no mother aware that such a threat was hanging over her children could have sat back and done nothing. You would have wanted to act, to help, and in doing so you might have tipped their hand.

And I couldn't stand the thought of losing you, Nanesse.

I'm sorry. I don't know if you'll be able to forgive me, but I hope you know that everything I did was to protect you and our children.

And for six years—until this morning—I thought I had succeeded.

# 63

***The wool hole, near the Four Sons of Aymon statue, Bogny-sur-Meuse***

Kristof stood as close to the edge of the hole as he dared. The toes of his boots overhung the precipice, and his neck stretched forward as he tried to peer down into the darkness.

Kristof had never suffered from vertigo in all the years of his life. He wasn't going to fall . . .

. . . unless someone pushed him.

Was Amos tempted? Kristof suspected that he was, that he dreamed of being freed from his elder brother, who constantly reminded him of his promise, his duty, their vengeance. . .

But Amos was incapable of coping without him. He and Amos were united by their disabilities. It was a question not of love, but of survival.

Even so, Kristof had to fight the urge to turn around, to check that Amos wasn't coming up behind him. He forced himself to focus on the task at hand: watching for the slightest movement, in the trees, the undergrowth, the tall grass as it wavered in the wind.

He waited, then stepped back. Nothing was moving.

Kristof strapped the VZ 58 over his shoulder and then wrote: *"You're right. The kid must have fallen. We'll have to manage without her. The sheep should be here soon."*

He turned on his heel. His brother stood thirty feet away, his eyes filled with tears, his face deformed by grief. It was important that Amos didn't cry, though. All the doctors had told him the same thing: Tears were like acid on his cornea.

*"You bastard!"* Amos typed furiously. *"That girl is dead because of us."*

Amos's anger seemed sincere. Kristof smiled with relief.

So it was true? His brother really had heard the kid fall?

*"You're right,"* wrote Kristof. *"She didn't deserve to die. Hans Bernard wasn't her father, so none of Mina's blood ran through her veins. Poor little lamb—I just wanted to tie her to the stake, not sacrifice her. It was you who killed her, Amos, when you opened the car door."*

*Twenty-eight, twenty-nine, thirty . . .*

Lola was managing to hold her breath for longer now.

Between the branches of her hut, she watched Earless turn away.

He was the scariest one. The bad one. And he was turning his back on her . . .

*Now's my chance,* thought Lola. Her chance to leave the hiding place and run straight ahead. She could make as much noise as she liked—Earless wouldn't hear her. She should take advantage of his back being turned to get away from the hole and run, as far and as fast as possible.

She checked one last time that Earless was still walking away from her, that he had no reason to turn around, and she set off.

She easily pushed aside the branches of her hut, like the bars of a soft wooden prison, and advanced in a crouch before standing up as soon as she could. She still had a few more branches to snap to clear a path through the undergrowth, and after that she would be able to sprint. Another ten feet, and she'd be free.

She heard the heavy footsteps behind her.

*Don't turn around,* she thought. *Just keep running.*

But she turned around.

And screamed.

# 64

***Bogny-sur-Meuse***

*Hang in there, Lola!*

It was all Vicky could think about: saving her daughter, reaching that lookout point as quickly as possible, driving fast through every bend, not braking until the last moment, one hand on the gearstick, barely even listening to the story being told by that puppet. She told herself to keep driving, at maximum speed, even if—on this steep road full of hairpin bends, where she had to keep shifting into a lower gear and then stepping on the gas—doing so couldn't gain her more than a few seconds.

Hans encouraged her, his free hand resting on Vicky's shoulder, as if to say, *Hang in there, honey.*

His other hand was still holding Nanesse's. His mother was pressing Kasper to her heart while continuing to squeeze her sons' fingers.

"My boys . . . Well, what should I call you now? Robin and Axel? Hans and Pierre? I didn't realize who Hans and Pierre were until you turned up to save us from the fire. But before that, in the railcar, I was so full of doubts and fears. You looked so young, Vicky, and you even more so, Éléa. It just didn't seem like something Renaud would do, cheating on me with girls young enough to be his daughters. And another strange thing: You both seemed so convinced that Hans and Pierre were alive."

Vicky remained focused on the road ahead.

"I knew my lover couldn't be Renaud," she said. "As soon as Milana said that her son was born in 1977, I understood. My Hans was twenty-five; Renaud was almost twice as old."

"Yeah, same thing for my Petrushka." Éléa nodded. "The moment Mamina started talking about her grandchildren, I realized they were Hans and Pierre."

Nanesse looked at her sons and their partners with a mixture of tenderness and admiration.

"And to think I imagined you were my rivals . . ."

Nobody spoke for a few moments after that. The Berlingo's engine roared as Vicky sped through each new bend. Éléa was the first to break the silence. Without warning, she let go of Pierre's hand and pinched his thigh.

"Actually, my Petrushka, while we're on the subject of your grandmother's story . . . Those poems you published in Baou's fanzine, the ones that made me fall in love with you . . . they weren't written by your father, were they, by any chance?"

"Um," Pierre stammered. "Well, let's just say that . . . at some point, I picked up the family torch."

She pinched him again.

*Nicely done,* said Brain.

"My father kept his old poems," explained Pierre, "along with your handwritten letters. It was all in the railcar. When I found them, I was charmed by your platonic relationship . . . Once I met you, though, I wanted a very different kind of relationship."

*Smooth-talking sleazebag,* hissed Brain.

But Éléa kissed Pierre anyway. As far as she was concerned, his argument held water, since he would have taken over his father's role at the point when the paper letters were replaced by texts. Even so, she couldn't stop herself from pinching him for a third time.

"So what about your world tours?"

"Ah . . . Well . . . I would have liked to do that, obviously . . . but, um, life had other ideas. I'd missed several years of training, so . . . I mean, I did go on tour, but it was mostly on a more . . . local scale."

"Why didn't you tell me that?"

"Well, if you'd known I was a pretty average dancer, just starting out, because I didn't start until I was twenty . . . would you have loved me as much?"

Éléa didn't know whether to pinch him or kiss him.

"Idiot!"

"Besides," said Pierre, grinning now that he knew the awkward part was over, "maybe I *was* good enough to tour the world! But how could I travel to Sydney or Rio or New York with a fake, backdated passport? It was the same for Hans and his truck! Vicky, all those times you thought he was in Budapest or Warsaw, he was actually in Mulhouse or Clermont-Ferrand."

"Is there really any need to take me down with you?" Hans said coldly.

"Four days ago," Pierre went on, "when the police found Dad's body near the lookout point, Robin—I mean, Hans—and I realized that Libor and his sons had been able to trace us. So we decided we had to disappear. I left flowers at Mamina's railcar one last time; I checked that the police were protecting you, Mom; and then I met up with Hans in Florac, as we'd arranged. He tried to convince me not to contact you, Éléa, so I wouldn't put you in danger . . . But how could I just abandon you without a word? So I dreamed up that treasure hunt, to lure you down to Florac. I thought you'd be safer down here, in a small town far from Paris, and that we'd be able to keep an eye on both of you, since we knew Vicky would probably come here as well."

As they approached another bend, Vicky jerked the steering wheel a little too abruptly.

"I didn't agree with that idea!" Hans said defensively. "But if the burned men had figured out how to find us, I thought we needed to burn our bridges with you."

"Sure," said Pierre sarcastically. "Except for the postcard from Japan that you left in Vicky's mailbox! But then you never had my gift for imagination."

*Nor your modesty,* added Brain.

Éléa wished she could pinch her brain. She found it even more annoying than her lying boyfriend.

"Obviously we didn't expect Amos and Kristof to track Hans all the way down to Florac, but thanks to Bruno Pluvier they did. They got a jump on us and kidnapped Lola, and it was only when we heard the villagers yelling that we realized they must be following the Tarn. We were about to break cover and go after them when my cell phone told me that you were on your way there, Éléa . . ."

*That bastard was tracking you!*

"I sent you a photo of the Fayet Bridge, the only road down into the valley. There was every chance that you would find Lola's abductors before we did. And, well, you know the rest . . ."

"No," Vicky said softly. "We don't."

"When you decided to come to Charleville," Hans explained, "we thought we'd just follow you down here."

Éléa was holding Petrushka's free hand again.

"So it really was you that I saw in Place Ducale, near Baou's stall?"

"Yes," Pierre admitted. "I guess we weren't the most discreet bodyguards . . ."

Hans's hand squeezed Vicky's shoulder.

"Those bastards Amos and Kristof trapped us there with their stupid bomb alert. Our car was parked in an area sealed off by the police, so we had no chance of getting out. We ended up hiring a taxi to take us to the end of the road near the abandoned railway line."

"And you got there just in time to rescue us!" Éléa smiled before kissing her hero again.

"But not in time to save Lola," Vicky said tearfully.

*Oops,* said Brain.

The five people in the Berlingo fell silent again. They gazed up at the schist peaks, about fifteen bends above them. No more than three hundred feet away, as the crow flies.

Nanesse had not let go of her sons' hands. She clung to them even as the car's engine whined and Vicky frantically changed gears. She leaned down to the puppet, briefly examining his ridiculous knight outfit, then pressed his chest to her own and muttered:

"Keep talking, Renaud. I need to understand. Why did you go up there, alone, five days ago? I need to know what truth you were hoping to find.

"I need to know the name of your murderer."

# 65

***The wool hole, near the Four Sons of Aymon statue, Bogny-sur-Meuse***

Kristof lifted Lola out of the undergrowth as easily as if she were a kitten. He saw her eyes widen with terror, her mouth open, her face twist, her teeth snap shut as she tried to bite him.

Kristof had to admit: This was his favorite moment.

When the face of one of his victims was deformed by fear, when a cry of despair arose, undetectable by him, from their throat; one last instinctive attempt to beg for mercy that bounced off him like a bullet made of feathers.

He had done this so many times, with rabbits, dogs, pigs, and cats.

In that moment, and only in that moment, as he imagined the unbearable yowls, yelps, and squeals of his dying victims, could Kristof savor the silence of his world; only then could he consider it a blessing. A world of peace that nothing could disturb. Not even the horrifying sounds of death.

Lola continued to struggle in his arms, hitting and kicking him. But she weighed less than fifty pounds and he weighed more than two hundred, so what chance did she have?

As he moved away from the wool hole, he caught sight of his brother's red eyes. Amos had carefully wiped them, but Kristof knew that they must still be burning intensely, and that it would be hours before they returned to normal.

*"How did you know?"* the blind man wrote. *"Your back was turned."*

To reply, Kristof had to hold Lola in a viselike grip between his arm and his torso.

*"I turned my back on the kid, but I was facing you. And watching you. I knew your expression would betray you if you heard anything. You are my ears—never forget that."*

Amos's eyes welled with tears again, but this time he managed to hold them back. In a rage, he lifted up his insideONE tablet, and for a moment Kristof thought his brother was going to throw it away or drop it on the ground and crush it underfoot.

*"Don't worry,"* Kristof typed hastily. *"I always keep my promises. I'll spare the girl . . . as long as she plays her part."*

Amos had lowered his tablet again, but he had not yet replied.

*"Talk to her, Amos. Calm her down. Tell her we're going to tie her to one of these trees, but only for a few minutes. Say her mom will be here soon. All she has to do is call her, as loud as she can, so Mommy will come and save her."*

Lola, exhausted by her struggles, was gradually calming down.

*"What about us? Where will we be?"*

Kristof looked up at the schist peaks that reared high above the meadow. The Four Sons of Aymon, petrified. Or so the legend said. His brother wasn't capable of admiring the savage force of those rocks rising above the trees. And he certainly couldn't imagine the ideal observation post that they offered.

*"Up on top of the first rock. From that watchtower, it'll be impossible to miss them."*

# RENAUD'S STORY

## The Superhero Costume

***Wednesday, September 13, 2023***

I thought we were safe. Six years had passed, without any sign of Libor or his sons. I often reread his letter, and I gradually convinced myself that my father was sincere, that he had given up on his desire for vengeance, that it had ended with my mother's death. Or, more reasonably, I told myself that Libor and his sons no longer had any way of finding us. They didn't know my first name, my address, or my face, and they didn't know anything about Nanesse either. The only clue they had was my sons' appearances, but Robin and Axel were a long way from Charleville now.

They were also different people. Robin had become Hans, and Axel had become Pierre. Robin was working for a small transportation company, and he loved the lifestyle of being a truck driver. Axel was just about making ends meet between his classes, occasional performances, and badly paid regional tours.

Robin drove a truck and dreamed of traveling the world; Axel strung a few words together and dreamed of being a poet. Neither of them seemed in any rush to abandon their new identities, even though they were supposed to be merely an interlude, a temporary refuge. But

Robin liked himself more as Hans, and Axel felt the same way about being Pierre . . .

Especially now that they had both found love!

Love comes in many varieties, of course. Robin's love was like a sailor's, and Axel's like something from a novel. They would call me sometimes, and it seemed to me that they had become lost in their lies, fully immersed in their double identities. Hans told me about Vicky and Lola, the little girl who called him Daddy, and how he was ready to do anything for her, even to stop driving. Pierre told me about Éléa, the young autist he had met through my poems, but to whom he didn't dare admit the truth.

Stupidly, I told them that when you love someone, when you truly love them, you always create a character, a second version of yourself that is worthy of being loved by the most amazing woman in the world. You give yourself new qualities, and you give up your faults. Loving someone means trying to impress them every day by donning your superhero costume.

Yes, I genuinely thought we were safe. I was even planning to confess everything to Nanesse on her birthday. And then, last night, she took me by the arm and said: "Look!"

Two of her foster children were playing on the merry-go-round in the yard. The sun was setting over the Ardennes, turning the tops of the pine trees an incandescent red. Outside our house, beyond the privet hedge, stood a man.

"Have you seen his face? My God . . ."

Yes, I had seen his face. It was almost completely burned.

I knew then that the Slaviks had tracked us down at last. They had not given up on their quest for vengeance. This was only a passing visit, but the message was clear. Wherever I went, whenever they wanted, they could come back.

I told Nanesse that I had to go to Luxembourg the next day. I waited for her to fall asleep, then I went out into the yard, holding my father's letter and my cell phone. I sat on a swing and pushed myself back and forth.

*LoukaSK@yahoo.fr. 07 11 26 36 31*

*This is not a trap. It is a hand that I am holding out to you.*

I called the number. My father answered right away. As if he'd been eagerly awaiting my call these past six years.

But why? To start the war again? Or to end it?

It was on the cusp between yesterday and today, around midnight. My story ends there. I am recording these final words, alone in my car, next to a sign that reads **FOUR SONS OF AYMON STATUE—2½ MILES**.

I will be there in less than ten minutes. I parked in front of a mailbox. When I have finally finished recording this message on my phone, I will slip the SIM card into the small envelope on the passenger seat.

*Baptiste Marou—Librairie Baou*

*3 Rue de Venise*

*75004 Paris*

Since he has been selling the puppets that Mom used to make, and later, mine—slightly improved models that could also speak—Baou will know which one to hide my secrets in. Maybe the one I gave to Lola through Hans, the little girl that he adopted. The little girl I will never know, if I don't come down from that mountaintop.

This is a possibility that I cannot ignore.

Libor arranged to meet me at the lookout point, just before nightfall. There will be nobody else around then.

You who are listening to me now, you probably think I'm naive.

You who know the whole of this story, you would have tried to stop me. You would have told me it was a trap, that Libor Slavik could not have changed.

But even if that is true . . . What choice do I have?

To run away again?

To continue living as though nothing had happened, exposing my family to terrible danger?

Forgive me, Nanesse. Forgive me, Axel and Robin. I have to protect you.

I have to believe in forgiveness, in redemption. I have to put an end to this curse.

And, as strange as this might seem to you, Nanesse . . . yes, I do believe that I will be there to celebrate your birthday tomorrow. Yes, I do believe that my father's letter is sincere. Yes, I do believe that he won't kill me, that he will tell his sons to call off their vengeance. I believe he is more afraid of me than I am of him, because of that ridiculous prophecy.

I am leaving you, for now. I need to be up there before the four peaks disappear under darkness or rain. I am about to climb to my death, or to a new life. Whatever happens, I want you to know . . .

I love you, Agnès, more than I ever expected to love anyone.

I love you, Axel and Robin, the two miracles of my life.

I'm so proud of what you have become. I have discovered that when your children pick up the dreams you had to abandon, when they wear your old clothes so that they look like you, it's as if you never really died.

Robin, Axel . . . take care of Hans and Pierre. They are only cloth orphans, ghosts of my past that will outlive me, fragile yet immortal, as all puppets are.

The puppet fell silent. For good, this time.

"I love you, Renaud," Nanesse whispered, "more than I ever expected to love anyone."

Suddenly Vicky stopped and pulled on the hand brake. Nobody else had noticed that they'd reached the parking lot for the lookout point.

Beside their car was a Skoda Karoq.

Empty.

Vicky unbuckled her seat belt and, although Hans tried to grab her shoulder, her hand, her shirt, she was too quick for him. She was already out of the car, sprinting straight ahead and yelling her daughter's name.

Hans ran after her, while Pierre helped extract Éléa from the back seat, and Nanesse got out of the car too. They left the Berlingo with its doors standing open.

"MOMMEEEE?"

The little girl's howl chilled their blood.

A heartbreaking cry for help.

Lola was right there, perhaps three hundred feet ahead of them.

They rushed toward her without a second thought.

All of them, that is, except for Brain, who warned Éléa: *It's a trap! And you're heading straight into it.*

# 66

***The Four Sons of Aymon, Bogny-sur-Meuse***

Kristof looked down from his observation post. The first rock of the Four Sons of Aymon was the ideal position for a sniper. The barrel of his VZ 58 was resting on a slab of schist. From where he lay, he could remain invisible while enjoying an uninterrupted view of everything below, from the lookout point to the parking lot. And, of course, the wool hole in the center of the plain.

The five people had just emerged from their car and were coming toward him in a scattered group, less than six hundred feet away. His gun had a range at least three times more than that, so he would have no trouble killing them from this distance.

Now he just needed to decide who to shoot first . . .

He aimed at the most distant figure from the little lamb bleating *Mommy*.

Agnès Duval. Their *sister-in-law* . . .

The mere idea of that made Kristof smile. She had not been easy to find, to say the least. He and Amos had possessed only one clue: the surname Duval. The name that Mina had chosen when she first arrived in France. The Ardennes alone contained more than a hundred Duvals. Kristof and Amos had researched them all, then approached each one in turn. It had taken years before they'd found the right couple. *Agnès and Renaud Duval.* They had become certain only after they'd spied on the surroundings and called the storekeepers of Bourg-Fidèle to ask questions. Renaud was a gray-eyed man who had lived in the village with his wife for five years. Not only that, but the couple had two grown-up sons whose descriptions corresponded to the faces of Mina's two grandsons that Kristof had seen on the stage in Place Ducale.

Kristof focused the gun's crosshairs on Agnès's heart. He knew that as soon as he squeezed the trigger, the other four sheep would scatter in panic. He had to be quick, to fire at them one after another, even if the path they were on, between the parking lot and the wool hole, offered hardly any shelter or hiding place.

He took one last look at Vicky Malzieu as she ran toward her daughter, at Hans as he tried to catch up with her, at Éléa and her Petrushka as they leapt through the tall grass with the ludicrous elegance of young dancers.

In a few seconds it would all be over.

Their deaths would be painless compared to the suffering he and his brother had endured.

His finger stroked the trigger. He was ready.

The tactile tablet, which was also balanced on the rock, vibrated under his wrist.

*"Wait,"* wrote Amos.

Amos had decided that he would not move. He would not intervene. Kristof had promised that he would spare the kid. As far as the others were concerned, Amos was prepared to close his eyes.

He was used to it, after all. Living in constant darkness did have the advantage of drawing a black veil over his guilt. But what did he have to feel guilty about, anyway? He was only obeying his father's orders.

He remembered the precise words.

*If I don't come back and you hear a gunshot—just one—then you must pursue our vengeance . . . you must hurt Renaud Duval, his children, and his children's children—everyone that shares his blood.*

"I promise," Amos had sworn.

There had only been one gunshot that night, and Libor had not come back.

Amos had waited for him in the Skoda, beneath the oak trees that surrounded the parking lot. The rain had suddenly started falling when Kristof went out to piss. And then it didn't stop. For four days.

After Kristof returned to the car, he had opened the door, grabbed a flashlight, and typed a message.

*"Follow me."*

*"Dad told us to wait here."*

*"Just do what I say!"*

They had walked, with difficulty, through the mud, in the pouring rain. When they reached the lookout point, Kristof had described the scene for him as he lit it up with the flashlight's pale beam.

The two bodies—Libor's and Renaud's—had fallen over the barrier and down onto the rocks sixty feet below. Nobody could survive such a fall. Kristof had handed Amos the flashlight.

*"Point it straight ahead."*

Amos had obeyed.

*"Lower."*

Amos had obeyed again, and then he had frozen.

He had heard Kristof climb over the barrier and carefully descend the steep slope, clinging to trees. He had heard him breathing heavily, grunting and grumbling, for what felt like forever.

*"Is . . . is he dead?"*

Amos had heard the effort it took Kristof to drag the body back up the slope. At eighty years old, Libor was a mere shadow of the Bohemian ogre they had once known. His body had shrunk in on itself like the trunk of an olive tree, growing wiry and bony. Kristof panted as he laid their father's corpse out on the grass near the lookout point.

At first Amos had refused to believe it.

Libor, dead?

Then he had touched and recognized his father's skin, his hands, his face, his hair, every detail of his anatomy, drenched as they were by the rain.

Libor, dead!

Amos's hands had touched the places where his father's heart had once beaten, where his eyes had once sparkled, where his breath had gone in and out, where his thoughts had once been nurtured . . . But he had not found a bullet wound anywhere. Libor had not been shot.

*There had been only one gunshot.*

Libor had killed his son, and then he had jumped. They had died together. The prophecy had been accomplished. Their vengeance was not over.

What had Libor talked about with his youngest son? Had they taken the time to have a conversation? Had Libor been expecting excuses or apologies from Renaud's mouth, a single *Papa* that had never come? Maybe Renaud had merely spat in his face, and that was why their father had jumped, making the curse come true?

Kristof never asked himself such questions. Or at least he never wrote them to Amos. He had carried his father's skinny body to the trunk of the Skoda. They had covered their footprints as best they could, picked up a pistol that had fallen on the lookout point but failed to find the CZ 75, then driven away into the night.

A night that, for Amos, would never end.

*"The mother is dead,"* Kristof had written before they drove away. *"And now the son is dead too. All that remains is to kill the grandchildren. That is the mission that Papa left us when he jumped."*

Throughout that car journey, Amos had wept until his eyes burned, the flesh of his eyelids dissolving in the lacrimal acid. But how could he protest? Start a discussion? How could he ever escape from this endless night?

One gunshot. He'd promised.

The tactile tablet vibrated under Amos's fingertips again. Kristof was growing impatient.

*"Wait for what?"*

Amos knew he couldn't save them all, but he had to do something. He hated himself as he typed:

*"Just kill the men. The women have nothing to do with this."*

*"How do you know they're not carrying other children in their bellies?"*

Amos gasped with horror. Had he underestimated the extent of his brother's madness? How far would Kristof push this pitiless logic? And what could Amos use to oppose him? His lack of willpower? His cowardice?

He was about to write another message, as if his braille words could delay the inevitable, but he heard Kristof typing first.

*"No more messages. I need to focus."*

A second later, Amos heard the explosion of his brother's tablet being smashed on a rock.

He froze. Kristof had just cut off their sole means of communication. Their only connection. The sound of breaking glass was followed by a terrifying silence. Amos couldn't hear anything now, except the distant weeping of the lamb tied to the stake.

*Just kill the men.*

Kristof moved the barrel of his rifle a little to the side until the crosshairs were targeted on Pierre's forehead.

Amos was right: He should start with the men. The women would be easier to slaughter, afterward.

Agnès Duval was the slowest among them; Vicky Malzieu would not leave her daughter; and pretty Éléa wouldn't let go of Petrushka's hand.

Kristof enlarged the red dot until it was perfectly clear in his sights, just above the dancer's gray eyes. It was an easy shot: The young man was standing still, more or less, as he waited for his girlfriend, who was now struggling to walk through the long grass.

But she needn't worry. Her turn would come.

Kristof looked back one last time to check that Amos was not planning to do anything heroic. He smiled as he saw his little brother sitting with his head between his legs, hands covering his ears, as if praying that his hearing would be taken away too.

Kristof settled back into position. The dancer hadn't moved. His tattooed ballerina had halted too, probably because Vicky and her truck driver had already reached Lola. Hans was a head taller than Vicky, and more than twice as tall as her daughter, so it wouldn't be difficult to kill him without touching the kid. He wanted to keep his promise to Amos. He couldn't guarantee that the girl would get away without being splattered with blood, though. But she could hardly complain about that. Unlike burns, bloodstains wash out.

He placed his left hand flat on the gun's cold metal barrel to keep it stable. The dancer would be the first to lose his life. Kristof stared at the close-up of Pierre in the rifle's scope. He tried not to concentrate on those gray eyes, which were so like Libor's, not to mention his own—and Amos's too, before the fire.

His forefinger tensed around the trigger.

Before he could fire, pain tore through his stomach, and for a moment he was completely motionless, uncomprehending.

Someone else had pulled a trigger, before him. A bullet had pierced his abdomen.

A clean hole, between his chest and his navel. A surreal red flower spread across his shirt, under his unzipped leather jacket.

Kristof pressed his hand against it and the blood ran between his fingers. He looked up, frantically searching for the spot from where the sniper had shot him. Obviously the shooter must be somewhere above him, on one of the other rocks of the Four Sons of Aymon.

Kristof's eyes widened.

Was he hallucinating?

On each of the other peaks he could see a dozen blue figures.

Police officers, in uniform.

And in the middle of this army was a single dark-haired figure, mouth covered by a megaphone, shouting out words that he was incapable of hearing.

*Captain Katel Marelle, back from the dead.*

Kristof had dived for cover behind a schist boulder. Amos, too, had crawled into this crack in the rock. His left hand immediately covered his brother's, trying to help him stem the bleeding. Amos's right hand was still holding the tactile tablet and his fingers were dancing across the screen as he frantically typed the resurrected policewoman's orders into the tablet.

*"Surrender."*

*"You are surrounded."*

*"Throw down your weapons."*

A few warning shots sent fragments of rock flying around them. Amos pressed his hand more firmly against his brother's wound. It felt like the blood had stopped flowing. The combination of their two hands was applying enough pressure—for now.

Kristof tugged at Amos's arm as if urging him to move the tablet closer to him. He put his blood-covered hand on top of Amos's and left a series of sticky dots and dashes on the tablet.

*"You told me the captain's heart had stopped beating."*

The brothers' fingers intertwined on the tablet.

*"You were my ears, Amos, and my ears betrayed me. And yet I had faith in them. Blind faith."*

Amos pressed one hand as hard as he could against his brother's open wound. If only he could go back in time . . .

*"I just wanted to . . . spare her."*

*"Pity is a weakness, Amos. By trying to save her, you killed me."*

The warm blood, the cold screen, the torn flesh, the vibrating glass. Their four hands were touching, conversing, belonging to the same body, relying on the same senses, protecting the same vital organs.

*"I'm sorry, Kristof. It's all my fault."*

Suddenly Amos could feel blood flowing from his brother's wound again. He let go of the tablet and pressed both his hands against it. As hard as he could. He could have stayed like that for hours, days, the rest of his life.

Kristof pushed the tablet under his brother's fingers, forcing him to read what he had written.

*"No, Amos. I'm the one who's sorry. Before I die, I have something to confess. I was your eyes . . . and you trusted them unquestioningly. But I betrayed that trust."*

# 67

***The wool hole, near the Four Sons of Aymon statue, Bogny-sur-Meuse***

Nanesse looked up at the four columns of rock that rose above the line of trees.

"What was that?"

"A gunshot," Pierre replied instantly. "Up there!"

"Lola!" Vicky shouted. "Get down!"

Hans dived on top of her.

"You're crushing me, Daddy!" the little girl protested.

Pierre reacted too, grabbing Éléa's hand and forcing her to lie down in the ferns.

*That was a gunshot from a HK G36K,* Brain told her.

"It's the police!" Éléa yelled.

Nanesse was also crouching in the grass. But she abandoned her caution to poke her head out.

"It's Katel! She got my message."

Hans was still holding Lola and Vicky close to the ground, ten feet from the wool hole.

"You called her, Mom? But I thought we weren't supposed to—"

"Let it go, honey," Vicky said in a muffled voice. "If your mother hadn't called the cops, we'd all be dead by now."

# 68

## Four Days Ago

***Wednesday, September 13, 2023***
***Parking lot near the Four Sons of Aymon statue, Bogny-sur-Meuse***

Amos and Kristof were waiting in the Skoda. Anxiously. Silently. It seemed like a long time ago that their father, armed with his CZ 75 semiautomatic pistol, had gone off to meet Renaud Duval. Amos heard his brother start moving around, showing the signs of impatience that Amos knew all too well: cracked knuckles, rapid breathing. Then suddenly he opened the door and stepped outside.

Amos typed as quickly as he could on the braille tablet.

*"Where are you going?"*

*"I need to piss."*

*"I don't believe you."*

*"Whatever . . . Anyway, you heard Papa. You have to stay here. To listen. And to count. One gunshot or two. He didn't trust me to do anything. As always."*

Kristof knew that this was his best line of argument: making his little brother feel guilty. Reminding him that Amos was the favorite son, always handed the responsibility of monitoring, listening, deciding. As far as their father was concerned, Kristof was just a rabid dog, to be kept on a tight leash. Every time Kristof touched this nerve, every time he hinted at a jealousy that might damage their fraternal complicity, Amos was so desperate to reassure him that he let Kristof do whatever he wanted. In any couple, thought Kristof, there is always one who complains and one who feels guilty. And whenever there is an argument, the former always defeats the latter.

Kristof walked away from the Skoda, toward the lookout point, following his father's large footprints. It was not yet completely dark. A crescent moon appeared to have come loose from the bend in the river. It was the hour of shadow puppets, of black tree silhouettes that resembled vampires, of figures without eyes or smiles . . . The favorite time of day of the Great Puppeteer, if he existed. The hour when the big white sheet can be drawn tight and illuminated with a blinding light, so that the silent actors behind it, reduced to shadows, can play their parts.

Kristof was careful not to get too close. He had found an ideal observation post—about three hundred feet from the lookout point, hidden behind some brambles at the edge of the meadow—when the rain began to fall.

Standing on the lookout point, face to face at the base of the statue, Libor and Renaud each pointed a pistol at the other.

Papa had been wrong, thought Kristof. Renaud Duval, the cursed son who was prophesied to be his killer, had not come unarmed. Hardly surprising, of course. Renaud Duval wasn't crazy. He had hidden for years, had changed his identity. After being taken from Bohemia to the Ardennes by his mother the murderess, who had taught him the caution of hunted beasts. Renaud Duval had not come here tonight to atone or apologize; he had come to defend his family. To put an end to this quest for vengeance.

Kristof squinted as the rain streamed down his face. He liked the feel of water on his scars. He liked to imagine that the drops could put out the fire that devoured him. He could stand under a shower or a rainstorm for hours, hoping that the course of fate would be reversed, that his face would become again what it had been before: the handsome face of a boy with honey-colored skin and gray eyes who seduced the girls of Bohemia.

Kristof concentrated. Between raindrops, he could make out every expression on his father's face. Over time, Kristof had trained himself to see far into the distance with supernatural precision, to focus with greater speed. If a blind man's hearing could become more sensitive, why shouldn't a deaf man's sight grow sharper?

Even so, Kristof could hardly believe his eyes.

His father was smiling! Libor was having a conversation with his son. He was still aiming the gun at him, but they both looked relaxed, like two old friends reunited after years apart. Never before had Kristof wished this desperately that he could hear again, instead of being doomed to watch the distant projection of a silent movie. He wished he could read their lips instead of having to guess at what they were saying to each other.

To judge from the sincerity of his father's smile, though, they were not exchanging expressions of undying hatred.

To judge from the gentleness of his gestures, the words they were speaking were words of reconciliation.

Words of love, even, to judge from the look in his father's eyes.

Kristof bit his lip so hard that it bled. He was wrong. He must be wrong! His father was playing a part, so he could trap this Renaud Duval, so he could protect himself from his patricidal son.

As if to fool Renaud completely, Libor opened up his arms, like he was initiating a hug. A gesture of peace. Or of sacrifice, if the other man refused the embrace. The CZ 75 semiautomatic in his hand was now aimed up at the sky. Facing him, Renaud hesitated.

Libor insisted. He raised his hands even higher.

His body language, now, was not difficult to translate into words. Kristof guessed what his father was saying, as the rain lashed down on his face.

*Go ahead, Renaud, fulfill the prophecy. Shoot me, and it will all be over.*

A new thought struck Kristof then: His father simply wanted his life to find some meaning here, to make sure that his existence had not been one vast waste, that from the mud and ashes of Pilsen at least one flower had grown. That he had not merely raised two worthless creatures with burned faces . . . That there would remain some beauty, born of him.

Kristof finally understood. Their father had used them. All these years, he had dangled vengeance in front of their eyes like a carrot. The more he had kindled their hate, the more his own had died down. And the more he had hated them.

He looked back at his father. Libor had closed his eyes now.

*Shoot me, Renaud. Shoot me, son.*

Renaud did not shoot. He continued to aim the pistol at his father, warily eyeing him, assessing his every expression, every word lost on the wind, trying to work out if this was a trap . . .

And then, as suddenly as Libor had opened his arms, Renaud opened his.

He stared at his father, and this time he smiled. And, like a farmer sowing seeds, he tossed his gun into the darkness.

He would not fulfill the prophecy. He refused to kill his own father. He offered himself to Libor, unarmed, sketching a reconciliation, the first signs of complicity.

Libor lowered his pistol, then, and pointed it straight ahead.

At that precise moment, Kristof recognized his father again. The father he admired. Not the failed puppeteer or the disillusioned alcoholic . . . He saw again Libor the fiercely determined, the man who had led this hunt with an iron fist, the man who had never given up, who had spent years navigating between the Communists of the StB and the new leaders of the Velvet Revolution.

The cunning Libor, who had succeeded in making this naive son feel sorry for him. He had bluffed and coaxed him into not only lowering his guard but throwing away his weapon. Now all that remained was for Libor to finish off this stupid, defenseless beast, and it would all be over.

Libor aimed his CZ 75 at Renaud Duval's heart.

Kristof had to admit that his half brother had courage. He didn't flinch. He stood straight and dignified, as proud as a partisan before a firing squad.

Libor fired.

The detonation would have been loud, even in the rain. At least Kristof assumed so.

Amos must have heard it anyway. One gunshot.

Renaud Duval hadn't trembled, hadn't even blinked. As if the bullet had gone through him without touching him.

Or, more likely, as if . . .

As if Libor had deliberately missed.

Everything happened very quickly then. In the long hours and days that followed, Kristof replayed the scene in his head, in slow motion, isolating each gesture, like a choreographer breaking down a complex dance.

Libor turned the pistol on himself, the barrel pressed against his throat.

Kristof realized that his father had decided to commit suicide. Now everything made sense. Libor had planned it all in advance.

Two gunshots, and their vengeance would come to an end.

He had told them this a few minutes earlier, in the car: *If I kill him, and then myself, then it's all over. And you are free.* But he hadn't been able to shoot his own son . . . He'd decided to let Renaud live, to cut short the prophecy himself, to die for his son.

Two gunshots, one sacrifice, and the curse would be lifted.

Kristof refused to watch, refused to see the second bullet rip through the flesh under his father's chin and exit his skull twelve inches higher. He was about to close his eyes when he saw Renaud rushing over to Libor, his mouth opening, crying out a word that, for the first time, Kristof was able to lip-read.

A word that neither he nor Amos had ever dared pronounce.

Renaud's lips opened and closed. Once. Twice.

*Pa-pa.*

Renaud managed to push the barrel of the gun away from his father's chin. Libor struggled. Renaud was younger, but his father was more powerful. Kristof hoped that the gun would go off during the struggle, and that the bullet would—by chance—hit his half brother. But fate decided otherwise.

As they fought, Libor and Renaud didn't notice that they were getting closer to the safety barrier, which was less than three feet high. They didn't notice that the rain had turned the asphalt beneath their feet into a skating rink. They didn't realize that all it would take was one false move, and they—

Their bodies vanished simultaneously, like two judo masters caught in each other's grip, vanishing into the void as the mat opened up under their feet.

Then Kristof could see nothing but the rain.

When Kristof returned to the Skoda, Amos confirmed that he had heard only one gunshot. Kristof grabbed a flashlight and led his brother to the hillside. When they discovered the two corpses, sixty feet below the lookout point, they ignored their dead half brother and concentrated solely on the body of their father.

# 69

***Statue of the Four Sons of Aymon, Bogny-sur-Meuse***

*"It was an accident."*

The tactile tablet was like a raft floating on a sea of blood. Kristof's fingers shook as they typed, leaving behind sticky red confessions.

*"Our father wanted it all to end, Amos. I was your eyes and I betrayed you. There was no second gunshot because Renaud stopped it from happening, but Libor wanted to shoot himself. Everything that followed—the hunt, the murders, the fire—that was my choice, not our father's."*

Amos kept his hands pressed against the gaping wound in his brother's belly. His ten fingers were like bricks in a dam that was about to burst. The flow of blood grew inexorably stronger, like a rising tide.

*"I've always been a monster. You know that better than anyone, little brother. I could read it in your eyes, in Papa's, in Mama's . . . even before the fire."*

A grimace of pain twisted his face.

*"Amos,"* he continued, *"did you keep our father's ashes?"*

Amos nodded. They had cremated Libor near the border, in the middle of the Ardennes Forest, surrounded by a guard of honor of oaks and spruces.

*"Take them back with you. To Bohemia. Scatter them in Pilsen."*

*"We'll scatter them together,"* lied Amos. *"I promise."*

Kristof knew this was one promise that his brother couldn't keep, but he didn't have the strength to argue. His life hung by a thread, like a puppet whose strings have frayed one by one.

Amos let his big brother slowly fall asleep in his arms, and he cradled him. The tablet was too soaked with blood now, and Kristof too weak, for them to communicate, so Amos just murmured words to his brother that he would never hear. Amos thought about his father's ashes. He would never take them back to Bohemia; he had scattered them a few hours ago, near the railcar, while Kristof was preparing the fire.

He had scattered them where Mina's ashes had been scattered years before. The two of them intermingled until the end of time.

But how could Kristof have understood that?

Amos saw them again now, the way he used to see them on every sleepless night, inside the caravan, his face pressed against the bedroom window. He had watched his father and Mina so many times, had watched them fall asleep together so many times, under the stars, after making love . . . Or at least that was what Amos had believed they were doing, since his father seemed to believe it. He had learned from Mina's story that what had happened between them actually had another name. Rape.

And yet a child had been born from that cursed bond, and Mina had loved that child.

So perhaps the best had been born from the worst.

Before meeting Mina, his father had been Louka, the brilliant puppeteer, the libertarian poet, the anarchist artist . . . broken by poverty and pride, by violence and desire, by socialist Normalization and Soviet tanks, by life and history.

Could the best become the worst?

Scattering his ashes close to Mina's was what his father would have wanted, Amos felt sure.

Besides, what choice did he have? He would never return to Bohemia.

Kristof had fallen asleep in his arms, and he was never going to wake up. Amos squatted down and delicately laid his brother's head against the few tufts of moss that grew on the rocky peak.

He patted the ground around him until he found the VZ 58, picked it up, and thought about the best way to hold it, to make it look convincing.

Then he stood up.

He immediately heard people yelling.

"He's standing!"

"He's armed!"

He aimed the gun in the direction that he thought he could hear the voices coming from, although the echoes made it impossible to locate them with any precision.

"Don't shoot!" Katel Marelle shouted.

Amos squeezed the trigger. The recoil almost knocked him from his feet. Gunfire rattled through the night. He had deliberately aimed high, as high as possible, as though trying to shoot the stars.

"He's blind!" Katel shouted. "He can't—"

The crackle of automatic gunfire drowned out the rest of her words. Amos felt the bullets pierce his body.

The Great Puppeteer was summoning him at last.

# ALL BEINGS ARE FATED TO BE HAPPY

*A Season in Hell* by Arthur Rimbaud

***Seven Years Later***

"Lola! Lola! Are you coming to play with us?"

Romy and Marius were running between the swings and the slides. Four-year-old Romy was quicker, but her cousin Marius, though only two and a half, refused to give up trying to catch her. He sprinted, fell, then got up again, his knees grazed and his face dusted with sand.

"Don't pester Lola!" called Nanesse. "She's busy."

Lola did not mind being pestered, at least for now. At almost thirteen, she had not yet definitively left behind the age of grace, that brief period—between six and twelve—when girls are all laughter, curiosity, and empathy for everyone and everything around them, whether human, animal, or puppet. That magical moment before life takes hold of them and they become women. Lola was on the cusp between these two worlds, eager to leave the first, excited to discover the second. She had promised her grandmother that she would bring in the tablecloths that had dried on the washing line, and she managed to reach them now, without asking for help, by standing on tiptoe.

"Lola, we need you!"

Romy and Marius were sitting on the swings, waiting impatiently for the wind or some helpful adult—or Lola, the target of their pleas—to come and push them.

"I'm busy!"

Big people were always busy!

Romy and Marius looked around them at the cascades of flowers, the labyrinths of gravel, and the ramparts of leaves that surrounded the house in Bourg-Fidèle. They loved visiting Nana Nanesse.

Nanesse's yard was even better than a normal playground. Not only did it have swings, slides, and a merry-go-round, but it was all for them.

Her house was even more fun than the yard, with its puppets hanging from the walls and ceilings and sitting on every piece of furniture, even if they weren't allowed to touch the ones with strings attached.

The cousins stared at each other for a few seconds, each hoping that the other would decide to get off his swing and push. When that didn't work, they started looking around to see who else they could ask.

Not old Baou, that was for sure. He was asleep in the sun, lying on a lounger, with a book open on his lap.

Maybe one of the five adults sitting around the living room table and talking? Nana Nanesse? Or—

Suddenly Romy and Marius went flying upward. Lola's laughter exploded behind them.

"Higher, Lola! Higher!"

Lola pushed them two or three times, as hard as she could, then waited for the two swings to slow down. Then she leaned toward Romy and Marius and whispered: "Quick, come with me. I've got a secret."

"Where did they go?" Vicky asked anxiously. "Robin, can you see them?"

Nanesse was bringing over a pot of coffee. The autumnal Ardennes landscape was aglow with stubborn sunlight. The remains of the birthday cake were still on the table amid the clutter of torn wrapping paper and the instructions for the Magimix Intelligent Pressure Cooker that her boys had given her . . . Did her own children really believe she was going to make cacasse à cul nu while chatting with a smart oven?

"Robin," Vicky said, "can you go and check on them?"

Hans pretended not to have heard her. He was feeling good, having eaten and drunk a little too much. A few glasses of cold Riesling. He would not touch alcohol again for the next six days. He was on his way to Helsinki to deliver some wind turbines on a wide-load truck that would travel all across Europe. He might get up if Vicky called him Hans, he thought with a smile. That was what she called him most of the time . . . but not in front of Nanesse.

Vicky, grumbling, pushed her chair back. She had changed since Marius's birth, thirty months ago, and she knew it. Hans's absences bothered her much more these days. She wasn't the perfect sailor's wife anymore. Her guesthouse was a success—almost too much of a success. She had twelve rooms to look after, not to mention her quiet, dreamy daughter, Lola, on the verge of adolescence. And a hyperactive son who could not be left unguarded for more than two seconds without him running off to play with the hens and the ponies.

"Don't worry, Vicky," Éléa said in a gentle voice. "Marius is with Romy and Lola. They're preparing a surprise for us."

Vicky hesitated, then put her hand on Hans's shoulder and kissed his neck. Would she still love him as much when the day inevitably came that he gave up his truck and moved in with her and the kids full-time?

This time, it was Pierre who stood up, grimacing. Like Hans, his hereditary chondrocalcinosis was starting to make his joints creak.

"I'll go and see what they're up to."

Éléa grabbed his arm.

"Stay here. They're allowed to have their little secrets."

Secrets? Pierre wasn't sure about that. Pierre, too, had been changed by the birth of his child, Romy. His dreams of being a dancer, a poet, and an artist had all been forgotten instantly, and he had chosen to devote himself to being a good father.

He had decided that they had to leave Paris so they could buy a house with a yard. He didn't mind if the building was a ruin—he could renovate it. And while it was true that he'd never held a drill or a screwdriver before, well . . . he could learn. And he had done just that. Romy had been born in Germigny-l'Évêque, on the banks of the Marne, in a princess bedroom decorated entirely by her daddy. And Pierre hadn't stopped there. Next had come a game room, a doghouse, a tree house . . .

*Will Romy ever imagine that her father was once a poet full of dreams,* Éléa often wondered, *before he found that job in the highway maintenance department of the mayor's office? Or will she always see him as a serious grown-up? And what must she think of her mommy, in her four-year-old head?* Éléa felt certain that Romy was also on the spectrum. Her symptoms were less obvious than Éléa's own, less easy to diagnose, but the signs were there all the same: a need for solitude, an excessive concern for a crushed ant, the way she always identified with the most damaged Playmobil figures. Éléa also felt sure that Brain had vanished since Romy's birth. As if he'd just evaporated. Or moved into another head, one more receptive than hers.

"I'm going to check on them anyway."

Before Éléa could object, three figures flashed past the living room door and out of the house, running toward the fence: Marius went first, followed by Romy, with Lola bringing up the rear.

"Pollux is here! Pollux is here!"

"Who?" Hans and Pierre both asked.

The barking of a dog drowned out the children's squeals of joy. The fence gate opened and a Skye terrier came bounding into the yard, then ran around the three children, yapping. They all sprinted toward the merry-go-round and the slides, with Pollux clumsily trying to catch the punctured ball that Lola, Romy, and Marius threw to it.

Katel Marelle came through the gate several seconds after her dog.

"Be careful, kids—that little furball is stupid . . . And stupidity is contagious, you know!"

Without giving her pet another thought, Katel went into the house, sat down at the table, and warily tasted the slice of cake—or, to be more precise, the slice of *gâteau mollet*, a local specialty—that they had saved for her. She apologized for being late, but the truth was that she preferred family meals when they consisted of nothing more than cake and coffee.

Pollux continued to run around after the punctured ball, covering it with his drool.

"What an adorable dog," Nanesse said.

"Adorable? Are you kidding?" Katel replied. "That animal is a total rip-off! I waited fifteen years before my stupid cat, Oggy, had to be put down. He could have run off to a neighbor's house or gotten hit by a car before that, but no! I wasn't so lucky. Fifteen years I spent feeding him, changing his litter box, removing ticks from his flesh, and he never showed the slightest gratitude. Nada. He just slept, meowed, ate, and fell asleep again. Worse than the worst lover in the world! So, people said: 'Well, you've tried men, you've tried women, you've tried cats . . . now you should try a dog. There's nothing better than a fluffy puppy when it comes to hugs,' they said. Yeah, right! All that dog does is drool, run around like a lunatic, steal my steak as soon as I have my back turned, and take up all the space on the couch . . . Worse than the worst husband in the world! His only virtue is that, being a Skye terrier, he probably won't live long. With a little luck, he'll be gone in ten years. So what would you recommend for me after that? An Iguana? An inflatable Chippendale? Or one of those Baou-Duval robots with prerecorded conversation?"

The others laughed at this as a lock of Katel's salt-and-pepper hair fell over her right eye. The children had already abandoned Pollux and his airless ball.

"See?" said Katel triumphantly. "Even the kids get sick of him in less than three minutes."

"The kids!" Vicky cried suddenly. "Shit, where are they?"

Pierre, equally worried, started to get up.

"Let's go look for them."

Nanesse smiled reassuringly. She had spotted three shadows behind a sheet hung on the washing line. Lola's voice called out:

"Is everybody there?"

All the adults at the birthday table turned around to look at the large white sheet.

*Yes, Lola,* thought Nanesse, *everybody is here. Even if, for me, there will always be one person missing.*

On the other side of the sheet, Romy and Marius were nervous. This was their first performance, and it would begin the moment that Lola pulled the sheet away.

Marius's hand tightly gripped the controller that moved the arms and legs of his puppet. Lola had showed him how to avoid getting the strings tangled. He really loved it when his soldier hit the other two with his big wooden sword.

Romy was equally unsure of herself. She had been practicing making her ballerina dance. But would she be able to overcome her shyness, with all the adults watching? Would she remember all the movements and words?

*Don't be scared,* Brain whispered reassuringly inside her head. *I'll remind you of everything you need to do.*

Suddenly the sheet vanished. Six adults and a dog held their breath. Then Lola cleared her throat, and a figure dressed in a white shirt and harlequin pants appeared from behind the cardboard puppet theater.

"Hello, my name is Petrushka."

# About the Author

*Photo © Céline Nieszawer*

With over thirteen million copies of his books sold in France, Michel Bussi is one of the most successful French authors of all time. His books have been sold internationally in thirty-eight countries and translated into thirty-four languages. Known as "the master of the plot twist," Bussi has published seventeen suspense novels with Presses de la Cité. Three of his books have already been adapted for French TV. The author lives in France.

# About the Translator

*Photo © 2024 Kayla Brint*

Sam Taylor is an award-winning literary translator and author. His novels have appeared in a dozen languages, and he has translated more than seventy books from French, including Laurent Binet's *HHhH*, Leïla Slimani's *The Perfect Nanny*, Joël Dicker's *The Truth About the Harry Quebert Affair*, and Marcel Proust's *The Seventy-Five Folios and Other Unpublished Manuscripts*. Taylor grew up in England, spent a decade in France, and now lives in the United States.